DUST IN THE LION'S PAW

'Miss Stark is a great traveller, a woman of astute judgement, and an extremely sensitive writer.'

Sunday Times

Dame Freya Stark was born in Paris in 1893, and now lives in Asolo, Italy where she grew up. Of the many books she has written, she says: 'even in my poorest days ... they were written for their own sakes'. This fact, together with the spirit of adventure which inspired their author, perhaps accounts for the extraordinary immediacy and imaginative appeal of her writing.

This present book forms one of the most significant volumes of Dame Freya Stark's autobiography in that it covers the period of World War Two, recalling the vicissitudes of 1939 and the subsequent tide of war. The author herself was living and working in the Middle East for the Foreign Office and the Ministry of Information where Propaganda and Persuasion were the tools of her trade. In *Dust In The Lion's Paw* she uses this war-time experience to offer an informed historical perspective of the war, and of Britain's rôle.

'One of the best of the many autobiographies that Miss Stark has written. Her talent for friendship amounts to genius and she was able to establish relations of confidence and even affection with Civil Servants, sheikhs, bimbashis, peasants, camel drivers, monsignori, and the plump denizens of oriental harems.'

Harold Nicolson, The Observer

'It is difficult to know which to admire more, her vivid description of her experiences or the realism of the lessons which she draws from them. Few recent books have provided as much food for thought as well as material for entertainment as this one.'

Illustrated London News

Also available in the Century Travellers series:
EOTHEN by A. W. Kinglake
SOUTHERN CROSS TO POLE STAR by A. F. Tschiffely
SOUTHERN GATES OF ARABIA by Freya Stark
THE VALLEYS OF THE ASSASSINS by Freya Stark
A TRAMP ABROAD by Mark Twain
HOLY RUSSIA by Fitzroy Maclean
A THOUSAND MILES UP THE NILE by Amelia B. Edwards
FORBIDDEN JOURNEY by Ella Maillart
FULL TILT by Dervla Murphy
A RIDE TO KHIVA by Fred Burnaby
GOLDEN CHERSONESE by Isabella Bird
THE TOMB OF TUTANKHAMEN by Howard Carter
VISITS TO MONASTERIES IN THE LEVANT
  by Robert Curzon
WHEN MEN AND MOUNTAINS MEET by John Keay
LORDS OF THE ATLAS by Gavin Maxwell
SOUTH by Ernest Shackleton
ONE MAN'S MEXICO by John Lincoln
OLD CALABRIA by Norman Douglas
ISABEL AND THE SEA by George Millar
A WINTER IN ARABIA by Freya Stark
SULTAN IN OMAN by James Morris
TRAVELLER'S PRELUDE by Freya Stark
BEYOND EUPHRATES by Freya Stark
WHERE THE INDUS IS YOUNG by Dervla Murphy
THE CRUISE OF THE NONA by Hilaire Belloc
GOOD MORNING AND GOOD NIGHT
  by The Ranee Margaret of Sarawak
IN MOROCCO by Edith Wharton
PERSEUS IN THE WIND by Freya Stark
A PERSON FROM ENGLAND by Fitzroy Maclean
THE STATION by Robert Byron
WANDERINGS IN SOUTH AMERICA by Charles Waterton
WILD WALES by George Borrow
IN ETHIOPIA WITH A MULE by Dervla Murphy
TRAVEL AND ADVENTURE IN SOUTH-EAST AFRICA
  by F. C. Selous
ALEXANDER'S PATH by Freya Stark
THE LEISURE OF AN EGYPTIAN OFFICIAL
  by Lord Edward Cecil
A YEAR AMONGST THE PERSIANS by Edward Browne
WHEN MISS EMMIE WAS IN RUSSIA by Harvey Pitcher
TWO MIDDLE-AGED LADIES IN ANDALUSIA
  by Penelope Chetwode
A PILGRIMAGE TO NEJD by Lady Anne Blunt
EIGHT FEET IN THE ANDES by Dervla Murphy
TRAVELS WITH A DONKEY by Robert Louis Stevenson
SAILING ACROSS EUROPE by Negley Farson
THE COAST OF INCENSE by Freya Stark

FREYA STARK

DUST IN THE LION'S PAW

Autobiography 1939-1946

CENTURY PUBLISHING
LONDON
LESTER & ORPEN DENNYS DENEAU
MARKETING SERVICES LTD
TORONTO

Copyright © Freya Stark 1961

All rights reserved

First published in Great Britain in 1961 by
John Murray (Publishers) Ltd

This edition published in 1985 by Century Publishing Co. Ltd,
Portland House, 12–13 Greek Street, London W1V 5LE

Published in Canada by
Lester & Orpen Dennys Deneau Marketing Services Ltd,
78 Sullivan Street, Ontario, Canada

ISBN 0 7126 0451 0

*The cover painting is from the collection at the
Mathaf Gallery, 24 Motcomb Street, London SW1*

Printed in Great Britain by
Richard Clay (The Chaucer Press) Ltd, Bungay, Suffolk

DUST IN THE LION'S PAW

*

'I am but as dust in the lion's paw . . .'
from THE SHĀHNĀMA *by Firdausi (941–1020)*

This book is dedicated to the memory of friends in Iraq who were imprisoned or murdered.

My thanks are due to many people, and particularly to John Grey Murray who went over the growth of this book with endless patience, to the Marchioness of Cholmondeley, Lord David Cecil, and Lord Horder, who kindly read the typescript with helpful advice, and to the editors of *The Times*, Chatham House, and *The Geographical Magazine* for permission to reproduce extracts from articles written for them.

Contents

FOREWORD ... 1

Part One

1. SYRIA, 1939 ... 7
2. ADEN ... 11
3. FASCISTS IN THE YEMEN ... 19
4. WAR IN ADEN ... 41
5. THE RED SEA ... 51
6. BAGHDAD: THE FIRST CRISIS ... 75
7. BAGHDAD: THE SIEGE OF THE EMBASSY ... 88
8. BAGHDAD (1941, 1942) AND CYPRUS ... 117
9. END OF A CHAPTER ... 146

Part Two

10. PASSAGE TO AMERICA ... 165
11. NEW YORK TO CHICAGO ... 175
12. CHICAGO TO CANADA ... 189
13. LAST OF AMERICA ... 210
14. ENGLAND IN 1944 ... 222
15. INDIA ... 230

CONTENTS

16. ITALY 1945   252

    EPILOGUE   276

    TABLE OF MAIN CHRONOLOGICAL EVENTS 1938–1945   284

    INDEX   287

Foreword

The mood in which this book was lived seems gone beyond recapture; partly because the greatness of the background in those years makes trivial any story of one's own.

The writing of autobiography is anyway a fragile uprooting—we sift with a constant surprise at finding our life so inextricably interleaved with lives of other people: its complication, in which we are so intimately involved, appears to us three-dimensional against the apparently flat and simple surface of our neighbours. Yet as we unravel our thread we find—there, in the lives that touched us—the origin or echo of every mood we thought of as our own. It is less through us than through *their* alien or divergent mirrors that the light we had in us has been allowed to shine.

And how imperfect, when we recapture them, our own feelings appear, shorn of that 'other people's' background which was the atmosphere in which they lived. It lies around us persuasive as air, and, though we cannot identify or portray it, our voice is a phantom without it. We speak an unfamiliar language in an empty room when the life-giving echoes are silent; the climate which once caught every intonation is lost—only to be recovered, if at all, by labour and interpretation.

The Second World War began over twenty years ago, yet it is not the mere interval of a generation that has produced the unusual change. History in that time took one of the rare turns that intensify its course: like the break-through of the Iron Age into the Bronze, nuclear science brought a radical difference into the everyday life of mankind. Most particularly the concept of war has altered. As its menace grows clearer, the avoidance of it at any price is already a commonplace among thinking men, and science will usher in through necessity what Socrates and Christianity long ago offered by choice. Persuasion alone looks like the weapon of the future, with annihilation as the alternative.

This gives the coming world a hopeful tinge, and makes one happier for those now venturing upon it. But it was not the world of my generation. What my book tries to record is something that from the beginning of history persisted almost unchanged to yesterday—a conviction that war is not the ultimate disaster. To those who remember the pre-1914 stability, who came to know the German terror, or who like myself lived for years in Italy under the Fascists, there was comfort and certainty in the comparative unimportance of death. When the news of the Dunkirk beaches came over the morning wireless to Aden, it was not relief or the hope of safety that struck us, but a flash of gratitude and assurance that the honour of England in her history was safe. I would not feel this now. The damage of war has risen beyond all human right to wage it and the feelings of 1939 are out of date. Yet this book deals with those feelings: and they had their validity, and should be measured in their own right and not in the light of what was then unknown.

What I hope to describe is a task of seven war years during which my immediate colleagues and I tried to convince the Middle East—the area in which we chiefly laboured—to trust in our eventual victory. We believed in it ourselves, and during the war we succeeded. I have sketched the Arab side of this work in *East is West* which can be read as a companion to the present more personal and more exclusively English volume. It was written in 1944 during success, and this is written after Suez and other phenomena of failure; yet both I hope have kept the vicissitudes of time in sight. If the past were ever past there would be little use in recalling it; but it lives with us in never-ending variation, as if it were a magic carpet on which we travel through the middle air. The contours of our destination were long ago woven in its fading colours and half-obliterated mazes, and the time to alter or improve them passes quickly while the landscapes of our world race by below. Our future is uncontrollable if we are unable to read our past.

Many things that are in my records of this time I have discarded.

There was a private life—of friendships and of love that have lasted, that cherished and sustained me. There was ill health increasing till 1943 when I reached Canada just in time to be operated on for peritonitis; and there was long and terrible anxiety over my mother, marooned and then imprisoned in Italy and finally rescued, and over the fate of my remaining niece and nephews and my home. All this, though important to me, I have taken to be irrelevant and mentioned lightly, while I have filled in with more detail the backgrounds involved in the advancing or receding floods of war, and snatches of news or diaries that, though not intrinsically valuable, may give to some neglected moments *a local habitation and a name*.

My task was propaganda, in south Arabia, Egypt, Iraq, America, India and Italy, and the interest of my book—if its mouse-squeak is ever heard among the generals' memoirs—is a fortuitous one due to the developing urgency of this art. The world is already largely relying on persuasion rather than war, and our danger in the vast corruption of words is increasing. A correct estimate of the formidable instrument of persuasion, its legitimate and illegitimate uses, seems to me as urgent as the study of any of the other engines of our day, and the more important since it lies open in the hands of ignorance for any inconsidered rashness. In one form or another, conscious or unconscious, we have all become propagandists; integrity alone can keep us truthful.

I came to what I think are a few fundamental conclusions during my seven years' study of this subject, and my book, in the shape of autobiography, is a description of how the conclusions were gradually arrived at, by experiment, thought and error, through the war. The adventure is one I like to think of for it was done in a heroic time, facing unequal odds in the first few years, and always with the friendship, guidance and help of people far more able than myself. Of these friendships many remain to make me happy, and some have become a part of that past by which our present lives; five in particular went deeply into my life and my world is the poorer for their absence—Lord Wavell and Brigadier Clayton in Egypt, Sir Kinahan Cornwallis and Adrian Bishop in Iraq, and Bernard Berenson in Italy when I came home: Nuri Pasha too, a friend of thirty years, must never be forgotten.

FOREWORD

I have included some of their letters because I love to think of them and often read them, and like to share them, looking out from the warmth of their memory as from a peaceful tower.

PART ONE

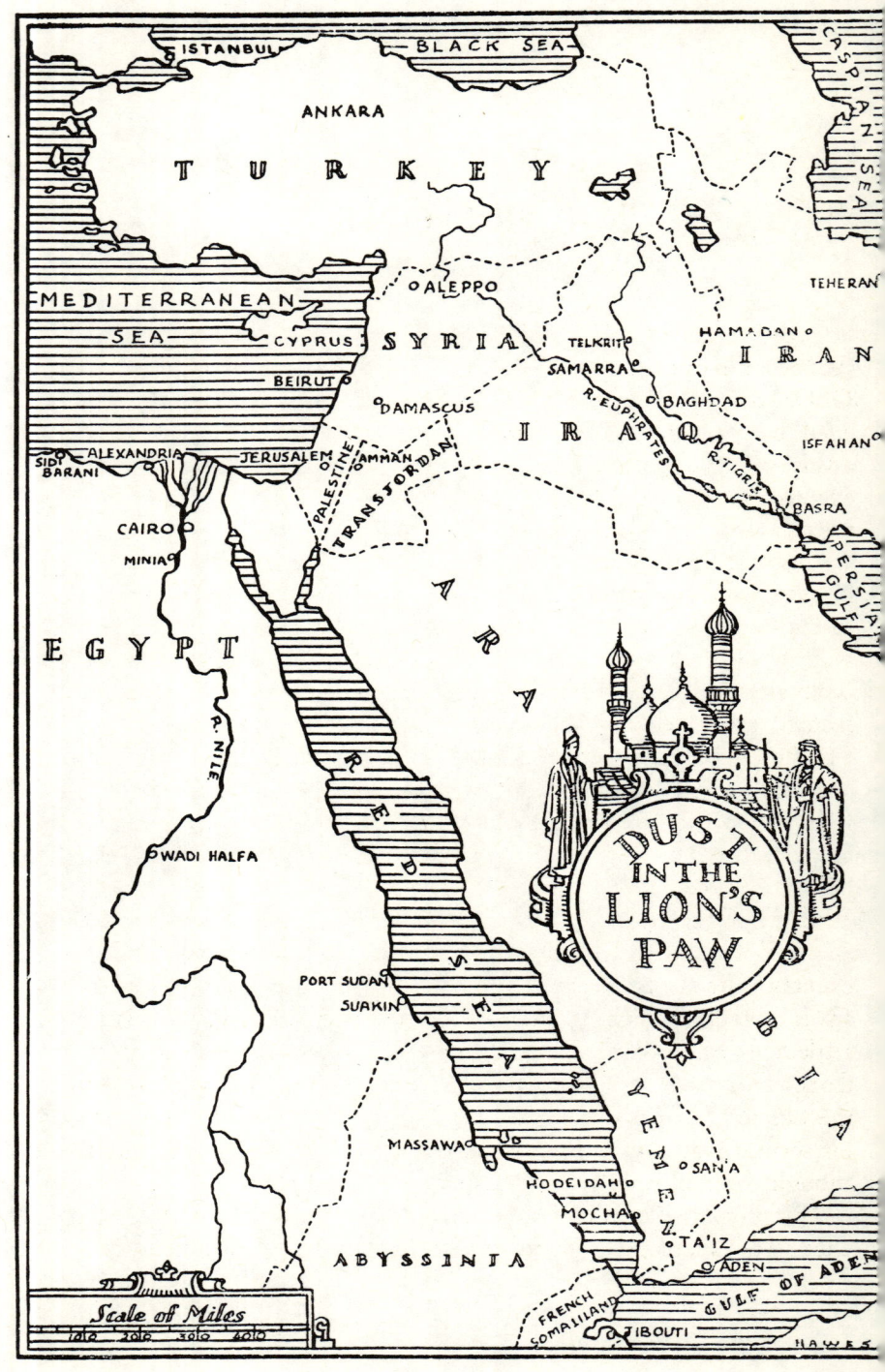

1

Syria, 1939

In 1938 I reached London while Neville Chamberlain was declaring the 'peace in our time' that filled us with bewilderment and wonder. Of Germany I knew little, though I had been there that year, frightened by its dangerous seclusion. But in Fascist Italy we were aware since 1933 of Abyssinian plans. These could only mean an eventual grab for the Mediterranean which English oscillations between threat and appeasement were making deceptively alluring to the historically uneducated régime. Italy—I never doubted—would fight us if she thought she safely could. In the spring of 1939 I wrote to the Foreign Office to ask if my Arabic could be of use in case of war; went home to pack our most valued possessions and distribute them among friends for hiding; and with a few months in hand, as seemed probable, travelled to Syria and Greece, to look at things I might never again see in a possibly ruined world.

As far as I was concerned, the war began in that spring weather. I wandered for some weeks among the Templars' castles and the fortresses of the Assassins in their almost unvisited hills. In some hollow beneath the snowline among the Syrian flowers I read William of Tyre and the memoirs of Usama, until time forgot itself and the prose of the delightful lord of Sheizar and the day-to-day events of the crusaders entered my life as I haunted their footpaths. I was now descending, making for Aleppo and picking up letters in settled places on my way. In Hama there was one that I desired, from a friend asking me to marry. Two days later in Aleppo I found the obscure news of his death. No investigation could be pressed, his service was anyway beyond the law; he had written to me, I thought later, already with foreboding.

This shock made, as I look back upon it, an almost physical difference. The landscapes, remembered in sunlight before it, I could see, after it happened, only in shadow. I was in the house of friends who ran a hospital in Aleppo and were used to grief in and out of its doors; they were good to me, and left me alone to weep as if all my tears had to be shed. For three days it went on, and surely I shall melt, I thought, if this cannot stop. It was a sorrow unlike any felt before, a nakedness uncomforted by the majesty of death. This harm done without personal cause in the name of some blind formula, and the warm life annihilated, left me despairing in a world built with despair.

When I was a child, I used to watch some blacksmiths at work along a canal in Piedmont, beating out scythes for the reaping of corn. Two men would bend over the heated iron and hammer alternately while the sparks responded, and the curved triangle of metal shone with a rusty glow as if already it knew the colour of sunset on harvested fields. A lad with a pair of pincers would suddenly seize and dip it hissing to be tempered in the stream, as we too have to be tempered for war.

Through spring and summer the history of Europe reeled drunk from crisis to crisis, while I lingered on the Syrian coasts and the beauty of the world in spite of all continued to speak its detached intimate language to the heart.

Dearest B [I wrote to my mother]:

... The Altounians[1] took me to their country place, above Alexandretta—*so* beautiful—that incredible bay, the snow-capped Taurus behind it, the green and mauve of early spring, the Muslim village hanging white on the slope, the jagged tilted hills. Down below you see Alexandretta and its ships, small and flat—and wonder what will happen next. Europe does not loom so large—everyone wonders whether this province will be given to the Turks and when.[2] Already their flags flutter everywhere ... All that Altounian property, and their model dairy farm and boathouse on the lake of Antioch—all may go from one moment to the next. I can't tell you how lovely that plain is—water avenues of yellow iris and white flowers: a strange cold colour like shot silk and a sort of Parisian elegance of landscape. It is done with so little: a ribbon of water, a patch of green on a bare slope, a thin little crescent of cypress trees—and

[1] Dr. and Mrs. Ernest Altounian.
[2] It was ceded in June 1939.

the evening light thrown over—it is something poignant and beautiful no one will ever forget. The Orontes flows by, muddy and full, and one can see the wall that Bohemond scaled at night[1]—hesitating because no doubt he knew that some rung of an Arab ladder must always break.

I followed that shining coastline south to Lebanon, and have many letters sent home describing it—one at the end of April from Tartous,

... the loveliest Templar church in Syria. Strength and beauty combined in these old fortified churches. The floor is sand, the stone a lion yellow, a little pre-Christian shrine is embodied in the nave, the deep windows have smooth receding walls to shoot from and let in streaks of sunlight.

Huge blocks of citadel and wall in a triangle from the sea have all been grown into and over by the modern houses: you see a pendent arch over some tiny courtyard, and whole blocks built into the vaults of the magazines. No one stops in Tartous; there is only a dingy place to sleep, rather picturesque over columns in a garden, but the sort of sordid bed one gets in Syria; a man obligingly turned out of it to make room for me. It takes hours for the exhaustion to wear off in the morning. People dash by on the main coast road. But there is lovely country rolling away full of corn and little hills of olives and the snow ridge of Jebel Akrum behind ... A crusader ruin is there, lost on a green hill in a green landscape with Safita and its tower in sight far away. A monastery on the next hill provided a horse with fine red double-pommelled saddle when the car could go no longer, and I rode up under oak trees, the land scented with flowers, remote and unimportant and pleasant, all its active life and wars forgotten. When I came back to the monastery the monks gave eggs and curds and sat and talked with their buns of hair tied neatly on their necks. They have a fair up there on August the 20th. The little monastery is built of good stone, safely shut in its own courtyard with carved windows opening high up on to that peaceful rolling view, the sea on the west and the snow-range on the east. After lunch I went wandering over more country filled with sheets of marigolds or borage, with buffaloes ploughing and the Alawit girls hoeing in bright dresses, and came to another small square castle called Yahmour in a hamlet not far from the sea ... Men there, in companies of six or seven, were catching quails and small birds with hawks. They beat the corn with a stick held in one hand and when a bird flies out the hawk pounces from their other wrist. They

[1] During the First Crusade in 1098.

decorate him with a bell and he has saffron-yellow eyes. This is a forbidden sport and the people were frightened when they saw us, but they let me photograph them after being talked to. When we left them we came to a headland with a few monoliths—a Phoenician city that once welcomed Alexander and is now a lonely stretch of shore.

One clung to the spacious world as it was falling. I crossed the Aegean by Istanbul to Greece in an almost empty ship while the war in Ethiopia was ending and Italy and Germany announced their 'pact of steel'. By October our own war had come, and I left England for Aden as Assistant Information Officer to Stewart Perowne under the Ministry of Information: 'I waited at the coast for the tide and left in the afternoon—all with lifebelts on—and had eventually to sleep in Boulogne, pitch dark. Paris deserted and the shops far more shut than London, Italy all deserted: Milan station about ten people, and Venice pleasantly empty with only Venetians—all pained and surprised because we "want to fight". You would think it was a caprice we indulge in for fun!'[1]

---

[1] Letter to Jock Murray, 15.10.39.

2
Aden

In Aden Queen Victoria presided in a bronze—or was it a marble?—crinoline over the Crescent and the colonial smugness of the oriental shops. A French or Italian town would have had an esplanade, bandstand and café, and some flights of fancy in its buildings; but Aden made its effort in a confident age and rested there, and we still sat under *punkahs* in the Marina Hotel. If the volcanic stone, which depressingly repeated the colour of the cliff behind it, had been whitewashed it would have made the town better to look at and cooler; but the myth that utility and beauty are alternatives was disproved by an absence of both, and where the black houses did go in for ornament, one was glad that it happened so seldom. Here and there the older Arabian architecture showed what beauty could be achieved in the country's traditional style; and the site—with its volcanic background, the opaline bay and sharpness of Little Aden's then still solitary outline, and its inlets and skyline of Yemeni hills (seen only at sunrise)—was such as might delight the architect's heart. Against it the ugly streets leaned, the bank and the gothic of the church emerged with a few of the more prosperous stores, the hospital and the Governor's residence were run up in an untidy way as objects of minor importance, and the whole—clustering round the Prince of Wales' Pier—managed in spite of all to touch one with an absurd tenderness for the tenacity that pieces together a small travesty of England in any unlikely corner.

My little trader purred down here early in November along the Red Sea highway, and every turn of the engine brought us more dreamily out of the atmosphere of war. The dim and rustling waters, the tropical night that moves in shadows from star to star, as yet held no menace. The small western towns of Arabia twinkled carelessly on their flat shore. Only at Perim, when we turned its signal, did we realize that from here eastward the continent lay unlit: black with bony ridges like a limb of Satan, it was cradled in the darkness which it had known for ages; the searchlights played their flickering fugues across the bay of Aden, and traffic had to wait to enter with the dawn.

It is difficult to put oneself back into the world as I then saw it, and the Arab world in particular. 'In Arabia,' I wrote at that time, 'there is something of the same state of mind as once obtained among the Greeks: a sense of kinship loosely held, constantly infringed by particular divergences but kept alive by such general events as the Olympic Games in one case and the pilgrimage to Mecca in the other.... Their pan-Arabism we think of as Utopia, and it may be so: but a strong and united Arabia would be to our interest; its divisions are a source of danger and an occasion for intrigue; and even if the dream of federation is a dream for the future, and a misty one at that, it is well for us to do all we can to further it, using to their full extent the three great assets for unity they have—the common language and religion, and the consciousness of common interests we can help to encourage.... The main danger that threatens is foreign interference ... and it is fairly obvious that we shall very soon require an Arabia as strong, as peaceful and as favourable to us as we can get.'[1]

I mentioned Egypt at that time, 'independent, prosperous and friendly'; Saudi Arabia at peace and 'the Yemen coming to understand the difference between a satisfied and an unsatisfied (Italian) neighbour'; Iraq 'unique in being a kingdom imagined, fashioned and established by an alien race'; the whole of the eastern coast and the whole of the southern loyal in friendship; and even Palestine, tossed and troubled for several thousand years, less unhappy than a century or so ago. 'Not all has been done by Britain; but all has been made possible by the mere fact that she is interested in the integrity of Arabia. If anyone doubts this, let him look at the map of Europe and think how different the fate of many small nations might have been if our commerce had made it necessary for us to keep their frontiers safe.'

It will be seen that I was what is called an imperialist, with perhaps

[1] Chatham House lecture, February 1939.

some reservations. 'We have, since the First World War, admitted one important new idea into our theory of empire: we have accepted it as a trust that is temporary and does not interfere with people's final independence ... and our chances are now bound up with that theory. It means that in Arabia, as elsewhere, our guardianship is not static; it allows a sort of elasticity for growth. Many in England seem to think of empire as a possession we hold external to ourselves. But those who labour for it and in it mostly look upon it as an opportunity for service. I believe these are right, and if all felt in this way our foundations would stand against all storms, nor would it be possible in such a commonwealth ... ever to think of lopping off any branch against its will, whatever the race to which it might belong.'

Such principles are now taken to be typical of a new and more liberal world: yet I shared them with practically every friend in Government service some twenty years ago. In Aden and along the southern and western coasts our community was made up of such people who had influenced these lands through peace and were now busy girding them up for war; and our task was made easy by the personal popularity of the officials who had laboured here before us.

I think of many of them—a tough, innocent and friendly little crowd, disciplined by solitude and evenings at the club: of Sir Bernard Reilly our Governor who, when the need arose, left his golf and came to sensible decisions of his own; of Count Bentinck, his A.D.C., who was also the cypher officer, kept awake half the nights by telegrams. We were all fond of the Count, and made him recite the 'Waterloo' cantos of *Childe Harold* whenever a crisis approached, and saw him off later to the commandos of the Abyssinian jungle. Colonel Lake was Political Secretary when first I arrived, and would take me for walks up one little valley and down another in companionable silence, by beaches spoilt by the new barbed wire, where shreds of the old were still rotting since 1914. Harold and Doreen Ingrams[1] were in the Secretariat: and there were many others—police, education, justice and transport; the doctors and hospital

[1] W. H. Ingrams, C.M.G., O.B.E., British Resident Adviser at Mukalla, S. Arabia, 1937–40; Acting Governor of Aden 1940.

nurses; our Air Vice-Marshal[1] and his wife, and the R.A.F. who lived on the flat ground where flamingoes walked among hillocks of salt. Mahrattas danced their torch-dances or wrestled, or climbed in patterns over tall poles on their playground; and the 15th Punjabis were stationed next to them, whose band we inveigled to learn 'The Blue Danube' for the Governor's ball. The Navy I came to know as I lunched with them daily at the Marina Hotel; and now and then, beyond this circle, young men passed in and out from their districts, where they lived among the bedawin whom they loved. So did we all, and the charm and forthrightness of the South Arabian Arabs was perhaps the chief pleasantness of our days. Beside them and the official world, I would escape twice a week or so to the old town of Crater, to see Hilda Besse and Anton sparkling with gaiety and malice. King of the Red Sea coasts and their commerce, and living—as befitted the manipulator of so many of its complicated strings—a little and not uncritically apart, he would take me climbing over the dead crags of Aden, quoting proverbs: 'If the speech is sweet, the bananas are dear' or 'The gift of a crow is but a worm' (if some nit-wit had annoyed him; for he enjoyed his enemies with unfailing gusto). He was distressed at this time because he could not help making money during the war; it piled itself up *malgré moi*. He too is one of those whom one misses, and St. Antony's College in Oxford remains a monument to one of the most vital persons of his time.

These were the fringes of life, whose centre for me was our office with a balcony over the harbour, a large and open room where sparrows nested. Stewart dipped in and out (for much of the work was outside) and was gay and easy and would sit on the balcony of an evening when the desks were cleared and drink vermouth which we could still get from Djibouti and watch the ships slip in or out. I bet him twelve bottles that Italy would be against us by the spring.

I had never lived close to shipping before, and at that time, with our hearts so far away, the gliding shapes moving quietly when the boom was opened would seem to me like veins that carried our own bloodstream across the sick body of the world. The news came

[1] Air Vice-Marshal Sir Ronald Macfarlane Reid, K.C.B., D.S.O., M.C., Air Officer Commanding British Forces, Aden 1938–41.

regularly in that first false winter of the war. Pamphlets, pictures, letters kind and encouraging and cheerful came pouring from our Ministry in London, and there too the group we had left as new acquaintances were soon becoming friends and so remained. From our side a constant stream was carried, moans for films, wails for pictures from Mr. Primrose's 'paths of dalliance' in the photographic department, a plan for an Arab college, and another, more fortunate, in the same file but resuscitated by later hands to flourish in the Lebanon. How comforting is any small result out of the living forests sacrificed for the making of paper! Jock Murray was getting my book out before he joined the army—so much a part of my books that I sometimes think he has written them. 'Be very careful, fair, conscientious, unbiased, impartial, my dear Jock,' I wrote, 'over this heavy responsibility of correcting, which makes you the arbiter of my, I hope, semi-immortal reputation—150 years if you use the best paper.'

To my mother I wrote all the pleasant news I could think of to amuse her: about riding in starlight before sunrise, and back in time for office at nine; 'there is only one ride here; no doubt one's thoughts can vary it.' About the Governor's ball 'with the full moon on the terrace behind the Union Jacks, and nearly everyone wearing decorations'. About Miss X who has had to lodge with two bachelors because 'one has to put up with anything in war time'. About Christmas, spent as a holiday on the plateau of Dhala,

... in Alpine air, delicious: it pours in cold and pure through the windows at night. The rest-house is a square little stone building and you look from it over a great basin, its rim the hills of Yafa'i and Yemen. The enemy country of the upper Yafa'i is there on the skyline, high level hills with blue shadows under clouds that float from the sea. No one much has been into Upper Yafa'i, but my servant comes from there and thinks he might take me if I were not now tied by official ties; how lovely it would be just to go off. We have now been for a walk to a little Wali saint's tomb on a hill. He is not even whitewashed because 'none of his family are left'—the ancestor worship is here very much mixed with the saints: from his altitude, all alone on the edge of the plateau, one looks round at pointed or flat-topped hills, ranges and ranges, every gap is filled. On the level they grow furrows of *qat* and eat it all locally. Colonel Lake has arrived and inspected our guard of honour, their officers with drawn swords before them and the men painted blue with ballet skirts also blue. The little boys are left white and are learning to play peaceful cricket, but the Yafa'i neighbours have just had nineteen murders over the beating of a drum.

We had one of the best Christmas Days I have ever spent: started off in a procession of five horses and a foal, and three donkeys running in and out with servants, soldiers, small boys, rugs—we wound up three thousand feet (we are already six thousand up here) to where the Emir has a mountain fort. I think we saw as great a view as anywhere in the world—mountains studded on their lower peaks with fortress towers, with here and there terraces and cultivated hollows, and ahead of us the blue wall of the Yemen. At this height there are villages; a Jewish one we passed, the Jews with their curly side-locks grouped on rocks to see us, looking very biblical. We looked rather nondescript, except the Count in a wide-brimmed hat that might just have come from Biarritz and Colonel Lake and Stewart correct and handsome in *keffiahs*. Our last day was as lovely as the rest: Stewart and I doing letters and in the afternoon a ride with the Emir and two feudal vassals and about five barefoot soldiers among the horses' heels. They are nice little locally-bred mares with Jaufi parents, and went deliciously. Next day we saw the Sultan of Lahej on the way, and came back to the heavy air and loads of work to deal with.

I wrote now and then to our most helpful of chiefs in London, Rushbrook Williams, and told him of people weeping at the reading of our bulletin in the square. "Many go to listen, but many stay away because they cannot bear it." "Why can't they bear it?" I asked. "They think what it would be like if their country and their families were being treated as the Germans have been treating the Poles."

On another day I described the censoring (which I usually did) of a film just out from England, where a kiss seemed unnecessarily prolonged for our simple audience. "'What does it matter?' said the Arab manager beside me. 'One kisses even one's housekeeper when starting on a journey.'" It was hard to keep pace with the sophistication of Asia during the war and has continued to be so ever since.

The reading of the news was the climax of our day, and Stewart organized it and handed over the writing of it to me when I came.

Having no newspapers, we recast it in English for the Arabic translator, and loosed it from a loud-speaker, after the sunset prayer, in the chief *maidan* or open space of the town, where it was pleasant to stroll in the mellowness of evening and the darkened houses. The cafés at the corners did business under shaded lights. A lantern, dimmed with the dust of years, showed the seller of *qat* (*Cathula Edulis*) from Yemen, brisk at his trade in the leisurely hours. It is a mild intoxicant which can only be chewed fresh, and the green tips of the boughs are the best. They came in bundles from the northerly hills, pitching slowly on camels that usurped the sidewalk. There was much coming and going, and yellow splashes from the booths showed the city gowns' dilapidated whiteness. The news was now a ceremony and Stewart, like a prow in surf, would approach the scene through greeting, tossing hands, dive into the police station, and be lost among the switches. In a dim harmony under the stars the cheerful crowd—coloured turbans, Somali caps embroidered with birds or fishes, gold-embroidered Indian or black skullcap of Parsee—would squat in the dust in rows as if it were a theatre. Through the fasting month of Ramadhan there had been holy readings, chapters from the *Qur'an*, before the news was given; but after I came we began with music, the slow and plaintive songs of the Yemen, accompanied by a lute. It may have been the mere gentleness of open air, but the notes had a melancholy like the solitary songs of country people, like the reaper heard by Wordsworth, heard for ever:

> For as she cuts and binds the grain
> She sings a melancholy strain—
> Oh listen, for the vale profound
> Is overflowing with the sound.

These pastoral melodies carry their own loneliness and bring into their notes the quiet horizons, the days of seafaring or mountain pastures, the empty easy hours of noonday when they were first conceived. It was pleasant to have this calm contrasting prelude to the European news, which came dropping slowly in tempered accents, for we were lucky to have an announcer with a beautiful voice. He picked out every syllable, giving it full value in a way that Arabs, who all adore their language, appreciate and understand.

It is indeed a man's language, so measured, rich, precise and grave; a language meant for council or for war. Its emphasis, for one thing, is on the verb, which all right living should be. The events of the day, the sinking ships, the burning aircraft, the internal horrors of Germany bloodstained amid her conquests, the vast slow girding of the loins of resistance: they pass before us in phrases which for many centuries have informed the Arab peoples of distant vicissitudes of empire. They have spoken of Abbassid wars in Spain or Khorasan, of Turkish battles under the walls of Vienna, even of those days of dawn when the Prophet's banner first moved across the frontiers of Arabia. Perhaps it is this long tradition that makes the rows of many-coloured turbans turn with such easy keen absorption towards our news. It is no new thing for them to belong to a commonwealth that stretches across half the inhabited world in a single many-peopled sheaf of nations.[1]

[1] From *The Times*, 2 February 1940.

3

Fascists in the Yemen

Towards the end of 1939 Sir Kinahan Cornwallis, then in Political Intelligence, wrote to ask if I could help by letting him know, 'as often as you like, how things are going in your part of the world,' especially in regard to the Yemen where our propaganda was said to be nil while the Germans were active, and the Italians active and pro-German. 'In consequence it is stated that ninety per cent of Yemen is in favour of Germany. Do you think this an exaggeration? . . . I see that the Imam intends to maintain his neutrality, but he is an old man and life must be precarious in those parts. I have no background and will be very grateful if you can supply it. . . .'

Dear Ken (I answered),[1]

Our Intelligence is filled with sorrow at the thought that the F.O. has not got the Yemen on its finger-tips; it appears that files and files about it are reposing at the Colonial Office and you might give them a look.

Aden and Hadhramaut are, as you say, satisfactory . . . the Yemen we have hardly touched and may count it as a Fascist preserve . . . This is, in my view, entirely our own fault. The Italians should naturally be disliked there (and so they are in a subterranean way). Italy is more dangerous to them than we are, and her power would not be great enough to make her feared if we were anxious to prevent it. The fault is not here; our hands are tied and we have to sit still under every infringement of gentlemen's and every other agreement. Now this seems to me quite idiotic (if you will forgive the unofficial language) . . . Italy in being with us or against consults her own interests entirely: and the Yemen is not a sufficiently big one to sway her into enmity on its account alone. Her policy is being shaped in Europe; we can safely use her preoccupations there just as she is using ours—to consolidate ourselves out here.

We are far too prone to say: 'Italy doesn't matter.' We said it in 1935

[1] 8 December 1940.

when, by attending to her in time, we could at any rate have saved ourselves the trouble of the Abyssinian war. Even when that started, in 1937, very few realized its implications, but in three years' time the threat which had been obvious years before had become a commonplace. The same thing is happening now. Nobody thinks much of her penetration in the Yemen—but what is the point of allowing it *unnecessarily* when we could so easily put a stop to it? I do not suggest being provocative: but I do suggest a *riposte* to every Italian step, however veiled—and the result would be satisfactory not only as regards the Yemen but as regards Italy: the one way to impress on her the value of our friendship is to accentuate such powers as we have of being disagreeable if we wish. We are thoroughly bad at dealing with Italians, chiefly because we insist on treating the whole country as Fascist, whereas we have there (far more than in Germany) a small governing faction which will always be anti-British at heart, and the larger number which, if Fascism is overturned but not otherwise, would easily become genuinely friendly.

I hope to go up to the Yemen in seven or eight weeks' time if this can be managed. The idea is to sit there, rectify rumours, and alter the atmosphere as much as one can from the standpoint of female insignificance, which has its compensations, and Sir Bernard and Stewart Perowne have both agreed to this with their usual broadmindedness. It was in fact only because of the Yemen that I was allowed to come from Cairo at all. I may not be able to do anything; everyone says it is very difficult, but I shall enjoy going.

The plan was particularly to smuggle in, and to show, a portable cinema—a religiously forbidden object which could at that time make some noticeable difference to opinion. At the beginning of February, in a lorry with cook, servant, three men, and the cinema unmentioned among my suitcases, I made the six-day journey from Aden, up the torrent beds of the northern frontier which was all the road there was, to the sub-capital of Ta'iz, down to the sandy Tihama, through Mocha with its fort and few straggling houses on the sands, through Beit el-Faqih and other brick-built decayed forgotten seats of learning, to Hodeidah, and thence to the plateau and San'a the capital, refreshingly cooled with high showers after the heat of Aden.

★ ★ ★ ★

FASCISTS IN THE YEMEN

It is difficult to recapture the feeling of danger which hovered over the Red Sea coastlands in those years when Mussolini's schemes were in the ascendant. These were unrolling themselves in a perfectly consistent policy of which the stages were marked in Libya, the Dodecanese, and covertly in Egypt; and the Abyssinian war only accentuated what had been the actual state of affairs for a long time. The Italian propaganda increased steadily. When I first travelled about the Hadhramaut in 1934 I heard of only a little bribery in ministerial circles, but during my second visit, in 1937, practically every trouble there was had some Fascist flavour about it. As these Arabs emigrated for a living from their poor and scanty valleys, many found their way to Eritrea, where their being British caused them numerous vexations. But when the Abyssinian war came to an end, the Italian Government noticed that we had meanwhile completed the transfer of Aden from the Indian Government to the Colonial Office; and discovered—with some disgust and for the first time—that we were in peaceful possession of the long strip of country which stretches half-way across the Indian Ocean seaboard. We had long had rights here, but had done nothing to implement them, and the Hadhramaut was still marked yellow and not red on most of the maps, a fact which they apparently noticed with annoyance: that we should not trouble to colour our own possessions on our own maps must have been irritating to a country exhausting the resources of publicity in the new gloss of empire.

The Yemen was a far more serious proposition, and increasingly so with the gathering threat of war. In the years gone by, one pounce had already been tried on Hodeidah, and had been thwarted by a British sloop under a commander not afraid to make up his mind in a crisis. Mussolini, manœuvring like a cobra with a lizard, now presented the Imam with a gift of guns placed just beyond our frontier in the north. We were poorly situated, since we could prepare no sort of defence without offending the Yemeni ruler. In any case we had nothing much for defence at our disposal. Italian doctors scattered about the country in four useful places were all accompanied by technicians with sub-military equipment, while we could only send two very unarmed doctors, and Colonel Lake on a brief official visit. Because of this threatening background I had been spoken to in Cairo by friends in the army, who pressed £100 for expenses upon me, and suggested that I should go. My only private reason for not doing so was my mother, who had moved back to our Italian home: but private reasons carry little weight in war, and I knew what she would have wished. The distinction between Fascists and Italians, so difficult for our people to grasp, was plain enough to us who lived among them: almost all the friends we had there would have checkmated Mussolini if they could, nor did they want a victory which would turn their country into a German province in its wake; and now without an excuse in the world we were threatened, nor did my conviction falter for a moment that Italy would attack us when she could. 'The Anglo-Italian friendship,' someone said at that time, 'is the friendship of the English for the Italians.' And my feelings about the Fascists were (and are) expressed by Benedetto Croce, who said that they could never be intelligent and honest, for 'if a Fascist is honest he is not intelligent; if he is intelligent, he is not honest; and if he is both intelligent and honest, he is not a Fascist'. For this reason I use a word which has had some of its venom dusted over by time, but is more appropriate to the people I was to meet in the Yemen than the name of a country I love.

In San'a the walled city gates were still locked every evening. In the one of the three quarters where the Turks had built agreeable little houses, H.H. the Imam turned out his Director of Artillery to provide me with a lodging. Here I spent six weeks, learning my first lesson in the dregs of propaganda. As this is the subject of my book, and as these weeks conditioned the whole of my later work, my letters to Stewart in Aden are left to describe them.

SAN'A *8 February 1940*

Dear Stewart,

I have come back from a pleasant tea-drinking with the Qadhi[1] and his charming chief wife. It is one of the ridiculous superstitions that orientals are not fond of their wives: she is no longer young, but so lively and sensitive and temperamental in a pleasant way that he is obviously

[1] Qadhi Muhammad Raghib, the travelled and cultured Minister for Foreign Affairs.

devoted to her. She could hardly bear to talk of the war—the thought of women and children drowning (which we are in danger of considering as a part of journalism) genuinely upsets her. So we talked of Stambul instead, and cherry orchards. We have arranged to call together on the wife of Prince Qasim, who will then arrange a visit to the royal harim. I described my cinema, but said I did not like to show it unless the Imam permitted. An offensive was then directed on the Qadhi in Turkish: the harim *insist* on seeing it and we are going to have a small private soirée in his house. I *do* hope you will be able to feed me with films.

I am sending our own Queen's photograph as a present, wrapped in a chiffon veil embroidered with silver, to Mme Qadhi.

Do you like to hear all this gossip every day or does it bore you?

9 February 1940

The chief Jewish merchant came to call and tells me that Colonel Lake was exchanging nine eastern oases for Sheikh Sa'id [the point near our frontier which the Italians had just supplied with guns]. I did my best to rectify this monstrosity and he then took me to his house and is going to find you a beautiful *janbiya* [dagger]: is there anything else you want?

The head of police came to call. His name is Hanesh. He went away with his hand on his heart saying my Arabic is *bulbul* (alas it is not!) and would I count on the police in any difficulty whatsoever?

I am beginning to disentangle four among my bodyguard of soldiers. They get six dollars a month, with good bread for sergeants and bad for the rank and file. Poor people, and they comfort themselves with *qat*.

Nagi [my cook] has just been advising me. 'All things in Arabia,' he says, 'are done by the harim; get them to wish what you wish, and you will get it.' It might be said anywhere. Anyway we hope for the cinema.

10 February 1940

I am feeling awfully tired: I hope it is not malaria as, if it is, the doctors say cheerfully it is bound to be malignant. I think it really comes from losing my sleep today so as to translate King George's telegram into Arabic. Any time would do, they said, but I thought you might like something expeditious in Aden. After that Mme Qadhi came here and was staggered by the print of our navy which I took from my wall. 'No wonder,' she said, 'that a few ships more or less make no difference to you.' She then took me to a sumptuous tea with Prince Qasim's wife and two most charming red-cheeked boys dressed grown-up with daggers in their diminutive sashes over dark blue gowns. It is worth being an Arab child to be allowed a real dagger at your waist at the age of five. As we sat a thunderstorm poured over us, and as we came back through the twilight everything smelt good. I thought of you with a pang in the heat of Aden. Everything will be at its very best here they say in a month's time.

I hope to go to the Imam's harim next week. One *cannot* hurry.

The Arab town and *suq* are fantastic with their decorated houses, but, for real beauty, I think no one with any taste can fail to prefer the Hadhramaut. The ornament here is *plastered* on and far too much; there, the sense of proportion and value is always exquisite: here it is the inheritance of those South Arabian profiteers getting more and more debased. If one felt feverish it would turn into a nightmare. As it is, I think it most beautiful seen through a mist of blossom from my roof.

Tomorrow the cinema is to be shown to the Qadhis and Prince Qasim. The thought of having to do the speaking makes me feel slightly sick.

12 February 1940

I am writing from bed, having gone under completely, what with the colossal dinner given yesterday and the effort of the cinema after. You can't guess half the agony it is to me to speak in public, and when I showed Nagi how to start the engine and the thing actually went I felt like one of those amateurs who succeed in calling up the Devil! But it went without a hitch and Prince Qasim talked about the rule of the waves for the rest of the evening. For the first time since coming up here I was told how necessary it is to strengthen our friendship with the Arabs. He asked me: 'Do not the Italians rule the Mediterranean?' I said, 'You would hardly call yourself a ruler in a house when someone else has both the front and back door keys?' and I could see the really tremendous effect of the film afterwards. But whether I shall be able to show it more widely is very doubtful.

PS. I am sure the first idea of a Turkish mosque came to someone who saw two cypress trees, one on either side of a small round hill. I look out at such a landscape and it is like Saint Sophia with a minaret on either side of the dome.

13 February 1940

The Royal Family *must* see the cinema tomorrow night. You are implored to send more films. I am to go at 7.30 p.m. and, as far as I can see, spend the night there. *Do* wish me luck. If you knew how I wish it were you! But I am pleased, and hope you will give me a pat on the back, for walking on eggs has not been in it these days.

The Qadhi sat for a long talk on frontiers, [the Yemeni-Aden frontier] all very hopeful of a friendly solution. He said: 'While Reilly was in Aden nothing ever happened; when he goes on leave these young men want to make themselves conspicuous and there are forty troubles at once. They say Lake is old-fashioned—they do not know that it takes forty years of kind manners to make oneself beloved.' It would indeed be criminal not to send Colonel Lake here when he is free, and you can quote my words as much as you like.

The invaluable Nagi meanwhile has been teaching the Imam to make butter. I send him out in the morning to chat in the royal *majlis*, and there they were pouring fresh milk into an Italian butter machine; nothing happened; try again; then Nagi stepped out and said the milk must be one day old and saved the situation. So that in a week we have made butter, have translated King George's telegram and have shown the British Navy to the ladies of San'a. It makes one feel like a dictionary.

14 February 1940

I enclose out of my mail a PS. from my mother to show you prices in Italy—it might make an item in the bulletin? All copper there is being requisitioned for shell-rings! Another letter from Italy looks very like war in the spring.

I never thought to rise to such heights as to draw the German radio! What fun! By the way Mama writes that the B.B.C. is now being listened to all over northern Italy and *much* appreciated.

I have had a charming visit from the Governor of San'a, a cheerful old boy, voluminous in white silk dressing-gown embroidered with yellow flowers. We went over the usual ground—the *hudud* [frontiers] and Palestine. I pointed out to him the advantages of having us as neighbours. What the old boy answered was: 'If we got rid of the Turks, who know how to fight, don't you think we could deal with the Italians ourselves?'

We then talked about Himyarites and Marib, and looked at the Navy picture which is a perfect godsend. I tried to defend our Cabinet from charges of corruption (rather amusing as coming from him!) and told him it couldn't be judged by people like So-and-so who came from no noble house. So he told me the story of some Muslims who asked Muhammad how they might know that the Day of Judgement was near. 'By the fact,' said the Prophet, 'that the reins of government are in the hands of the lowest of the low.' I pointed out several states in Europe where the Day of Judgement may reasonably be expected, and he pointed out that Musso's father was a blacksmith. This rather snobbish argument is almost the most effective of all. I shall be able to write a treatise on propaganda when I get back.

15 February 1940

Am a shattered wreck again after last night, but it went off without a hitch except for one ghastly moment when the engine wouldn't start and I felt as one does on the doorstep of the dentist. Nagi could be allowed only as near the harim as the court below, with the engine-cord coming up through a window, and I had to cope upstairs in dimness and tumult; wives, daughters, female servants and Princes of the Blood all seething round me. The Imam, himself, I suppose I shall never see as women are beneath him, but his two wives were there (the elder Fatima; so very nice) and four daughters-in-law, three sons and *at least* five daughters.

The microphone explosions were the greatest success. Do impress how vital it is for us to have lots of *good* 16 mm. films. *Ordinary Life in Edinburgh* is the present rather surprising favourite: they adore it—just people walking up and down Princes Street! When the performance was over, I showed them which of the ships they had been seeing (on the map of the Navy, which I left for them to talk over with the Imam). I don't really think it matters not seeing the Imam himself, so long as one gets to the harim: the two wives live in two separate palaces, the Palace of Happiness (for the elder one) and of Thankfulness for the younger, with a garden between them so that they can see each other and live 'as sisters' and the Imam is very fair and stays one month with each. It seemed to me that there was a lot to be said for this arrangement, but Fatima says it is worrying to see one's husband's heart go wobbling to and fro. It is awfully hard work to combine social affability with the running of the cinema all by oneself, but I sat afterwards and chatted over this and that. I don't really *like* the job, because I hate having to be pleasant with a purpose—I mean going out to make oneself liked irrespective of whether one really wants to like people. As soon as a real liking comes it is all right, but otherwise it makes one feel rather like a commercial traveller with the rival firm round the corner. However, I think it is a good work, both for them and for us, and I believe the sight of the Navy has really done something. The children had great fun talking through the microphone.

Today I am meeting all the foreign colony here.

16 February 1940

Darling B. [my mother],

Yesterday I went again to work the little cinema in the house of the second Queen, very young and pretty but gauche, dressed in white and tinsel. They wear charming indoor clothes, long to the ground, gathered at the waist, sleeves with cuffs, just like dolls, and white panties with frills to the ankles. Sometimes they wear a tight-waisted coat of brocade, like a riding-coat, and their heads are wrapped in chiffon and tinsel swathed to the neck, or else they tie two handkerchiefs, one under the chin and one like a circlet round the brows. The smaller girls wear little pointed hoods.

I went to see the Friday review. Most of the troops are barefoot and the whole thing lasts four hours, and they showed no sign of fatigue. The Syrian pasha was smart on a white horse and watched them; he has been training the reserve who serve four months and then go to their homes, and after only two months they came by in quite creditable style. They look poor compared with the ironlike Turkish soldiers, but the people here think a great deal of them. They wound through the gate in the dust with slanting rifles over their dust-coloured tunics and shirts—a pale yellow handkerchief on their heads, with a scented sprig inside it. The crowd that watches is not very large, the Imam's orphans in saffron yellow, and *Sayyids* in striped gowns, their sleeves hanging a foot or so below the hands: when they want to do anything they tie them at the back of their necks to free themselves up to the elbows. What was strange, was how little the modern weapons, the slanting bayonets, the guns and machine-guns, affected the medieval look—the round towers in the background, the varied faces, the dull, sun-bleached lovely colours. The men, they say, love the Imam and think to go to heaven if they die serving him, because of his holiness. He is everything in their country. I went along a street and they said it was the 'Street of Ghouls' and there used to be ghouls, but they have all left since the coming of the Imam.

16 February 1940

My dear Stewart,

Nothing new has happened except that I have finally got an *'alim* to read with me every morning: he preaches in mosques on Fridays and I have promised to send him stuff from Aden to inspire him in his sermons: a few words, he says, are enough for him to embroider to any extent, and he treats me, as Mr. Gladstone Queen Victoria, like a public meeting.

FASCISTS IN THE YEMEN

I returned the Governor of San'a's call and was pleased to hear all my own sentiments about the Germans served back as original thoughts!

I have written you a little report. I would much rather you improved it and have no wish that it should go about in my own name. If you agree, I think it ought to go at once; if Italy does mean mischief, every week here will count.

The Fascists are bringing all their guns to bear against me. Nagi says 'their hearts are boiling'—long may they boil. But, dear Stewart, I do *dislike* this job.

You can't think what *riff-raff* the Fascists have got here! I met the whole colony (except the one who has left) and you never saw such an unenticing lot. There are three innocent young men, but the rest just the worst, commonest and *low* products of the régime. The only person I took to was a German (?), who sat chatting about antiquities. He comes from Egypt and goodness knows what he really is. His German is very bad, and he evidently thinks in Arabic. He is a nice dishonest man I should say and tells me he is the only one here trusted by the Imam! One hopes, as the Egyptian Government sent him, that we saw to it that he is not anti-British?

I hardly know how to break it to you that he says he can quite easily arrange for me to go to Marib![1] A woman, he says, is possible as long as a woman attendant goes too. I have no idea whether he really can, but anyway will keep it over to the very end; you *must* come, even if you have to dress in a crinoline. I shall not press the matter at all, but cannot humanly resist if it is offered.

The things in the Yemen that I longed to see, these cities of Sheba and their like, could not be pursued while I was busy with the magnates of the capital. As in most Arab countries, they themselves found their nomad tribes quite as difficult as a visitor might have found them, and all exploration had to be renounced. San'a meanwhile went on ringing with my cinema.

I soon showed it to the royal harim—about fifty women and the Imam himself probably looking through some crack, while the Fascists, who had spent weeks getting permission to import a mere wireless, were more furious than ever.

[1] The pre-Islamic capital of Sheba.

18 February 1940

My dear Stewart,

I had a charming visit from the son of the Governor of San'a, full of enthusiasm about ancient Himyarites and so friendly. After the usual complaint about Palestine (absolutely *universal* from both friends and enemies) he said what is very true: 'The peasants and tribes here do not even know there is a war between England and Germany; but they have *all* given their money for the Palestine revolt, and they all take an interest in that.'

Both my visitors' harims have sent messages clamouring for the cinema. The Qadhi's younger wife told me that when she lies down to sleep the pictures pass before her eyes every evening.

I am feeling awfully unwell, and after wondering if it was incipient malaria, now believe it is the height and keep as quiet as I can. It does apparently often affect people.

21 February 1940

Darling B.

I paid a pathetic visit today to my landlady, a gay little elderly Turkish barrel of a woman, with a silver-embossed belt very tight over a yellow-and-black striped silk, bunched as if it were the middle of a bolster, and an orange head-scarf above. She is kind and friendly and brought a present of two agates—and told me such a sad story. Her thirteen babies *all* died, so she adopted two girls as her own and lived happily in a big house with her husband who looks after the King's cannon. Then one girl died; and the other suddenly left and went to the house of one of the King's sons and works there like a servant. I saw her there; she is very pretty and seemed happy, with something rather resentful about her. And my poor little woman was wiping away tears as she told me, and really has very little to live for, here in a strange land for forty-five years.

I did the cinema again last night and feel tired: the high air has sent my wretched blood-pressure bang down, and I long to be in Aden to feel normal again. How lucky I am in this war: not a single week of tedium since it started! How few can say that—and I feel sure that tedium is the *real* horror of war—the hours and days wasted, the doing of something quite out of the stream of one's life. I have been lucky enough to carry on what I have been aiming at for many years, and indeed to find now the help and comradeship which I never had before. Personally it has been a great increase of happiness. I hope too that we are succeeding.

FASCISTS IN THE YEMEN

21 February 1940

My dear Stewart,

Your letters are my great and only pleasure. I should hate it if you became conceited all through me so I hasten to add that very few other pleasures are available.

Last night we had a delightful evening in the house of the Governor, turning to Berlin on the radio to hear if all the ships we had just been seeing in the cinema had been sunk. They are sunk by the Germans regularly once a week; I explained this and can't help noticing that Berlin is less credited than it was.

This morning my teacher arrived with a second savant who had refused to believe that a *Mullah* would come to read *Tabari* with a woman. So we had a seance rather like *Les Précieuses*, so very high-falutin, with florid phrases turn and turn about, and I listened while my teacher told us the state of Europe: he has a wonderful memory, almost every word was repeated. The only inaccuracy was that he insisted on my being an M.P. (because I had described how Parliament opens with prayers) and all my *istaghfar Allahs* were of no avail.

22 February 1940

I think you ought to have an Arab harim—you would enjoy it. When the Master enters, all the women (who have been chattering like *bulbuls*) fall silent: not a whisper (except the chaos outside where people have mislaid teacups and things). If he desires solitude, he waves them away; if he feels sociable, they bring him his hookah, and sit round agreeing with all he says (which I should hate myself) and, however they may feel, they always look amiable. If the war is going to last for three years, you ought to think about it: you could have four, and lots of relations, and get rid of them simultaneously with no trouble at all at the end! The Governor of San'a was pleased when I compared him with Abraham!

I have just been listening to the Berlin radio—a speech on the Imam by one Saki Kerim: its effect would have been greater if he had not absconded from this country with 500 dollars.

I have been to visit the Qadhi, who really is a dear, about your coming and hope to hear tonight. I said all sorts of nice things about you, but what carried most weight was the fact of your being the son of a bishop. Nothing, he said, could be more suitable for the Yemen and asked if you wore a turban. I said you were too young for anything more exalted than a *Keffiah*! A propos of bishops, could you let me have the Navy prayer (even six copies typed) as everyone here has been very pleased to hear about it and it explains our victories.

23 February 1940

The pseudo-German asked me to tea. He appears to have none of the Public School virtues; it is only my penchant for scamps, I rather fear, which makes me like him. I tried him in halting French, German, Italian and Arabic and at last found he spoke fluent Russian, born in Dresden, childhood in Kiev, educated Switzerland, years in Egypt, emigrated to America and now here: no Public School virtue would stand that!

The Fascists have been made to close a shop they had opened for the sale of literature and all the Italian flags distributed to riders on bicycles have been abolished. I helped them with information about the fortifications of Aden, and told them it was now almost as strong as the Rock of Gibraltar (those poor barbed wires!) and described an imaginary (German) fleet wiped off the surface of the bay by cannon fire every week for practice. Unfortunately I couldn't remember *where* anything was or even how the troops were housed: they were all over, and so many new ones coming and going, one couldn't keep count. After that we left politics and turned to literature. The three young ones are so delighted with *anything* in the shape of a woman in San'a that they have thrown politics to the winds and lay themselves out to be pleasant. Perhaps they may become anti-Fascists!

A little deputation just appeared—two small boys in gold-embroidered skull-caps asking for the cinema. I would not show it unless they got a *rukhsa* [permit] from the Imam, but we pulled crackers instead and tried the fireworks inside. They have such nice manners.

23 February 1940

Darling B.

The Jews here remind one, with their silky curls and soft eyes and lips and long gowns and barefoot walk, of the conventional picture of Christ. They are so intelligent, and this great plateau, held by Religion, is very like a prison for them. I went to one of their weddings yesterday. The bride of twelve was an idol, her hands blue with indigo, her breast plastered with gold necklaces and silver beads as big as eggs, and in the middle, hanging to a gold torque, a triangular thing like a pincushion covered with gilt coins. Wedding guests are allowed to try the bride's bonnet on at a dollar a time.

26 February 1940

My dear Stewart,

The Qadhi came and sat for two hours this morning, going through the whole story of Anglo-French relations from the time of Edward VII, with extraordinary knowledge and insight. I then had my *Mullah*, with a Koranic reader from the Great Mosque, and his brother a judge. We had your bulletins and I was anxious to get the opinion of these poetic experts. I am sorry to say that their chief criticism was the *badness* of the printing: you will have to bring yourself to say a word, light as thistledown, to the incomparable Ali.

In the afternoon I sat in my daily harim and had my fortune told in a coffee-cup; came back in time for a visit from the King's goldsmith and then from my 'Pseudo' who is lending me his house for a general cinema show, European and Arab, on Thursday. I don't quite know what language to have: two of the Princes have asked to come, so I think there must be an Arabic version, but the presence of all the Axis is rather cramping.

Your bulletins came open. If there was a letter, it had fallen out. I have made a bit of a fuss, as it is very careless (if that is the word).

I have been sent the most delightful book of Chinese philosophy, and feel I need it all.

28 February 1940

As if there were not difficulties enough to deal with, our poor telegraph man yesterday fell and drowned himself in a well—the sort of thing one only expects to happen in Ruthless Rhymes. He was a friendly mild creature (and I had *lavished* bakhshish on him) and it always gives one an unpleasant shock when the unsafety of the world is brought home to one. I find he charged twenty-two dollars for my telegram, but even so, Providence seems to have been drastic.

I have your telegram and have replied. Everything *English* that is not understood here goes to Mme Favetti to be translated (you may tell Mr. Howes in case he doesn't know!) so I have been rather obscure, but not I hope for your ingenious mind.

It is *awful* to live in this intriguing atmosphere, with everyone practically pro-German. I go as carefully as I can, but the very fact of being successful rouses the other side: I no longer hear that Germany will win the war; the cry is 'Poor little Germany, so much weaker, why drive her to despair?'

Yesterday I had a call at 8.45; paid a harim visit; back for my *Mullah* at 11; call from *Sayyid* and arrange for cinema; rest till 5; three veiled ladies to tea; call with them on new neighbours; cinema to the *Sayyid's* harim after dinner; typical day! It is most amusing to see the difference of a Great Man in his own home; you find him sitting in happy deshabille in what looks like a late Victorian nightdress; he then goes wandering about, picks up a gown here, a scarf there, gold cap and turban, *janbiya* and belt, and goes out the venerable immaculate you see in the *Majliss*: all done while entertaining the lady visitor!

This morning I have had the head of police, always rather a nerve-racking visit—but it was only to quote poetry as far as I could see.

29 February 1940

A Hodeidah mailbag with Phyllis's letter of the 20th has come, but nothing from you. If it is just natural forgetfulness, it is horrid, and if your letter has been pinched, it is worrying. The envelope sent overland with bulletins was opened; the aged postman is an Albanian who wants an Italian passport.

1 March 1940

The fat has been *sizzling* in the fire or, in other words, the hearts of the Fascists have, as Nagi prophesied, boiled over. It all began yesterday morning when their Lady Doctor (both nouns doubtful) found me chatting in the house of the Heir Apparent which is their preserve. We were, however, on friendly terms, and cordial, and I went as usual on Thursday to their general tennis reception, and left on the understanding that they were to come at eight to a neighbouring house for my cinema—all except a fat little man called Rossi who was outside and to whom I repeated my polite message when I met him. Would you believe it, he boiled over then and there: said he was the head of the mission and I should have given the show in *their* house. As he went on blustering, I said that if we *were* to be formal, I would not even know of his existence till he had called on me—whereupon he simply *frothed*, said he had called on Colonel Lake (as if it were a concession) but that I was just a supposed tourist (long pause before the word) and that he had been very polite in asking me to their house!! Whereupon I could but bow in as lofty a way as is possible for a small person, and retire, and the whole of the Italian Mission missed the cinema (the Favettis came, and are very upset about the incident). The silly little man remarked that 'We are the *chief* people here' which (as I have been saying to all who gossip) is not particularly polite in someone else's land. The extraordinary effect is that this morning even strangers beam at me in the street.

Tomorrow we give a show to the harim of the Amir al Jeish.

FASCISTS IN THE YEMEN

3 March 1940

There is no doubt that the Italians here expect war with us. They think of the place as completely in their pocket: Favetti yesterday said, 'if one can come to an arrangement (i.e. give Italy chunks of whatever she wants) you will be able to come up again and we shall be able to go to Aden.' (I believe he said it without noticing.) I think they are out for my blood, and only hope H.M.G. will support my mother when she is turned out of house and home.

Yesterday a man came for me and the cinema, saying he was from the Beit al Wazir. Luckily I suspected, and insisted on seeing the Imam's permit, and he went away: that is the second try-on.

I hope I shall not find you worn to a thread!

Quotation from my Chinese book: 'It is only the upper classes that can maintain their principles without a settled income'.

I was now hoping to leave and waiting impatiently for the arrival of Mr. Champion[1], then District Commissioner in Galilee, who later became Governor of Aden. He had been proposed and accepted as a visitor to the Yemen to discuss the matter of the Shabwa frontier. This boundary, meandering through history and geography, obscure and until quite recently unidentified, has been a recurring source of contention like nearly all desert boundaries whose scanty supply of water and of grazing makes them subject to the wandering of tribes. I sometimes think that more than half the troubles of governments come through the effort to impose fixed barriers on what nature has made fluid: it must at all events be remembered that all normal people will break through a frontier rather than die of hunger or of thirst—whether it be the crossing of the Danube in the decline of Rome or the watering of camels at illicit desert wells. Mr. Champion delayed as if the Colonial Office had become oriental: 'they had got all the reception here ready,' I wrote, 'and denuded me even of soup-plates; and you know how bad it is when expectation falls flat.'

The Fascist efforts to get rid of me had now become more and more harassing; and a letter, which Aden rashly sent up in an O.H.M.S. envelope, had been opened and caused me some trouble. Life went on however, filled with picturesqueness and intrigue.

[1] Now the Rev. Sir Reginald Stuart Champion, K.C.M.G.

FASCISTS IN THE YEMEN

5 March 1940

Darling B.

Little pitfalls are laid for my every step. I do hope they won't take it out of you.

I spend my time sitting about in houses—rooms with cushions down three sides, all covered, and the floor too, with bad rugs. In the middle a brass tray holds hookahs, spittoons, stands for water-bottles (which are needed when chewing *qat* which makes one thirsty), old rough boxes for tobacco inlaid with mother-of-pearl, and a few brass candlesticks, all this kept very bright and nice. Niches round the walls with an untidy little assortment of teapots, papers, and scents: the gilt daggers and their brocade belts hang on nails. Cushions all round the walls. And every window shut.

It is easy and pleasant, and entertaining goes on all day. One sits down, covering one's legs decently; 'How are you? Well, please God?' 'Praise be to God. How are you yourself?' The women all gather; then the children; the servants in a corner; until the Master announces himself and the visiting ladies have to scatter. They marry at the age of seven and onwards, beget children about twelve, and then, when they grow old, throw off their cares and *every* regard for their appearance and become really cheerful. The fat old lady who takes me round with so much gaiety is sixty-five; I pleased her by guessing forty-five (quite honestly) and she pulled out her breasts and patted them to show that they were still 'firm as a girl's'.

5 March 1940

My dear Stewart,

Socotra sounds like that peep into Paradise of the fairy-tale (only I am glad you did not find yourself three hundred years old when you came back). Relieved, too, to think you had that interlude.

Surely you are right about the Arab. We are drawn to him because his sense of values is not material; even when he takes bribes he does it light-heartedly; he doesn't sit and concentrate on heaps of money. I am sure it is this that makes one feel so happy among them and that makes them and us, too, so unhappy when caught in the trammels of industrial intrigue. Your remarks on the passing and enduring things made me think of a sentence in the Ricketts life I have just finished which speaks of artists who 'in every age and every clime (why not *climate*?) have created in thought or form things which endure the longest'.

I continue to write this diary, though probably no safe means of sending will be found till I take it myself—but there is such a lot of marvellous gossip to put down. The Fascist eye has been wiped right away by a nice young Greek and Mr. Perkins between them: they have collared the coffee trade, and armaments they hope will come. Favetti has been sending agonised *billets doux* to my Pseudo: Qadhi R. has been opposing all he can; but the contract has gone through Prince Seif Ali who, in spite of my Aden dossier, is so little pro-Italian that he refused 40,000 dollars bakhshish from them and took 20,000 only from a Greek for the new harbour. The fact is that the only way to do real propaganda is to be a genuine well-wisher. There are only two parties in Yemen: one pro-Italian, dependent entirely on bribes; and the other pro-Yemen; and if we can help with that one, we shall be all right. I hope we may have the sense to see it. A charming story for instance about Seif Ahmed[1] who is also, and I am told wrongfully, supposed to be pro-Italian. When the four Fascist guns arrived at Mocha, it turned out that there were fifty men and fifteen officers accompanying them. Seif Ahmed went down, said that two Italians only need disembark, and shut himself up away from protests.

I spent yesterday p.m. sitting beside a small new-born baby no bigger than your hand (the boring things I have to do!) and then went through pleasant sunset gardens with the three ladies veiled and draped to the Qadhi's house, and told him the story of the tiff with Rossi. He looked very thoughtful! He is a wicked, amusing old boy, but I am quite sure that he *likes* the English, while earning his living against us.

All the army officers now want the cinema; the Imam is being approached. The old head of police came to call this morning almost lyrical about it; his five fingers were put up before his face in sign of admiration almost all through the visit.

I get about nine hours sheer talking every day and hardly ever manage a walk at all. You will have to give me a trip for fun among nice friendly tribesmen, to forget all this ghastly intrigue!

6 March 1940

I paid a farewell visit to the chief Queen, who is one of the nicest women you can possibly imagine. She took me by the hand all over the garden, cornfields and fruit trees—fig, quince, pomegranate, plum, apricot and peach, with a cemented stream-bed running through and a little private mosque. The palace soars up from it, half brick, half stone. Ladies of the other harim, whose doors also open to the garden, were praying by the *birket* (well), robed in white and very like Tanagra

[1] H.H. the present Imam.

figures. Our party were all gaily coloured. They make their dresses themselves. A crowd of children is always in and out. As for the Imam, I don't believe I shall see him at all; nor will I see the Qadhi al Amri. Some people are too exalted to talk to women.

Meanwhile I have made a social blunder by asking to call on Prince Abdullah's wife. He is the Minister for Education and I was told to write to him for permission to visit the cloth factory: after that you would not expect him to be *also* in prison! People said in an ambiguous way 'he lives in the Qasr', but I couldn't know that this meant prison, especially as he was allowed out for the cinema! You will see how difficult life is here! Another blunder I have made is to ask to subscribe to the local paper. There would be no difficulty, they said, in having it *free*, but to ask to subscribe looks like spying and needs a special permission! Poor Dr. Walker has to get a permit all over again for his wireless, which has been mended and sent back from Aden.

7 March 1940

Your telegram just here—two days *en route*! I am getting Nagi to say things to the Albanian postman. The film arrival is excellent news, though it will mean an extra fortnight at least here. You can't think how I shall appreciate being a mere harim again and having you to do the real work!

This morning I went to visit the cloth factory. There seems to me always something pathetic and rather heroic in these first struggles in the East with machinery. The poor Yemeni apprentices (at three to six dollars monthly without food) standing by those clattering engines—and really turning out quite creditable stuff in appalling designs from Manchester. The Yemeni head and the Egyptian teacher are coming to tea. They were so pleased to show it all. When they have got a spinning plant, they will be able to do the whole thing, from growing of the cotton to the finishing off of a *dhabit's* [officer's] uniform by an ancient Yemeni tailor who held up a pair of impossible trousers and said: 'This is Europe.'

The Italians are fuming over their lost contract. Favetti strode in on the Pseudo and said, 'I have to thank you for this.'

I think I have done as much damage as one could in the time, and this place is now fairly convinced that Britain is *strong*. The next thing is to convince them that we are not dangerous as neighbours, and that I hope will be done by Mr. Champion!

I don't think I could bear this for very much longer. Every day the Fascists send their soldier to scrounge around with my bodyguard and report my every movement: every cinema show except those in the royal palace has been given in houses that take secret bribes.

9 March 1940

The Imam, it appears, was amused by the story of my tiff and the Fascist claim to be the 'chief people here'. My old gossip told it to his wife, who told it to him—and they were all laughing about it.

What with (1) Colonel Lake, (2) me and the cinema, (3) loss of the coffee contract, (4) Mr. Champion, (5) the most opportune business of the German coal which is causing a sensation here, the Fascist nose is badly out of joint.

A small domestic comedy is going on in the house of Qadhi al Amri who is too religious to have a strange woman in his house or to ask to see the cinema. But all his sons and harim are dying to see it and are the only important people not to have done so. They tried to lure me into a neighbouring house where they would have gone, but I discovered at the last moment that there was no Imam's permission and refused. I am sure it is wise to be very strict about this; it also makes the cinema even *more* sought after than it would be otherwise. They are now waiting for the arrival of an uncle to ask the Imam.

14 March 1940

All sorts of things have been happening. For one thing I paid a funeral call and was made to stay for the baked meats, *helbe*, which is flour and water and vinegar beaten by hand, and a very nice dish called *Shufut*. About twenty women sat, all in black, while the bereaved family brought copper cauldrons of sheep, soups, rice, and then coffee in a monumental ewer. The nieces of Seif Ahmed were there and I have made rather friends with that house, where all the women are delightful. I went this morning and photographed the little girls in a row in their best dresses, and was shown a Bestiary with the picture of an animal with human face and scorpion tail which they told me is 'a sort of lion but not common now'. The lion is a noble animal: it looks at footprints in the dust and never pursues a woman. Monkeys (male) on the other hand are horrid; you should never have them in a house *ma'a al banat* (with the girls). I longed to possess the Bestiary: seventeenth century I should say.

19 March 1940

I hoped to be off to you tomorrow but it is no *good* trying to hurry here. Five days ago Mr. Champion was arriving in Ta'iz, due here yesterday, I thought I would take his car back and get the good boat from Hodeidah with a hairdresser on it on the 21st. Yesterday I heard that the elusive man is not even in Ta'iz. I feel rather desperate, because I have a headache whenever I *look* at paper. That is why I haven't written these five days, not for want of news. The trouble, I hope, is due to the altitude; if not, all I can see is that we shall lie side by side in hospital while Ali in his lovely new uniform runs the office. The point of Champion's car is that most of the local ones break down for anything from one to six days *en route*, and the good ones are all away meeting this rush of Ambassadors.

The new cinema films at last arrived, rescued—already opened—from somebody's office just in time (my own undeveloped negatives had already been subtracted from the post and spoilt). A first European soirée was given and our tanks came rushing at Herr Hensen in the audience in a lifelike way. The Italian Mission kept aloof, but the independent Favettis—who were charming though on the wrong side—always came and would then bribe the Qadhi to try and stop the next show. The Imam protected me, and in all this time was generous and kind—sending only to ask to know beforehand what I had. I became fond of him although I never met him, merely from the way in which his people spoke of him, with voices of affection. On my last evening I showed all the new films to the Royal Family, 'with one agonizing moment when a princess (very small) sat on the wire and I thought the thing would burst. In the middle I blundered to the men's side to ask if all was well, and suddenly noticed a wall of agitated princes standing up between me and royalty itself.'

There were doubts and delays to the last and exasperated notes in my letters.

20 March 1940

If it had not been for chance, which I like to think of as providence, those films would *still* be in Hodeidah together with the food and toys, in spite of all orders from here. And why Mr. Champion should increase the uncertainties of Arabia by turning himself into a Myth I can't understand. It seems easy to send a telegram from Aden a week before one starts with the general dates of one's journey. Anyway, I plan to leave on Thursday and am hunting for something that looks as if it did not break down. I can't help feeling that when I reach Hodeidah an earthquake may have destroyed the shipping! I have taken to *dreaming* in Arabic! Dear Stewart, do take things easy meanwhile. I hope you have sent me news. You might send a wire to Hodeidah to say how you are—I shall probably be stuck there a few days.

When by the end of the month I reached our office it felt like home. The high towns of the plateau with their contrasts, the sun- and shadow-barred streets, lay behind me, and the endless parley where enemies lurked. I remembered the black and white houses, the kindness and the friendly harims and should like to see them again with no task to accomplish. And I had learnt my first lesson in propaganda or persuasion. Behind speech, light, deep or subtle, I had seen the other powers—tensions perhaps of old and younger gods—a struggle, ultimately, in this case, for life itself. Speech, our instrument, had shown itself the scabbard with the sword of reality inside it.

4
War in Aden

I received a letter from London full of kindness over the Yemen, though it added a rider to say that 'H.M.G. still desires Italy to be regarded as a friend'.

This ostrich attitude of Government, which by April 1940 was constricting General Wavell's defence measures in Egypt,[1] mattered little to our colony, since we had nothing much anyway with which defence could be connected. We continued to encourage a most willing and steady people, with a feeling of events round any corner. 'Sirens went, fire-engines (half an hour late) came rushing up to the Secretariat. What had happened was that an Arab threw a match from his cigarette into a barrel of Very lights that stood beside the telephone.'[2]

My own belief that Italy would pounce was far too long established to be shaken by any official optimism; and by the first of May, with the real heat of summer upon us, the Red Sea war was plainly clear to all.

1 May 1940

Darling B.

War is very near today and we quite inadequately ready.

Stewart put up a piece of talk to prepare for Italy's entry. The people listened in silence, then walked away clapping—a very rare thing for Arabs to do.

Women may be evacuated. I called on Mrs. W. and found her packed. The harbour has filled with Norwegian ships taking refuge. Two cruisers

---

[1] 'As the months passed Britain remained, officially, friendly with Italy, and he [General Wavell] found that his Government's wish to preserve this position with the Italians hampered his efforts to be ready against them.' (*The Campaigns of Wavell*, R. Woollcombe, p. 16).

[2] From a letter to Jock Murray.

are in. The five submarines have crept away. Soldiers are to wear uniform: officers to remain in reach of telephones; leave is cancelled. The air is soft, hot with cool ribands through it; the lights flicker on shore, red on the wireless staffs; they glow from the hills where belated caves are being bored to store the Aden oil.

With the serious opening of the war I began to keep a diary.

4 May 1940

Miss Patel has called and asked what she is to do with her Parsee school in an air raid. She says the mountain refuges are too dangerous, full of Arabs (who would surely be distracted by air raids from any more everyday amusements). Miss Patel goes on to say that her ladies would prefer to sit quietly in their houses till they are dead.

Stewart and I dined with the Italian Consul. He is very jittery, kissed me on both cheeks . . . says all look coldly upon him (possibly because he flew the Italian flag round the aerodrome). Our broadcast, which gave a premonition of war, has filled him with perturbations and he asked us not to damage Italian prestige!

This man sent the reports which landed my mother in prison, so that I think of him with repulsion.

5 May 1940

The Dutch airlines stop calling at Naples; *Ala Littoria*[1] takes no passengers. Question of evacuating children here referred to England. The municipal garden opposite our office is open at night, so I can sit beside Queen Victoria's statue in a raid.

6 May 1940

Bathed this a.m., so calm: tide full; tame gull trotting on the pier; myriads of small fish all turning round simultaneously like a regiment by some obscure radar signal of their own. Rest of the day is all work.

11 May 1940

B.B.C. says Whitsun holiday will be cancelled. Another notice this morning recommends to inform police if one sees parachutists descending in England (Switzerland says shoot at sight). Public here quite calm. I

[1] The Italian air line.

feel constant heartache for Mama and Herbert [the old friend who shared our home] and wonder where they are: wherever it is is irrevocable now as Switzerland is closed. Italy may keep out if things go well for us—otherwise no.

21 May 1940

Little heart to write the news these days, but France has counter-attacked, it seems as if the German advance may stick. Italian attack from Somaliland expected: women and children here evacuated (none of my friends comply).

Improvement in English *style* since the war. Feeling makes it: Samuel Hoare's and Hore-Belisha's banality was just that they did not *feel*. Now events face us with terrible visions and the clichés die: a most moving speech on the B.B.C. on what captivity is, from a Belgian. Alas.

Tonic influence too of uncomplicated people trained in control. Colonel Lake on the worst day said he thought things 'better than in 1914': this subduing of immediate feelings is the triumph of Reason? Not the intellectual who attain it, but the *disciplined* mind accustomed to danger. Courage, I feel more and more, is something that can be taught—a matter of practice very largely.

23 May 1940

Worst news so far—Amiens, Abbeville, Arras lost: Arras retaken. Curious exhilaration together with the gloom—'and we are left or shall be left alone'—finality about one's back to the wall. Favourite place of the English—the last ditch!

Arabs here worried over their families, and whether Lahej is safe for them. Good many gone to India. 'Hitler has no religion—he must lose,' they say. Up to now he had the religion (of a sort), and he won. *Passion* transcends every other human power. Now we, too, step into that arena, we no longer talk of Whitsun holidays given up, of 'London just as usual', of 'team spirit'—we say we mean to fight—and as we are saying it passionately, we will win.

28 May 1940

Belgium has surrendered. The Italian ship is scuttling out of harbour—sandbags being piled up everywhere. We are for it, and the sick fear is going: a *clean* feeling that all we have to do now is to fight while we can . . . There is even a sort of gaiety since the burden of choice is removed.

What will history make of it? If the Germans won their inferiority complex would go and perhaps with it their revolting cruelty? They would respect us, for we are going to fight like hell—perhaps collaboration and friendship might come out of it for another generation. The Empire might go, but the ideas of co-operation which the Empire has sown will survive—I believe that even losing we should emerge as leaders, because we are the only people visibly fit to lead: and if the material benefits are taken from our leadership, its spirit will be all the stronger. But what lies before us now for the time being, for a long time, is the job of fighting. May we be tempered for it.

I wonder if Germany will ever wake from this folly. She has lost already over 500,000—for what? She does not even stop to pick up her own wounded: her tanks just go over them— after 2,000 years of Christianity!

29 May 1940

Darling B.,

I hope your decision is right:[1] your letter (undated) after receipt of my telegram has just come, and I cannot help wishing you both safe in U.S.A. We are ready here for anything—but I wish myself a V.A.D. like twenty-five years ago, somewhere in France! All night we hear the drone of aeroplanes, and see the searchlights moving, and the armies go marching in one's dreams. If there is a comfort, it is in the affection of all: every race here steps forward, ready to help, ready even to be *buried* together! When it comes to it, it is shown that no one except our actual enemies wishes the old Empire to fail. In its trouble, it gathers more loyalties than one had ever imagined.

I hope this gets to you: and then if writing is possible will you tell me:

(a) About coal for next winter—what arrangements have you made?
(b) Who shares your house? *Very* advisable to have someone.
(c) What about correspondence if U.S.A. joins in?
(d) What about money? Jock says he will send whatever necessary from my account.

Your organdie dress has come—looks *so* pretty; it is a great pleasure.

After a rather ominous week, there is an Italian ship in harbour, so I take it that all is well for a day or even two!

[1] **To** stay in Italy.

[Diary] *30 May 1940*

It seems certain that Italy will join against us. Without a reason, except what would inspire an apache, she attacks when she thinks all danger of losing is gone. No decent man, whether German, British or Neutral, will ever do anything but despise her. I think of the many friends whose hearts at this moment must be sore and ashamed.

Stewart is back, and has taken from this office the loneliness of the last ten days.

I have been buying materials—the shops are selling fast as they can, anxious for money rather than goods. Later, no doubt, when things are unattainable the problem will be reversed.

1 June 1940

No one, even on our three worst days, has doubted the final outcome. My low-down pub is crammed with sailors—sometimes a bit drunk—and I must say the sight of them gives a happy confidence.

Streams now pour off one's arms as one writes: the warm weather is fairly here. One works under difficulties: the little dim lights make many things impossible—I can only just see my food by the open window, and have to write with shutters shut in the blackout. The Italian ships didn't come in at all today but waited in a nervous manner outside to pick up passengers and then make off. I hope one will yet come back with the Paris models!

Stewart has bought a tiny yacht. We went out yesterday: all so still that a *water beetle* was going faster than we! It was lovely to get away among quiet unemotional things like fish, so beautiful, browsing among the coral.

I have a constant pain about the heart which would be cured if I *could* know them safe in Asolo.

7 June, 1940

Darling B.

I feel so sad when I think of you, and only hope that in our garden you can forget the unpleasantness outside. I hope this will reach you. Every time an Italian ship goes one feels it is like a run at cricket, the only sort of cricket they play just now: they must not be caught in the open, and we feel safe every night we have one of them in harbour!

I am reassured about you, but fear the Fascists may be as unpleasant as they can because they do dislike me. So do look out.

We sail about the harbour of an afternoon. It is fun, and one forgets all trouble. I do nothing, but begin to learn a few of the unnecessarily abstruse terms. Today we are going visiting on a warship—full of recent shot holes. 'I'm afraid they're very small ones,' the Commander said apologetically.

One of the Colonels' wives here has her son in Flanders and no news of course: so brave, she just keeps on doing her war work, with very tired eyes.

We are full in the heat—luckily it suits me, but I wish the secretary would stop being ill! I hope to be an air-raid warden. I fear it is all going to take very long.

PS. You will have heard that the dresses came! My mouth waters for the Paris frock, and perhaps a ship with some friend on it may yet slip in. But one has little hope of pleasant news for a long while.... It would be a mistake to think that we are not on our own peculiar expensive and exasperating road to victory.

On the 10th of June the expected news came and war with Italy began at midnight. I heard it as I was dining with Harold Ingrams on his terrace above the dark shore and darker headland below. But I was thinking of Asolo, and France—and in that night of stars it all seemed far away, not insignificant but merged into one vast significance, mercifully free of hate.

The air raids now came regularly, doing extremely little damage in the hard Aden soil that scarcely splintered. They mostly came by night, in a halo of gold shell-bursts, while the silhouetted hill-walls of the crater dulled the explosions. Or they would crash below our office windows into the harbour, where cruiser and destroyers lit each other in jagged flashes like a Nelson battle-scene whenever they loosed their guns.

There was exodus from Aden. Even down at Ma'ala where the dhows lie in shallow water, graceful as butterflies, leaning one-sided, their delicate tangle of spars like stitchings on a tapestry sun-bleached with age, their crews, the men of Dis and Sur who lived happily careless of bombs and news, had left not because of war but of the monsoon. Of the shopkeepers on the Crescent, some went to India, some merely to their branches in Crater which they seemed to think safer.

On the 16th of June I find written in my diary:

At the bottom of the turmoil of our time one thing only—the absence of *truth*: in all parts of human life the importance of truth is now less regarded: it was a love for this alone that raised Greece to the peak of civilization. To think of your public rather than of the truth of what you say is, for instance, quite common and not regarded as a crime: but it *is* a crime. It means that you flit from point to point of the circumference while, if you go deeper and try merely to be true, you find yourself eventually not only at home in your own centre, but in the universal centre of all human hearts. Only so by *truthfulness* can we reach the universal, and therefore a hope of concord among men.

On the 17th of June the news reached us that France had surrendered. It came to the office in the mid-afternoon, with a flash of thought in the stillness of the heart that here was Pitt's day again and the map of Europe rolled up for twenty years. And again the strange feeling of elation—we must rely on ourselves!

I hunted for Stewart to tell him but, not finding him, went out to try a horse belonging to the Government Guards. It was three years old, very Arab and all over the place with a friendly skittishness. I led it past our police, who recovered a little cheerfulness by talking; and then listened to our announcer who was lost and garbled the news. All night sad processions walked through my brain. However this might go, our civilization, the easy-going culture we grew up in, was at an end.

I was much alone, for I had no car and the distances in the blackout were too great for walking; the windows, both of the office and my room behind it, could only be closed with shutters, and this was now a breathless thing to suffer in the heat. So I would sit on my balcony looking out to the silent darkness where town and ships were hidden, and the thicker darkness of the heavy summer sky above it, even more detachedly silent but with a comforting punctuality of stars. I would turn on the wireless and often come upon the wandering German music, and listen, and wonder what it is that makes the language of a *country* speak to the heart. Patriotism of all things is an emotion one cannot take for granted, as it would be different if we happened to have been born inside some other geographic lines. Together with colour, it seems to me to be the most arbitrary of all human divisions, since pure accident determines them both: skin has no more relation to one's being than, say, the eyes or hair; and as for the frontiers in which we were born, they have mostly been changed a dozen times in history with all their implications. Yet these feelings exist: not colour, as far as I am concerned, for the likenesses of human beings strike me far more than their difference; but the pattern of my own country is very strong, hammered like metal out of forgotten strokes that have all left their impact, till the unified surface bears only a richness, a patina of workmanship, to tell the lives and centuries through which it was made. Yet the mystery remains why an irrelevant line drawn by men should limit our affections, when the same sort of world stretches beyond it. Perhaps it is language, more than any other shackle, that circumscribes our freedom in the family of men? I would think of this, and listen to the German music, and think of the man I would have married whom they had killed, and of my mother then being imprisoned (though I did not know it) and my two nephews one to be lost in Russia and the other killed in the Resistance: all pawns in the human procession where there should be one heart only, one 'army of unalterable law'.

The raids came at night or in the dawn, and I lay on my balcony to watch their terrible beauty, for the old house swayed like a treetop in the explosions and I had a childish idea that the balustrade would keep splinters off my head. Fear came and went in an unreasonable way connected with *noise*; any sound louder than a certain pitch gave an unpleasant feeling just below the waist; but the sight of the flame-shod things descending cast a spell like the beauty of Medusa. Very little damage was done, though the harbour below our windows was the enemy objective and I would always be surprised at Stewart's matter-of-factness, arriving without a remark, in the morning after a noisy night, with no apparent doubt as to whether his office (and I inside it) were still bound to be there.

The month of June brought one event that cheered us. Our trawler *Moonstone* captured an Italian submarine, shot fair and true at its conning tower as it surfaced beyond Aden harbour, and wiped out all officers except one lieutenant at a blow. I was borrowed to translate the prisoners' interrogation and gathered that they had come up when depth-charges were dropped, hoping to shoot away the trawler and escape.

'Depth-charges?' said our Naval Interrogator, seriously ruffled, 'no one would surface for *depth-charges*. Ask again!' But so it was: my prisoners thought it natural to get away from a depth-charge if possible, and the divergence remained unresolved. There were ninety-three of them, nearly all opposed to their war. I sent off letters for them which they dictated to me before the interrogations, and our Provost Marshal, a kindly man from Kenya, told me that it made them answer more willingly than any prisoners he had met before. He soon cherished them as if they were pets, though quarters were cramped owing to their unexpected numbers, and the crew of a Savoia had to be added. It had flown across the Red Sea by night without noticing, looking for Djibouti, and was much relieved to be rescued, far in the Hadhramaut, from the indigo-painted Arabs of the coast. The cause of this geographic vagueness was the fact that the airmen never knew their target, since sealed orders were opened only by squadron leaders in the air. 'Our faith in our Government,' they said with dignity and truth, 'is blind.'

The affairs of the sea penetrated life in Aden and I had quite a lot to do with them for I translated the captured papers, and there in the operational orders were the movements of two other submarines within the next few days. In little over an hour destroyers got up steam and streaked away to trap them both at their appointed places. I could now think that in my life I, too, had sent out ships in a modest way—with far less fun than Helen. At the time, faced as we were with so great odds against us, we thought of little beyond the bare fact that we meant to save the sort of world we cared for, but I have often thought since how strange a twist the divergent codes of war and peace give to the innate reasonableness of men. Eventual harmony, if we ever reach it, must surely be the same all through. I was, for instance, asked to find out a structural Italian submarine detail from the only surviving officer if I could. It seemed not possible to put such a question to someone in captivity, but I thought I could try if he were trusted to me for some hours of freedom, and the Provost Marshal brought him on parole in the Admiral's car; we took a long walk along the Aden beaches, with the monsoon blowing heavy and damp upon us, and ended over the best that the Marina Hotel could do. That devotion to gadgets so mysteriously potent in the masculine character worked its magic in the course of a long detour devoted to machinery, and the detail —whatever it was—emerged, without visible prompting, in a natural way. The young lieutenant had, I hope, a happy evening and, as I had watched various torpedoed ships burning on the outskirts of Aden, I had no feeling of remorse: yet it is not a thing I would have done for any *private* reason, or except in time of war.

The only other event of the summer that immediately touched us was the defence and loss of British Somaliland in August. Troops came, disembarking and re-embarking all day long; the deserted Crescent looked as if waves of khaki were submerging it: they went and after a short time of anxiety were back.

'All in the dark on the terrace with searchlights, and sound of breaking glass below,' we gave a party for the two commanders, who came late looking desperately tired, 'the first to lose a bit of the Empire,' said General Godwin Austen miserably, not mentioning impossible odds. They left, and the *Royal Sovereign* left, a mighty hill of guns and towers; and we relapsed into the uneasy ineffectual bombing at dawn, while *Carlisle* and *Kandahar* remained to look after us, with friends on board to take us out of an evening, as we settled from being a centre to a suburb of the war.

In July I went for a few weeks to Cairo for liaison consultations, with the problem of departure from Aden on my mind.

5
The Red Sea

We were the first Red Sea convoy after Italy's declaration of war, and the *Carlisle*, under Captain Langley, led us out. The foam washed her sides, a streak of paler water widened behind her, and her turrets were the colour of the sea. *Kandahar* slipped as if unleashed across our bows, and the horizon enclosed us all in a hazy circle of sunshine. We were carrying 70,000 tons of oil, and the cargo on my ship—a B.I. liner converted—was ammunition.

Perim, long dismantled, had been bombed that day, and cruisers and destroyers—*Leander, Kingston, Kandahar*—aligned themselves beyond it to let us pass protected through the straits. The last daylight caught the grey hulls and the White Ensigns, the night fell with southern speed, and shafts from the lighthouse lit the black buffalo silhouette of *Carlisle* leading, wickedly showing a tiny careless gleam. A match, they told me, will shine for three miles at sea. Safe through the straits, safe from the air in friendly darkness, we sped along the unlit Italian shore.

The Red Sea was as hot as it can be in July. The men, many bearded and as near naked as possible, lay through the worst hours in any patch of thin transparent shade; and I—the only female on board and officially non-existent at that—felt the absence of clothes must be more agreeable to them than the presence of women, and did the best I could for myself in the suffocation of my cabin below.

'Most of my life is in the Man's world,' I find written in a rather morose note of my diary at this time. 'Women are apt to think of it as the real one, but it is not so to me—filled with jealousies and now bloodshed. If women live more in the spirit, theirs is the real world —but I don't know that they do.' The closing sentiment is more like me than the rest, for I was brought up to the man's world and have always liked it through its ups and downs. But a rift at this time with Stewart and Harold Ingrams over my departure was making me unhappy. In the dearth of people who could talk Arabic, it was unreasonable to keep two of us in a post like Aden, now withdrawing out of the actual zone of war; Stewart, a very brilliant person, was perfectly able to deal alone with these beloved coasts; and ever since the end of Somaliland I had been feeling that it was wrong of me to stay. It was not conceit to know that one was needed; for very few people, men or women, were available with a knowledge of the language at that time; and though any number knew more about one or the other among the Arab countries, there were not many who had visited them all (except the very east and centre) so generally as I had. These reasons made Cairo remind me that I had been assigned to them in the first place, while Rushbrook in London agreed with them and left the choice to me; when I returned in a few weeks' time to Aden and the actual decision had to be maintained, I was hurt by what seemed to me a masculine obtuseness in two friends who appeared to think that mere caprice was ruling a change which I made with so great reluctance.

★ ★ ★ ★

Cairo in that straitened summer was not the place of hope and glitter that it became within the next few months. General Wavell was preparing to face the desert against tremendous odds,[1] and 80,000 Italians, nearly all tied to Fascism by their purses if not by

[1] 'General Wavell at that time had a total of 36,000 men in Egypt and just under 28,000 in Palestine. In the Sudan and Kenya, along nearly two thousand miles of frontier with Italian East Africa, he had 17,500; and another 3,300 in Aden and Cyprus. He therefore had under his command some 86,000 men, of which no single formation or unit was equipped up to war establishment, at the end of a thirteen-thousand-mile supply route to Egypt round the Cape. On one side of him were Italian forces totalling some quarter of a million men under Marshal Graziani in Libya, and on the other side an army of nearly 300,000, including native units, in Italian East Africa under the Duke of Aosta. The R.A.F. in the Middle East in June 1940 had some 360 first line aircraft, with a bleak prospect as regards immediate replacements and reinforcements; the Italians had rather over 300 aircraft in Libya and the Dodecanese, their home strength in Italy on call, and about 325 in Italian East Africa. The quality of Italian aircraft at this moment was much as ours, although the same was not to be said for many of their pilots.' (From *The Campaigns of Wavell*, R. Woollcombe, pp. 17–18).

their hearts, were loose in the capital and even more so in Alexandria. Their Party chief had transformed himself into a Swiss diplomat for the duration and was therefore unassailable; he held the schools, hospitals, charities, workmen's clubs, etc., open to Fascists only, and these walked about with an exuberant confidence in streets dimmed with blue lights against their bombers, and bought up all stocks of green, red and white material suitable for the making of flags to greet their advancing troops. A small, devoted but disunited band of anti-Fascist Italians struggled against them, under the exasperated guidance of Colonel Thornhill[1] and Christopher Sykes. The Colonel, a most dogged and lovable man, was thrown into that world like a Christian to the lions—convinced like so many colonels that he was an author by immaculate conception. In an office seething with Latin feelings he sat, worn away like a sea rock, and busied himself with the creating of a paper which was to convert Italian prisoners when we got them. The prisoners in a short while appeared; but few people could be spared to look after them, and their camp commandants preferred to have them run by their own Fascists on lines that gave no trouble, although this entailed the beating-up of anyone who favoured us, and the boycotting of most of the colonel's efforts. This was still in the future. In the summer of 1940 the only suggestion about prisoners that I can remember is that they should be marched through the streets of Cairo instead of slinking round it, to show the Egyptian public that so rare a species really did exist.

Of the fifteen million Egyptians, most thought we would lose the war. The gap before we had any trump card in the way of a military success was a very long one, and the atmosphere remained friendly chiefly, I believe, because of a personal trust and liking for individual Englishmen in the Egyptian service of the past. People like Russell Pasha, Walter Smart, Reginald Davies, John Hamilton and many others are still remembered, and twenty years ago their influence carried over the sticky summer and all Mussolini's intrigue. Yet,

---

[1] Colonel C. M. Thornhill, C.M.G., D.S.O., a lifelong friend of Lord Wavell was sent to Cairo in 1940 to work for S.O.E. with Captain Christopher Sykes as his personal assistant. His branch, G.S.I.K., was intended to stimulate anti-Fascist activity in Egypt.

with many exceptions, sentiment was unfavourable as one reached the richer society. 'We are getting ready here,' I wrote to a friend in the autumn of 1940, 'without a united country behind us. If we took to leaning against anything it would turn out to be a fifth column no doubt.'

* * * *

I was flown back to settle my affairs in Aden, in a long-nosed Blenheim bomber where one sat transparent, watching the world spinning below one's feet—five hours to touch at Port Sudan among the meagre cluster of our fighters, who had nothing but the blackout to rely upon against the Fascist Savoias when they came up from the south; four more across an opaque sea cut into solid creases, as if it were the wrinkled granite of the Alps. Far below we noticed four hurrying destroyers, but could not dip to see what they were since I had been taken on instead of the usual load of bombs. It was a sad return, for Stewart and Harold were still vexed; the office had changed, and the sparrows I had tamed there—cutting snippets of string off the publicity parcels to help them with their nests—had fled. Even Said's canary had been removed, and I missed his tweeting conversation as I went in and out. The wind swept, shaking and rattling in a hard, bright way and cutting one's nerves: and noises seemed louder than ever, though the bombing had stopped. Before my time came for departure, peace was restored; Stewart took me out to the smallest of Anton Besse's steamers, to join the second Red Sea convoy on its way; Harold, who had been torn between the official and the friendly, came down handsomely on the kinder side. 'You're a great dear,' he wrote to me in Cairo: 'and I hope all goes as you wish.' All this made a pang at leaving, and I have a warmth at my heart whenever I think of Aden, its gaunt pinnacles and the brightness of its solitary bays; the friendships and the people I knew there share its same quality in my mind, set in remoteness, independent of time. I was never again to feel such safety, of everyone united about one against a common danger, until I came home to England in the last year of the war.

I left on the 4th of September with fifty-five Sikhs on board: they sat cross-legged with a small harmonium, playing their Indian tunes, smoothing their long black beards round their chins under nets. Steaming in mist and sunset, we picked up our convoy off the southern coast, and made for Perim through a phosphorescent sea. It was moonlight strewn with diamonds in our wake. Next morning, opposite Massawa, the Fascists attacked out of the sun; we were thirty-two vessels in sight, scattering like poultry—our destroyers, led by the cruiser *Leander*, watchful round us. The bombs spouted higher than her funnel. 'The rattle of the ships' guns is almost continuous; *Leander*, firing, one sparkle of gold flame *coruscante*, very fine indeed. Sea is dark blue—a northerly breeze.'

At Port Sudan, John Marriott[1] was busy with the southern war, and took me with two of his colonels to Suakin. While they looked at wells I wandered among the coral-built houses of dead merchants, bleached with white-painted woodwork and roughened by the nearness of the sea. Among the stuccoed alcoves through ruined doorways, I saw a Venetian chandelier. Pigeons nested on the terrace of Kitchener's rest-house, and sails of the nautiluses came skimming up the estuary where an old dhow lay stranded. A number of forts built by Kitchener stand round the landward side.

Here I left the never-revisited Red Sea world and travelled to the Nile. In the month of September an air like fire moved over the polished water. Winds as from a furnace swept the banks, with cool threads that came from who knows where caught now and then between them. The desert landscape was gritty rock and barren water; and Abu Simbel, as the stiff-eyed statues greeted the morning sun, impressive but unlovable in grandeur, looked like an incarnation of their inexorable land.

At the end of the second day we anchored near the temple of Phylae, green with lake-weeds but unharmed from its yearly immersion, risen like Ondine. In the desert calm and the evening light, the Luxor Express sat at the end of its shining rails with an air of leisure while the Worcesters were de-training and, gradually cooling, carried us to Cairo through the night.

* * * *

[1] Major-General Sir John Marriott, K.C.V.O., C.B., D.S.O.

Cairo

Cairo was the centre of our world during the first three years of war, the stage on which all glances south of the Alps were focused. To see it even in 1943, when the tide of Alamein had receded, or more so today when it has returned to be one of the uneasy national provincialisms of the East, is to miss all that made it unforgettable to those who lived in it or near it during the three great years. It was the goal of the pincer movement of the Axis, the artery of our oil and our communications, the keystone of our Middle Eastern arch. It had returned to the days of the Ptolemys when Egypt was the gate to Parthia and India and all the spice trade. You would hear every European language (except German) in its streets. In the wartime epilepsy, people travelling from everywhere to anywhere would have to pass through Cairo: they would come from Scandinavia or Chungking, and salute you unexpectedly on the terrace of Shepheard's or the Continental. To describe, or even to think of it now is as difficult as to evoke the magic of dead *prima donnas*, those moments—Nijinsky poised in air or Pavlova among her white feathers subsiding—which may have been artificial but are remembered more living than anything alive, and yet they cannot be conveyed. Nor will any peace prosperity restore the incantation, for—like diamonds on velvet—it was set in danger—in the orbit of advancing armies, the drama of existence or death. Exhausted as all were at the end, the threat was an enhancement, and no one can forget the gaiety and the glitter of Cairo while the desert war went on.

It changed a great deal during the time I knew it—from September to April 1940–41 and then to and fro at intervals during the next two years—yet it always presented, like the two-way-facing Janus, aspects of surprising contrast—the unobtrusive hard work and private anxiety, and the confidence which the Army, the Egyptians, and the outside world were made to see. It was quiet at first—the G.H.Q. typewriters clicked from private flats (liable to be overheard by the houses around) and dinner parties at the Embassy were easy among English or Egyptians who came to know each other well. *Cawasses* in gold and scarlet bowed one into pleasant informal evenings of talk with the Lampsons,[1] Miles robust and Jacqueline light as a fairy. The Embassy gardens at that time still stretched to the Nile, and one rested under a light rug after dinner, on chaise-longues in the soft night, where the lisp of the great river's journey joined the conversation.

Sometimes it would be Mena House, round a swimming-pool in the open with lights dimmed so that men late from their offices would peer among bare jewelled shoulders and mess uniforms that still existed[2] to find their party at the little tables. These dimmed blue lights bewitched Cairo into the *Pelléas and Mélisande* remoteness that seemed to belong to the precarious time.

The Lampsons were very good to me, and, now and then when I was free, asked me for a night to a cottage taken over from the Fayyum archaeologists, where one could wake in desert air and ride, under the eyes of a police guard on a camel poised on every height.

Less official company had the desert to itself. I soon acquired an assistant and friend,[3] and she and I and three airmen would get away on donkeys now and then on a Sunday. A fine of ten piastres punished anyone who mentioned the war, though the R.A.F. commanders could not help casting up their eyes eloquently enough to some aeroplane sailing home above us, to see which of our scanty numbers it might be.

The Egyptian Court was lukewarm during that autumn when—to most Arabs—our chances seemed hopeless. Yet there were many faithful friends. Jaunty in spite of his age, Prince Muhammad Ali, the heir, was in and out at Momo Marriott's[4] tea-table, sitting on the edge of a chair, his tarbush on one side and an emerald the size of a sparrow's egg on his little finger. The Emir Abdullah would come from what was still Transjordan, plump, draped in white and gold, with the Hashemite look of Ali and Feisal appearing in his

---

[1] Sir Miles Lampson (now Lord Killearn), British Ambassador to Egypt and High Commissioner for the Sudan 1936–46, and his wife.

[2] Given up when the Dominion troops arrived with only the more austere luggage of war. The regiments of 1940 had been stationed for a long while previously in the Middle East.

[3] The Hon. Mrs. (Pamela) Hore-Ruthven.

[4] Wife of Major-General Sir John Marriott.

face with age, ready to spot a winner on the racecourse; and his son, Naif, with him, curly-haired and seventeen, in search of a bride.

People came from overseas, by detours to skirt the citadel of Europe. Anthony Eden was there, among Pashas congregated in tarbush clusters on divans under chandeliers. He was popular then and Turks and Arabs liked him—happy, charming, and lucky to have been born with great events around him, 'for he does not seem quite strong enough to make them for himself.' I have wondered whether those days in Cairo may not have added their witchcraft to paint a picture of the importance of Egypt which showed itself fallacious even during the progress of the war. The Canal was out of action for days with no perceptibly fatal results.

In 1941, the desert victories held the early spring. Then came the Greek defeat and the Libyan pendulum against us; between March and June General Wavell had five fronts on his hands. While this went on, Cairo became more anxious, more cosmopolitan, more brilliant than before, with the flight from Greece and the added impact of Europe; royalties and diplomats, officers, commandos, and agents showed like bits of glass in a kaleidoscope, to change and dissolve. General Wavell left as C.-in-C. for India, Sir Arthur Longmore, our Air C.-in-C. went to London and new actors stepped upon our stage. Pat Hore-Ruthven (my Pam's husband) and the Long Range Desert Group to which he belonged continued in and out with their far stories. The Free French appeared and De Gaulle passed through, 'rough and unfinished—like a Rodin, with carefully done bits here and there, such as his eyes and brow which are very sad ... we talked about the Druses and not war (for one can't help feeling that one might get on quicker without the Free French in Syria).' This was a few months before the Syrian campaign, when the full implication of the French defection appeared. When that was over, Oliver Lyttelton was our Minister of State, Air Marshal Tedder was in command of the Air Force and General Auchinleck, our new C.-in-C., was on his way. 'He looks much younger than Wavell,' I wrote, 'with a Scotch face like a rough untidy bit of rock, and a great directness. He misses the *greatness* which General Wavell carries about with him, but you feel that here is a soldier who would remain a soldier in any circumstance, and a man who thinks with his own brain and not with formulas.' A few months later the great tank battles came to accentuate his personal ability during the worst crisis of the Egyptian war.

The loss of Wavell was almost individual to many who scarce knew him, for he had this quality of greatness. Stories were current about him in Cairo. His engine conked out in the desert, and he sat reading Browning, waiting to settle for the night, when headlights appeared. Jeffery Amherst[1] was with him and advised him to walk into the darkness, till the lights turned out British after all. A general could easily be lost in the desert war.

Before I knew him well, and while I was still involved with Italians, a raid on the hinterland of Genoa in the country of Masséna's campaigns seemed to me possible, to encourage the anti-Fascists who were numerous in that region. I felt this so strongly that I penetrated the barbed wires of the new grey building into which G.H.Q. had expanded. I was handed by the outer guard to the Cypriots who stood at the doorway; escorted through lifts and corridors; until in the map-room the General himself stood before me. By this time I had realized the enormity of my position and no voice came from my frightened throat. General Wavell looked kind but was notoriously silent. After a second or two of mutual contemplation somehow I brought out my idea and, still without a word, he stepped across to the map of the Mediterranean and looked at it in silence. 'I have no troops to spare,' he said at last, without a trace of impatience and as if with regret; and I retreated, still overwhelmed, but with the picture of him in my mind which I have often thought of, counting inadequate resources and looking at the map.

As the war went on, he and all his family came to be among the dearest of my friends. In the letters to my mother, in which I tried to write what I thought could amuse or please her, I described a dinner in my flat high up on the Cairo island above the 'blind Nile' looking westward: 'only six, and we talked of everything but the war, the General twinkling with his one eye, quoting Oscar Wilde on Samarkand.' This friendship I count among the greatest fortunes of that year, or of many years.

[1] Earl Amherst, then serving with the Guards.

In and out of the official world was the Levantine society of Cairo dripping gems and substantially unchanged from the days when Thais wore Alexandria's most expensive togas. It would gather in the Muhammad Ali Club where fatherly waiters and huge chandeliers preserved their Victorian solidity, into which cheerful troops broke now and then and asked for drinks. Having got them from the shocked fifth-columnist head waiter, they would ask for women, and the police were sent for; as I left once I found my fat chauffeur with his head in his hands, rather bashed in by a South African annoyed with him for not being a taxi.

Beyond these quarters, the whole of Cairo itself buzzed like a hive, carrying from age to age, from foreigner to foreigner, from dynasty to dynasty, its blind traditions and long poverties. In these crowded quarters I came to have many committees—teachers, clerks, workmen or the lesser rank of government servant, living in small alleys up narrow stairs, hard lives not untouched by dreams. And in the crowded Muski I would discover Aly Khan's devotees among the Persian merchants, and would sometimes lure him[1] to sit sprinkled with rosewater in a carpeted twilight, while a poet festooned in his own fat chins recited beside a small splashing fountain of peacock-coloured tiles.

★ ★ ★ ★

The German invasion of Russia[2] brought a temporary easing of the desert war that did not last for long.

19 November 1941

Our people from Russia are hopeful and seem to think that their line may be established. One may have to evacuate here. One goes on putting things together which life and the Germans continue to pull apart.[3]

The desert battle was ever in our ears, advancing or receding, while the greater war moved beyond it in shadows of its own.

[1] Then serving in the Army as a colonel.
[2] 22 June 1941.
[3] Letters to my mother.

6 December 1941

We are hanging anxiously on to the Libyan news. It is the most fantastic battle: till the things are almost on top of you, you can't tell if they are German or British. All the wives are anxious enough, as no news of their husbands comes through.

23 November 1941

The battle is at its height out in the desert; we are smashing their tanks—we took them by surprise, a feat almost unparalleled [the range of our tank guns was eight hundred yards to the German fifteen hundred].

A grim little story of our Poles: a German aircraft crashed into their camp. When they were asked where the airman was, they said: 'There is no airman.'

10 December 1941

For the first time in this war there have been German deserters last week. The Libyan news is very slow, but the people who know seem calm. It is fantastic to be here with that monstrous battle going on two hours away by air, and life just as gay as usual, cinemas full, restaurants crowded, evening dress [I had bought a last Molyneux from Paris], and people with arms in slings or bandaged heads going out to dinner-parties.

15 December 1941

The U.S.A. are in after Pearl Harbour, but we are morally certain the French are going to let us down in North Africa.

In January 1942 I wrote from Alexandria, where the fighting seemed very close:

Nearly everyone here wears the good thick battle dress and luggage is coming and going all the time. It is amusing to watch the 'oppressed' Egyptians strolling dressed to the nines, a porter carrying their little bags, while our tyrannous soldiery slog along half buried under rifles and packs!

I had been moved to Baghdad and when I last came back through Cairo, on one of my temporary visits in the summer of 1943, Alamein and the danger were over. It was as if a dust had settled on the town. Athena's grey eyes that cheer the matadors and soldiers, the tang of life and death which belongs to the bull ring or the battle, had disappeared.

★ ★ ★ ★

Principles of Persuasion

The old-fashioned Arab chivalry had relieved us by halting the Palestine guerrillas when our larger embroilments started, but as the German pincer movement developed in the East it became ever more urgently necessary to keep the whole of the great peninsula friendly.

Closely interwoven with the life in Cairo just described, which existed as a necessary relaxation for the armies, and also as a bridge with Egyptians and others who were our lifelines at that time, a vaster and less visible network, the ordinary arteries of warfare, spread their countless ramifications of which the departments of propaganda were one.

... I am not very happy about the Middle East. Are you? [Sir Kinahan Cornwallis wrote in the summer of 1940] ... If it were only the Italians it would be all right, but it won't be and we must expect a huge German stiffening. Even so I believe we shall pull through if we have friendly countries behind us ... That is what I'm nervous about and I don't believe we are doing enough to keep the Arabs on our side ... they are all waiting for a sign about the future and they aren't getting it ... They have been very patient so far and, considering that most of them must believe we are losing the war, pretty loyal, but it won't last for ever. The Jews seem to me quite mad not to come to some arrangement with them, for if we lost they would be annihilated and when we win they can hardly expect us to fight on their behalf. It is very unfortunate how much influence they have over people who don't know the Middle East. I suppose it will all work out in the end, but we do seem to be handicapping ourselves unnecessarily.

These views have now become a commonplace merely because, immediately before 1940 and after, they were shared by practically everyone who had to do anything intimately connected with Arab affairs. Among their many other consequences they had brought me to Cairo under Reginald Davies in the Embassy Publicity Office, to work out a plan already sketched in Aden when the Yemen journey left me so deeply conscious of the danger and the power of the human word. To use and build it up on sound foundations was my hope, and during the three following years I hammered a more or less coherent structure into shape. But when I began in Cairo it was with a deep uncertainty before a task much greater than all my experience; nor would I have succeeded without the sympathy of chiefs and companions kinder and more helpful than anyone has a right to expect so many people to be in so diversified a world.

Few of us were available in Egypt at this time to deal with the persuasion of the fifteen million whom the Fascist Italian colony was trying to undermine. In its oral aspect, apart from the other varied activities of our office, two more experienced colleagues[1] dealt with the most tricky propaganda—the Press and the Pashas—while I was given as much of a free hand as possible with the rest. I lived in my flat and bought a Baby Austin with a hood like a Salvation Army bonnet, an ugly little thing which I hoped, 'like a dowdy wife, to love in time.'

A few driving lessons let me loose on the Cairo traffic, and an incident at Mena House soon made me get a better model: "Why are you savaging that innocent hotel?" Sir Arthur Longmore asked as he happened to see me go back into a wall instead of forward. He sent his driver, who recommended a Standard Eight painted midnight blue, on which I spent instalments of salary and affection, and drove in it from committee to committee, and to and from the office of the anti-Fascist Italians in between. Pamela Hore-Ruthven soon joined me and kind voluntary helpers moved in and out: a clerk was added later and before I left we had Ramzi Bey supervising a busy office and Lulie Abu'l Huda added to our staff. The work was largely social and took us into the general life of Cairo, among all sorts of people who came to my flat for parties, regardless of frontiers or rank. The desert news—as much of it as could be told—

[1] Such as Mr. Grafftey-Smith, and Mr. Williamson Napier whose business was said to be 'wining and dining with the gentlemen of the Press'. Both were on the Embassy publicity staff, who all touched on oral propaganda among their many activities.

would be brought by Brigadier Shearer,[1] dropping in for breakfast on a Sunday morning; hussars would come from their camp near the Pyramids for the occasional luxury of a bath; we had friends too many to mention though all are remembered—for we were all working together, comforted by the greatness of the background and the excitement of the odds.

I have already described the Arab aspects of this venture in *East is West* and they need not be repeated; but the principles of persuasion which underlay the *English* aspect have never been published; I gave them every ounce of available thought and energy during the next six years; as they were my life, and, apart from this, are still just as urgent today, I will make an effort even at the risk of dullness to explain them.

A main obstacle was the unfortunate word *propaganda* itself. When first adopted by the Church of Rome it was simply used in the gospel sense of the spreading of a faith, until a reputation for subtlety whether or no deserved gave it a new and sinister twist of deceit. Two opposite ideas, the truth and the hiding of the truth, thus became sheathed in one term, and have been shuffled promiscuously inside it ever since. I soon decided to leave the unhappy word in the climate of its acquired darkness, and to use *persuasion* (for want of a better) to express the spreading of ideas that are genuinely believed. A missionary told me in the middle of the war that she could not take sides because of her religion (the Archangels were less particular, though the occasion had been less ambiguous no doubt); her confusion was, however, I believe, chiefly brought about by language; if the good word *gospel* had been used instead of *propaganda*, her mind would have been clearer, and if some such definition had been generally connected with what our Ministry was saying, we should have realized that it was not only desirable but also honest to distribute our persuasion as truly as we could. There would have been less reliance on statistics of things like pig-iron to make the nations of the world believe that our cause was just. What we were dealing with was the originating and spreading of *ideas*, whose dynamic force, whose almost unlimited consequences, we are so strangely unaware of. In physical disease,

[1] Then D.M.I.

international medicine and co-operation promptly intervene; political laws are combated in a lukewarm way merely because most people—and Anglo-Saxons in particular—are unwilling to admit that thoughts can matter; and as these clothe themselves in language, it follows that the importance of words is underestimated too. While originality can be left to a natural variety in nature, truthfulness (one's own attainment of it at all events) is a matter of constant renewal and the only lasting foundation for style. Clear thinking must show behind it. Perhaps nothing but a sacramental attitude—a feeling for the sanctity of utterance in general—will nerve one for the labour. These are vast matters: the whole of civilization is in their orbit; and their neglect made a war possible at a time when most of the world had ceased to believe in it. Seen against such livid consequences, the only excuse for not attempting *persuasion* would be a weakness, a want of knowledge or conviction, in ourselves.

My visit to the Yemen brought me to some conclusions on which I tried two little ventures out in Aden. The basic rules both then and later were:

(1) To believe one's own sermon.

(2) To see that it must be advantageous not only to one's own side but to that of the listeners also.

(3) To influence indirectly, making one's friends among the people of the country distribute and interpret one's words.

This last point, not quite as vital as the other two, I shall deal with first, because it is still related to the subtleties of language which we have just been considering.

The nature of words is that none of them express a meaning exactly and when we speak or translate in a foreign country a far greater divergence is brought in than we think: for in our own language, being aware of the shortcomings of words, we supply a thousand lights and shadows to correct them. All this has to be reconstructed in a foreign tongue and is hardly ever obtained direct in a translation: the best we can do is to inspire a limited number of people not with our words but with the ideas behind them, and cause these to grow as it were all over again from the beginning in their own way, in whatever the climate of their transplanting may be.

When this was done properly, two consequences followed, the

very opposite of our usual propaganda. Since we were not trying to convince our enemies, but were intent on encouraging our friends, we avoided any repetition of the enemy's arguments (which gives them an advertisement free gratis and for nothing and which every publication I read during the war seemed to begin by doing). We built up our own story, on the fundamental assumption that there is not room for more than one idea at a time in the average head. What the other side says matters scarcely at all if one's own message is sufficiently interesting. We did, however, use the enemy catchwords if they suited us: these inventions, even on a false side, are the unconscious tributes paid to human decency, and if you hold them you capture a whole series of feelings and enthusiasms with which they have become connected. The word freedom had been misused for years by German agents; we chose it for the title of our society, emphasized it on all occasions, and brought it over to our own side (where indeed we truly felt that it belonged).

The other consequence of encouraging friends rather than proselytizing enemies brought us up against what I think is one of our chief mistakes in the East—the idea that it is a waste of time to employ people in capacities for which they may be inadequate. This frequently cuts away nearly everyone we wish to make a friend of. The dangers of such rigidity were apparent as early as 1930—or seemed so to me—in companies such as the old Anglo-Persian where the good jobs were kept to the West; even then I thought that it would pay commercial enterprises to duplicate their salaried posts even uselessly rather than remain extra-territorial in an oriental land. In Aden I tried to get together a body of local young men to do fire-fighting and such things during raids, and came up against the same objection—that they 'would be no good'. This seemed to me quite secondary: the point was that we wanted them as friends, and to have them idle while we looked after them was not the way to keep them so.

The fact that we were proselytizing only through our friends brought another consequence in its wake, which I soon adopted as the second of the three corner-stones of all persuasion: *if we wanted them to help us, we must preach in their interest as much as in ours.* It was most important to raise a banner which the Middle East could follow for its own sake, and the misuse of such words as 'freedom' and 'democracy' in Europe was not to blind us to their potency among a less sophisticated crowd. The Brotherhood of Freedom was non-national and not particularly British, except that it stood to further what we were ready to fight for. It was based on the axiom that it is more blessed to give than to receive. Instead of influence or payment our members had a chance, denied at that time (and now) to so many, of working for what they believed. All confidence, all self-respect lay in that liberty. A feeling of inferiority under Western culture chiefly poisons our relations with Eastern peoples: if we can remove it, we bring harmony and friendship. One cannot do so by *giving*—that may help *us* but not them; but by encouraging *them* to be disinterested, generous and enthusiastic the real equality appears.

The first corner-stone and the most essential was (and is) our own belief in what we say. If that is absent it is better to be silent, for nothing but failure can come of one's preaching, and it was our great strength, in this war that had been thrust upon us, that we could stand and fight undoubting with our backs against the wall. I saw no reason why our values of 'democracy' should not be adopted by every town in Asia. Never for a moment have I doubted the possibility of universal persuasion or hesitated to think that Socrates was right. Nor, in the whole of our service, did we ever spread a rumour we thought to be untrue. Sometimes indeed we had to risk a statement before we had time to authenticate it. In these cases I always risked. Truth may be compared to a building whose general symmetry does not depend on the substance of all the separate bricks: their quality must be good but it would be foolish to subject every one of them to a chemical analysis before setting it in amid the mortar. Since it is easier to be accurate than truthful there have been many cases where pedantry about single facts has resulted in a perversion of the whole: and in oral persuasion it must never be forgotten that accuracy is but the starting-point; a yard this way or that will be forgotten by the first repetition; but truth is the whole direction of those forces which our words are intended to set off.

To speak what we believe; to tell it to those who in their turn will tell it to their own people; and to see that it is directed towards the welfare of this people—these seemed to me to be the only justifiable rules and the only ones effective in the end. 'It would be a pity,' I said, 'not to follow some such lines as these in future, and disastrous to allow a way of life we truly believed in to succumb for want of the capacity and the machinery to diffuse it. Because we dislike *propaganda* we should not refrain from persuading with all our weight what we do hold to be essential. We neglected this in the past and paid the price: and the aim of our Brotherhood is a sincere attempt to differentiate and to establish the legitimate principles of persuasion.'

'Your idea is worth trying,' Iltyd Clayton had written to me. 'Why shouldn't we have some of these societies in favour of us instead of against us?' And I had experimented the actual method of working such a society in Aden—with a small committee of locally influential people who continued the 'whispering campaign' after my departure. They sent me news from time to time, but it was rather static because in Aden there were very few opponents on whom to lavish the resources of persuasion, and it was only in Cairo that the Brotherhood of Freedom developed, with a system which my friends described to me as an imitation of Bolshevist cells.

They had, as a matter of fact, nothing to do with the Bolshevists but were based on the Christian and Muslim religions: for I argued that no form of persuasion could improve on what—before the days of paper-pulp or printing, before newspapers or radio—had converted millions of men. The spoken word is the traditional way by which every great movement in the Arab world has spread, from ancient beginnings to the last revolt which freed it from the Turks. The Abbasside Empire was established by 'oral propaganda'; the *Old Man of the Mountain*, Hasan i Sabah, said in the eleventh century that with the help of two friends he could overthrow a kingdom—and he did—by 'oral propaganda'. Like most powerful things, the instrument has a good use and a bad; and in one way or the other one can watch it at work right through the history of Asia. The results we gained were not the fruits of chance but tallied with what we had expected—parts of a coherent whole based, as I think, on the permanent character of human beings.

Rushbrook in London was eager from the first; 'I am sure you are on a winner if we can get the thing going' he wrote in September. Reginald Davies, made careful by many years' management of the Alexandria Municipality's finance, was doubtful of any movement based on disinterested Egyptians; but he arranged everything to be easy for me notwithstanding, and so did everyone at the Embassy, from the archivists to the Ambassador himself. They became converted and the Brothers blossomed with new committees in unexpected places, until it began to look as if we might grow *too* strong. After nearly a year Rushbrook wrote: 'It looks to me as if the Embassy are a little alarmed at the size and strength of your lusty child! At any rate they are profoundly concerned that the direction of it should not fall into the wrong hands.'

This reasonable fear was influenced by the most ominous of fallacies—the belief that things can be kept static by inaction. Action and inaction are merely two facets of activity, and when in danger it is better to hold a sharp knife by the handle rather than so to blunt it that no one, friend or foe, can find it useful. The young Nationalist, whom they feared, was bound to increase, whatever anyone might say or do; that he has done so all over Asia under *every variety of régime* proves his predestined progress; the utmost that any policy could hope for was to keep him on our side. We have now temporarily failed in most of the Arab world to do so—and I will come later to what I think are the two chief causes of our failure; but during the war we succeeded, and that was our concern at that time.

By the end of 1940 I had about four hundred members and more work than I could do. The dining-room of my flat was still the office, and Azmi, the clerk, and Pamela were inside it, Samaha[1] and Lulie were busy with a weekly bulletin where the main questions in men's minds were to be answered, and the few English helpers[2] who had time to spare came in and out, or looked after committees.

Before another year was out we had spread up and down the Nile, and Azhar University was being converted by seventy small

[1] Mr. Samaha, a journalist in Cairo who gave us his spare time for translating.

[2] Mr. (now the Rev.) and Mrs. Michael Pumphrey, Mr. Fouracres of the Sudan Service, Mr. G. W. Murray of the Desert Survey and Mr. Ronald Fay who was to hold the Egyptian Brothers together until the Nasserites demolished them.

'democrat' committees inside it. In Alexandria, in the commercial quarters and among labourers in the port, ten thousand members stuck to us through Rommel's invasion, publishing leaflets at their own expense.

Pamela wrote in the spring of '41: 'We leave tonight to see all the Brethren in Luxor... Bakir says "all but a few insects believe in a British victory," so we must convert the insects... I wish you were coming. I hope to have an early morning ride on Lovely Sweet. Met lots of Government Officials and others and started a committee.'

From Luxor where I spent two Christmases with the Lampsons I wrote to my mother:

31 December 1941

This has been no rest cure with a committee and a speech in Arabic every day. Miles decided yesterday to come also and see the Edfu temple—so we went upstream by train in the special coach and found a red carpet waiting... horses with silver amulets round their necks, magenta saddle-cloths and high-pommelled gilt saddles—and were driven in a cabriolet with a crowd shouting 'Long Live Democracy'. We coffeed... saw the temple, Miles went back to his train, and then—with shrinking splendour—I attended a committee I suspect never meets unless there is someone to visit them. As soon as one goes in grandeur one sees a look of 'benefits to come' lighten the eyes of members—non-existent when one is poor and obscure as usual! Last night some were in turbans, some European... such a difference from last year, when Pam and I went tentatively to people who had never thought of such a gathering: now there are five committees in Luxor, and the fifth column they say is more or less eliminated. The schoolboys sent me off with four cheers, one for me, one for liberty, one for Great Britain, one for Egypt—the order not quite protocolaire.

Under the shadows of greater things and in spite of the illness of my assistants through the summer, the Brothers of Freedom flourished. They were to start in Iraq as well as in Egypt if we could find a head for the whole, while Ronnie Fay in Cairo and I in Baghdad looked after the parts. 'I am the only person in the Middle East,' I wrote, 'who willingly suggests that someone be put above them.'

CAIRO *21 November 1941*

Darling B.

Owen Tweedy,[1] sitting with his coat off in his office and his lovely *kilims* hung on his walls, promises me an assistant if I can find one. I have to set about quickly on the hopeless quest. One unknown woman is on her way out and Lulie is to be taken on permanently, both at £600 a year; and two more if we can get them. Sir Walter Monckton[2] says he wants to help all he can, and has heard from everyone, including the Minister of State, that we have done good work. I hand on these bouquets to give you pleasure, and if you knew how many reputations have been lost this last year and how few survive in their jobs, you would be quite impressed. Anyway I do the best I can, rather looking forward to a quiet time at the end of it all.

Before 1942 we had not yet got our supreme man to leave in charge. But Sir Walter Monckton told me he had a 'sweet' letter from me, 'and as it was asking for £9,000 for the Brothers, I was delighted he thought it so.'

By the end of the year, Christopher Scaife, recovering from a desert wound, had agreed to take over as soon as he was fit. He was brilliant and imaginative and interested from the beginning, with good Egyptian Arabic and experience and we were all delighted. Our numbers under Ronnie Fay's devoted care increased progressively, and by the 21st of January 1942 I could write that everything was ready for the next person to carry on. 'In sixteen months, beginning with two young students, we have gathered over six thousand people all pledged to fight the fifth column and none of them paid; all except five, including Ronnie and myself, are Egyptians; and if we had a more numerous staff we could treble our numbers in a month.'

* * * *

The growth of the Arab work drew me away from Italian problems,[3] and in any case we had failed in the main objective—the

[1] Assistant-Director of Publicity for all the Middle East.

[2] Director of Publicity for all the Middle East.

[3] See *Memorandum on Anti-Italian Propaganda in the Middle East* by C. M. Thornhill and F. Stark, 8 August 1940.

converting of the colony in Egypt. A suggestion to kidnap the king-pin from his shelter with the Swiss was welcomed in a genial moment by both Lampson and Wavell, but the army, though delighted to co-operate, asked for an impossible written order; and our other plan—to prepare a fan of anti-Fascist scouts for a hoped-for landing, also petered out against the lethargy of the camp-commanders. We succeeded with a few minor innovations such as the change from an Italian to an English Apostolic delegate and the interpolating of prisoner greetings into the Italian news; and Colonel Thornhill and Christopher Sykes continued to battle with and for their paper, in the emotional waves of their office.

This I was now out of, but my thoughts were still in Italy, for news of Herbert Young and my mother's imprisonment[1] had met me in Egypt, and a shock is none the less severe because it is half expected. They were taken to the jail in Treviso where the prison doctor saved them from a concentration camp by refusing to remove them. Our friends, everyone except the sons of the régime, did all they could with the gentleness Italians show for personal relations and in human suffering, and after three weeks Marina Luling's[2] strings pulled them out of prison into the peaceful confinement of a country inn at Macerata Feltria, until they returned to three rooms allowed them in our house. With help from every quarter a passage to the United States was fixed at last, but Herbert fell ill. He was eighty-six, my mother seventy-nine, and weeks of anxiety went by while she waited: until he died happily without being driven from the world he knew. He had given us the house we loved, and we could never count what we owed him—the feeling of a home one goes back to and finds always the same. My mother was ferried across in the summer of 1941 to John and Lucy Beach, our friends in California.

This anxiety gave me headaches that lasted through the war and never let me feel quite strong again till it was over, so that I was haunted by the fear of illness long after my mother was safe and we could communicate freely:

[1] See *An Italian Diary* by Flora Stark, published in 1945 by John Murray.

[2] Contessa Luling-Volpi, our neighbour and owner of the beautiful Palladian villa of Maser.

CAIRO *30 June 1941*

Darling B.,

It still feels like a tempting of Providence to write my daily diary to you—the telegram was not clear, but anyway you should be on the way. I shall not feel safe till I get a telegram from the U.S.A.

Of all my letters only one seems to have arrived, so you know very little of my surroundings. I wish you could see them. My flat is so nice now, after its iciness in winter: a cool north breeze blows through it from the lesser Nile, and barges filled with straw, or cotton, or bricks, come sailing by, their masts taller than the landscape of houses and palms behind them. The first room is the dining-room, with one of those *terrazza* floors and white-painted chairs and table and cupboards. I bought a Persian picture to look at during meals, all reds and gold, with a view that leads you away into a sort of Samarkand: and a most amusing silver urn which is Turkish imitation of Louis Philippe I would say, and stands on a little mirror on the table. The drawing-room is double and opens all white with brown curtains and two lovely *kilims*, blues and dull pink, which look beautiful with red roses. It has a few Japanese prints I found in Aden. Then there is a spare room, furniture all painted yellow, with a wardrobe used as my cellar, and then my bedroom, which is almost all windows, and furniture mauve, with curtains dark blue and magenta stripes and a violet bedcover. I have a Kurdish blanket given me in Baghdad, crimson purple and green with gold threads, so that it looks very rich. I wish you could see it all, and my little car which is said to be one of the chief menaces to the general safety of Egypt.

My dearest Heart [my mother wrote],

What a joy, what ineffable joy, to have a real letter again and in a short month and three weeks. Incredible to have a diary again, I never believed I should have another! I never hoped to see you again ... I do so love your descriptions, and your flat ... am not very sure of purple— very good in itself, but is it becoming to *you*? And hats? I am so sad to think of two lovely evening gowns reposing in Marina's cupboards: a black moiré—very spreading flounces, and a brilliant slim one, with a burgundy velvet little jacket—the last Paris models to come to Venice.

I eventually let my flat in Cairo and moved to Iraq, where I was made (temporary) Attaché to our Embassy. At intervals during the next two years I would cross the desert with a pause in Jerusalem, where the MacMichaels[1] lived wise and remote from city turmoils in the wartime stillness of the most beautiful of Government Houses. It was (or seemed to the visitor) a haven at that time, between the eastern and western anxieties of Hitler's pincer movement; and a refreshment to see terraces of lavender and rosemary with Nesta MacMichael planning herbaceous borders, in a deceptive landscape of stability that sloped between the stones.

Little memory stands out from these desert crossings beyond a confused shimmer of heat and fatigue.

'I am sure you ought not to be trusted by yourself in your little car,' Jock wrote after one of them. 'I mean you can't always have a charming major to turn the wheel when you go to sleep. Anyway you must be very *blasé* about majors not to keep awake in their company... Whatever chance is there for a poor second lieutenant?' On the next crossing, before taking up my Baghdad job, I had to promise Owen Tweedy 'to take a Man across the desert, as he says he can't afford accidents to his staff.'

---

[1] Sir Harold MacMichael, High Commissioner and Commander-in-Chief for Palestine and High Commissioner for Trans-Jordan, 1938–44, and Lady MacMichael.

6
Baghdad: The First Crisis

The idea of spreading the Brotherhood to Iraq was mooted in the spring of 1941, I cannot now remember by whom. With the appearance of Rommel and our withdrawal on Tobruk, the desert was then swinging against us, and in Iraq itself the situation—according to my diary—'was frothing like milk about to boil.' At the end of March, within the first few days of my arrival, I was caught unexpectedly in a student procession in Baghdad. With the window of my car open, I made an island in the main street while the lanky young figures and excited chanting flowed by on either side. The first Arabic word that came into my head was *Meskin*: it means *poor thing*, and I said it whenever they seemed about to stop or hit me. I must have repeated it fifty times or more, watching (with some anxiety) while a human gleam came back into their fanatic faces. Nobody hit me.

Shortly afterwards the English Ambassador left for Afghanistan in a Buick and Sir Kinahan Cornwallis replaced him. Could he have come earlier, the April *coup d'état* might perhaps have been avoided: as it was, with twenty years of Iraq experience as Advisor in their Ministry of Interior, he guided us through the rebellion with a wise and steady hand. He had become a friend of mine, first met when I reached Iraq twelve years before, and known better and liked even more when we shared a table at the Ministry of Information during the first month of the war. With the Arab Bureau behind him, and the election of the first King Feisal, and all the early problems that brought modern Iraq out of the Turkish province of Mesopotamia, there was little he did not know about the Middle East. I used to enjoy the way his pale blue eyes became small, with the pupils like pin-points, when he considered an idea or a person, listening with an air of leisure long ago acquired. He once told me that he did all his paper work when the day was over and kept his office hours for visitors and coffee; but never missed a Friday's[1] shooting in the years of his service. His wife and daughter, who had not been out with him before, also became dear friends.

There had been years of quiet German preparation in Iraq, in the skilful and rather pleasant hands of Dr. Grobba the German Ambassador. The historic restlessness of the country against its governments had already shown itself in 1937 in the military dictatorship of Bekr Sidki, ending with his murder; and now again a mixed minority—students, politicians out of power, and chiefly the same discontented army elements with a German victory in prospect to sustain them—were gathering to a head under four generals later known as 'The Golden Square' and Rashid Ali al Gailani[2] as a political leader. In the spring of 1941 a first attempt failed with the escape of the Emir Abdullah the Regent, and the brilliant tactics that landed our troops in Basra: the main revolution was then forced on before German help was available and was defeated by an extremely slender force sent across the desert to lead back the legal Government, to relieve our air base at Habbaniya, and to rescue a small Lucknow of imprisoned British in Baghdad and the north.

This campaign, though small, was a turning point in the Middle Eastern war. If we had lost it, Hitler's pincer movement could have succeeded, and oil, our access to India, and our desert strategy would have shown in a new and very unpleasant light: so that the investment of the Baghdad Embassy made history in its way. So far as I know, its details have not been published,[3] and I will therefore consider the jottings of my diary through the crisis and the siege as a minor document and give them as they come. They begin on March 22nd over tea in Amman, watching the Emir Abdullah[4] wave away the Vichy attitude of the French in Syria[5] with his well-

[1] Friday, the Muslim equivalent of our Sunday in the Iraq Government offices.

[2] A rather distant connection of the Gailani family in Baghdad and not held in much esteem by them.

[3] Except for a brief extract in *East is West*.

[4] Later King.

[5] General Weygand and the French Army on which the Middle Eastern defence was to have relied went over almost entirely to Petain after the surrender in France.

kept hands. "Let them go," he says. "It will mean a year or eighteen months more, but England will be alone at the peace...."

When I reached Iraq, the first abortive plot had failed.

[Diary] BAGHDAD *3 April 1941*

Crisis as usual only a bit more so. The army has got post office and radio station; Government resigned, and Rashid Ali Gailani has seized it; Regent disappeared, some say to the British at Habbaniya.

Yesterday a poor little English array and one or two very solitary Iraqis went to meet Sir Kinahan at the airport, but only a message came, to say he was detained—possibly with the Regent. We have a chance to be firm: whatever happens in future, the present lull in the Balkans would allow us to dish the Iraq Army first, and they know it.

Drove by back way unchallenged to the defences of Harthiya; nothing but absent-minded looks from bridge guard. Useful to remember.

Visit the Museum director, of Syrian origin and perverseness. 'We will discuss politics and I will speak frankly,' he says. Tired of people who 'speak frankly', and wonder what would happen if one did it oneself.

The Regent was got out the day before yesterday, lying under cushions in the U.S.A. Minister's car with the Minister sitting in it. No one looked, though the bridges were guarded. Rashid Ali's men searched the palace from floor to ceiling and would no doubt have murdered him.

5 April 1941

Went to lunch with George Antonius[1] and found him with the Mufti,[2] a young-looking though white-haired, handsome man, wearing his turban like a halo, his eyes light blue and shining and a sort of radiance as of a just-fallen Lucifer about him. He looked at me in a friendly surprise . . . most courteous and very different from his companion, sad and black-haired, with venom in his glance.

News of our crisis grows worse. Palace telephones cut. Basra Governor arrested. Rather feeble manifesto from Regent said to be on British sloop at Basra. All depends on whether Wavell can spare troops: the fall of Benghazi adds no little to our troubles in a propaganda way. The town here is polite and quiet, but the German radio is beginning to invent: says we poisoned Feisal and killed Ghazi. Rumour that four

---

[1] Author of *The Arab Awakening*.

[2] Haj Muhammad Amin-al-Hussaini, the ex-Mufti of Jerusalem.

doctors went to the Regent's palace with a certificate for heart failure all ready—but he had gone!

7 April 1941

Everyone is watching the crisis get worse in a fascinated way. The Big Four[1] seem very competent in the management of news: the Regent's broadcast is jammed; Reuter's fatuous message about 'perfect tranquillity' in Baghdad is already scattered by them in leaflet form; anxiety to continue British friendship stressed, though the German tone of Press and Baghdad wireless are already more pronounced. Bazaars peaceful: it is still very pleasant to row up in a *bellam* under the eaves and overhanging balconies and look into river courtyards with gardens.

H.M.S. *Falmouth* reached Basra full steam: Rashid Ali protests that no permission was asked: H.E. says he doesn't recognize the right of the present government to be asked.[2]

They are being marooned in the Embassy. No Iraqis have been to see them there.

8 April 1941

I expected no Iraqis at my tea party, but twenty-nine turned up, all very friendly. How right it was not to cancel! It would be a great mistake not to encourage those who are prepared to show themselves on our side. Furious with X's who, when asked to co-operate in this way, one and all refuse 'because they are annoyed with Iraq'!

I wrote to Sir Kinahan:

My dear Ken,

Abd el Qadir[3] is going to see you at twelve tomorrow. He suggests that they are very worried, particularly about Turkey. I said we need not

[1] The four Iraqi generals called 'The Golden Square', who ran the rebellion.

[2] We were allowed by treaty to land troops in Basra, including the use of railways, ports, aerodromes etc., in time of war. Sir Kinahan used this clause, and the rebel (Rashid Ali) government was forced to accept the first landing: the *second* landing, before the first had moved on out of Iraq, precipitated the explosion in May: the rebels could not afford to wait for German help while more British troops accumulated in the country.

[3] Minister for Foreign Affairs under Rashid Ali and one of the deeply respected Gailanis with whom Rashid Ali was connected at an inferior level.

even fight Iraq—all we need do is to murmur that we are no longer interested and plenty of people will fall on her on their own.

If you get concessions—acquiescence in the landing of a battalion or brigade, a complete volte-face of the Press, the establishment of cordial relations between our Mission and the Army, and such things—against the recognition of their Government, it seems to me you gain a way out without loss of prestige. The landing of troops would counterbalance the recognition. You would drive a wedge between the Rashid Ali people and their Axis allies, and the odium of the Government's rapidly approaching unpopularity would fall on their shoulders and not on ours.

The not-helping of our friends I believe would only be temporary and Abdullah himself, if consulted, would probably agree to it. The ex-government has simply done nothing for itself and is not at all deeply rooted in any popular affection, and for a foreign power to put in a rather unpopular government by force is nearly always a failure.

Forgive me for piling more paper on your devoted head, but this is the outcome of endless talks with moderate Iraqis and I thought you would not mind my condensing it for you, for what it is worth. The idea of using this crisis to establish our forces peacefully and wean the Axis allies does appeal to one!

(This was the line actually followed and had already been decided on before my letter went.)

[Diary] *12 April 1941*

Conversation with George Antonius. He asked what were the reasons for our interest in the Iraqi crisis which appeared to him entirely an internal political problem.

I disclaimed any knowledge but gave personal opinion that the whole matter would be much simpler if we could feel convinced that the present Government is not acting for Germany.

G.A. Admitted he had heard in Cairo that Rashid Ali is in German pay—but even if this had been so in the past, it did not follow it need be in the future.

I. Agreed, but remarked that something tangible would be required to convince.

G.A. Quoted R.A.'s assurance in the *Majliss* (Parliament).

I. Put it to George that *if* R.A. were in German pay, would he not have said exactly the same?

G.A. 'Then you think him in German pay?'

I.   'I don't know him and therefore have no opinion. All I say is that his public statements are no proof one way or the other. Anyone suspected of being pro-German is *ipso facto* suspected of being both untruthful and untrustworthy since these are among the recognized virtues of the German policy.'
G.A. Thought this over and asked, 'What could he do to prove his good intentions?'
I.   Suggested that for one thing the revolting tone of the Press might alter.
G.A. 'You know that the Press in the East does not represent the people.'
I.   'No, but it represents the Government. If R.A. in one day could make all the pro-British papers anti-British, he could just as easily do the opposite to the anti-British papers.'
G.A. Suggested he could easily bring such a change about if that were to be sufficient to convince H.M.G.
I.   Said that I had no idea at all of what would convince H.M.G. and thought that a change in the tone of the Press by itself would most probably *not* be sufficient by any means. All I suggested was that the chief difficulty will be to persuade H.M.G. that R.A. is not acting for Germany and that anything short of conclusive proof would most probably be unacceptable.
G.A. 'Do you mean that England would prefer civil war in Iraq rather than accept R.A.'s assurances?'
I.   'If R.A. is acting in German interests, I imagine that England would naturally prefer civil war: it is obviously better to have half Iraq pro-German rather than the whole of it.'
G.A. Ended by saying how gladly he would offer his services as intermediary if Sir K.C. would like to see him again.

14 April 1941

Libya very disquieting. Looks as if Rommel means to push on to the Delta with patrols, but I feel pretty sure he cannot. I write, however, to arrange for my flat as I would feel sorry to lose my goods if women should be evacuated.

15 April 1941

Stefana Drower[1] goes to see the Queen[2]. Has to wait for ages while

[1] Lady Drower, D. LITT, HON. D.D., writer and lecturer, scholar of Middle Eastern religions, folklore and languages, particularly of the Mandaeans.

[2] Widow of King Ghazi and mother of the little King Feisal, then aged six. The Regent was her brother.

the Line of Defence asks for leave. Queen is very worn—life intolerable—everything watched. Miss Borland[1] cooks and tastes all the King's food.

16 April 1941

S. (owner of a factory in Baghdad) complains bitterly of our want of propaganda—he suggests there should be a common office run by a Britisher and Iraqi in collaboration. This might be a promising idea. He emphasizes, as everyone does, the mistake of past governments in keeping out all the younger men.

I dined at the Embassy and had a long talk with H.E. afterwards. Very pleased to be at his old job but shocked at the way our touch with outlying districts is lost. Says he is going to delay the recognition of the new Government till sure of its good intentions.

17 April 1941

Last night an agreement was reached accepting the landing of our troops in Iraq. It was expected to be published this morning but there is nothing in the papers. The fact is that it converts the whole business into a victory for us, no matter what rebel government is in, and no doubt they are anxious to give it as little publicity as possible.

20 April 1941

Electrical effect of our landing. The new Government tried to keep it dark and even denied it, so that our broadcast describing cordial reception by local officials, etc,. came as a surprise. Most people seem pleased.

In the lull of this excellent news I reverted to my own business, and wrote what still seems to me sensible today:

17 April 1941

I believe there is a large body of opinion here opposed to us only *accidentally*—young Nationalist opinion, which had become anti-British chiefly because the older generation was pro-British and kept all the power in its own hands. This young opinion has been caught by the Nazis, but a divorce should not be beyond our skill. Its strongholds are Pan-Arabism and the Mufti (matters of higher policy beyond our propaganda); the Army; and the Press.

The Army. Our Military Mission should see to it that *every young Iraqi officer* has some sort of social relation with the English here. When

---
[1] The King's English nurse.

it is considered that such a labour during the last few years could almost certainly have prevented the present crisis, it becomes clear that a much closer social feeling in the Mission is necessary. There are plenty of our officers keen on foreign languages and customs—and it should be one of their chief qualifications for countries of this sort.

The Press. Every Iraqi I have spoken to is astonished at our failure to make the local Press useful to our cause. The fact is that it is hard for us to plumb the iniquity of oriental journalism, and the best suggestion was that it should be directed by one British and one Iraqi in collaboration. We might point out that it is not enough for the Press of an allied country to abstain from actual vituperation of its allies. In Iraq, when it has 'acted right it has taken special care to act in such a manner that its endeavours could not possibly be productive of any consequence.' Burke said this and continued: 'This innoxious and ineffectual character, that seems formed upon a plan of apology and disculpation, falls miserably short of the mark of public duty . . . *What is right should not only be made known but made prevalent* . . . When this public man omits to put himself in a situation of doing his duty with effect . . . it frustrates the purposes of his trust almost as much as if he had betrayed it.' Only an Iraqi I believe can successfully deal with the Iraqi Press: the British should be there to stiffen, sustain, guide and occasionally corrupt him.

The fundamental fact to remember is that it is only when we can induce the Iraqi to do our propaganda for us that our propaganda will be effective.[1]

The basic principles of my theories of persuasion were being driven in to me by experience, though the word was not yet adopted.

A letter from Rushbrook a few days after these notes were written makes the gloom of the situation even clearer.

30 April 1941

My dear Freya,

It was a great joy to get your letter. I congratulate you upon being in Baghdad while the *coup d'état* was in progress. At the moment the storm clouds seem indeed to be gathering. I only hope that you yourself will suffer no personal inconvenience . . . do remember that we cannot replace you if you are put out of action.

I am sure the way you suggest tackling the problem of propaganda in Iraq is fruitful, and will—if conditions allow it to be pursued—yield good

---

[1] From a memorandum on Propaganda, 17 April 1941.

results. We have been desperately weak on the liaison side; and I think this is perhaps not wholly the fault of the specifically publicity organization. But I agree that the results have been lamentable, and have spent a number of sleepless nights turning over in my mind what, if anything, can be done this end. At last, I arrived at the conclusion that the first thing was to send you to the spot. Our thoughts must have been moving along parallel lines; because almost at the moment your telegram came...

I am still not quite clear in my mind as to why the country has gone sour on us in this way. The Mufti had been a constant source of trouble; and to him I feel inclined to attribute much of the mystery... I earnestly share your wish that Sir K.C. had gone a few months earlier. I am sure things would not have been so bad.

19 April 1941

My dear Rushbrook [I had meanwhile written],

You will see that the essentials of propaganda here depend in all their main points on Government action at home. There is no doubt that under Hitler, the Mufti is the main immediate cause of trouble: his removal or pacification entails action far beyond the scope of the wretched propagandist and I feel I must add the usual wail to my report—namely that the Palestine question lies at the root of all our troubles. Everyone who knows these lands has been saying this for years, but it will have to be repeated as long as we continue in the sort of morass we are here involved in.

The problem of the Military Mission too requires action beyond the range of our propaganda powers. It rather involves a change in the policy behind the Mission and, as a consequence, a very considerable change in the grounds on which the personnel is chosen. Vyvyan Holt[1] says: what is the good if Government is asked to do it all? I, on the other hand, feel that one can't produce even the smallest chick without some sort of an egg to start with—your propagandist merely acts in the nature of an *incubator*, not as a conjuror producing the non-existent from a hat!

For years I have been unable to see why our Government should not take every public opportunity to give a blessing to the Pan-Arab cry. What are they frightened of? The sentiment would please every Arab, even if the realization remained as Utopian as ever.

However, to leave these distressing surveys. We are having very

---

[1] Later Sir Vyvyan Holt, K.B.E., C.M.G., M.V.O. At that time Oriental Secretary and Counsellor at the British Embassy. Died 1960. Referred to henceforward as V.H.

anxious days here. I miss being on the inside of the news as in Cairo and wonder how things really are, and whether our Brothers of Freedom stood up well to the idea of a thousand tanks on the road from Mersa Matruh.

Here there was a sticky day or two, but the volcano looks like sinking to the usual simmering point of Iraqi politics. I am told that we are unpopular only with the Baghdad part of the Army: it seems a sad reflection, as Baghdad is the only centre for our Mission. It is depressing to think what a large amount of government machinery has to be put in motion just to try and make us liked! And how little it seems to succeed!

Forgive these wails of a Depressed Propagandist! I am leaving for a week in Persia and will then hurry back to Cairo a few days after the end of the month. I haven't been able to get to the north at all with all these troubles but have sat solidly talking Iraqi politics in Arabic instead of looking at the lovely spring flowers from the Shammar tents.

As the crisis seemed over, I started on April 25 for a week of consultation in Teheran, in an empty train going north to fetch Iraqi soldiers: ominous, I thought, when the bad Greek news was taken into account.

The Iranian frontier was a florid palace in the wilderness, with a garden full of flowers and small trees, the Customs Director's office spotlessly kept, with French novels by his desk, and himself a pleasant man from Tabriz. From there we went on over hills clothed with faint grass, like hair on a baby's head, to Qasr Shirin, and then by lush sweeps under a chorus of larks, through breezes weighted with sweet and sticky scents of grasses thick with flowers. The nomads were out in their tents like flocks of black goats against the hillsides, and new villages were started here and there: one I remembered just begun, now hidden in pale poplars and blossoming trees, though the poverty of the people prevented anything else developing but squalor.

At Kermenshah a great vision came suddenly of Mount Parau and its neighbours, their tops mist and snow above green shoulders —a cold spring landscape of the north; and when night had fallen we drank tea on Kangavari's new boulevard, with lanterns on poles all down it. The latest civilization seemed to consist of boulevards, regardless of what backed them. At the foot of the Asadabad Pass, a bridge was away and a band of coolies were helping lorries across a small but tumultuous river in the darkness. The steep bank shone with mud in the headlights and so did the coolies' thin wet legs: their skullcaps and pale turbans, their ragged light felt coats, looked beautiful against the background of night.

Mist and snow at the top melting to slush as we came down, and buckets of rain in Hamadan. A fire was lit in my room, and food brought up, and in the morning the sun shone like varnish on the young leaves and the snows of Elvand. But what had become of Hamadan?—a square surrounded by cupolas, symmetrical and hideous: the wide new spaces—seas of mud; the women's pretty *chadurs* changed to drab scarves, and the men with any old bit of European clothing, all dingy and mostly black.

The landscape continued grim and beautiful—hills black with rain and white, cold bands of snow, or ponds of water. Mineral streaks made the lower folds rusty and red and jade like autumn Scotland. The mud-bastioned villages looked well with their low lines, and the peasants in the fields, the ragged strips of their clothes fluttering about them. Kazvin seemed unchanged, with brick-vaulted descents to the bazaars that I remembered; and as night was again falling we caught one glimpse of Elburz sunset-lit. Then lorries in the headlights at Karaj rescued through slush and sleet from the silt, while a white bird, a duck, started up illuminated and perpendicular like a Chinese painting against the background of the dark.

In the morning I woke to a scent of wallflowers in the Legation garden, where two happy bachelor ducks and a library of good books solaced Sir Reader Bullard's[1] harassed leisure. The shadow of the Greek retreat hung over us, and anxiety for Egypt, and absence of Iraq news.

[Diary] *28 April 1941*

The general feeling in the country is that of a rabbit hypnotized by a snake—we are not masters of events and things have gone beyond ordinary methods. None of the two thousand or more technicians of the Axis here are over thirty-five!

I had a dream and woke up saying: '*Je me permets le seul luxe de ne pas*

[1] Distinguished expert on Arab and Middle East affairs. Minister (later Ambassador) in Teheran 1939–46.

connaître des Allemands,' and when Mr. Churchill in his speech last night said he was going to make a not inapt quotation, I thought it *should* be—'Say not the struggle nought availeth, etc.[1]—and it *was*.

There was nothing to be planned at the moment. I spent a quiet morning or two being painted by Gerald de Gaury,[2] wondering idly where that canvas might end. The Victorian Legation with its Persian mirror-work and stucco, its comfortable compromise of two traditions, its Oriental dignity and English country-house ease, made a curious contrast with our precarious tenure. 'The snows of the mountains behind us and their visiting clouds all combine to give a feeling of remoteness only broken by the News.'

As the aeroplanes were full and there was no means of returning for a week, I decided to spend the two spare days in Isfahan; but I left sooner, on the 30th of April, after waking up with a presentiment. The crash in Iraq was not foreseen immediately, yet I suddenly felt that it was coming and that I might not reach Baghdad if I delayed. I renounced Isfahan and hurried by special car at my own expense to Kermenshah, back over the Asadabad—its chrysoprase landscape of grass and corn almost transparent under a rainbow. Liberty, the loveliness of Persia, was all about me: those groups of riders, those herds and flocks, the town-free spaces, the limpid air. As I drove along, with my foreboding, uncertain of what the frontier might hold, I thought of all the things good and bad that I had seen in my short journey—the larks and the honey-scented air; the bird in the night; the snow-slopes and poplars of Teheran; a boy with a bicycle, on a boulder in a stream, reading; the errand boy strolling with a bunch of roses; four gazelles crossing the road; the flocks of sheep adrift on the *dasht* like fat summer clouds; black tents where the hill slope breaks like a wave above them; the crescent moon reflected in the stream-bed of a village street, with the old moon in her arm; three villagers round their pool where the little splash could mingle with their talk; fields of blue hyacinths; the shepherd's fire high up on Kuh Parau and the outline of Bisitun rocks under the moon. I thought of Persia sitting like a frog in front of the German

[1] A. H. Clough.
[2] Then Attaché at the British Legation.

python; of the poverty of the people and the ugliness of their clothes; of what some people drank and some of their wives said; and how mixed the world, with a balance on the whole in its favour.

It took thirteen hours to reach Kermenshah, and I was off next morning, asking the kind Vaughan Russells at the Consulate to say to the Oil Company that I had already departed. A message for me had been sent there from H.E. in Baghdad, and I thought (rightly as it turned out) that it might try to intercept my return. There was no difficulty, but a great deal of rumour and many good wishes on the Persian side of the border; and it was only when I reached Khanikin, the Iraqi frontier town, that a young lieutenant put me into police custody in the railway rest-house, to wait for the evening train.

7
Baghdad: The Siege of the Embassy

I got off so easily at Khanikin by asking for a lady's maid. This old-fashioned product, obviously unobtainable there, which I pointed out to the police officer as an indispensable adjunct to a civilized female prisoner, made him prefer to send me off to wherever I wished to go. I had taken care to have no return visa for Persia; and the result was a long but polite evening with a policeman, and a sleeper on the night express, instead of the prison camp in which other people spent a month of discomfort.

During the short five days of my absence events in Iraq had precipitated with unexpected speed: on the 30th of April[1] our landing of the second brigade of the 10th Indian Division, before the first had moved on, proved to 'The Golden Square' that their game would be up if they waited any longer, while our forces might indefinitely grow. The German reinforcements were not yet available and the battle of Crete, in which almost all German transport aeroplanes were lost, was only just preparing: faced with this dilemma, the Iraq Army moved west from Baghdad to invest Habbaniya, where such aircraft as we had took the initiative and attacked them on the 2nd of May at five in the morning.

At about this time, trundling along the deserty landscape in my sleeper, I could begin to look out into the dawn and to see the familiar outlines of the Baghdad plain with some relief—for I had feared at every station through the night to be shunted away to some prison siding. The police came up to me in a friendly way on arrival, saying that I must be going to Dr. Sinderson's[2]; if not, to

[1] See the official history, *The Mediterranean and Middle East,* Vol. II, Ch. IX, for a detailed account of the Iraq campaign.

[2] Dr. Sinderson Pasha (now Sir Harry Sinderson), known to us all as 'Sinbad', head of the Baghdad Medical School and physician to the Royal Household, whose gallant cheerfulness sustained us all.

the Y.M.C.A.; and looked grave when I said the Embassy. But they put me into a gharry and I drove through shuttered streets with not a cat in sight. A dead sort of animation of Arabic leaflets was flickering from the sky; as they were ours, I read one out to the driver, who asked for a double fare 'because of the danger', handed down my suitcase in a hurry in the narrow alley and made off while I squeezed into the Embassy court through a postern, where the *cawasses* crowded round to shake my hand.

[Diary] *2 May 1941*

Leslie Pott, our Consul, called by a soldier to identify, is so dazed with want of sleep that he doesn't recognize me at first. The Chancery is a bonfire, mountains of archives being burnt in the court, prodded by the staff with rakes; black cinders like crows winged with little flames fly into the sunlight. State of siege has been going on for three days. All ask how I came from the station, and furious when I say 'in a gharry'.

Dormitory upstairs; uprooted women; horrid look of places meant for few people and crowded. All desolately tidy—an oriental camp would be far less tidy but also far less desolate.

Petrol tins of sand everywhere for bombs; cars parked on lawn; men sprawling asleep round the blue-tiled fountain in the hall to be cool; nurses. Lucknow feeling, very disagreeable. Pathetic looks of doglike trust of Indians; gloomy looks of Iraqis; imperturbable, hot, but not uncheerful looks of British. The courier from Teheran who was to have brought me, had I waited, has been wired not to come. At Habbaniya the women and children have not been able to leave and are surrounded by artillery shelling the aerodrome. Iraqi planes fly overhead: ours too busy I suppose. We have shelled the Basra radio.

My possessions appear to be lost to me—(No, Mr. L. sent them to Vyvyan Holt's office).

3 May 1941

News was not good when we last had it (at present even wireless confiscated, except one hidden). Mystery why the Iraq Army were allowed eighteen hours to go quietly and instal themselves round Habbaniya instead of being held up at Fallujah bridge. Notice of their going was sent ahead by the Embassy: and Pat Domvile[1] sent a wire on his own

---

[1] Group-Captain Patrick Domvile, O.B.E., formerly 8th Hussars and British Military Mission to the Iraq Army. He held R.A.F. Intelligence posts in Iraq, Jordan, Palestine and Cairo.

to advise holding them at Fallujah and not throw the advantage of the Euphrates away. We have a big V on the lawn in white sheets to tell the air that we are lost to news. We are trying to rig up a receiving set, but it makes a noise like a machine-gun and the police rather naturally object. Police are 'protecting' us, patrolling constantly up and down the river in front of the antirrhinums and our long low terrace wall, where a look-out or two of our own, in grey flannels, or khaki, or tweeds as the case may be, is lounging.

No one has much to do today except people busy with sandbags. A mob came against us with war chant and drums—black silhouettes and their banners crowded against the sunset over the eyebrow arch of the Khota bridge.

I was given a mattress, pillow, and blanket, and laid it out with my Sulaimaniya rug on a terrace above the river and the police. The sunrise draws flaming swords behind the black of Baghdad's river houses and low domes. The sky turns green to blue; the clouds red to orange. The purple river—a hurry of small triangular ripples—rushes like the German armies to meet Eternity. There is a sound of bells I had never heard here before, though perhaps they always sound them; they seem friendly now, like a Christian message (Iraqi Christians are not mostly among our friends). I dress in the early sun. Two aeroplanes overhead: hear the power in their engines—British bombers, black in the blue sky—about 5,000 feet up over east Baghdad.

Came down 7.30 to breakfast at H.E.'s table: very nicely laid, no eggs. Electric current is cut off (no lights, bells, fans or ironing) but daily paper arrives and so do letters. No telephones. V.H. comes in looking tired, reads out the Iraqi *communiqués* which claim twenty-nine of our aeroplanes. It seems certain that we must have lost a good many on the ground. The women and children are still nearly all in Habbaniya.

H.E. very calm: gives the certainty of feeling deeply with no means of knowing how he conveys it—by great honesty in his words I think. He has been through many a stormy sea before. *Mens aequa*. The General[1] goes about with a busy eye for detail and preserves his calm by not investigating the abstract. H.E. is tempered steel, the General simpler metal: but will not fail all the same.

Men are doing guard and arranging sandbags, and happy because of the manual labour which helps them not to think. Indians and Iraqis are not so happy, this Lucknow atmosphere of rather silent and not rhetoric preparation for unpleasantness is getting them down. They answer little

[1] Major-General G. G. Waterhouse, C.B., M.C., head of the Military Mission.

bits of conversation with pathetic eagerness. Yesterday the hungry *cawasses* were able to send out one of their number, escorted by a policeman to the *suq* to buy provisions. Today this too is stopped. It is thought that relations may be broken off between Iraq and Britain! [Diplomatic relations continued in an oriental way while the troops fought it out at Habbaniya.]

In our dormitory are two Polish women, one with a little boy of nine, a widow from Warsaw. She leans over the balustrade above me in the moonlight, the outline of a plump, delicate continental arm and hand waving as she talks of the long misery of it all.

Our new wireless was dismantled yesterday in obedience to the rebel government's threats to come in and force us.

I can't help feeling we have been idiotic in our leaflet distribution these days, while the issue is being fought out; we should not have sent these insulting leaflets *till we were in sight of victory*. It naturally provoked retaliation, the capture of our distributors, and the impossibility now of either distributing or going out at all.

British outside now seem mostly to be prisoners. No news of the remaining oil men from Khanikin. No news of Bill Bailey, distributor of leaflets. [He was in prison.]

6 p.m

The Iraquis sent two officers to remove our wireless—(did not find all however). They also asked us to take the flag off the top of the Embassy: it now flutters modestly on a black metal staff beside the front steps. We have no means for news to or from Habbaniya.

4 May 1941

I played bridge last night distracted by the news (false) that Rutba was taken. Extraordinary to see how a rumour spreads: four people had actually *heard* and all efforts to suppress were vain.

About 4 a.m. in faintest beginning of light, five of our bombers came over to plaster Rashid camp and machine-gun the airfield—wild and ineffectual popping of Iraq firearms. A very beautiful sight—a great Wellington, slowly sailing along at about 1,000 feet, up the river from south to north, very dark against the green sky and the sleeping houses. The sound of bombs dull but clear: the A.A. very sharp and crackling: the police launches swish up and down, police with *sidaras* [caps] off grasp their rifles firmly and shoot sitting, whenever they pass the Embassy. The raid lasted about three hours. I spent my time among the women of various nationalities soothing their nerves. Our room has Iraqi Armenians and Jewesses and an Indian family above; a Greek with two or three Armenians and a Jugoslav *prima donna* below. We are nineteen females altogether.

We now make a daily bulletin of news from the B.B.C. and I help to take it down in a nice untidy little office with translators all devoted to the British cause, touching and friendly. Ernest Main is there, for whom I worked on *The Baghdad Times* so long ago; Pat Domvile, diffident, imaginative, unselfish; H.G. like a large bearded embodiment of *la mouche du coche*; Seton Lloyd, full of shy and quiet enthusiasms—with a mouth that smiles up at one corner and down at the other and a long thin figure looking as if it were 'stylized': good colleagues.

The most constant sound is the cooing of doves, like pacifists; as soon as the cracking of rifles stops they are at it again.

Ripple of agitation: *the Superintendent of Police*. All it was, was a friendly escort to take our lorry to buy food. Turns out they can't because all shops are shut, terrified by our bombing. The police at the gate say they would like to please us in any way, if a bit of *bakhshish* is available.

I made friends yesterday with those in the launch moored outside our wall: promised them tea for today.

One of our dormitory ladies has a bad character, not supposed to be safe with property. A horrid feeling. She has quite a human smile. Difficult anyway to know a good woman by sight.

5 May 1941

Yesterday passed uneventful. Our gardens look like those of a country-house when opened to the public. Domestic trouble in our publicity section. We have *two* daily conferences dedicated to sustaining the public morale under H.G., our *Ras*, whose manners are bad. The fact is that a *Passage to India* element is brought out by circumstances, and it is too easy to assume that ordinary social manners cease in a crisis: should be most important just now to stick to them.

Pleasant rest on my rug in the garden, coloured like the lupins behind it. In the pergola, dark and shaded, the two who watch our long and rather vulnerable wall walk up and down. The police-boat outside has added one of the *Futua*, the Youth Movement, to its strength. The police lie stretched there asleep on the thwarts: they have a square of shade on the water, but shade too is getting rapidly hotter. Soon the siesta hour will be safe for anyone to go in and out! A man with a bundle of fish on a pole has already been seen in camp.

Yesterday having been asked what, if anything, was causing gloom among the Iraqis inside our compound, I said it was the absence of their own bread. 'That,' said our *Ras*, 'is a matter for Colonel Smith's department.' Seton Lloyd and I left it at that but wandered off and looked into the matter among the stablemen, who were cooking over a few planks on an iron *sarge*. A woman is what they really need but an earthern *tannura* [oven] would be next best. Got over the difficulty of its belonging to Colonel Smith's department by giving a present of 3/- and leaving it to them to get the *tannura*, which is seen this morning walking in on someone's shoulder. V.H. enraged (a) that I can get one for 3/-; (b) that it comes walking in with no trouble at all. No idea of how it is done myself!

Such a very friendly reception at the cooking place: blessings poured on one. The Muslims in one corner squatting: in the other, at a spotless table, the Hindu priest with a long beard is pasting flour and prayers into a yellow dough. We have arranged for guests to go to and fro from the Indian mess and our canteen: the Indians have two ping-pong tables to eat on under palm trees near the stables. The six horses are rather bored. Take them dates every day. Syces are Kurds: gardeners are Persians: *cawasses* Kurd or Arab. Two-thirds of them have remained. The rest left and were, we are told, taken to prison.

Today five airmen from Habbaniya captured by Iraqis are being brought in to us—we hope.

Monstrous leaflet dropped by British Government to say they will bomb Government buildings in Iraq, so condemn all here to destruction—and of course it can't be carried out. Why spread *empty* threats? H.E. telegraphs urgently to stop *violent* leaflets written by ourselves.

Mr. Edmonds[1] is now sitting here in V.H.'s office: quiet, except that the shuttered windows are being barbed with wire. He is writing suggestions in case we reach an official state of war. If the British have to remain here, should they try to go to their houses or be kept in the Embassy? V.H. meanwhile is called off to *most* friendly talk on the telephone with the Iraqi Minister of Defence.

A pleasant walk with Adrian Bishop[2] among hibiscus, buddleia and pomegranate—so lovely looking *from* shade at the flowers and the brilliant green like stained glass that lets the sunlight through.

---

[1] Mr. C. J. Edmonds, C.M.G., C.B.E., then Advisor in Iraq to the Ministry of Interior.

[2] Assistant Public Relations Officer 1941–42; killed in September, 1942. The most brilliant personality of his year at Cambridge, he had become an Anglican monk shortly before the war.

BAGHDAD: THE SIEGE OF THE EMBASSY

6 May 1941

V.H. depressed and tired struggling with question of women and children in Habbaniya. The Foreign Minister telephoned to say that they are ready to let them out: a reply was drafted that this was a matter for A.O.C. Habbaniya and the Commanding Iraqi Officer—which more or less dishes the suggestion, for the A.O.C. will never trust the women (and there are over a thousand if Iraqi, Assyrian, etc., are counted) to be entirely in Iraqi hands and on the other hand he can't spare sufficient escort to protect them. I am personally convinced that the *less* escort they take the better: the Iraqis would not do anything to them—their feeling in this matter is *very* strong.

Food is getting lower: we have strict rationing, but quite sufficient though one could easily eat every meal twice over. Breakfast: cocoa, one sardine on bread, one bread-slice and jam. Lunch: rice, corned beef, half tomato, two small bread *bibi*; two prunes and half slice pineapple. Evening: fish, curry and stewed fruit: very little of each.

I enjoy watching the crowd of sparrows splashing about in the garden where the hose is watering the grass. One of them has swallowed so fat a worm, he can't shut his mouth after it—goes hopping round with it open and a surprised expression. I stroll to talk to the four police in their guard boat. They apologize for being on the other side: one lays his hand on his heart and says, 'We would like you (*British*) to be happy.' Notice that the Shiah boatmen are much more friendly. A boy in a *bellam* comes close up and says, 'Would you like fish for a *dinar*?' 'Yes,' I say, 'bring all the fish you like—but not for a *dinar*.'

Have got *soap* for our Iraqis and Persians. Their food is still a problem. They told Seton Lloyd yesterday that they had not told me they were hungry when I asked because: 'You are all hungry too and it would have been a '*aib* to mention it.' This is manners and very touching. They say one of them knows a policeman and can get food—so S. L. has given them £5 to buy enough for two days; hope it may work.

We now divide into two monitoring shifts and my afternoon one is 4 p.m. to 10 p.m. A surprising offer comes through from H.M.G. of friendship if Rashid Ali withdraws: it looks as if it meant friendship with him, but must be badly put. My transcription is suspected, the thing being so deplorable—so that I begin even to doubt myself: but heard it repeated over the Palestine news. The mischievous effects begin to be apparent this morning listening to Baghdad radio which declares us to be suing for peace.

All rather languid at our committee—because we are hungry. Our *Ras* says we shall make Rashid Ali and his friends 'tidy up the mess with their women looking on—do I approve?' I don't. Nothing more revolting than that sort of attitude, apart from its futility.

Sinbad gives me a piece of chocolate. Salama comes with a present of two apples. Rather grim to be so appreciative when this is only the *beginning*.

The six people expected from Habbaniya have not come in. No R.A.F. in sight. B.B.C. report Habbaniya garrison almost intact. A few Iraqi aeroplanes floating about.

7 May 1941

Try to deal with the *cawass* problem. They have had nothing to eat all day. The truth of this obscure subject almost impossible to get at, the *cawasses* being too polite to say they haven't eaten, except to me in private: it finally appears that they were given two days' rations and ate it all in one. The money we gave the day before was handed to a contractor who brought it honestly back saying he could get nothing. Have now agreed to be the *liaison* for the *cawasses* with Mr. Bourne and Colonel Smith, who do food. Would like to know whether communication with the outside world is to be encouraged or not; this morning fifty rounds of bread got across the wall and were being sold for 10 *fils* each.

As we were at supper in the dim moonlight round the canteen, bombers came over again: explosions from Washash—and sound of machine-guns. All hurried back and the women sat in the big drawing-room. No one panicky now. There was another air raid just as I went to lunch with the Indians, and I sat a long time in their shelter (very comfortable and cool). A Lahore doctor there with his wife and Sarah, seven months old: very good-tempered people they all are. The Hindu priest with long beard who was making bread the other day comes and eats with us. He used to be a compositor on *The Baghdad Times*. He says he loves this opportunity to cook and work for his people. His religion enjoins that every opportunity for service be taken. A pleasant friendly atmosphere in the speckly light shade of the palms. The lunch there was rice, two dates, quarter small cucumber, and lentils, and very good *chupatti*.

Last night we had a concert, but were not allowed to applaud, fearing that the sound of it across the river might be thought of as rejoicing over the air raid.

This morning cool and pleasant. There is a feeling about of depression as the idea creeps in that this may not all be ended so soon. Adrian Bishop is not too optimistic: must admit that in the map of the whole Middle

East we are not so very important, but console ourselves by reflecting that our neighbourhood to Oil will prevent us from being forgotten.

8 May 1941

Yesterday ended with very good news: the retreat of the enemy near Habbaniya with loss of 1,000 casualties and 300 prisoners. A series of R.A.F. visits followed, flying quite arrogantly in formation. They must have dropped bombs near, possibly on the railway station, as we shook and rattled. I was chatting to my boat-load of police as three Wellingtons came sailing along, and, when they grabbed their rifles, said, 'That's absurd; they are much too high to hit'; whereupon they put their rifles back again, much to my surprise. About 7.30, when all our garrison is gathered to hear Dr. Sinderson read the news, a Gladiator came swooping almost to touch the palm trees on the lawn and drop a letter from Habbaniya—all very satisfactory, and all except thirty-two women and children safely evacuated to Basra. I did not see this; only heard a huge roar, and saw the rotund behind of our translator under the office table in the twinkling of an eye, with a general impression that the enemy were on us.

Find my way through mazes of barbed wire and lorry barricades to the front gate to chat with police there. Quite quiet and apparently friendly world outside.

After dinner at 10 p.m. when my shift was over, I went with V.H. to see if a gift of whisky might be acceptable to my police. They won't move, however, but continue to sit in the moonlit stream, suggesting I should go to their boat—rather shocked.

General Waterhouse has just come in, says he has lost *everything* at the Military Mission, his gold chain, hat, and his temper several times. He looks so pleasant, tall and simple, with a great faith in things like sandbags and rifles.

I had a talk with H.E. who complains that there is no means of keeping in touch with feeling here—a state of affairs already painfully visible four years ago. One should have made use of the oil people's opportunities ages ago. So annoying to see that we *have* all the machinery the Germans so elaborately fabricate—and never trouble to use it. Now that the news is better, I hope we are rubbing in the betrayal of the Germans—who apparently promised aid within two days of the outbreak. Churchill's words are rather ominous however, so I suppose we must wait before crowing.

A pleasant conference in the absence of our *Ras* this morning who sent word three-quarters of an hour after its time that we should go on without him. We had just happily finished, and wandered down to the gate where the policeman smiled broadly but refused to give news: '*Kull shai maku*' [Everything is not], he said. The Iraqis claim to have knocked down forty-five of our aeroplanes and lost one of their own.

Last night a huge panache of fire and smoke hung over Baghdad and the steely river: it came from an I.P.C. oil-tank on the east side, which looks as if it had been set alight accidentally by an Iraqi: difficult to think the R.A.F. would bomb our oil-tanks. [They did, however.]

A horrible beauty there is about a fire in a town. The great convolutions of the smoke rolled northward above the quiet houses: still there in the early morning, when Baghdad above the water looks like some dingy but still beautiful version of the Grand Canal in Venice.

9 May 1941

V.H. took me into the inner Embassy to tea like a lady; very pleasant to see polished mahogany, flowers, silver, and not least a little solid food like cake and biscuit. Sit about on the lawn till, just before dusk, again a small fighter swoops down to visit us. We hunt around but can find no message dropped. Pamphlets are being dropped just now, a spatter of machine-guns is going on.

Last evening I gave a lecture on the lawn in the moonlight—Aden in Wartime.

V.H. and Edmonds very irritated by a long conference full of Lucknow spirit of vengeance with plans to humiliate not the *present* Government but the one that will be replacing it and will presumably be composed of our friends, and I wonder anyway if proscriptions have ever done much good. It would be a pity if the energies we should keep for German dangers be directed to Iraq. I should deal with the five top people, the Mufti, and only such others as we know to be working for Germany: then concentrate on discrediting Germany with the army here (easy, as they must be feeling rather badly let down): and for the rest, treat it as what it is, one of those too frequent ripples which continually ruffle the surface of Iraqi politics.

Walk up and down in moonlight with V.H. The garden is full of pitfalls, and barbed wire connects the cypress trees, a trap to the unwary. I regret to say that my police, when I talked to them this morning, made most unrespectable suggestions: 'Become a Muslima,' one of them says, 'and I will keep you myself.' Apart from this indelicate point of view, I am sorry to see their minds dwelling on loot and rapine—evidently the result of the Mufti's preaching of a holy war last night. Cannot understand why we, seeing the effect other people manage to obtain through propaganda, persist in thinking it quite useless for ourselves.

10 May 1941

No aeroplane visited our lawn last evening to our relief, as we felt sure the Iraqis had trained their machine-guns and might get it. A few explosions far off and the drone of engines show that our Wellingtons are busy from time to time. The B.B.C. says we are in Ramadi and Fallujah and talk of the Western Iraq Army as 'dispersed' and of the Iraq Air Force as finished. Yet here, we continue provided with food through V.H.'s correspondence with Abd el Qadir Gailani, our one means of communicating with the outside world.

The Lucknow feeling is settling down to one of ease and boredom. I should be delighted to take it as a rest-cure while one can, and hate the constant efforts of people to make one *do* things. How pleasant to sit on the grass and revive *The Decameron*! Adrian Bishop is the only man with a mind leisurely and playful enough to do this.

Dined with H.E. last night: good to sit at a well-set table and wear an evening gown (no one need do that as a matter of fact). But the talk is rather shaky, as the guests are chosen in turn in order of merit and that has nothing to do with the art of conversation.

After many struggles I yesterday secured the only lot of cigarettes in camp for the *cawasses*, and everyone had a box. I can at least feel that this is useful work, as they were getting neither food, soap, nor smokes—and Mr. Bourne is thankful to have that part of his job taken off his very overweighted shoulders. He is a kind conscientious man, with a look of surprise because he has round eyes and round eyebrows on top. Colonel Smith, with him on the Food Supply, is well groomed and always tidy in a military way. Both of them very pleasant to deal with.

Pat Domvile tells me he wants to become a *cawass* so that I shall have to look after him. I now have a family of forty-five including the Embassy servants, the syces and personal servants, the gardeners and all. All seems to be going quite smoothly for the time being. Washing and ironing goes on in a steamy little room whence you would think nothing could ever emerge clean and tidy, so great is the chaos.

11 May 1941

The heat was like an oven yesterday: a hot wind from the north, made damp by floods—one blinks one's eyelids as one goes out of doors. I could not face a siesta in the garden, or our dormitory of the seventeen ladies, or my own balcony—so subsided in V.H.'s office and he laid Bishop's mattress out for me on the floor—delicious sleep. One comes to take great pleasure out of small and natural events, like sleeping and waking, a cool breath from the river, a tendril of the vine pergola. Prison gives one t*i*me: I am still enjoying that delightful boon, though soon there will be too much of it no doubt.

The moon is almost round already. I sat with V.H. listening to the dry rustling trees and watching the dusty light—glad to be here though one begins to see the end less speedily ahead. There is a want of privacy in the garden: heaps of sleeping people everywhere, and everywhere else barbed wire. This morning strolling with Adrian Bishop, find S.L. asleep on his mattress on the lawn, looking like my Himyar [the pet lizard I once cherished]: I think he has the same amiable sort of character too.

Church this morning—only about thirty people, and a poor little service shown up by the circumstances which ask for something more profound.

It is 114° in the shade today.

Our Blenheims were over this morning and dull substantial thuds follow their track. The police are growing glum. My family of *cawasses* agree that they are less amiable since the Mufti's speech and now call them *Ingliz* and promise massacre. They have a Lewis or some such gun on the roof overlooking us from the north and unpleasantly convenient for hitting our visiting aeroplane.

H.E. asks whom we should have (later) for dealing with Anglo-Arab or any other human relations. It would be disastrous to have the wrong man for with luck this may be our chance, and our very last chance, to set good relations with Iraq on their feet once more. There is bound to be resentment, but it should not be beyond us to switch it against the Germans.

12 May 1941

Very tired yesterday, what with heat and the natural wear and tear of having to listen to blaring and depressing radio matter at intervals from 4 p.m. to 10 p.m.

V.H.'s office is nice and cool: the Secretariat congregates there for the news. A rifle and three boxes of cartridges stand ready by the door. Horrid shock this morning to find both big doors, front and back, shut, their locks tied up with rope: one has to creep in by devious kitchen ways, but this is against the heat not the Iraqis. Even the rosebuds are now protected by barbed wire, and the Indians begin to hang their laundry on the *chevaux de frise* which gives them a domestic look.

This morning two visits from our aircraft, one Blenheim and one fighter—both swooping low but not over us—either to see if we are still alive or to explore the homes of the machine-guns. It is rather depressing every day in the news to hear 'all quiet in Iraq', with apparently complete forgetfulness of our existence.

Mr. Bourne is going to try and get some face-powder out of the enemy for us.

13 May 1941

Yesterday an aeroplane with strange markings came down upon the airport. No one knows her: may be Iranian though not the usual weekly mail. One of our Gladiators flew over, low, and examined and we then heard machine-gunning and the foreign craft has not re-emerged into the sky. The news of the Soviet recognizing Iraq, and Von Papen flying to Ankara has come to depress us; the taking of Hess in Scotland to puzzle us; and the third day of hearing of Rutba being in British hands, to irritate us. They do this morning add that the *possibility* of an advance farther east is hereby opened up. My expectation is to be here another ten days, or a week *at least*. Some seem hopeful for the day after tomorrow.

I have made out a list of cosmetics, soaps, etc., for our ladies: I can get them by murmuring to the man who goes out for provisions, so it only seemed fair to try and make this advantage general and push my list at poor V.H., vainly protesting. It is his negotiating with the Minister of Foreign Affairs that produces all our food and Sinbad yesterday mentioned his name with thanks in the evening talk.

We have Union Jacks spread out flat on our roof.

Woken up with heavy crumpling bombs over Rashid in the early sunlight. More at night, but they did not wake me.

14 May 1941

It continues hot. The big doors are closed except in the evening and we have been told to wear topees (as if one could go out shopping) and to guard against heat-strokes. The people one is really grateful to are the gardeners who go about their ancient pleasant toil just as though this were still an Embassy and not a siege. We have put Dr. R. to organize a play for Sunday, so immediate is our hope of rescue. He is a young man with a round forehead and longish yellow hair who becomes serious and animated only when you talk of Drama: otherwise he is serious but not animated. He lives among the finer feelings, but they are a shadowy food for wartime, and he is faced with the discovery that all these blossoms of civilization by themselves will neither feed, protect, nor even comfort you. I am sorry for him for I don't believe he can temper these refinements and turn them into the true steel they should be made of. The thought of the play makes him much happier and he is talking about entrances and calls as if his stage were really a world.

Others are beginning to show here and there slight gleams of impatience, especially those whose work is calling outside.

A spent bullet tied with a piece of string to a notice has been paraded before us all to impress on us the dangers of walking in the garden when people shoot. As the whole place has been snapping with machine-guns and only one bullet was picked up, it seems to me that the argument works the other way, but that may be just my undisciplined mind.

What is sad is to see how easily all those traits come to the surface which we think of as Nazi: just the sort of thing we are fighting against with all our resources leaps at one from all sides as soon as the Lucknow atmosphere develops. So far, however, we have kept our Nazis well under and a general spirit of amiability prevails.

The Ladies' harim very pleased with the arrival of face-powder!

15 May 1941

Small female sensation caused yesterday afternoon by our *Prima Donna* who appeared coated and hatted, with two valises, on the lawn. Her luggage has arrived from the hotel—no one quite knows how, but presumably through the police. Apart from this she is causing some scandal by strolling about in nothing much more than a camisole and sleeping in the downstairs' ladies' dormitory 'mid noddings on' at all where—the Greek lady says—'We do not like all to have to look at her body.' So Mrs. Pott is to speak to her. N.B. A siege no place for people with temperaments.

Apart from a visit high above, yesterday and today, of a black-and-white Andan, like a delicate butterfly overhead, and noises of invisible explosions, we have no news. A rumour brought back from marketing that Grobba[1] is back and German aeroplanes in Mosul. The former quite likely. B.B.C. talks of reinforcements, but only in Basra and Habbaniya (R.A.F)—no visible prospect of a rescue from the West.

Last night I walked up and down with V.H. talking of possibilities of escape—very thin. This morning I went with Bishop and saw the police reclining under the awning of their hot little launch holding strings with fish-hooks. Two fish called *bunin* with flat round mouths were twisting their tails there and the police were very ready to come and

[1] The German Ambassador in Iraq in 1939.

give them, while I handed over 250 *fils* with the other hand. The disagreeable policeman was not there and the other four are very amiable.

The news two days ago of Grobba's return and German plane in Mosul is probably true,[1] as today's news mentions the use of Syrian aerodromes, the destruction of German aircraft there by the R.A.F., and Germans in Iraq. The mysterious aeroplane with disguised marking is now explained.

16 May 1941

Last night at one a.m. one of our fighters came low, dropped a flare on the airport, and went—looking, no doubt, for Germans. We may, of course, be here *weeks*—but anyone could have seen that days ago. Meanwhile we are all being inoculated for typhoid to fill in the time.

Our *Ras* got at the General and put up a very nice open-air cinema against the advice of all the rest of us—and H.E. at once said the showing of light was far too risky. Bishop and I agree that our lower natures are delighted, though I must say that I do regret it really: indoor amusements are almost unbearable this hot weather, and the inside of the house altogether dreary: somnolent figures in all the drabness of masculine *déshabille* plunged in semi-darkness of dismantled rooms, with whirring of fans overhead. Only the blue fountain shoots up its little splashing grateful sound. The ballroom is like pictures of the first emigrant ships. The oriental is much better at the nomadic life even among the trappings of the West: his carpet and his *samovar* are usually at hand, and he instinctively settles in a circle—while we, each defending his own privacy, vainly try to make small barricades of our boxes and belongings. Yesterday the Lahore doctor's wife, mother of baby Sarah, appeared in a peach-coloured *sari* embroidered with silver, and was a pleasure to all to look at as she moved about the withering grass.

Loopholes are being made to the front-door sandbags. Also more permanent eating arrangements, and our two offices are given as dining-rooms instead of the out-of-door table where all went to get their cup and plate and ate when and how they could.

The policeman at the gate, staggered by the mass of cosmetics we sent for, said he couldn't think how the harim which is to be murdered in a few days could still be thinking of things like face-powder.

A woman asked if I didn't think it time for us to give up using our lipsticks but I mean to be killed, if it comes to that, with my face in proper order.

---

[1] It was true.

17 May 1941

The Vichy French today say that it was only by accident that twenty-two out of thirty German aeroplanes force-landed in Syria. Nauseating. Eight hundred tons of ammunition are said to have been sent from there. Yesterday I saw my first Messerschmitt of the war—a locust creature buzzing out north-west against the white clouds on the tail of two of ours that had come over. This morning two Germans were seen to fall in flames over Rashid camp.

A feeling of gloom I do not share, since one could not have a better field to meet an enemy than this of Egypt—Palestine—Iraq so far and difficult for him. We must wait, hoping that our importance on the Indian route may bring us relief—but not I imagine very speedy. The gloom I think comes from a silly habit of trying to hide the dark prospects instead of frankly asking the whole community to share. This treating of everyone as if they were small children would make a saint gloomy. Have also decided that I will not submit to any education while here: lectures, informative papers, uplift of all sorts, is henceforth to flow innocuously far above my head. I sat through half a lecture on Iceland about which I have not the faintest curiosity and then strolled in the hot and restless wind to see the river still flowing swiftly though less full. It looks in the early morning like metal pouring hurriedly to sea. The stars were faint in a dusty sky that eats the lower constellations. The days now climb to 112°, 115° in the shade.

We have moved office and are in the upstairs untidy purlieus of Chancery, a little world of its own far more cheerful than the dim railway waiting-room atmosphere below.

I walked up and down with H.E.—lonely and harassed but with a steady strength in him—a rugged, tall old bit of weather-beaten rock. Talked with him about the General's bombs: beer-cans filled with paraffin and a cotton-wool fuse to ensure our massacre in most certain fashion if we ever use them. Only useful thing here is to rely as completely as possible on the Iraqis: preferably quite disarmed.

V.H. has to write a daily letter to the *Chef de Protocole* for our food supply. Today's list includes ten tins solid brilliantine, Kotex, and mothballs—the latter *must* be the order of a pessimist.

18 May 1941

Last night great flares were dropped by the R.A.F. I climbed to a roof where no one would be shoving me down and saw a yellow star above Rashid sinking slowly into the lacework of the palms. Little fans of light spread out and spluttered from the ground, but there was no noise because the wind was downstream. I walked to the flagged path by the river and called to the police in the dusk: 'That is our airmen beating the German.' 'Yes, indeed,' said they with the greatest cheerfulness. The Baghdad radio has not yet mentioned the Germans' arrival though they had a grand funeral for their commander, Von Blomberg's son. An Iraqi soldier, shooting in his light-hearted way at anything in the sky, sent a bullet through the side window of his aeroplane into his throat, and he was dead when they touched the ground.[1] Iraq takes the credit for anything done in the air, on either side; the two aircraft shot down yesterday were said to be British—strangely sitting on Rashid aerodrome! As I was out by the river another flare appeared, over north Baghdad—and descended rather suddenly: the parachute cord must have snapped. Only hope it wasn't over the hospital. It threw a sword-like luminosity upon the river, making the long line of houses black above it. The flares in this dusty atmosphere give a warm reddish light.

We work in our new quarters upstairs where numbers of people of Chancery live. Our only terrace gives on to the river and might be cool if not screened off with sacking: I ask why and am told it is to stop the sniping—and that is the first I know that we have been sniped at—apparently at dusk and dawn from houses on the other side. Bullets do come pinging over as one does one's hair behind a pillar on the terrace, but I thought they were casual.

A note has come asking for all our Iraqi servants. Yesterday V.H. replied protesting Diplomatic Usage: if this has no effect, we shall have to send them away, as they are threatened with death: but even now they would probably be oppressed if they leave us. Another German sign is the first jamming—this morning—of Arabic news from London.

Newton, the butler, kindly offered to clean my white shoes this morning. What makes this camp life go is that everyone is out to help instead of to crab—and if ordinary life were run on the same principle there would be hardly any problems left.

Loveliness of the river before sunrise—so *much* water; it looks like a solid thing, some great dragon hurtling to the sea and the ripples are the swing of its muscles as it moves. Its light has a million little breaks where every ripple pushes up a tiny crest, so that it is a multitudinous light, holding shadows in its heart like happiness, or grass in sunshine. And the

---

[1] The Rashid Ali Government, full of consternation, sent a deputation to assure the German Ambassador that they would rather have lost 7,000 soldiers than suffer a disaster of this magnitude. Dr. Grobba's rather endearing reply seems to have been: "Nonsense, no man's life is worth 7,000 soldiers."

houses on the other side have fascinating detail: dark mouths of steep streets that go down: a pointed *bellam* moored here or there below the walls: small patches of garden, a trellis of vine or orange where some rich Jewish merchant now lives in fear. The jade-green bridges upstream and down, whose curves make the only hills we have for miles, and the finger-minarets and domes, make the view more like a book than real life. One can't think of this as real life at all.

19 May 1941

I went to breakfast with H.E. this morning and discussed arranging some means of communicating with Iraqi friends outside in case of need which might arise.

Delhi news this morning says, 'Baghdad situation obscure because all communication cut, but it is believed the Ambassador and Military Mission are safe.'

Another B.B.C. gem last night describes us as 'calm' and goes on to mention the taking of a police post twenty-five miles south of Basra *five* days ago. This morning's news says, 'Iraq situation developing satisfactorily.' Adrian Holman[1] says he can't see the satisfactorily: I say I can't even see the developing.

No answer to our protests against the *cawasses* being threatened with death. On the other hand yesterday a letter asking for Colonel Smith's car, which is State property.

Today our water supply has stopped. They say it is throughout Baghdad but very inconvenient. Pat has been washing his head all over with hair lotion. He has a very pleasant sleeping place for his mattress over the river, with a big tree and the bridge visible beyond, but just beside the terrace at which they snipe.

I now go every morning to see that the *cawasses* really get their proper rations and there is a great tussle for things like onions, oranges, etc. We ought to be laying in stores, as nothing much can be arriving in Baghdad from Basra or the West and things will be getting short—but it seems very difficult to do.

This morning I went for the first time at 6.30 to a gymnastic class, pleasantly barefoot on the fresh lawn. What John Macrae considers very light leaves us quite breathless.

I walked about the lawn with Adrian Bishop in the late afternoon and read the Latin psalms in his breviary—soothing lovely language, clothing so fitly that deep and pure and early faith. Life, to be happy at all, must

[1] Attached to the Baghdad Embassy 1940; now Sir Adrian Holman, K.B.E., C.M.G., M.C.

be in its way a sacrament, and a failure in religion is to divorce it from the holy acts of everyday, of ordinary human existence. The Greeks saw in every drink of water, in every fruitful tree, in every varied moment of their living, the agency of a God.

I forget if I noted down that all the women and children from Habbaniya got safe away, though one of their aeroplanes was shot at while taking off.

Though Von Blomberg's son has been killed and Rashid Ali went to his funeral, the presence of the Germans is still not yet officially admitted by Iraqi wireless.

20 May 1941

Events today began with the scrunch of heavy bombs over Rashid and twenty-six of our fliers in the sky. The little Gladiators sail over us in threes, their black made grey by the sunlight shining from above them so that in size and colour they look very like the grey and white doves that circle agitated from the garden trees. Over Rashid the bombers sail and dip and the dull noise follows; they circle in far wide curves in the early sky. One fighter flies the whole length of New Street almost touching the minarets, dropping leaflets, and the first burst of ground fire comes only from beyond the line of defence in Baghdad north. But when the sun has risen and we have all had breakfast, another fighter comes and answers signals at risk of its life, swooping down to the palm trees of our garden while the machine-guns which seem to encircle us on three sides spit out with most venomous barking.

I am a little ill and feeble and therefore lying on Bish's bed in V.H.'s office under my Kurdi rug, and pleasantly engaged with *Alice through the Looking Glass* and Bish and V.H. to talk to. First really nice meal for a long time.

Now, four in the afternoon, just heard that Fallujah is taken, bridge, town and all. Thank God. No details except surrender of town; leaflets were dropped, air and ground attack, and the whole given over. Really brings relief in sight. Hope Ramadi and tribes may follow.

Played bridge last night with Pat, Bish and Tom Arnold in the latter's room—all surrounded with Aids to Living such as soda-water bottles, suitcases, and mattresses, and people coming in all the time to find their bedding, etc.

21 May 1941

News today that the German attack on Crete has failed. Fallujah was invested on three sides by air-carried troops in spite of the Iraq attempt at flooding the intervening land; it surrendered at 2 p.m. on Monday the 19th, and the bridge is intact.

Only novelty this morning is a large guard of army instead of police at our gate. Watch them from upstairs checking our food as it comes in: tins of bully beef are tipped out of one box into another—I suppose to discover letters. It looks as if the house opposite the gate, whose upper windows dominate our court, were to be Army H.Q. for our guard. Message sent in, would we mind not waving, running, or showing ourselves unnecessarily when our aircraft are about as 'bad people have guns' and might shoot. Some, it appears, have been taking a few shots already.

22 May 1941

News this morning is that the Regent is to be back in Baghdad shortly to resume his duties and Gerald [de Gaury] is representing H.M.G. till the reunion with H.E. is effected: he is 'Cornwallis's vice-regent on earth' says Bish.

Fallujah news is evidently abroad for the police knew about it. Talked to them last night. A soldier is in the boat with them, surprised but pleased at our chat from over the wall. I talk to them after dark: they say the Germans are '*Shiql ash-Shaitan*' (of the kin of Satan), and say '*Al hamdu lillahi*' (thank God) when I tell them we have brought six down between Habbaniya and Syria. 'We have burnt forty of yours,' they add dutifully. 'I take refuge with God,' say I—and they shout with laughter, not having believed for a moment. Can't help thinking the Germans must be disappointed in Iraq.

Two sentries stand very wideawake at the other gate, but perhaps because the officer is sitting near them in the shade.

The day is very hot and stuffy, but I feel better, and pain less. Very difficult to be ill here—and V.H. chafing rather under the infliction of feminine oddments in his office, says it looks like a *boudoir*.

Mr. Eden telegraphs in answer to our forwarding of Iraqi complaints. Threatens drastic reprisals for any injury to 'defenceless civilians', i.e. us. No further news of the death sentence on our Iraqi *cawasses*.

First apricots come into camp today.

23 May 1941

Unofficial report this morning says the British troops are twenty miles away—by Khan Nuqta presumably. Soldiers were on the café roof opposite to our west wall last night, but this morning all our soldier guards have vanished and the friendly police are back again. Martial law is proclaimed in Baghdad and Kirkuk, and guns and lorries crash over the bridges in the night.

Busy with Bish writing our report for Cairo. Last night I sat out with V.H. on the hot damp lawn, the stars thick in a tired sky: two dull rifle shots—but no one pays attention. I bet him 50 *fils* that the British will be here by Sunday.

Have now got my *cawasses*' meals well in hand. The kitchen complains that everyone has to wait till they get served. I turn upon them rather severely when they ask for the *first* apricots. 'You never *buy* the first things in season, do you?' say I.

'Yes, indeed we do—we are obliged to buy and divide them for the dead.'

'Well there aren't any dead here yet, thank God,' and the matter ended with two handfuls carefully hidden under the bread flaps.

Tom Arnold has had toothache for three weeks and the Minister for Foreign Affairs today sent a dentist together with a policeman wearing the Red Crescent for this suitable occasion. I think one should send a letter of thanks to the Ministry of Foreign Affairs, they have been so kind and considerate.

24 May 1941

The B.B.C. this morning tells us that the Regent is in Iraq—presumably Basra. The Iraqis counter-attacked at Fallujah and were repulsed on Wednesday night. [The Regent was at Habbaniya.]

Lengthy argument with my four Jewish sweepers who, trampled on by all, cling to Religion which forbids them to eat animal fats. They were convinced that *ghee* is mutton. With difficulty I get them to accept 'Spry' out of a tin instead, staking my soul it is only coconut.

I sat a long time in H.E.'s cool office this morning while machine-guns pattered about across the river against some passing aircraft which we are now blasé about. H.E. has written a very fine farewell speech for the moment of our release. In his measured way he always comes straight to the centre of the matter.

Evening bridge in the newsroom. The game takes one's mind off the terrible uncertainty of Crete. One of the Polish sisters played, neat and *élégante* as ever with an air of being self-possessed in an unimportant world. I go back to undress in pitch-dark dormitory at 11.30.

25 May 1941

A little Gladiator came swinging over to look at us this morning, turning in the sunlight quite low across the river, while we were awakened by machine-guns crackling remarkably near. Could not find in myself the slightest trace of fear—I suppose one gets accustomed very quickly. The relieving army is held up round Fallujah by floods. The Amarat and Naseriya tribes seem to have sided with the Regent. Otherwise yesterday went by without news of any kind. Bish and I finished our report. We have fallen into a routine here, not unpleasant if one could forget the outside world. There is something rather touching about all these middle-aged men doing their various jobs: there is no zest about it for them as there is with the young.

26 May 1941

News that Ramadi was bombed, that Nuri[1] is returning. Rumours (from our river police) that there is trouble for the rebel Cabinet; and news of Ministers and families rushing off to Turkey or Iran.

A rather weary feeling here, as we seem to be forgotten. News that a post five miles from Basra is captured when weeks ago we were told of the taking of Qurna so much nearer comes rather like a douche.

Yesterday I lay most of the day on my mattress in V.H.'s office. Very touched by offerings brought in—Seton with barley sugar and Harold (Pennefeather) with a priceless half-bottle of champagne, consumed in the blue mausoleum light which allows V.H. to keep his windows open, while I take my dinner off a tray. Bish is induced to taste a little in a tumbler. Never was champagne so good.

6.30 p.m.

An aeroplane has just swooped to about a hundred yards over the lawn and dropped a message: little weighted packet sewn up in calico with two long streamers of calico, red, blue and yellow. It came with engine cut off, and no shot was fired.

The packet just opened is full of private letters—and a half-sheet from Gerald telling all the news we know already: no word of a relief—really an unimaginative effort.

Three notes today from the Ministry of Foreign Affairs, the most important being a protest against our having (they say) rigged up wireless on the roof. V.H.'s reply, which is polite but slightly badinage, is not approved of. Wonder if it will ever be known how much our comfort here is due to his handling of the correspondence.

Pat, walking up and down the lawn, remarks that never more will he enjoy an Embassy garden party here.

[1] Nuri as-Said Pasha, the 'Grand Old Man' of Iraq, murdered in 1958.

27 May 1941

News gloomier daily from Crete and delay here very dangerous. Called this morning to read H.E.'s speech which is good as ever. I am fond of his plain rugged face and the slow smile beginning to curl his mouth and ending with a sideway look of his light blue eyes. He got three letters from Madge [his wife in Basra] and looks quite renovated.

Spatter of machine-guns wakes us as a Gladiator sails over. I go to the General's in the morning to get notes on 'The Golden Square' for my article and find the police in the boat with three fish flapping on a string. They climb up the outer side of the barbed wire; our hands just meet for the necessary exchange (250 *fils*); I say, 'in a few days the Regent will be back and we shall be out and you will be comfortable too.' 'If God wills,' they say.

I found the *cawasses* heaving all their meat over the parapet into the river because they said it smelt. So it did, but apparently Dr. Mills had seen it and said it was all right (I didn't go with them, feeling rather ill still but it shows how necessary it is to go). We had all eaten the same meat and it seemed good enough when cooked. I must give a little homily tomorrow.

29 May 1941

Gunfire has been thudding steadily since four this morning, coming gradually nearer. They think it is by Aqqa Kuf and may be cutting across country towards Kadhimain. Now (8 a.m.) it begins to shake the window-panes slightly.

Small arms they say have been heard from the direction of the iron bridge. There is something quite indescribable in the slow approach of this noise, so full of fate, so full of all the unknown, and so much a contrast to our stagnation here.

30 May 1941

The guns died away in the afternoon, and started again, they say, at night. Curfew in Baghdad was put on to 8.30 and our police guard doubled in case of trouble. Cavalry led their horses across the bridges eastward at about ten at night. This morning we woke to the sight of twenty bombers and a fighter above. Explosions shook the walls. They seem to be bombing artillery at Kadhimain and probably along the road from Khan Nuqta (sixteen miles away). The B.B.C. speaks of 'our advance on Baghdad'.

Everyone here begins to look a little pale and feels the month's internment has lasted long enough.

Yesterday H.E. and most of Chancery and I lunched with our *cawasses*—flowers on the table—fruit salad.

Quarrel made up. It started by Ishak (Christian) dipping his Unbeliever's cup in Shi'a tea.

A military Governor, Yunus Sabawi, is just named in Baghdad.

11 a.m.

Our aeroplanes fly over continuously, keeping high and going to the north. The police are building sandbag defence posts at our gates to protect us. We have cut our rations today in case no fresh supply comes in tomorrow.

3.30 p.m.

Just heard that the Amin el-Asima [mayor] has sent to say the Government has gone and Baghdad is in his hands: the army *inside* the town turned the rebel army *out*: all the preparations we saw and which had disturbed us, such as taking *bellams* to the east bank, etc., were directed not against us but against the rebels.

The position and whereabouts of the 'rebel army' are still 'obscure'. At present the loyal troops in Baghdad are only two battalions. Some of their guns they put on the mosques.

6 p.m.

A delegation has come—police, young Ghazi Daghestani, and the Amin—to ask for an armistice, and beg that the constitution of Iraq may not be taken away from them. H.E. has made a wonderful speech in Arabic telling them that as he and King Feisal *made* the constitution, it is safe in his hands. The armistice request is forwarded to G.O.C. The little Amin, in lovely dove-grey suiting, is smiling three times round his face: the young officers are also very friendly—a feeling of family reunion and bygones be bygones about it all. Much touched by the *cawasses*, syces, and gardeners, who all came up with shining eyes to say *al-hamdu lillahi* and shake hands.

The American Minister came, looking as if he were just off a yacht, and told us quite cheerful news of their prison. Their cars were all taken away and they spent an hour in cellars having been told they were to be bombed—but nothing happened.

Everyone then hung about for hours with nothing much to fill them. Then the visitors left and H.E. spoke from the steps.

'The Golden Square', Rashid Ali, the Italian Minister and the Mufti[1]

[1] The Mufti slipped through.

are all interned at Qasr Shirin, and the armistice is telegraphed for. After this, in a sort of golden mist of sunset our bombers and fighters came sailing: they came in troops and societies, their outline sharp in the luminous sky: they separated and circled and dived, going vertically down at dreadful speed, like swordfish of the air. The crack of bombs followed at few seconds' intervals. It was like graceful and gigantic play—nothing more lovely than that dive, start, and re-breasting of the heavens. But it makes one think with a sick sort of feeling of Crete at this moment.

At about eight, V.H. brought two Iraqi officers into the office, anxious to arrange the surrender before tomorrow dawn. Young Daghestani, a nice lad, speaks perfect English, Staff College at Quetta: the other is an older man from Mosul very much on the defensive.

The difficulty about the white flag is that at night anything will be shot at, but a wire is to be sent to Habbaniya and V.H. is dying to go and risk possible bullets on the road. Arrangements are suggested for recognizing the car, which is to move slowly and show undimmed lights full on.

Today for the first time I stepped out of the Chancery gate and asked the police to pose for their photographs—which they did.

31 May 1941

Fighting ceased 4 to 4.30 a.m. This morning H.E. went out with Gerald de Gaury who got here for breakfast to arrange the truce. Absolute orgy of activity all over the Chancery with typists flying in and out.

Bill Bailey arrived last night. He was seized while scattering pamphlets on Friday, the 2nd of May, and has had vicious treatment—five days hand-cuffed to the wall, scarcely any food, water thrown over his face when thirsty, *Futua* [The Youth Movement] coming to bait him, and then taken to filthy cells with murderers. He looks very thin and strained but called it 'a glorious experience; you would have given anything for it' (extreme overstatement as far as I am concerned!). He drove from one prison to the other and saw our flag down and thought we were finished. The warders were quite human and decent: the police all abominable—and all the crowds brought in were as horrible as possible—a sad story.

I realize strongly how lucky I was in Khanikin—all other English out at that time had wretched experiences. The reluctance to put me on the Baghdad train was not accidental as I then thought: they were carrying out orders and only my bantering shamed them into letting me go.

Yesterday a horrid, aggressive Colonel came asking for the armistice in a hurry to save further pounding. V.H. left this representative with me and I was confirmed in my feeling that the Iraqis' manners when bad are the worst of all the Arabs. With great labour I began to tame him when Pat came and dealt beautifully, but evoked no response to anti-German remarks. It seems that Grobba, the German ex-Ambassador, came here for four days and gave it up as a bad job.

Many houses appear to have been gutted by the sequestrators who were to look after them. The camp where about 150 British and 300 others were interned was quite well treated. About 150 British were also in the American Legation.

The armistice is signed—terms very lenient—but I take it the fighting is not over as Grobba is still in Mosul. They will doubtless hold the north if they can.

1 June 1941

All gates were open this morning; H.E. made a moving speech—was cheered—and all available cars went to meet the Regent. I jumped into Ernest Main's car with Seton Lloyd. The crowd looked, I thought, very ugly—remarkable change from a month ago. This ugly temper confirmed by people who went out later. We drive across the iron bridge— no visible damage anywhere except at the corner of Feisal Maidan. Police all along. Army cars try to pass us. No friendly spirit visible.

Mounted police every fifty or hundred yards all along in the low scrub and weeds where we turn right from the iron bridge: then left through barbed-wire entanglements unfinished, and along the canal (waterless and unfinished) on right. Rather derelict Iraqi outposts; and then we reach the British—marvellous look of solidity. I am the only woman in all this gathering (and worried at having no stockings and very short skirts) and reap perfect harvest of smiles. Long line of cars glittering in the sun; through the dust their back windows send sword-like flashes. Armoured cars. We have done this with only two battalions—colossal bluff.

Regent's car sighted. Army, police, Ministers, British, coalesce. Regent very smiling and gentle—Nuri looking finished.

I join Gerald standing there very cheerful. Tells me how he waited last night for the Iraqi surrender in a lonely place with marshy patches, holding on to a white flag while the Regent's representatives, getting more and more jumpy, finally disappeared in his (Gerald's) car. They were turned round again by British troops. The surrenderers arrived quite correctly but late, and the fighting ceased.

As we drive back we meet the visitors leaving the Regent's *majliss* in the *Palace of Flowers*: *Mujtahids* (Elders) in black turbans, Christian bishops with red and black, sheikhs, politicians, none I feel looking very friendly. The military band is smart and the Regent's soldiers seem very fit and fought well, shooting from trenches round Kadhimain.

2 June 1941

Yesterday afternoon was a time of general departure. Glubb leaves with his legion; Gerald leaves for Jerusalem. People visit their houses, many—such as Sinbad's, Holman's, etc,—left like a *shambles* and filthy beyond words.

Mistaken idea that all is over.

I see H.E. with the war correspondents in the evening. He surprised me by saying he thought the town looked friendly. I feel it very much to the contrary and think it is a pity we did not bring the Regent in with a good show of troops or aeroplanes. Always the choice between placating one's enemies or encouraging one's friends. But the pretence that this is an Iraqi spontaneous Restoration is just nonsense, so we might as well get the advantages as well as the disadvantages of being behind it.

However, we kept well in the background. Ernest Main, who is a first-rate man, asked to take over Press and radio at once: was told it is not our affair but Iraqi—so nothing done except total cessation of propaganda of every sort, and now we have a night of snapping rifles, police posts doubled, Jews murdered (reports vary between a dozen and five hundred, and Abdullah Ezra says he was 'wading in blood' up Ghazi Street). The shooting is getting momently stronger. The mayor is telephoning to say he wants to resign: and the new Cabinet is not yet formed.

Rashid Ali, meanwhile, is issuing proclamations.

A batch of our own prisoners were brought in today—looking very worn and many wounded: about thirty of them given breakfast in the canteen.

Had hoped to leave tomorrow, but it begins to look remote.

R. was in the Iran Bank when the looting and shooting of Jews and Christians began; machine-guns in River Street; he was locked up in the safe. The bank clerks crossed with him in a boat—a very brave thing to do: six looters leaped into it and were pushed into the river: and they got across looking like a peaceful summer party and hailed me as I was talking to my police (not putting up my parasol because of all the sniping). Lucky for R. I was there as the police would not have let him land. He just missed a bullet anyway.

Pat telephones from an hotel to say there is looting all down Rashid

Street, chiefly by army and police taking a rake-off. He suggests a launch to rescue the people in river hotels, under the impression there is no firing on the river. Eventually thinks better for everyone to stay where they are.

H.E. is closeted with Generals. V.H. has been twice to urge sending for troops and dare not go a third time, and one realizes why battles can be lost by a sheer inability to get the data to the people who make the decisions.

8 p.m.

The riot has died down. Curfew at five and everyone showing is shot. I brought Husain, the policeman, in to tea and he said they had been told to fire real stuff and killed sixty or seventy in the afternoon. New Street from the air looks as if strewn with confetti, the loot lying out in the street. Number of killed will never be known: a family with three children came in today—had seen two dead Jews in the street and their own house gutted. Reports say the police were helping to loot yesterday.

Ernest Main flew to Mosul where ninety-seven have been shut up in the Consulate and tiny garden. Found the airport completely deserted, even by the police, on his return here, and got out very gingerly fearing surprises.

My *cawass* comes with a new topee—says he got it from a heap of loot collected by the police at our gate, and paid for it with one of my boxes of cigarettes!

Gerald tells me that the army in Basra expected their advance up the Tigris to take twelve months less than in the last war—i.e. two years only.

Sat this afternoon quietly embroidering on the lawn, with Bish and Bill Bailey—pleasant peace. Cypress trees smelling aromatic in the sun. Very few people; but now in the evening isolated houses are being rounded up and lots of old friends reappear.

The little King who was coming today was turned back at Ba'Quba.

Extraordinary sight the bridges: stream of people going empty-handed eastward, coming back laden with spoil.

Our Mosul people are to be evacuated tonight by air. We are anxious to occupy the town.

Everyone is slowly gathering back here. Rather desolate feeling. Judge Pritchard telephoned from Alwiyah this afternoon—shooting all around and he alone in his house with his servant. Advised to make for American Legation. The American secretaries' cars have been shot at as they went about tonight.

3 June 1941

All quiet this morning and the inmates of the Embassy are allowed to go out freely. Pat came back with grave accusations of police helping the looters. A new Government under Jamil Madfa'i is now in power. V.H. has been to the Serai where it operates in completely sacked offices. News of Germans in Syria darkens our horizon. I think the main stream will turn Egyptwards, but who can tell?

Coming and going makes the Chancery like a railway station: officers from Habbaniya, colonels from Basra, Cawthorn[1] from Cairo, Iraqis, people here leaving, cars scrunching, *cawasses* returning. Eighteen still in prison: V.H. went to rescue them. Two Britishers in Kadhimain were, we hear, shot out of hand.

In the afternoon Bish and I leave in a Lockheed with Colonel Cawthorn and a few other officers who had come over to confer. We refuel at Habbaniya which looks spick and span from outside though there is a good deal of debris here and there inside, they say, if you look close. Fallujah looked intact too and its minaret is certainly standing. Fascinating to look down on the battlefield, the low waves of the plateau where the Iraqi guns were placed, and the watery blue flats into which we pushed them; and Fallujah and its little bridge like a miniature beyond. Reach Lydda just as daylight goes in a glowering sunset, and Jerusalem and the King David Hotel in the dark. What a dinner, with champagne, at 10.33 in the *Régence*! The people dancing look quite awful compared with our nice shabby crowd to which we have grown accustomed!

---

[1] Now Major-General Sir Walter Cawthorn, C.B., C.I.E., C.B.E., then Head of the Middle East Intelligence Centre.

8
Baghdad (1941, 1942) and Cyprus

In the King David Hotel in Jerusalem, under the eyes of the barman who was known to be a German spy, the whole of Cairo seemed to be packing its kit to cross into Syria, for a war which opened next morning with an old-fashioned cavalry charge: commanders with field-glasses on opposite hills—the Spahis and the Cheshire Yeomanry against each other. General Wilson[1] was housed in a modest little H.Q. in the valley; General Catroux[2] looked ten years younger with a war of his own in prospect; Aly Khan in the hotel lounge rushed up to embrace me and said he had feared me dead; and Crete, which had filled our captivity with the echo of its eighteen days' resistance, now showed itself to us in eye-witness accounts, with all the gravity which the B.B.C. had cautiously suppressed; few recognized it at that moment as the successful turning-point of the Middle Eastern war. The massed parachutes had made a deep impression. "It seems very noisy," our Ambassador said at breakfast one morning, having reached the island from Athens, and scouted the idea of an attack. "If you look out of this window, you will see the parachutes, Sir," one of his staff replied.

As for my Brotherhood—Pam was at the King David, in bed with jaundice, Phyllida Pumphrey down with sandfly fever in Cairo, and Ronnie Fay carrying on alone; any idea of a few days' leave was done away with. Two friends in the 4th Hussars gave me a lift across Sinai; Ismailia in moonlight was stiff with troops; Bill Astor

---

[1] General Sir Henry Maitland Wilson, G.C.B., G.B.E., D.S.O., now Field-Marshal Lord Wilson of Libya and of Stowlangtoft: G.O.C. British Forces in Palestine and Transjordan, 1941; C. in C. Allied Forces in Syria, 1941; G.O.C. 9th Army, 1941; C. in C. Persia and Iraq, 1942-43; C. in C. Middle East, 1943; Supreme Allied Commander, Mediterranean Theatre, 1944.

[2] Commanding the Free French.

was stationed there and found us a camp-bed somewhere; I was in Cairo next day to arrange my handing over; and in less than a month had returned to Iraq to take up the peace-making jobs of persuasion.

In writing the story of an enterprise, it is easy to give an illusion that the whole, rather than one small facet only, is being presented to the reader. In Iraq there were many colleagues on my job—assistants in education, Stewart Perowne extracted from Aden to take over the Embassy Publicity, Adrian Bishop and his group, the British Council and the Political Officers in their districts—they were all engaged in one way or another on this labour.

'The British Council particularly, offending no nationalism, should,' I wrote in some report, 'take all the weight it can carry. When everything else withdraws, there is every chance that these institutes will remain and flourish . . . and where we have first-rate people as here, the good it is doing is immense.'[1] The teaching service for the Levant never got properly started and many present troubles derive from that omission. The influence of my own Brotherhood and of Adrian Bishop's little group[2] has been drowned in the nationalist sea: yet they did their work in the critical years, and held their sharp instrument by the handle: and so did an unobtrusive set too easily overlooked—the Political Officers in the outlying provinces of all these lands. Below the turmoil of politics their names are still recalled in the districts where they laboured, and their communities remember them as friends. I returned later after an eleven years' absence and found this to be so. 'Iraq was in a mess and it required a concerted effort to get it right,' Sir Kinahan wrote to me later on. 'You will remember that I always attached the greatest importance to that, and so in order to get at all grades of society we had the Political Advisors in the districts and the Public Relations Officers reaching the public by means of . . . reading rooms, etc. . . . and your Brotherhood and the British Institute, and the Military Mission [reconstituted first by General Bromilow and later, more fundamentally, by Major-General J. M. L. Renton] working in the Iraq Army, and a large number of individuals. The British Army

[1] 1943.
[2] Teddy Hodgkin, Aidan Philip, Seton Lloyd and William Jones.

by its correct attitude and the senior British officers by their friendliness also helped.' This is a fair and true presentment.

My Brotherhood belonged officially to the Embassy Publicity, but actually continued on its own lines as before, a little apart. It dealt with a tougher problem than Egypt had presented. The country was soaked in German doctrines; the Berlin radio blared from every coffee-house; the army was surly over its defeat and none too pleased to discover that it had been effected with less than two British battalions; and the worst of the Middle Eastern war was beginning. The German advance in Russia, the entry of Japan, the fall of Singapore, Sebastopol and Tobruk lay ahead. The enemy plan of July that year foresaw a Panzer corps through Persia in the winter. Ten divisions would traverse Anatolia to Iraq.[1] It meant a lifting of the strain in the western desert, but the threat in the east was increased. Once through the Caucasus, it would take an army, I was told, not more than two days to come down from Azerbaijan over the passes. By the end of August, after a quick and bloodless advance into Persia, extremely modest preparations, consisting as far as the outsider could see chiefly of British tank traps and latrine huts, began to mark the Iraqi border in the north.

This atmosphere made great demands on 'democrats' and few were prepared to label themselves as such. When I first returned, though the bazaars seemed unchanged in their dusty half-sunlight shadows, and the ramshackle amusing crowd was much the same, our soldiers were kept strictly in bounds and now and then sniped if they wandered beyond them. It was 'a rather artificial calm' and when I gave my first party H.E. asked for a list of the guests in case of touching pitch. I sent it with a note to say that all were pure more or less, and the cloven hoof, if any, 'hidden in official slippers.'

By the end of the autumn, relations were mellowing in the extremely friendly atmosphere of the army which was moving everywhere. General Wavell came through. He sent his A.D.C. for me in the midst of his conferences because, he told the Embassy, he had heard that I had seven new hats (and in the course of conversation remarked apropos of Syria that 'we are always good friends

[1] Winston Churchill, *The Grand Alliance*. Ch. XXIX.

with the French when we are enemies'). Johnnie Hawtrey,[1] who had trained the Iraqi Air Force and sent a message through one of his imprisoned airmen to congratulate them on their performance, went up to Mosul to treat for the surrender: he shook hands with his old colleagues as if nothing had intervened, which so disquieted them that they fled into Syria that night. Ladies whose husbands had murdered each other now began to drink their tea together at opposite ends of the table; and a new cabinet was formed like a mouse from the mountain with many labours. The Regent had grown a little fatter, still with the same gentle brown eyes and charming manners and the fine look of his family 'like portraits in old houses, almost too delicately bred'. The King was a little boy of six who had just learnt to swim.

By the end of October the Emir Abdullah came over from Transjordan and sat covered with decorations at the end of a long ballroom. At the banquet given for three Arab rulers together I was placed next the old Chief of the Senate who kept his end up in conversation by the simple expedient, when he reached the end of a story, of beginning again at the beginning in the same words, relying no doubt on a general female lack of Arabic to save himself the wear and tear of thought.

I sympathized, for the whole of my work was talk and it sometimes seemed endless: men in long gowns would be sitting in a row waiting for me before breakfast, and it went on all day with only a break for the sacred hour or two of the afternoon.

The first difficulty had been to procure a house, without which I could do no good, 'and have wasted a month of this precious summer for want of one.' I had hoped to find something on the river, to look out over people splashing or eating their water-melons in the shade, with the red furnace of the sunset across the wide water and the slim arch of lights over the bridge's shadow, and lighted candles floating downstream on Thursday evenings in honour of the Prophet Elias; but the only house available there belonged to a man

---

[1] Air Vice-Marshal J. G. Hawtrey was Inspector of the Iraqi Air Force in 1940 and in 1942 was on the Air Staff in India. After distinguished service in Europe he became Senior Air Staff Officer at Headquarters Far East Air Force in 1951 and in 1952 returned to Iraq as Air Officer Commanding, Iraq. He died in 1954.

whose brass plate said *Father of Dust, Lawyer*, and was as dilapidated as its name. Finally I secured one of the official bungalows in the suburb of Alwiyah. I could sleep out here in a garden and be wakened in the early morning by a chorale of small birds and by the sun before dawn beating on the underwings of doves. They flew all one way, to or from their morning drink, the shadow of their bodies against half a wing and the rest of them shining in the sky. Beneath them the dates hung like heavy udders round the palm stems—columns in some temple of fertility rather than trees. And in the cooler mornings an old man would scythe the lawn and I could shut my eyes and smell it for a moment and think of England in June.

Pam came over and did the buying for the house, so that we hoped to be 'less like a Chinese baby on a doorstep' in future. It was pretty—three rooms opening one from the other, washed a faint pink with white furniture and striped curtains of white and pink and grey. Everything had to be bought and much was unobtainable:

It is a fearful strain to get these things started [I wrote to my mother].
There are innumerable wheels and it is not one's own superiors but people running parallel departments who are apt not to see the necessity for one's existence. But I can't complain: I have such affection and help that it would be ungrateful indeed not to be thankful... It is only myself I feel doubtful of—I do so badly need a three months' holiday! Telephoning alone takes an hour or more a day, and, of course, here it is mostly in Arabic which one has to do oneself... The polite exchange says 'Do not mention it, Madame', whenever I say thank you.

I got one month's holiday, even in this tricky summer, and spent most of it in the solitudes of Carmel, in a *Kurhaus* among the pines:

9 September 1941

... you see nothing before you but the hill slopes and the sea: sometimes a white sail as lonely as life: but a party was sitting under a pine tree eating water-melon slices: black veils showed them Muslim, apart from their unprogressive way of spending the time. I was invited and sat with a slice of melon, and they told me they came twice or thrice a week to breathe the air and enjoy the sunset, just husband, wife and two daughters. They were so pleasant and restful among the money-grubbing of Haifa.

This sanatorium is the last Jewish outpost: the hills and paths beyond it belong to Islam. One day I climbed to a headland of tillage and found a lovely girl in her best—enormous full red bloomers and a flowering dress of magenta satinette with green braid round the skirt, and hands all hennaed for the holiday. She said, 'Come to the wedding', and led me along a path to a tiny cottage where the mother was kneading bread and eight or nine women danced to the piping of a youth with bleary eyes. They seized my hand and I was soon dancing in the circle, stamping and waving a handkerchief and saying *hah* to the beat of the music. They never asked who I was, but said I must not leave without eating and presently produced a plateful of excellent stew and bread and then a cup of water and set me on my way.

There is one very nice German-Jewish doctor here, and he and his wife took me to one of the colonies on the foothills of Carmel, that have been there ten years and are self-supporting: already forests cover the slopes behind them and wheat fields lie on the ground below; and they have a finely built school and a little general garden. Each family has one room to itself, some in houses, but most in wooden shacks as they are poor and the money has to go largely in machinery. But they have good crèches for the children, who are brought up by nurses and taken for two hours a day to their parents. The babies are kept very hygienically in pens surrounded by wire-netting against flies. They eat in common. Most come from Poland and they all look happy. Well, there it is! There seems nothing to be said against it, but if I were there I should run off and live uncomfortably and unhygienically in a hovel with the resentful Arabs just outside. One can give no reason—but I can't help wondering what Jesus meant when he rejected all the kingdoms: no doubt they included sanitation, and baby welfare and all, and his own carpenter's shop was a dingy old-fashioned affair. It is just that *something else* is also needed!

The shores of Galilee on my way were lovely in the quiet evening. They have still kept their ancient spell; and looking down from here is Athlit, the last port left to the Crusaders, its ruins moored to a hook of land that juts to a low bay. North is the bay of Acre, lovely in shape, and, far, far beyond, the cloudy vision of Hermon, its huge landscape now only attainable with a police pass—beautifully solitary except for good-looking young men of the police patrols, all fit and bronzed. You come upon them camped in olive groves, lodged in villages, running lonely posts in the hills, looking as if they were settled there for life, starting little gardens, perfectly self-composed and happy, and ready to run the country, any country, and all its inhabitants if asked to do so. All the Middle East is a huge armed zone; as Churchill has said so, the Censor can't mind my saying so too!

We drove here when Stewart came to visit me, after bathing in a soft seaweed bay where waves froth round one. How flattering it is for women to be compared to the sea. It may be changeable, but no one could get tired of its playing, every wave different from the last.

I returned to Baghdad with friends by a deserty five-day route along Euphrates—through Latakia and Aleppo by Deir ez-Zor, in whose *Beau Geste* setting the Vichy aeroplanes were biting the sand of their airfield and café tables were set under riverside trees. Nearby are Justinian's fortresses whose angular enclosures the current washes, and the walls and gates, basilicas and cisterns of Resafa, once built of shining gypsum in the sun. The droves of gazelle leap round its solitude, as they did when the Palmyrene archers escorted the Roman or the Parthian caravans. Then as now, the battle line ran from Libya to Russia, linked by much the same roads, as fragile and as rare: and the army lorries of our day—ever in sight between Baghdad and Transjordan—were no doubt churning the forgotten Roman dust. A bedu in a yellow gown, with a gun, came slinking among the ruins of Resafa and murmured in a soft voice that he belonged to the *Children of the Wolf*. "What do you know of all this?" I asked him. We were in the nave of the church of St. Sergius, and he gave it a glance of indifference that might have belonged to Time itself. "You must know," he said.

My house was painted by the end of October and life in Baghdad settled into a routine which for the next two years it was to follow. After changing residence eight times in twelve months, I hoped to be able to live in tolerable quiet, and felt that we had the winter before us to make the most of. It was not long, but better than a matter of weeks only in which to get people fond of the British after the crisis of this year.

Letters gave the day-to-day comments to my mother: on the Baghdad ladies, 'so ready to be friends, so gay and pleasant; and many have never been inside an English house,' or on the English modesty,

by which when I say *pale mauve* the other fellow recognizes *bright purple*, and answers *shell pink* meaning *scarlet*: it takes years of a foreigner's life to know what we mean and then he rarely gets beyond the fact that it is something different from what we say. I think truth is more essential: it doesn't seem to me to be true modesty to say you are a poor tennis-player, when you know you are a good one; the only mistake is to take it to be a matter of importance.

An old Arab diplomat to whom I complained that the trains keep me awake said: 'I should not mind that. It is the voice of civilization.'

This morning a blue-eyed English bank clerk walked into the Chancery with a sad tale. As he was doing nothing much in Persia and as there were three other assistants, he asked to join the navy, and—as he wasn't given leave—just walked out, joined up in Basra, and was sailing for India when the authorities stopped him. It will be very unpopular if he is put in prison for wanting to fight!

The Americans are back from Moscow, hard put to it to stand up to the drinking: twenty-six vodka and red pepper mixed.... The Russians are giving away nothing: they say send them the stuff, they will attend to the using of it. Everyone is left with a high opinion of their soldiering.

I lit a fire last night—just to please Bish who came and dined and drank my best bottle of Syrian wine. I am his only solace (he says)—so few women and the men all living under strain. I sometimes think it may be more helpful to listen to their innumerable troubles than to do my work.

Am reading General Weygand's Life of Muhammed Ali. I knew how anti-British he—the General—was before Vichy even existed, but in this book he manages to describe the siege of Missolonghi without ever mentioning Lord Byron.

Under this temporary smoothness the violence of oriental life went on, nor could we forget it for long. In November Pam and I went to lunch at the Embassy where Fakhri Nashashibi, on a visit from Palestine, was invited. He was murdered as he stepped out of his hotel by a man on a bicycle who shot him and rode away. After half an hour's waiting, Vyvyan Holt came up to Lady Cornwallis quietly to say that the guest was not coming: it appears that after twenty years of Iraq politics, when he heard the news over the telephone, he merely said: "I suppose we needn't wait lunch any longer."

* * * *

At the beginning of 1942 the desert, relieved by the pressure on Russia, sent cheerful messages.

Tommy Elmhurst, writing in March far away on the pursuit of Rommel, described 'a day of battle, soldiers and sailors and airmen all fighting vigorously and I think successfully' and the 'great feeling of seeing our own bombers and fighters overhead'.

'For all its bleak and colourless character,' another friend wrote, 'this country has its little consolations, such as owls which pop out of their holes and sit blinking but in no way disconcerted, or a herd of curlew (believe it or not this is the right term for curlew and applies also to swans and cranes, three such dissimilar birds! rather odd!) making their plaintive call ... Then a big bee will suddenly appear from nowhere and if one shuts one's eyes his buzzing brings back memories of English gardens on a summer's day ... "Lying lazily, with eyes half shut, one sees as in a dream green boughs wavering or waters rippling in a golden light."'

In Baghdad my private life had become singularly pleasant. The relief brought by my mother's safety made me happy; so did my house with three friends[1] to share it, a room for an office and a coming and going of Brethren all day long. Pam had been forced, by the birth of a son, to leave me, and Peggy Drower, an excellent helper, had come in her stead with a knowledge of Arabic and of the country as good if not better than mine. And as the eastern Arab front now had an H.Q. of its own in Iraq, friends were continually passing by to give us outer news.

In the house we were ruled by Jasim, our Treasure, whose turban and black moustache were like my earliest imagining of the Arabian Nights. He steered us through small dramas—the milk watered (according to him) by the ingenious invention of making the cow drink abundantly just before the milking; or the laundry for which our neighbour Judge Pritchard (who had been angelically keeping

[1] Hermione Ranfurly (then General 'Jumbo' Wilson's P.A.), Barbara Graham (an assistant), Nigel Clive (in the British Embassy).

Pam and me in his house while ours was finishing) paid less than he should 'because he is a judge'. He was no doubt unaware of his privilege, but Jasim interposed when I thought I could do the same. With all of us busy, Jasim's rule was absolute and it was only by drawing my finger silently across the furniture to produce a dust mark that I would now and then gain a small temporary advantage out of his passionate pride in our house.

It was a time full of strain and overwork for everybody, and in looking through my letters it seems extraordinary to find so many oases of calm. Walks when Vyvyan Holt . . . 'chose the dreariest view where nothing but sand is visible while the gardens are all blossom. It is raining, and the green is rushing out, on the apricot boughs, in the willows, on the mulberries and in the grass: for a short week or two this ancient earth seems new. The little wild Kurdish iris are breaking along their stalks, one after the other like signal flags at a mast-head. When the lawn is being watered and reflects the trees it is like fairyland.'

I rode with Stewart through Muaddham, a pleasant suburb north of Baghdad, old-fashioned with quiet streets and houses overhanging, with dusty carved windows bayed out to get the maximum view for the harim—over the pontoon bridge, almost level because of the spring-rising Tigris—past the golden minarets of Kadhimain—along the river where fishermen sat beside round nets in huts made of palm fronds—through aisles of palms and walled flowering orange-gardens, languorously scented—out to tilled fields and vegetable patches—from mud village to village, the track built high to dyke the river which shone ice-blue like a mirror in the spring lights of the day. Islands were appearing, where the tamarisk was breaking into pale feathery flowers, coral and white.

Outings, too, with Nigel my lodger 'young and English and happy to be here', reading Plato in a garden full of apple trees and pomegranates, where a boy showered us with rose-petals, cool and smooth like hands under water. In the evening we rode back down the right bank to Baghdad, meeting the old horse-tram that trundled on rails, an antediluvian sight, packed two storeys high with women and police and peasants, turbans, sidaras and gowns, the craziest tram in creation.

As the days grew hotter we would drive out on a Sunday afternoon in a molten world and find the river among crocodile snouts of mud and thin lines of palms pressed between sky and water. New islands appeared week by week under jade-pale bushes and coarse grasses spiked like helmets; doves and rollers, bee-eaters, magpies and kingfishers were at home there, and melon plants were grown in pot-holes before another flood. The peasants walked barefoot, with hollow, sallow faces, very poor. Sometimes we would turn inland, across the Diyala River where the Lancaster Regiment held in 1917 'against overwhelming odds'—too familiar phrase—by strips of deserty steppe with flocks, shreds of oases in walled gardens, huts of the Jibur; till the road ended in a mud patch and the few tribesmen smoothed a way to a picnic place among ears of corn and roots of clover. One of them had a fair moustache and I asked how he got it. "My mother was with the English," he said.

It was 'boiling hot' by May, but the house was cool. The fan revolved gently, the windows were shut by eight-thirty till six or so when all was thrown open.

How lucky we are [I wrote] with fans and baths and frigidaires and servants, and a pretty house! One has no idea how long such things will last, but it makes them the more valuable. I have about six pieces of French soap left and enjoy it every time I take a bath. What I am pleased about, too, is that I am living entirely on my earnings.

My letters are filled with a kaleidoscope of people even more varied than Egypt, for by now the Middle East was like a broken sea with waves of refugees in every direction and every sort of military cross-current as well.

A pathetic visit from a Jew pedlar with a pack of silks to sell for other merchants: all his house and shop looted in May, so he begins the world again—the indomitable, impressive side of the Jew.

Did I tell you that the black-out here had to be stopped because everyone knifed everyone else in the dark? The papers said it had been such a success there was no need to continue. One is always on a thin crust—the most ordinary Iraqi ladies riding ten days in disguise to join their husbands in Cairo through the English lines.

A young airman rang up to say, 'Could a Persian lady who longs to meet you pay a call? She has been in jail six years.' This peculiar introduction brought a charming couple, the daughter of the famous Taimurtash who *made* the ex-Shah and died in prison for his pains, and now she and her husband are full of the wish to see their country strong and independent and who, I wonder, is going to help? It is a great mistake to be a small nation today.

What strange lives one comes across! I went to a Czech oculist—quite an elderly man, and he has lived here eleven years in an Arab house, clean and cool, in one of the back streets of the town, with a young Baghdad wife and two small children. He has two grown sons in Prague and no news of them, and he makes his living among the Arabs. A woman from Riga does one's nails, a blonde good-natured, plain, healthy Frau, also here eleven years with husband employed in a soap factory. A Hungarian does one's face, she came on a visit to a sister who married an Iraqi, and got caught in the war. There are a few Poles, and a Czecho-Hungarian-Rumanian played the 'Appassionata' to the troops. Lovely it was to hear something so beautiful! He played Chopin. I wondered what the listeners were thinking, so far from their homes. They live in camps among the dust-storms—full in summer heat when it comes—and one has such a time driving one's little car in and out of their convoys and lorries. They sing 'Land of Hope and Glory' with gusto in church notwithstanding the fall of Singapore!

Our prospects with the Brotherhood did not seem to me less hopeful than Egypt had been the year before, in spite of the bad start. Countries used to absolute rule are chary of voicing their opinions, and there was more friendship for us perhaps than we imagined. Johnnie Hawtrey remarking to his ex-pupils how poor their artillery had been against Habbaniya (which they could easily have destroyed), they always retorted that, on the contrary, their aim had been *extremely good;* not many of them had wished to destroy us; and this double current through the country (which probably still exists) was a factor of great though unassessed importance throughout the revolt.[1]

But now a gloomy spring opened and the Baghdad peace blos-

[1] It is my opinion that General Wavell's underestimating of our chances in Iraq was due to the fact that he did not, and probably could not, know the strength of this friendly feeling at the time.

somed as it were in the heart of a tornado. Burma and Malaya and the Farouk crisis in Cairo were leading towards the fall of Tobruk in June, and Iraq was as fidgety as a frightened horse. Her recent defeat kept her quiet and troops continually moving up and down to Persia, becoming popular, acted both as a deterrent and a balm. Women told me how surprised and pleased they were to find they could go, even to a cinema, among the armies, and luckily when Singapore was threatened our Brotherhood no longer waited for 'guidance' which always came too late, but we prepared our people a month before it fell. Even so, most were too frightened to commit themselves until the news improved.

You can't think, [I wrote 4.3.42] how beastly it is to be a propagandist just now. One's resource has to be endless, one's courage flawless, one's patience inexhaustible. The Brothers here are also a little dashed because two members were put in prison: however, as we undeservedly got blamed for their going in, we are now undeservedly enjoying the credit for their coming out. It is wearing, too, to be always ready to pack up with nowhere to go; but nothing matters so long as the Russians in the Crimea keep that vital wing of our huge front.

By the 29th of March: 'Here we still are: the Iraqis jittery and all of us wondering when the spring offensive starts. Hitler *must* make for oil or die. Meanwhile they are trying the rebels of last May and one hopes this state of uncertainty may soon be over. I can't help feeling it is a pity they ever arrived in Iraq: so many things could happen to people at sea.' Poor George Antonius, a gentle frustrated man and my friend, was dying too, and soon lay in Jerusalem in an open coffin, his face slightly made up, in a brown pin-stripe suit, defeating the majesty of death. And the spring went on with increasing strain, when an early night and eight hours' sleep seemed a boon. Peggy was splendid and my other assistant, not cut out for propaganda, was 'slowly waking to the fact that women must either work or weep unless they are *very* beautiful'. The Iraqis, corrupted by politics, seemed to think of friendliness as intended to snatch some non-existent benefit from them. 'The older ones know our strength and value us, and the young are difficult as can be.'

It was the young that mattered.

BAGHDAD (1941, 1942) AND CYPRUS

Adrian Bishop and I had written a report during the leisure of the siege on this 'growing force hitherto neglected, which we believe will soon be of paramount importance' and on the main problem ... 'to rally the forces of nationalism to our side.' Any other success, we thought, was secondary, 'a mere dabbling in backwaters when our necessity is to regulate the main current of the stream. Because we have no territorial needs in Arab lands, because our interests run parallel and not against the interests of the Arabs, there is no reason why national and pro-British feeling should not be united. Our aim should be to make nationalism friendly.' To do so we must gain to our side the army; the disbanded officers and men who might be a source of trouble; education; and the young educated population of the towns.

'We feel,' we also said, 'that it cannot be too clearly stated nor too often repeated that there is only one problem at the root of all our relations with the Arab world: this is the absence of any clear statement from His Majesty's Government of their intentions towards Arab nationalism, the future of Syria and Arab confederation, and the still unresolved problem of Palestine. The fact that this has been said *ad infinitum* must not be taken to lessen in any degree its primary importance and its essential truth; without such a statement the plans suggested cannot be expected to lead to satisfactory results.'

'You will see,' I wrote some months later to Mr. Casey,[1] 'that our general purpose goes very parallel to that of the British Institutes—with one big difference, and that is that we try to keep it as non-British as possible, basing ourselves on a purely *democratic* propaganda: in Egypt there are not half a dozen British in the whole show, and in Iraq it is the same. This is because the people we want are the young ones who have been, or are, or might become at any moment, ardently nationalist, and the object—to combine their nationalist feelings with a friendly bias ... is devoted to a time when we may have to do without political officers and almost certainly armies, when even the British Institutes may sound too foreign in the ears of Eastern governments, and when an Iraqi, Egyptian, or Persian organization may be our only means of influencing the

---

[1] Rt. Hon. R. G. Casey, P.C., C.H., D.S.O., M.C. (now Lord Casey) at that time Minister of State resident in the Middle East and a member of the War Cabinet.

population in general. It seems to me that some such system of *insurance* is very necessary and should be started while we are in control of the field.'

By the middle of June we had fourteen committees of Brethren and one hundred and fifty members.

The summer was hotter than usual for Baghdad. It rose to 127° in the shade. Even the nights were hot and infested by sandflies, and everyone looked thin and pale and most people were cross. All of this was twice as unbearable when the news was bad.

Poor Nigel is getting so thin, I am worried about him. I am all right, but incapable of doing a heavy day's work. However, I had two long committees and the Iraqi Military Chief to lunch yesterday. We are trying to get them to help us by allowing committees in the army, and it is all most delicate. I hope I have succeeded: I invited the Xs—I like the wife and she is very good to us; but neither Stewart nor Nigel could bear to look at her because they said she reminded them of a second-rate *procureuse* in Paris! It shows what a pity it is to know second-rate *procureuses*, if it spoils you for quite respectable army wives in Iraq! The poor woman sat between two averted men all through lunch. The news is as bad as can be and it is a miserable job going round explaining to frightened or secretly rejoicing people that all is well. I had sixty to my party yesterday but hardly any Iraq army put in an appearance: the Nazis there are furious with our gatherings and have been going round sabotaging them. If we get better news this will not matter.

My new committee consisted of twelve officers. Nobody had really got at the army so far, and it was largely Nazi at heart, so I was anxious about this *entrée* and distressed to find my chief partisan being sent off with the rest of the troops to the north. With some trouble I got him let off for a month; 'whether it is worth doing is another matter, but it is rather necessary just now. He was difficult to recommend as he interviewed his general and threatened in his ardour to commit suicide if not allowed to stay attending to democracy in Baghdad. He said to me: "I know how to deal with the army: one bottle of beer and it is finished—they are democrats." It was the best we could do to begin with.

By the end of the year forty officers had joined us, though the army was still largely Nazi in sympathy and our groups had to face a possible loss of promotion. They showed a falling off during the summer (after the fall of Tobruk), but were rallying well even before the news of victories in Egypt. We had a certain amount of natural opposition from the top chiefly due to a misunderstanding as to the nature of the Brothers—they were no more a political party than a union to defend 'King and Country' would be in England; but the Iraqi generals (whose wives were in our committees) accepted us, and a benevolent neutrality was promised by the heads of the British Mission. Our penetration, however, remained very slow and the army was, of all in Iraq, the least influenced by our efforts.

By the end of June we were pulling ourselves together after the bombshell of Tobruk.[1] Against most of my committee members I insisted, by some intuition like that for Singapore, on forecasting its loss a week before it happened, and this chance shot had a remarkably steadying effect. It was always better, I found, to be on the pessimistic side and then, if nothing happened (as in the case of Malta whose fall we were prepared for) the better news had the effect of a victory, and if the catastrophe occurred our people were forewarned. Meanwhile there was a mixture of panic among friends and silence, in our presence, among the fifth column.

Only one of all our ladies took the trouble to ring me up with a friendly message. Oh well, it is not a pleasant month for the propagandist. I do what I can and go out to about five different *salons* a day—and notice people are the better for being talked to. 'Keep calm and carry on' is all one can do. If we had had five years instead of six months we might have had a more solid body in Iraq to rely on; as it is, I am always surprised at the number who believe in us rather than at their scarcity.

My week has been full of committees and I have little energy left for anything else. The thermometer has touched 122° in the shade and the sheets are like ovens when you lie down on them. Hospitals are full of heatstroke and the thought that leave will be cancelled is almost as grim as anything else. One has to be awfully careful about little things, servants' tempers, etc., as everything is very explosive this weather—and of course very precarious with an offensive beating at both front door and back. We say that all has to be subordinated to help Russia (including the heavy

---

[1] It fell on the 20th.

tanks which might, and indeed would, have saved Libya)—but that is a poor sort of argument to those who are likely to be among the sacrificed! My one personal happiness is that you are out of it all, and in such a dear and happy home. I bless Lucy and John for it every day. The Government has bought my car, so I am rich to the extent of £500, and will try and send some, but may not be authorized to do so. If I leave I shall trust all papers etc. to Hamid.

By July the country was seething with disguised Nazis and swastikas were appearing everywhere—even on the back of my car. The Jews were doing us almost more harm than the enemy, afraid not so much of the Germans as of the Iraqis.

5 July 1942

And all the time one has a feeling that the fate of the East for the immediate future, perhaps for centuries, is being settled on that strip of western sand beyond the Bramley's house where one has spent so many happy hours. They are fighting there now. It is so hot that if one leaves the car ten minutes in the sun one can't touch the steering-wheel without gloves: a tank must be appalling. Poor boys, they come out of these tank battles looking almost distraught. Among all the depressing venality of the Iraqi friendship a few bright spots stand out. Twenty young mechanics came to enrol in our forces, saying, 'it is a time for deeds and not words.' Our committees do not fall off: we have about two hundred and fifty members—oh well. Nigel is wilting away; I am so worried about him I don't know what to do. Bish is just down from the north where he says all sorts of ugly things are rearing their heads; he embraced me and said: 'How far this little Scandal throws its beams.' He was most pleasant to see in this town of ragged nerves. In spite of all, my conviction is that the feeling is genuinely much better than last year! Peggy is very good indeed, and we begin to see results—some a little disconcerting, as when a rumour that the Allies had landed at Dakar flew like lightning round the *suq* and we traced it to a zealous Brother; he said he thought the people needed a tonic and so invented it, and sent the price of gold down by 4/- in one day.

By the 12th July things were better.

A fortnight ago I wondered if we would still be here—or at any rate if Cairo would still be there: and now we are less anxious on that side and looking with more anxiety to Russia. As we are just in the middle of the pincers, we are equally interested in either end! Meanwhile the summer is slowly passing and the rainy season not more than three months away in the north.

I have now got about thirty army officers in my committees and it is a toss-up whether I shall succeed or whether the Nazi sabotage will be too strong. They are being very active against us, which is the greatest compliment to our success. I had six young officers at my own committee yesterday, all making suggestions and very keen, and we are now trying to get Allied cinemas into their camps, hitherto a closed ground to all except the swastika.

Nigel is having a lovely birthday cake with icing, twenty-five candles, two bottles of champagne, and a dinner-party for his friends.

By the end of July the worst of the news seemed over. I asked H.E. if he would rather give me two months' leave or have me in hospital, and made for Cyprus as the nearest place where no Arabic conversation could take place.

★ ★ ★ ★

On my way through Palestine I met Christopher Scaife and heard the Cairo details of the 'black day' when Rommel came so near, and the Embassy burnt its archives. Many were ordered to leave, and practically all the members of the Minister of State's Department were evacuated to Palestine.

The Egyptian branch of the Brotherhood was attached to that department but as our chief object was to maintain morale, and as the departure of Christopher and Ronnie Fay would have destroyed the faith of our thousands of members and made them think themselves abandoned on the approach of this first real crisis, it was arranged that they should be allowed to remain under the aegis of the Embassy. By constant visits to committees in Cairo and Alexandria—where we had about three thousand Brethren—they were able to maintain confidence while the battle wore itself away on the outskirts of Egypt. Races went on and cinemas remained open, and the Brotherhood, too, came through with satisfaction to its godparents and credit to itself.

Christopher's next ordeal was to see me through my accounts—a large document had come allowing a little more money but all under different heads. To put £4,000 a year into its proper place drove me nearly mad, and there still seems to me no sense in not buying a typewriter with a surplus from telephones (when, as I explained to Christopher, like Macedon and Monmouth they both begin with a T). The figures, shy as animals, fled in and out of their elusive columns, and only after hours of misery I discovered that I had been counting the date of the year as a sum either received or expended—a dealing with Time which wrecks any arithmetic, however philosophically true. At the bottom of the document I was amused to read that they had considered reducing my salary 'on account of sex differentiation' but had desisted at Owen Tweedy's suggestion. I would have resigned. As for the accounts, kind Mr. Das in the Baghdad Secretariat now added them to the other troubles in his charge.

Christopher had much from his Baghdad branch to put up with, run as it now was on uncompromisingly female lines. 'Eve and serpent that you are,' he wrote, 'how often have I said to you, dear Freya, that a woman has powers of opening the dossiers of diplomats, the files of field officers, and the codes of commodores, which are totally denied to a conscientious man. When you ask for a tyre from army stores it is the appeal of a damsel in distress; when I do it, it is a nasty grafter's racket. But this doesn't diminish my joy at the news that you have been able to get some'—and that of course— not being a conscientious man—seemed to me the main objective. Dear Christopher, I always wonder why it should be derogatory to behave like a woman when one is one.

I was now free for two months. I drove along the coast to Haifa by clear little bays and along the Samarian highlands; saw again the vivid ridges of Jerusalem bathed in air, the country white at heart through the crust, green or brown, of its seasons, the city weathered to the hills on which it lies. I was depressed by Beirut, in spite of the kindness of the Spears[1] and their staff—nearly all old friends.

[1] Major-General Sir Edward and Lady Spears. He was head of the Spears Mission in Syria and the Lebanon and later, in 1942, our Minister to the Republics of Syria and the Lebanon.

The hilly places were alight—rather strangely, with the blackout in Palestine—and Joan and Aly Khan carried me off to dance in the mountain coolness: but 'those pathetic displays of porcelain vases or stamp collections in shops where everything one needs is missing, that touch of French mode through which the natural coarseness of the Levant has no difficulty in appearing, the visible men so few and their wives and sisters cheering the boredom of the armies at little tables all about the town so many'[1]—I was glad to get away to Cyprus by the kindness of the Navy, in a Greek corvette that had sailed out of Singapore the day before it fell.

Cyprus was full of troops in expectation of a second Crete. English women were nearly all evacuated—a discrimination inside the boundaries of empire which naturally did us no good with the Cypriots, but spread a beautiful solitude and peace over the island. Flat places were dotted with small earth cones, like nails on the soles of mountain boots, to deter airborne landings, and a fierce controversy raged as to whether they did not make things too easy for the enemy when once the landing had taken place. In this dilemma some ground was fortified and some not, and paratroop invaders could shelter behind the cones after landing on the open ground beside them; our fair-minded loss of the advantages of both sides seemed secure.

I had had to promise the tired Navy that under no circumstances would I ask to be evacuated, and now, after safe arrival, I convalesced beside water so limpid, so transparent, so green near shore and variegated—like the leaves of those hothouse plants—with such patterns of sunlight on its submerged sands that the sight of it alone made one forget all trouble.

The land stretched outer arms of hills with a foreground of orange groves and windmills; the old Famagusta in its walls was inhabited in a decaying way by Turks whose mosque was the cathedral of the Crusaders—the name of Allah was suspended on its piers. The eastern promontory kicked a tiny subsidiary island out into a sea fantastically blue, where bays were cut hard with dazzling beaches, and myrtle shot upright from the ground like candelabra, and villages were separated from each other by ridges of small juniper and

[1] Letter 5.8.42.

pine. The animals were sleek and the trees well looked after in contrast to the rest of the Levant; the people's looks seemed to have a keenness of Europe; El Kantara from a backbone ridge held the double seas in sight. All looked its best in the liquid bath of the sun. There was a *festa* in the castle village—children playing at garrison with spears of reed, and grizzled men in rough boots and baggy trousers dancing with rapt concentration to the music of two violins. Salamis, the ancient city, lay destroyed below in woodlands of fennel and mimosa.

From Famagusta a train jerked across the landscape, full of sheep and priests and peasants, to Nicosia and a few days' ease in a Government House so permeated by arts and crafts of the island that even the drawing-room curtains were cross-stitched with Crusader patterns. The Woolleys,[1] who were governing, were hospitable and kind, but what I needed was solitude; Mr. Davies of the British Council offered it with the loan of a cottage facing the western uplands: Prodromos, a peaceful natural village lay below, and ranges and clouds and a gulf, where the sunset dropped, were beyond it. Vines grew round the house, and pinewoods and browsing goats climbed to a minor Olympus. Bracken and arbutus flourished here, evergreen oak with little undergrowth, and whiffs of sun-heated sage and thyme in the open spaces. There were only about four hundred people in the village, and a big hotel which was closed, built by Sir Ronald Storr's inspiration on the model of a Crusader castle—a poor pattern for hotels—by an architect who was a mining engineer evidently intended by providence for a life underground, for he had turned it away from the finest view in Cyprus. North down the valley was the next village called Pedhoules, with a fifteenth-century chapel under a pointed roof, and frescoes sustained on dull-painted columns, pleasant and neglected. The women wove carpets, and recognized the subtleties of pottery, linen or weaving—they had a feeling for the beauty of everyday things, coming down perhaps from Neolithic times.

Except for Sim Feversham,[2] who was stationed near Nicosia and gave me the experience of a ride in one of his Crusader tanks and

[1] Sir Charles and Lady Woolley.
[2] The Earl of Feversham, then in the Yorkshire Hussars.

drove me down to Paphos, and Jock Jardine[1] in Famagusta, who came once to camp for a week-end in the cottage's other room, I spent a month of solitude. The river of the sun slept on the pine-needled slopes. Only once did I drive down the valley, and that was with J.J. to the palace of Vouni, that overlooks, as if it were an amphitheatre, the bay of Morphou from a flat-topped hill. Built two and a half thousand years ago, it still watches the marbled sea between its rows of columns and keeps its ease of space and leisure, and sees the coasts melt like silver into the burning furnace of the blue. In the sunset I returned alone to my alpine air and the outlines of woods far below against the dipping shoulders of the west. The bracken tips were turning brown with autumn; red hips were on the dog-rose and yellowing boughs in the plane trees; and the saw-edged leaves of the arbutus hung silvery against the dark ravines. I did nothing but walk all day or stitch at my embroidery, until I felt able to read, and then to write—in a sort of urgency and at Sydney Cockerell's request—the rough draft of *Traveller's Prelude* which I felt destiny might never let me finish. I had arranged for any bad Egyptian news to reach me, for 'the plans even for the next week-end depend upon the battle: one has come to take it as a matter of course'; and I wanted to reach Baghdad in case of a retreat. 'Did I tell you,' I wrote to my mother, 'that Goebbels refers to this peaceful island as a self-supporting prison camp?'

The Ministry of Information at this time wished to send me to the U.S.A. to counteract Zionist propaganda, which was producing anti-British feeling to an alarming degree. With the thought of my mother it was hard to refuse, but it would have meant the end of all the work in Iraq and there was no fair choice. 'I hope for your sake,' Peggy wrote, 'that it will only be postponed. We were glad you refused to go now—indeed we believed that would be your answer.' The delay was only of one year, and had I gone it would have been too late, for my mother died peacefully in November, three weeks after my return to Baghdad. Adrian Bishop, too, the dearest, gayest and deepest of friends there, was killed by an accidental fall into the well of an uneven stair in a Teheran hotel; and

[1] Then British Council representative in Cyprus.

Pam's husband, Pat, was missing. A few months later General 'Jumbo' wrote that he had been shot in the lung and died in hospital in Misurata, 'a great character and one of the bravest of riflemen.'

These were private sorrows. Apart from them, the autumn did well, and our Brotherhood was achieving its first seven hundred members, 'as much as could be expected after a summer of persistently bad news.' The unexpected effect of the good news when it came was that—apart from bringing in a certain amount of dross among our purer metals—it inclined the Brothers to sit back and renounce all further effort. We therefore now began to switch from war to peace, hoping to prepare a body of democratic opinion for later times with the help of the more educated young people. By December 1942 I was expecting an increase of about ten thousand members in the coming year.

When once this has been attained [I wrote to Cairo], I think there will be no further difficulty in expanding to any number required. Probably however there is an optimum beyond which it would be unadvisable to go. Ten thousand represents a little less than one per cent of the total male adult population of Iraq: it is the equivalent of about thirty thousand in Egypt. A much smaller number would not be sufficiently strong to influence public opinion: a much larger would perhaps become difficult to manage, and would lose the drive and cohesion of a minority; it is, in fact, preferable to be the leaven rather than the lump. When we have produced this band of friendly democrats we shall have fulfilled our wartime task. We shall have fashioned a powerful instrument which is not British and can therefore continue without offence under non-British governments. Its fundamental principle is that it is not based on bribery of any kind, but is intended to be beneficial and to obtain co-operation by persuading that it is so. This and the treatment of the idea of democracy and freedom as an essentially religious idea explain, I believe, its comparative success in a most difficult year.

I am personally convinced that a minimum of twelve carefully selected people can maintain a friendly state of opinion in Iraq. They would be sufficient to prevent a relapse into the conditions of 1939, and they would enable H.M.G. to economise on more expensive and less disinterested forms of persuasion. The whole success depends on the quality and devotion of the people selected.

This scheme could, I hoped, be enlarged to embrace the whole Middle East and forestall in some degree the totalitarian menace of the future. As early as the 26th of January, 1942, I had written in a letter to Cairo that 'Russia will be tremendously strong at the end of the war; it is more important than ever to have a reliable block of the Arab world.'

*   *   *   *

The Brotherhood did its wartime service but foundered in the peace, and the reason for its failure was no fault of the people who came after us, but rather an inherent weakness of our position in the Arab world as soon as the war ended. I was and am convinced—as I have tried to explain—that *the benefit to the listener and the belief of the gospeller in his own gospel* are two out of the three essentials of persuasion: Anglo-Arab relations were deprived of both these fundamentals by the problem of Israel, and without them we had no permanent chance of success. We succeeded during the war because in that interval the problem was shelved. After the war, in the height of our prestige, we had a chance to produce education to influence, not the young men of 1945 but those now grown up in 1960: but we left Egypt and not ourselves to take that opportunity. These two failures are quite sufficient to explain our situation today, without any other addition whatsoever.

A point on which I am anxious to defend my Brotherhood is the suggestion that they encouraged, if they did not cause, the nationalism which Europe already looks upon, and Asia soon will, as a disease. This is a silly accusation and would not be worth refuting if it had not been believed, even during the war. Its cause lies deep in that ostrich sentiment which makes an Englishman hope that an unpleasant object ceases to exist if he can avoid seeing it. 'Nationalism', long before the war, was as obvious as any thunderstorm on the horizon. The only possible choice was whether to have it with us or against us. If we had been able to keep it with us, the history of the Arab countries, of Iraq in particular, might have been different today.

I cannot think of these things now without grave sorrow because

—whatever the faults of the peoples of Asia—we too, I feel, have failed them. Freedom and independence is what they asked for, but the point is that when the child asks for a stone one does *not* give it a stone, one manages to give bread notwithstanding. They asked for freedom, but with it they needed experience and help, and to wash our hands and give freedom alone was not enough. Management they disliked, but without counsel they were lost. We understood this more than many other nations and often succeeded, but in the Arab world, by a very small margin, we failed. That the chief reason for this failure centred on Israel and our, and then the U.S.A.'s, handling of it, no one really familiar with the Middle East in those years would I think deny.

Yet during the war we succeeded and it was no small achievement, and in Iraq it was chiefly due to Sir Kinahan's wise and sensitive steering, wooing the country back to security and rest. Nor should we forget the Iraqi statesmen themselves—now pushed aside or murdered—and chief among them Nuri as-Said Pasha, the only *great* man of the Middle East in all those years. From the time of his youth in the Arab Movement his life was spent in the gradual construction of an Arab world as united as circumstances allowed. Policy is the art of the possible, and he moved within those limits. He will be recognized, even by his own people, when histories are written and these storms are over. To me, for more than a generation, he was a friend. I saw him last the year before his murder, in Baghdad, and asked about the future of Iraq. "It will be safe," he said, "if we can keep it quiet for ten years and let the middle class dig itself in. But can we?" He laughed. He had a young laugh with a sudden glance of blue eyes that usually seemed to sleep under tired pockets of darkened skin and eyelid. With his slight figure and the boyish charm that never left him he was yet an old and fragile man, and Kassem need have waited only a year or two for all he wanted.[1]

---

[1] Many rumours were current as to the manner of Nuri's death. Lord Birdwood (*Nuri as-Said*, p. 267) says little but is as accurate as possible, while James Morris in his brilliant but rather heartless sketch, *The Hashemites,* is not very informed. Iraqi sources which seemed to me reliable said that Nuri tried his telephone on this black morning, and found it cut: immediately suspicious, he made his way to a friend's house on the river bank below and found that telephone also cut. They put two and two together and went upstream to Mu'addham to friends who for some reason were

To describe the recent Iraqi revolution as a conflict of the new and the old is, I think, accurate only in part. English accounts have mostly been written by people unversed in the Mesopotamian background who do not see under the modern catchwords that pendulum-swing of murder, ancient and long familiar, which has made the pattern from the day when the first Ali was stabbed in Cufa and probably long before. Even the massacre of the Prophet's family is no novelty on that soil. How much of this story was private revenge I suppose no one will ever know.

During my last visit, in 1957, so many years later, I saw the young King. He was very gentle, dignified and small, standing by a vast desk among the shadows of his room and the greater shadows of his long history, 'the future stirring with such dim uncertain forces,' I wrote with some strange foreboding. He had kept the gentleness of manner of all the Hashemites, and a charming trustfulness in the kindness of his world; and as we spoke of his country—how to make it one land for peasant and effendi—it was like watering thirsty ground, he was so anxious to learn and do. Many centuries of tradition had gone to his making, of which I had known the last three generations, and thought of them as I came away: his grand-

---

unable to shelter the Pasha for long. He then drove, with a woman's black cloak as disguise and still with his friends, to another house in the Sa'dun quarter (on the left bank), where also there was no hiding place for him. They decided to try another friend, returned to the waiting car or taxi, and found the usual small group of loungers with a few children collected. In the maze of the new suburban streets and the usual Baghdad absence of addresses, they had to ask the way. By this time the wireless was blaring out advertisement and incitement against Nuri. In his impatience he broke into the discussion with a question, and a child said "but that is a man's voice, not a woman's". Whether Nuri shot first or a soldier who happened to be there, I did not hear.

The account of his burial I heard from Pat Domvile who was in a house opposite the North Gate cemetery and saw it. In the dusk after the curfew, with no one about, the new government sent his body to be put quietly but decently in the ground. Next morning, just before dawn, Pat was awakened by a noise and saw about forty men, most of whom he knew. They were practically all, he told me, connected with Rashid Ali and 'The Golden Square'. They dug up fourteen bodies in the cemetery before coming upon what they wanted (and this incidentally suggests that there was no collusion with the people who had buried Nuri the night before). When they at last found him, they threw him on to the road, made the passing cars drive over him, and treated the poor dead body with all the savagery for which Iraq in her long history has ever been notorious.

mother's exquisite Arabic, her erect little figure wrapped in an ermine stole in the serai palace now abandoned; and the other one in King Ali's house on the river, where the children played in house or garden and practically never came out at all and a huge eunuch kept the key; and then the gentle, good mother, widow of King Ghazi, in her new palace near the Damascus road, where she could walk about freely and—in a room clustered with silver mosques in glass cases and orange trees worked with gold fruit in filigree silver —the little boy would come with the same gravity and beautiful manners to greet the guests.

It is a long way from 1941, though the tragic end is never quite out of sight in Iraq. Methods which have sprouted under Kassem were there in the 1940's, and many young people who joined us soon left us, because at all costs we kept them from violence. '*Build*, and let the abuses die in their own time and of their own accord.' Hours and days were spent on this theme, and the endless repetition lost us many adherents, though it kept out of prison such as remained.

In a country like Iraq there were many difficulties—tribes and townsmen whom one had never thought of as coming together, and the schism of Sunna and Shi'a, as well as minorities Kurd, Christian, Jew, Yezidi—explosive nerve centres we tried to irritate as little as we could. As in Egypt, we went through anxious months with our own side, walking on a knife-edge while our numbers grew to such a level as would make them more difficult to disband than to keep on. What saw us through was the enthusiasm of Iraqi friends, the friendliness of the English Political Officers whether they believed or not, the willing ardour of our little office, which really has the credit of the toil, and above all the fact that what we were saying to the people of Iraq was genuinely in their own interest. In the years after the war the stream of such intercourse dwindled. 'If Nuri could have made fuller use of his publicity,' Lord Birdwood writes, 'he could have had the public behind him.'[1] I believe this to be true.

By the summer of 1942 we had visited every group of any size in the whole country. We had jolted in a most uncertain car over the sandy levels, ending the day in some town where a canal wanders through the High Street and the gardens are packed behind blind

---

[1] *Nuri as-Said* by Lord Birdwood, p. 277.

mud walls. There, round three sides of a crowded room, coffee was drunk, and tea in little glasses; the governors, doctors, judges, school inspectors, sat at the upper end; speeches were made and poems recited. Sometimes, when the war news became no longer a deterrent, people got in whose motives were not so pure; but mostly we came into a gentle atmosphere, a great and untutored anxiety to do well. I made my speech in Arabic, taking whatever point seemed most appropriate to prepare a body of decently disinterested public opinion for the days of peace. I explained how it had been done in England, in Anglo-Saxon villages centuries ago, through small groups such as these: how they had grown to send their delegates to London, and how this same living relationship between government and governed is what the young of every nation have to create in their own land.

Many pictures remain in my mind from these visits. The date groves of Kerbela where pomegranates, vines, oranges and roses are tangled among palms, and the dates slashed down on yellow shiny stems fall with a spatter of fruit on to strips of sacking, and the women in their black bundled clothes carry them to the donkey's waiting panniers: or the holy places, where the teachers of the Shi'a sit with their acolytes around them in old houses of pale yellow brick with turquoise woodwork, on dim alleys too narrow for wheels; holy men swathed in creamy draperies and turbans—nearly all Persian by origin—they lived in an atmosphere of intrigue, theology and greed. When they got very old they were run by their sons and disciples, sallow and fat with want of exercise, though sometimes one saw the delicate ascetic Persian face. They had no furniture but a cushion or two on the floor, and books in niches of the walls, rush matting or carpet, and behind that apparent simplicity a fierce contest for power, unimaginably contained in the same frontiers as the hill villages of Kurdistan where the chief rode out on horseback to do one honour with all his men behind him, his turban jaunty with tassels and a rifle on his back. Or the creeks of Basra where the long thin *bellams* slid like snakes under the palm trees, where the heads of our groups talked perfect English, and democracy was fostered by the ancient traditions of commerce and the sight of sea-going ships. Or the strange southern land of the marshes, where houses are built of reeds and men go from one shallow island to another by watery avenues between the knotted stems: or the middle Euphrates where there was always trouble, from floods or murders or wars, but the men who liked you were good friends for all that: or the towns of Mosul, Erbil, Kirkuk and all their districts, ancient lands in the north, green and carpeted with flowers, whose cornlands sweep over mounds that cover the forts and villages of the Assyrian dead.

To many who do not know this country's history, and to myself in moments of despondency, it seems now that most of our labour was wasted, with the murders of the immediate past and (no doubt) future in our mind. The Brothers after I left the Middle East thinned to an intelligentsia in Iraq, but not in Cairo, where they rose to sixty thousand and were only disbanded with the abrogation of the Anglo-Egyptian Treaty when fighting had broken out in the Canal Zone in 1952. In Iraq, in spite of Peggy's continued success with the women, the intake—lacking the broad pyramid base of our rather promiscuous earlier assortment[1]—declined to a trickle and died; and the passion for politics as opposed to construction, the constant nemesis of that unhappy land and the menace we had chiefly struggled to avert, swept back with its age-old familiar froth of violence. Into this later history I have no need to go.

---

[1] Christopher Scaife and I disagreed on this policy and I mention this here because I think the apparently more reasonable and fastidious academic trend is a dangerous one in the Middle East. Christopher is now a brilliant teacher at Beirut University where discrimination does nothing but good; but in the outer jungle of Middle East politics where the gulf between intelligentsia and public is already far too great, the education of the *whole* and not of the educated alone seems to me essential. Any movement based solely on the intelligentsia becomes, I believe, either unbalanced or so anaemic that it dies: and this is what happened in Iraq.

9
End of a Chapter

In the spring of 1943, before leaving the Middle East, I made several journeys, of which the farthest was to India, at Field-Marshal Wavell's request. 'There will always be a room for you in our house,' he had written from New Delhi in July '42, 'and I am sure it would be a good thing from the propaganda point of view if you saw a little of India's problems . . . So do try and come.'

This enticement had to be resisted, but a visit to be combined with an exploration of Brotherhood possibilities in Persia was agreed for the April following. Threatened at the last moment by the higher priority of generals who very nearly caused my three weeks to be spent in a Basra hotel, the pilot of our aircraft saved me by off-loading fourteen gallons of petrol and taking me on instead; and with this exact knowledge of my physical displacement I landed three days later in Gwalior and saw for the first time the richness and the colour of India. The Middle East, separated from us by language, is yet, by culture, tradition, and even religion, a part of our own stream; but the Mogul palaces dreaming in stone with their prisons beneath them, the tombs with their eclectic ornaments—Victorian lamp-posts carved true to every detail in stone—the brilliant tints after the black and white of Arabia, all opened a world unexpectedly remote. I spent three weeks of delight in a house filled with those who later, when I returned to India at the very end of the war, were to become among the dearest of my friends.

To drive back overland seemed to be the most economical as well as the most interesting way of making a report on Persia, and I bought a car. The Field-Marshal and all his A.D.C.s insisted on a driver as far as Quetta, where Johnnie Hawtrey was to join me for what he (mistakenly) thought of as a few weeks' rest; the Irish sergeant who attended to these things procured more spare tyres than

END OF A CHAPTER

I dare to mention; and I drove through the fertile Punjab that rises and falls to its rivers, where the cultivation thins or thickens as water is near or far—from Lahore by the tombs of Multan, rich places padded with a natural prosperity as far back in their past as one can look.

On the third day I reached the Indus, iridescent like mother of pearl, where we waited for forty-eight hours and played bridge in a blinding climate while guards were posted to protect the road through Baluchistan. The gigantic tribesmen shouldered their rifles, dressed in rich colours with the empty mountains and the sky behind them; they stood a few hundred yards one from the other, like an avenue, to guard the solitary car. It is a memory of empire in its greatness. At night I was entertained in lonely places—not forgetfulness but only space prevents my recording the hospitality and kindness of people on my way. In Quetta Johnnie appeared, insisted on driving himself, and we entered eastern Persia by skirting Afghanistan.

Tyres at that time cost £300 each, and it was the sergeant's spares that saw us through. They also contributed a danger, for they would be stolen at a mountain corner and the traveller left, if alive, with no wheels for his journey. Perhaps for this reason, no other civilian car was travelling on our way as far as we knew. But we now came into the military stream of help to Russia, that panted up from Karachi day and night: a river of metal flowed north across the wastes of the Persian borderland. By the end of the third day we reached Meshed and relaxed, and the Skrines, old friends at the Consulate there, took us to the Imam Riza's tomb, the holiest place in Persia, where the Governor was their friend.

From here on, the Teheran road was impassable because of floods: rather than risking a three weeks' wait, we made the six hundred miles or more back to the Baluchi frontier, took 'the first turning on the right', and crossed two salt deserts to Isfahan. In that lonely corner, near the district where an American party has recently been killed by bandits, an unusually sharp pebble pierced our tank. We had a driver for this mountain stretch, and he patched the hole with a paste of dates while providence sent a colonel of the Sappers. He had a R.E.M.E., he said, about two hundred miles ahead. Johnnie, by this time, was despondent, seeing a court-martial at the end of an overstayed leave; but the colonel's R.E.M.E. mended and set us (with one more spare tyre) on our way; we slept at Kerman in the peacock-tiled Consulate—now abandoned—and at Yezd beside the Parsees' towers of silence; until we again relaxed in Isfahan. It was probably an easier road to travel then than ever before or since.

The golden gates of Meshed have a rosy sheen, like lustre ware, and—seen in the cold and rainy spring, with men in ragged felts or *pushtins* (sheepskin coats) clustering along the water-course that cuts the square below them, they have a fine feeling of central Asia, the northern Muslim one imagines in Bokhara or Samarkand. But Isfahan is like a pale torquoise, its tree stems white, its sky light blue, a lovely skiey light about it all. In the fields around are huge circular towers like keeps, merely built to house innumerable pigeons. The whole of Isfahan gives the feeling of a great deal of labour and loveliness and thought spent on the light, airy, evanescent side of things. It was fun going about the bazaars where the carpets, miniatures and stamped patterned coverlets are made by tiny boys with long eyelashes bending over their fine brushes and bright paints.[1]

The history of my car caused some scandal, for I sold it for a splendid profit as soon as I got to Teheran, having omitted (by ignorance and not intention) to get the diplomatic permit to which I was entitled. There were all sorts of hindrances for people who came through with permits but none, naturally, for those who came without. Once already I had asked in vain in Baghdad for a car; I had bought one for the necessities of our office and had paid for it myself, though the office was allowed to rent it at army rates: this would have cost H.M.G. more in a year than the car had cost altogether, and it was only when we rather honestly pointed it out to them that the buying of the car was belatedly sanctioned. Like a human baby, a Government sanction even in wartime took nine months' gestation. Now, when I came curling round the Afghan corner, they would no doubt buy my car for what it had cost—and if on the other hand the bandits got it, my deficit and I would be left to do the best we could: so I was delighted when two Teheranis appeared who waved aside the absence of documents over

[1] Letter to G. de Gaury 28.4.43.

slim-waisted glasses of tea; and Johnnie and I divided the profit between us.

In Teheran, having planned a quick flight to Baghdad, we watched our aeroplane trundle from its hanger and subside, with one wing damaged, into a drain that gave way beneath it. We drove over the passes day and night with three equally belated army officers, and were back in the heat of Iraq in time for Johnnie to catch his aeroplane to Delhi. Never, he said, had he been so near a nervous breakdown before. He was the gayest of companions, and is dead.

To Owen Tweedy in Cairo I wrote a report which still seems relevant.

BAGHDAD *2 April 1943*

I arrived two days ago and found your letter waiting and am so touched by the kind and nice things you say. These are the wayside flowers on one's official path.

Now I have a huge letter to write to you: (1) about Persia; (2) about the work here; (3) about America in the autumn.

Persia: the fates provided a more or less comprehensive tour—one desert after another and no one about who wanted to be told about democracy, but I talked to the consuls in Meshed and Isfahan, and found both unanimous in saying that something on our lines was advisable and indeed urgent. In the Meshed district the Russians present a difficulty; it would mean taking a rather careful line! On the other hand, if something is not done soon, the whole place *will* go Russian; it is already going anti-British at a great rate. In Isfahan the consul told me there is a large industrial population now beginning to become self-conscious; also a number of rich and eager young men with nothing much to do; if these two sets of people are not attended to, they will very soon drift away into some other camp. Both consuls are ready to co-operate. In Teheran I found a great deal of pessimism. I don't mind if people refuse suggestions when they have some alternative, but it seems melancholy to confine oneself to negation. Sir Reader, however, also very depressed and tired out, talked about the Brothers and told me that, if it *could* be started, the thing might be good. The problem remains: *who* is to do the job?

The other thing I felt should be promoted in Persia to the fullest extent is the British Institute. The Persians are clamouring for it: for want of staff, thousands of eager learners of English have to be turned away: the students are excluded *en bloc*. This seems to me deplorable and

I can't see why, when everyone agrees on the urgency of a means of contact with the Persians, when there is a channel which they themselves are clamouring for, and when the only requisite is a sufficient number of elementary teachers of English—I can't see why this cannot be provided; one hundred men would make no difference to our armies and might do a very great deal of good in Persia. It is a question of getting the C. in C.s to co-operate in extracting the suitable men. Mr. Holman has written a very urgent memorandum and perhaps something may develop. I know this has really nothing to do with us, but our object, after all, is the same and, personally, if someone else can reach it more easily than we can, I am all for helping them to do so. The British Insitute could be got going with no difficulty and at once, and its influence if it were started everywhere, in big towns and small, could be felt within three months or so of its starting.

In Iraq the Brothers are in the full crisis of their growing pains and much in the state in which they were in Egypt in 1941, with the difference that here, unlike Egypt, we have a British administration spread all over the country. What you tell me about the importance of working in with it I agree with most fully. I have kept in friendly touch with all the politicals in the districts where I, myself, started committees; the only one I neglected to keep fully informed was Colonel A. of the middle Euphrates where the Brothers generated themselves of their own accord. This was very stupid of me and like the fairy-tale, where all the fairies were invited to the christening except one, who caused trouble (not that Colonel A. is a wicked fairy, because he is rather a dear). The truth, however, seems to me to be a real difficulty which needs more than just tact to clear up. The country at present is being run and kept in hand perfectly satisfactorily by a network of politicals backed by our armies: in this scheme our Brothers, difficult to discipline, full of inconvenient zeal and altogether non-official, are definitely a nuisance and—as things are at present—unnecessary. Their usefulness will come when and if we have to withdraw our armies and our politicals: then an Iraqi network, loosely organized and friendly to ourselves, could be very useful indeed. The question is whether the administrators are willing to put up with this inconvenience now in view of a future need. It is a problem which never occurred in Egypt because there were no British administrators (though when we did come up against any, i.e. the police, we had difficulties of exactly the same sort).

This is the fundamental question to answer. There is, however, a legitimate ground of complaint against the Brothers at the moment, as they are not nearly sufficiently supervised. This has been owing to my illness, which was most ill-timed, and absence, and G.'s not yet being experienced enough. What is quite obvious is that Iraq needs very much closer personal contact than Egypt and I would give anything to have someone experienced like Ronnie Fay to help me out here. However, I hope that a series of visits and meetings will provide a concentrated training and shall do all I can.

My visit to America I am most interested in. I gather I am wanted in September. This is a very long letter, my dear Owen : I hope you can read it to the end. I have come back very much better, though my trouble hovers and pounces still at intervals : but I think I should carry on now for the half of the summer. It is extraordinary how I revive as soon as I breathe the mountain air : it has an effect like champagne !

CAIRO 5 *May 1943*

My dear Freya,

I read your Persian impressions with real interest. It is not easy to comment. My own feelings are those of Lord Allenby's maxim, 'Step by Step', and I would prefer to feel that our feet were firmly on the ground in Iraq before we start expanding in Iran. It's not that we oughtn't to go there. I believe that we ought. My doubts are whether we can, and your comments on your Brothers in Iraq strengthened my apprehension. We are all at our wits' end for staff and when I was talking to the D.A.G. a week ago, he said he was desperate and that he hoped we would think twice before expanding . . . You know what I mean and think. I have talked on these lines with Christopher who, on the whole, agrees. But as I read your Persian letter and today your account of mid-Euphrates, off to Mosul, then four more towns—I was feeling more interested in you yourself than in the Ikhwan in Iraq. You seem bent on burning yourself out and that with your American tour to face in the autumn. You do know, don't you, that it is going to be a great strain on you physically . . . ? I know I am talking sense. Will you think it all over and then write to me with plans?

Owen Tweedy's friendly advice was followed in all except the matter of a rest, and that was unattainable : I had to visit outlying committees so as to leave as clear a field as possible behind me, and the next few months were spent in travelling from one flat, dusty, mud-brick townlet to another, divided by empty desert stretches and almost exactly alike. I slept in nearly every little centre in the country. The palm-trees thinned out to corn and then to bareness and back to corn, and only the river brought variety, looping in wide flood loops, brimming to the curb of its banks, and sometimes seeping through.

We had to make a detour of twenty miles, cutting over ditches and cornfields to miss the flooded patches. I passed by Ur of the Chaldees to Basra, and then up by Qurna near the two rivers[1] meeting at what was supposed to be the site of Eden, where a little committee of ours now sits on a terrace over the river, overhung with vines: then up the Tigris, with towns of the marshes along its banks. That strange region stretches, thirty or forty miles wide in meandering length, with island settlements at its fringe, but at heart nothing but a solitude of water, where forests of reeds grow intersected by waterways that only the marshmen know—clear water, or carpeted with lilies and flowers that sway on gentle waves. The rivers bring muddy silt into this clean world and every year a little more wet land is built up by hand, pushes out into the marsh, is cut by small straight channels, and grows rice. This process, they say, was the origin of the Genesis account of the creation. The people build their reed huts on the solid islands, beginning with sheaves of the tall stems—ten feet or more; they tie them in arches and roof them with mats of the plaited leaves, and they look, inside, in their twilight, like the aisles of churches opening on to the water. One moves between them in shallow, wide boats studded with nails, black like gondolas and I believe with some kinship to them. I had a last day with one of the great sheikhs who are now immensely rich with all the rice they sell; and we took five boats with five men in each rowing; upstream, they leaped out and towed us, running with light steps along the bank in and out of the intersecting channels.

These people are very friendly and stayed with us all through the troubles of 1941. Every day I make a speech in Arabic on democracy, and listen to a speech or poem, and talk to new members of my people—lawyers, doctors, teachers, the sub-governor, carpenters, builders, a dozen or more labourers, and a sheikh of the *bedawin*: such have never sat in one committee before. It is moving to meet them: so ready we are with material help, so slow to see how far more support the spirit needs, wavering and uncertain.[2]

[1] Tigris and Euphrates.
[2] Letter to Lucy Beach.

END OF A CHAPTER

The most remembered of the journeys was the northern tour through Kurdistan, a country I did not know and now visited with my earliest friend in Iraq—Muhammad Baban—whose ancestor in the 1780's had founded the capital and called it after his own father Suleiman. The dome of his tomb is shown there among the rough and undistinguished slabs of the other graves.

On a dusty April day we left Baghdad—the air like damp underwear and the tired spring colours of Iraq, jade green, white sky, pale sand, melting into each other with a charm of fragile horizontal lines like those faint pencil marks drawn by artists round sketches of sheep, perhaps, with a man in an abba before them. It is the secret of Iraq —that it looks so much more like a sketch than a photograph: a point or two is marked and the rest left fluid in dust.

Out of this patterned and travelling dust emerged Baquba and its bridge; the gardens of Shahraban; the similar ones of Karaghan. The names grew Turkish; the country rose subtly in differences of movement as between lake and sea. Wheat and barley were still poor for want of rain, and flowers, all but hollyhocks, were over; but the bee-eaters no longer looked startling as in Baghdad, like foreign jewels against the sand. They flickered naturally among the equally variegated colours of their background.

Towns stood here on mounds of departed generations: Kifri, Tauq (bird), Tuz-Khurmati (salt and apricot); each had its river running to it from the hills. We drew water at a village carved into a mound while sunset lay yellow over the thinly grown downs in a pale metallic sky and on a British landing-ground where the army was widening the road. The crocodile mouths of block-houses were scattered about the land, preparing the defences of Mosul.

Three and a half hours from Kirkuk, eastward over little hills, the flowers began: tufts of blue salvia, iris in the ditches, anemones red and presently white; and we came to Derbend, the gate of Kurdistan, and a white boulder just below it, where after long guerrilla wars Sheikh Mahmud was captured by us in 1919. He now lived in exile near by. Sheikh Ahmed Barzan and Jafar Sultan were also—and for the same reasons—in exile in Suleimaniya: we had fought all these chiefs during the mandate years.

We dipped from the Derbend into their lovely land, locked in snowy hills, rich in small clear streams, where the grape hyacinth lined the damper meadows. Everyone here rode with a gun; they dressed in felt coats or a few velvet, with barrel trousers cut in narrowing seams to taper at the ankle for riding.

The Suleimaniya road had been made only some ten years before this time. A deep ditch protected the town from waters pouring down the hills, and the one-storeyed houses had earth roofs supported on rough poles against the dripping of the snow. The low *subs* were like a north-Italian market in a small town, selling charcoal, heaps of corn, barrels of rice, white and good bread, socks knitted in Fair-Isle patterns, cottons, Japanese home-made cotton shoes and tongs and hammers to deal with the solid cones of sugar that hung, wrapped in blue paper, in the booths. The people were friendly and there were thousands of swallows.

Here we lunched while the brother and son of Sheikh Mahmud arrived to call, girt round with cartridges wherever cartridges could go. The brother had a charming weather-worn face with a sensitive mouth which quivered a little when he was amused, and tassels on his turban. The son was an effendi with hair *en brosse*, and the effendi's parrot cry that all is the fault of the English—even the fact that the Kurds cannot unite. They swung away with their guns slung round them and we too were off, across the gently-dipping, green, flower-splashed plain of Shahr-i-Zor, which is dotted with grassy mounds probably important in Islamic times—the Persian frontier like a wave on our left, sugared with snow and running more or less even in the gnawed horizon of Avroman. Poppies, anemones, ranunculi, pink campion, and, in the corn, blue vetch and sheets of borage among the flowers. From a height above Halabja as the sun sank we saw long comb-like ridges, the plain beautiful with mirrored water-patches, the flocks trailing home among the darkening gardens.

[*Diary*]

The house of Adela Khunum,[1] famous in the First World War, is dilapidated in the middle of Halabja. There is a photograph of her and her

[1] A constant friend to the British, this Lady of Halabja was a great character in the early days after the occupation of 'Mesopotamia' in the First World War.

two sons, one living still, small boys held by the hand while she looks out with wide eyes from a Mongol face, open, intelligent (or rather sensible), and full of character. Her house 'with mothed and dripping arras hung' is crumbling: the outer portico where the guards lounged is filled with chicken-coops, the upper portico—where Soane[1] sat as a Persian scribe forty or less years ago—is derelict with just a bed here and there where the harim still lodges. There are three fine ceilings of mirror inlay held up on stalactite squinches, and one room with a good stucco frieze. From the windows, one looks over the flowery roofs to the garden, also ruined, and wide spaces beyond: it was all only built forty-two years ago and was left at Adela's death in 1924.

We stayed in Halabja, and rode across meadows to villages whose streams leap out of the last patches of snow beneath their cliffs, and lunched under mulberry trees by the water—the horses browsing and our escort shooting at an egg on a stick. We were a small company, with three men on horses with guns, and about four on foot. At *chaikhanas* (tea houses) or by the springs where sycamores spread their shade, all stood up to salute our host, Hasan Beg. As I rode on in the sun I thought of Huxley's *Grey Eminence* which I happened to be reading, and how 'annihilation' comes through the sight of beauty and through love (only some loves, alas) and how—as far as I am concerned—the sight of a snow horizon gives me that happiness of almost non-existence! The Avroman ran in a long wave, and the downs in a grassy wave before them; and we returned to Suleimaniya by way of Penjwin.

[*Diary*]

At tea at the *Mutasarrif*'s the Mirza Faraj's wife and daughter sailed with tribal pomp into our European drabness. The dresses give an Elizabethan effect and Miss Mirza altogether is Venetian Renaissance and might have walked out of the Doge's ceiling or with a gold and blue ribbon under her chin like Beatrice d'Este. The curve and shine of a raven's wing showed her hair under her turban. The Mirzas, though mere merchants and nothing in comparison to the sheikhs, Jafs, and Babans, added to the gaiety of the party. Miss Mirza told me she stands before her glass and enjoys herself by looking at her dress—a harmless pastime. After two and a half hours at the *Mutasarrif*'s we called on Dr.

---

[1] See his book *Through Mesopotamia and Kurdistan in Disguise*.

END OF A CHAPTER

Georges, a Greek tossed here four years ago in his small Odyssey. The Greek-British flags were painted over his chimney and a red rose V for Victory below the portraits of our King and Queen. He has forty relations in the Greek army, whose fate is unknown, but he spoke of the future and left the past. He had come from Istanbul and gone to Athens, thence to Paris and Baghdad and eventually to this little haven, as good as any while it lasts. We came back at 10.15 to meet Jafar Sultan (the exile) who can only call on 'important people' at night because then the police don't know. His son brought him tottering, seventy-nine, very deaf, but full of determination. It is harassing to be treated as 'important people' in Kurdistan, where every word is explosive and one feels that one can do little good at the moment and might easily do harm. The fighting just across the Persian border is sending electric shocks all over this country. The Kurds do nothing but ask to be taken over by Britain, and nothing is less likely for Britain to do. All one can say is that it is obviously a British wish that hill regions should be quiet and happy while the Caucasian front draws nearer; and that if the war comes, the Kurds will no doubt help in the fighting and improve their case. As one feels it to be an excellent case already, it is rather depressing.[1] Old Jafar Sultan counted fifteen sons killed by Persians, two in prison in Kermenshah, seven in Suleimaniya, six in Kirkuk, and has been an exile for twelve years. His son has the same sort of long sunken face with sad eyes and a gentle look. At 11.30 they left and I went to bed almost sick with fatigue and the strain of these delicate subjects in my imperfect language; Persian is far easier to them than Arabic.

We drove out in Sheikh Latif's beige Hudson to lunch with Sheikh Mahmud, over fields patched with purple lilies, the kind of which the Persians make a tisane. Far away, in sight, rise the hills along the way to Kifri, Sheikh Mahmud's permanent residence now, with trees here and there. He is visiting his ruined estate here—houses burnt, inhabitants fled—and has only just been allowed back and Latif had a twenty-four-hour permission to visit his father. Our going was not welcomed (behind our backs). The meeting was rather pathetic—the robust old Sheikh, about sixty-three, shows some signs of age, a plumpish figure and lines about the eyes—but as full of fight as ever, and his followers in a group beside him, most of them with something on some black-list, their baggy homespun faded from brown almost to white in the sun, their bulky sashes faded too, their guns and cartridge-belts round them. The tent, a poor affair, belonged to the village. It was a delight to look out again on a

[1] Iraq policy towards the Kurds improved greatly after the war.

houseless landscape framed by the black woollen roof and slanting ropes and poles; a single line of hovels ran behind, mud-roofed and walled into a stony hill. The Sheikh was in dark green, with a black-dyed moustache and face round like his son's, and a round button of a nose that gave him an engaging small-boy look. He had a sense of fun and friendly feeling for us, his old enemies, unmixed with any particular admiration for our politics. 'You make friends, you cherish them, you make them ready to do all for you, and then chuck them away.' But he admired our present policies. He made up a quatrain to describe how Satan, tormented in Hell, was allowed after many ages to approach the throne of Allah. Far from complaining, all he did was to give thanks to the Almighty. For what? 'For not having been created a Baghdadi.'

We sat chatting for an hour and, Arabic not being popular, I struggled with Persian while our driver flung himself on Sheikh Mahmud's hand and kissed it, though I had no idea he was a Kurd. After lunch I talked to Khanem Ayesha, his wife, a kind old face and hands quite lovely, small and nervous; she uses them with exquisite elegance to take cigarettes from an old Persian box with silver scrolls of flowers. Across her turban and under her chin are ancient coins, some gold, some dipped in gold by the Kurds. Some are, I think, Seljuk; some Venetian like those the men of Hadhramaut wear on their daggers, some Hellenistic—but whether Greek, Parthian or Sassanian I don't know. They were found in two jars in Avroman. Somewhere the road must lie between the two Parthian capitals, from Takht-i-Suleiman to Ctesiphon, but where? I would like to spend a month or two discovering that range. The lady's head-dress proves that the settlements were not only Islamic, and probably went from pre-classic to Mongol times, like those of Luristan.

We reached John Chapman[1] in Kirkuk to hear that the death sentences on four of the 1941 rebels are to be carried out at dawn. It is still being kept quiet. Shansal is included, and I think of his horrid voice on their wireless gloating over our approaching end. Sad world that makes one welcome people's death. I also heard that I was made gold medallist by the R.G.S:[2] can't think what for, but delighted all the same.

Some ten months after this visit John Chapman, who even now long after his death is loved by the Kurds and still remembered, wrote: 'success in battle is soon forgotten, but you are building up

[1] The Political Officer.
[2] The Founder's Medal awarded for journeys in Persia and South Arabia and for my books.

something that will live': sad irony in view of Iraq now. Meanwhile I took a last day in the north with the sheikhs of the Shammar. They shot bustard and raced gazelle round the ruins of Hatra, where a few spare *bedawin* tents alone were propped beside the Parthian wells.

★ ★ ★ ★

Our Brotherhood was now well started on its way to peace. Our office was reported 'orderly, healthy and active', and it was hoped that our 'long-term views might receive consideration'.[1] In Cairo it was doing well with Christopher and Ronnie Fay devoted to it, and Eddie Gathorne-Hardy and Mary Berry new and excellent on our staff. Lulie Abu'l Huda was opening up the women's side in Palestine. In Iraq our numbers had nearly reached seven thousand and our committees had contributed £700 out of their own pockets. Yet we needed about six more people for our staff and were desperately in need of a good man to leave with Peggy after my departure. 'I'm beginning to look,' Owen Tweedy wrote from Cairo, 'into the future as it may unroll itself in this Middle East of ours. The future is a curious customer and you can't make rules . . . All you can do is to marshal your forces. When you have time, let me know what you think not only from the Brotherhood standpoint but from a more general one, embracing a world which will be extremely severe financially.'

22 February 1943

My dear Freya [Iltyd Clayton wrote from Cairo],

I've been quite amused at Nuri's telegrams and letters (on Arab unity) and am bound to say I find myself largely in agreement with them. If only he would not allow his higher political ambitions to distract his attention from the more humdrum but at the moment more necessary task of administering his country and extracting from the occidentals as much as possible, he would have all my sympathy. What a tangle we are in in Arab countries. We got into it in 1918 and don't look like getting out of it. I think they will quite likely cut the Gordian knot or knots

[1] From the Middle East Bureau, Cairo, to the Middle East Sections of the Ministry of Information in London.

themselves after the war and I doubt if the great British public will be prepared for further wars in order to impose untruthful policies. I think far saner and more objective views of all Middle Eastern questions would be taken if people would keep in mind one or two maxims. Firstly one must choose the right yardstick to judge these countries by. It is no use using the Indian Civil Service or the Sudan Civil Service ... one should take the Balkan States, or Portugal or Central America, or even French recent form. Judged by these standards they do not come out so badly. Secondly the Levant and Egypt, and to a large extent Iraq, is not oriental —they look to the West and, incidentally, all the Western ethics came from the Levant. We have a lot of history in common. Thirdly it is fatuous to say that they are not capable of idealism or sacrifice for a cause. They are corrupt, rather inefficient, prone to nepotism, but they *can* be inspired. The three great religions of the West had their origin within a few hundred miles of each other in the Middle East—and it wasn't crass materialism that enabled about two thousand odds and ends to tie up two divisions and 24,000 police in Palestine for a couple of years. And all this goes for Jews as well as Arabs. Lastly, is the state into which Western ideas, culture and progress have landed Europe anything to write home about? I think myself that we are the salt of the earth but am sometimes faintly surprised at others thinking so too. Lots don't. We must avoid smugness—rather a national failing, though perhaps a useful one. Now I'll get off my horse again. Today is the foulest day I've ever known in Cairo, blowing a gale and pouring with rain. Economy has removed all stoves and I am sitting in my office in a greatcoat.

The future and the peace were in our minds, and a great anxiety to avoid past mistakes now that the English reputation stood once again so high. We realized above all that a time of great economy must lie before us. 'No overlapping will be allowed,' I wrote, 'yet there should always be *two* sets of contacts in each of these independent countries—one official with those in power and the other non-official with those who are out: otherwise an unfriendly opposition will always be growing up, merely because we are exclusively identified with its opponents. This has often happened in the past, and it is essential to remedy it.

'The official contacts are made by the diplomats and it seems to me that much facile and undeserved blame is poured upon this service: the British Institutes and a sufficiency of good teachers should provide the unofficial contacts as far as the youth problem requires with no further addition at all. *We* deal with the next stage, and take on chiefly young men whether official, army, political, labourer or peasant;[1] and this influence should continue independently of who is in power, *provided it is kept well out of politics.*' With many other cherished visions, this proved a dream after the ending of the war.

* * * *

When the day for departure came I was sad to leave. In spite of grief, and illness growing upon me, these years had been happy in their private brightness against the stormy background. Friendships had come in overflowing measure, and some, now dead, went very deep—Cornwallis and Bishop, Wavell and Clayton. The world is not so good without them. Love, too, had come, easy, but perhaps happy for that reason. It is, I think, an ungenerous heart that does not give itself in wartime, when men's mere physical hunger for women is so great. (This, incidentally, may be the chief virtue of the semi-military female services, though obviously not one for publication.)

The Baghdad scene had altered, though Nuri stayed unchanged at the head of affairs, suggesting 'that we take over a mandate for France and leave the Arabs alone'.

General Wilson had gone to Italy—'Mark, Patrick and self,' he wrote, 'accompanied by dogs, parrots, etc. It was almost like Barnum and Bailey's circus on the move. There is still no news as to who is to succeed me in Baghdad but there will be a lot of troops there all the same. I had literally to eat my way out through farewell lunches and dinners.'[2]

Hermione had left to go with them all to Caserta; and Nigel was soon to parachute into Greece.

---

[1] We had succeeded in forming three committees among the working men of Iraq, whose intercourse with the effendi was so scarce as to be almost non-existent. 'Though rudimentary now, they belong to a class which may develop quickly after the war, and they are important because they touch the large illiterate body of the country which it is very hard for effendi influence to reach.'

[2] Letter 27.2.43.

END OF A CHAPTER

Stewart was driving in July across the desert and took me by Syria and Lebanon through Palestine and Transjordan; thence I flew alone, from Cairo along the desert route, where tank tracks still showed round the salt pans of Aghaila and the cliffs of Mareth, to Algiers. The Sicily offensive was in progress, and the sea almost to its horizon was full of ships. Harold Caccia[1] and Roger Makins,[2] with our present Prime Minister,[3] had found themselves a villa flashing with mirrors, into which the former kindly rescued me from the squalor of the army transit hotel. I spent some ten days here where I met General Eisenhower and visited Tunis and Carthage. In those six weeks between Baghdad and the West I spoke to most of the political people, both English, American and Arab, in preparation for the American venture. Everyone helped me and increased my sorrow at going, and I finally left for London with my Middle Eastern picture fairly clear. For the last time I strapped into one of those naked Dakotas whose memory is cold and spiky metal; looked on Fez with its tanks and domes of coloured tiles as we flew above it; spent an evening in Gibraltar, comfortably illuminated, since the bright coast of Spain made the blackout useless; and flew in moonlight over the Atlantic, with the risk of Fokkers pursuing, in bitter cold and silence, through a 'vertical storm'. In the early dawn we landed in Cornwall on grass drenched with dew. England from the air had looked small as a cliff-bound nest rocked in the waves, filling one's silly heart with tears; in her strong toils of grace she holds us. The people I was returning to were my people. The things they love, little or great, short familiar words I, too, love and understand. A letter from Jock, a letter from Pam awaited me—Jock a captain now: 'What little bird or jungle communication made you promote me? What evenings we shall have when we sit consuming the last bottle of claret in the country.'

And Pam, trying hard to get into her 'dull head that Pat died the best death man can die—that he has escaped the clipping of his spirit during a perhaps successful middle age when power and position does such dreadful things to us. He's got a flying start, and I can't

[1] Serving with the Resident Minister North Africa.
[2] Assistant to the Resident Minister at Allied Forces H.Q. Mediterranean.
[3] Minister Resident at Allied H.Q. North-West Africa.

help feeling terribly excited about my own dying; but if I have long years to grow selfish and self-opinionated and blind, shall I find Pat among the lovely company he keeps? I look at your godson and think this funny, gay and over-energetic little boy is going to live for ever and ever with the same excited twinkly look in his eyes and the same desire to do something funny to make one laugh: now it is only a silly face or noise.'

This was home, that spins our private time and space into eternity; and its comforting warmth, however bombed or weather-beaten, closed my first years of war.

PART TWO

10

Passage to America

In approaching the controversial landscape of Zionism one must bear in mind the basic rule that a part is not a synonym for the whole. Zionism is a part only of Jewry and the distinction must never be forgotten, all the more so since it often suits an advocate to see it blurred. The opponent of Zionism may be an anti-Semite: but he may just as easily not be so. In 1943 there was no anti-Semitism in British opposition: there was indeed so much sympathy for the Jews as such that it impeded our natural defences against what had already brought about an Arab war and was now threatening Anglo-American relations. The Zionist campaign at this time was aimed against Mr. Malcolm MacDonald's White Paper—produced in 1939[1]—to limit Jewish immigration into Palestine to twenty-nine thousand for the time being. It did not close the door for the future; but it was hoped that the small, harassed and explosive country might be given time to recover from what I described on my U.S.A. tour as 'indigestion'. The main point, however, about the White Paper was a stipulation that after the admission of the twenty-nine thousand any further immigration was to take place *only with the acquiescence of the majority*—i.e. the Arabs, who were there in the ratio of about two to one. It therefore stressed the principle of consent as against coercion, and the question really was whether or no the population of a country has a right to decide the matter of its own immigration. Britain was ready and willing to help the Zionists *as far as she could do so with the consent of the Arabs and no further*. There was no anti-Semitism in this attitude: it took away nothing from the general admiration for the Jewish achievement:

[1] When he was Secretary of State for the Colonies. In 1941 he had been appointed High Commissioner in Canada.

but it was a clear issue on a principle which—like so many others —we had allowed many extraneous sentiments to blur.

I had felt strongly on this subject for many years—as did most of the English men and women who, having come out to the Levant to look into the problem for themselves, thought that to force immigrants on a people at the point of a bayonet was an injustice which no other consideration could condone.

The Arab side of the question is given in *East is West*, and the reader of the following chapters will, if he has patience, become familiar with it as we travel; in this book I concentrate on the *English* point of view. The Arab world had given us a break; they had shelved the Palestine struggle for the duration of the war; they regarded the White Paper as 'a solemn undertaking'; its infringement would cause certain trouble not only in Palestine but in the neighbouring nations of Arabia; it gave us our one, eleventh-hour chance to get back to that position of *speaking with conviction to people in their own interest* which is, as we have seen, the only safe basis of persuasion; and our Government having at last reached a firm conclusion, seemed determined to maintain it. The Zionists therefore shifted their whole impetus to the U.S.A., where they fought the White Paper knowing that England could not put through an Arabian policy in the teeth of her ally. In the long run they succeeded and the Middle East is what it is; the discrediting of the West is now fairly complete. But in 1943 it was felt that the almost total ignorance of the transatlantic public on Middle Eastern affairs was a danger that could perhaps be mitigated; it was serious enough at that time to be seen as a threat to our friendly relations; and I was sent—a puny David—to see what I could do: my inadequacy is perhaps a measure of ways and means in wartime.

'Women are strongest, but above all things Truth beareth away the victory,' Stewart wrote to me as I left; and in the middle of November 1943 I shipped on the *Aquitania*—stripped, of course, for war, and carrying five thousand troops to Halifax—or to the Pacific beyond—who knows? Their hammocks were slung deck below deck in our view as we went down for meals. They filled the one saloon with a sort of collective haze, in which only khaki wreathed in tobacco smoke and punctuated with faces seemed to exist with an amorphous temporary life. Over their heads, cleared now and then by eddies of the smoke, the *Aquitania*'s luxury ceiling appeared and hid itself; and it was this sight of former splendour under the stripping, a gilt bracket, a tattered skirting, a bit of painted doorway gone dark with unwashed touches, that gave us our atmosphere of squalor.

There were few women, nearly all with babies who seemed (by the carefulness of his instructions) to weigh heavily on our captain's mind; at all costs infants are sheltered to grow up for another war. Their pink little faces wrapped in shawls were inured twice a day to deck-drill, with officers helping mothers to arrange the cork jackets for two. The Atlantic howled by in its usual gruesome hurry, putty-green flecked with white. The sea-gulls dipped sideways, their round eyes fixed on food. The day rolled low in the sky from squall to squall.

A cabin for one had been arranged to hold four of us. It looked like a slum, with all we needed for six or seven days hung out on various strings; but the heart of it was sound, with helpfulness and kindness inside it; and its worst irritations were the luxury gadgets made for a single occupant, which wasted valuable room, and the icy threads of Atlantic air that seemed like ghosts to pass through solid metal, for the porthole was battened down from seven at night to seven in the morning for fear of submarines.

We were, we soon discovered, not in convoy at all. The *Aquitania* was so big and so strong that she could do better by herself and relied on secrecy and swiftness to get across. Like a greyhound through grass, or the poet's words through the generations, she sped night and day with her strong thudding heart, and the Atlantic waves with their sodden possibilities of death inside them flattened themselves against her. The sea—as we came towards its middle fastnesses—stretched into long wizened sinews and even its foam seemed grey like the storm-clouds above.

On the third or fourth day I developed acute appendicitis. I was not told what it was, but the pain was so violent that a doctor came and looked at me with a blank young face of panic inspired, I thought, by the awfulness of having to deal with a woman in this world of men—for the ship's hospital was full, and there were only orderlies about. They gave me what I was later told was M. & B., and explained that I had a gastric cold; I was exonerated from boat-drill and had the relief of thinking that, if necessary, I could now drown in a quiet independent way by myself. For the next three days I lay in my bunk, fed by kind companions with such few things as are suitable for appendicitis out of the menu of a troopship in war. I had books; and the horizon kept itself quiet below the port-hole; but the weary nights dragged minute by minute in an almost intolerable absence of air interspersed with icy intervals whenever one had to walk down the clanking corridors of metal, groaning and straining almost in darkness as they pulled us through the sea. I longed for seven o'clock and the opening of the port-hole, and the sight of the sullen wind-ripped grey! And lifting myself to look out over the sunless ridges, tried to remember the existence of the blue Mediterranean, the little journeys from harbour to harbour in ancient grooves, the well-worn Greco-Roman world. When we berthed in Halifax, late on the fourth evening of my illness, I felt suddenly as if nothing could keep me alive through another night; the doctor, increasingly worried, evidently felt about it as I did, and at 11 p.m. I was tucked in blankets on a stretcher and lifted down a gangway on to land.

The five thousand troops must have thought that some pampered general was being allowed ashore while they were battened down for another set of hours almost as uncomfortable as mine. Tier above tier from the huge ship's side their dim crowding faces lined the narrow slits of decks as they leaned out with cat-calls of annoyance; until, in a slanting drizzle, preceded by a lantern and with four men carrying the stretcher, my cortège appeared like the funeral of Sir John Moore at Corunna, surrounded by shadows and rain. The five thousand looked down in silence, the stretcher-bearers stumbled on, and the smooth flank of *Aquitania* lifted itself out of sight into the starless region of the elements where she belonged. I was now on a pleasantly quiescent cobbled street; lifted into an ambulance; transported to an infirmary; unwrapped by a kind and soothing nun; put into a four-legged bed, and operated on at two hours' notice. As the appendix had already broken, the chances of survival seemed small. But I passed through it all without a hitch, and was tottering about in a fortnight—a remarkable feat which surprised all except myself who knew nothing about it. It was due to skilled surgery and devoted nursing which I think of with gratitude often, and also perhaps to the unsurpassed unpleasantness of the Atlantic which prepares one with equanimity for any other trial.[1]

25 October 1943

Dearest Jock,

I can now say that I am well, but the best part of it is that it would have been well anyway. I felt that I had done what I most wanted and was leaving no great gap behind: like a child crossing stepping-stones, I had been helped on this side and now, if the last bigger jump remained, most hands I loved were waiting to catch me on the other; I felt I can't tell you how detached, fluid and gay, and went to sleep looking at the Euganean hills in the afternoon sun. If that had been the end, who could have complained? But I woke quite calm and collected and lay thinking that perhaps some day I might regret not having slipped away on so easy a moment.

Anyway my poor Ministry whose perpetual Utopia it is to make People behave like Files, must be very worried, for here am I not even in the *country* in which their schedule puts me. I am awfully happy and comfortable. The voyage was a nightmare. It appears that, battened down in that horrible cabin, I started talking in my sleep and was heard to say: 'Life is real, life is earnest, how I wish it weren't.'

My mind, inspired by the natural and beneficial effects of illness, ran on these lines. I wrote to Pam:

26 October 1943

I have day and night nurses, all young and gay with husbands in the air or navy; they are Protestants and do the trained work and the Sisters are Catholics and do the overseeing and it seems a perfect combination of Martha and Mary. In fact if one realized how important it is to have one's Opposite about, how easy the world would be. Instead of saying 'I am extravagant and I hate mean people', one would say 'I *must* have someone rather mean about me', and vice versa! You see how much pleasanter everyone would become.

The doctor brought me a little wireless and I listened to Tchaikovsky's fourth symphony. It is very grand, with massed trumpets blowing as it

[1] *The Geographical Magazine*, April 1954.

were out of a purple and tumultuous battlement of cloud. It seemed to stretch along the sky, clearing here and there to show, closely ranked into the distance under banners, the celestial armies: you could not see them, but you could see at points in the long line the sun catch the curve of the trumpets as they answered each other, army to army, round the zodiac and back into the dawn. The radio made noises which I took to be the powers of evil, but the great trumpets sounded unperturbed. In a sort of shadow below lay the long dim horizon of earth and a causeway easy and plain but with a bad surface leading up. And presently the sound of the trumpets was broken by a rather cheerful human clatter and a jeep came sputtering up the causeway. The officer got out of it with a dazed look, murmuring 'I've lost our battle. I thought we were scuppered.' Then he looked and he saw in what ranks he stood. Instead of armaments he saw the sanctuary of Power, and in the place where the guns should be massed he saw Light irresistible and where the fighter aircraft should be rising he saw flashing, in splendour unendurable, the never-surrendering heart of Love. And the angels nearest to him said: 'Welcome, stranger.' 'I'm not a stranger,' said the officer. 'I belong to the sector just down that causeway. But I seem to have lost my people. Something hit us and I thought we were done. It makes no odds. I can turn the old bus round and fight here just as well.' Then, with an extraordinary air of cheerfulness he turned to his jeep and the two or three men inside it: 'Turn her round, boys; look lively,' he said. 'We're not where we want to be, but it's all the same battle. It makes no odds at all.' Perhaps it ought to have been a tank, because you wouldn't use a jeep in actual fighting. Anyway it seems to me as true a story as most.

I had leisure to think of these things in general and wrote to my friends describing the hospital—torpedoed sailors washed up here and petted back to life, and the nuns with their high Gothic headdress and peaceful faces.

'They welcome you with human charity beautifully different from our Economic age... Of course one notices at once that the point of view is more reasonable than that of a government office; it is obviously the presence of religion—but how does this work itself out? The office sister here tells me that she had a protest from the shipping company for accepting a sick man at midnight with his papers not in order: she wrote back that she would always continue to accept sick men at her door who needed help and it was for the company to decide whether they paid for them or not (they have gone on paying).... I don't believe we *can* have civilization unless we accept, right through private and public, national and international life, the doctrine that we are responsible for the human beings we come in contact with. I have often wondered why the tribal society with all its poverty is, on the whole, so contented, and believe it is just this feeling of human responsibility. To lay down economic well-being for all by law does not seem to meet the need; one can't make goodness foolproof, and, if one began with *feeling*, the economic laws would inevitably follow. Perhaps the result will be the same, but it is very much cart before horse. The plan to feed all Europe shows a beginning in an empiric way—but I think the Sisters of St. Vincent have the real approach.'[1]

Have you read Arthur Bryant's *English Saga*? [I wrote to Robin Maugham.] It does seem to put its finger on our modern weakness—the fact that power and responsibility do not necessarily go together. Wherever this divorce occurs—i.e. in big concerns of shareholders in no direct relation with the men they employ—everything worth while goes to pieces. Well now, it seems to me that wherever we undertake to serve foreign nations, whether as governments or private people, we should do so with a feeling of responsibility for them. I mean that if a British engineer accepts a job on Egyptian railways he should feel so responsible that either his railway goes properly or he resigns.

This standard is reached quite often but not generally enough to give that status that one desires to British employment. An unkind book like Jarvis's *Oriental Spotlight*, written after thirty years in their service, should not be possible. If you made the feeling of responsibility so cardinal a principle of your centre[2] that it came to be counted on as a characteristic of every British official who is trained there, so that it grew to be recognized as the basis of our service—I believe it would help more than anything else to make us cherished in the world. There is a dreary commercial morality that says that so long as you do what you have undertaken it is all that is required (Cain's remark that he was not Abel's keeper). I have seen it doing frightful harm all over the Middle East and it seems to me that our first effort should be to make people feel that Abel's business is our business as soon as we get our living in his neighbourhood. I don't know if I have expressed this very adequately, but you will understand. . . .

[1] Letters to Henry Channon and Iltyd Clayton 11.11.43.
[2] M.E.C.A.S. in Lebanon which is still doing excellent work.

To Aidan Philips one of Bishop's young men in the house on the Tigris, I wrote on the same lines about his left-wing friends:

... to make of ourselves one nation again, a homogeneous people: I don't suppose anyone but the young left-wing people can do it—but, Aidan, they are terribly uneducated! I mean by that that when I look back on what I have had in life, a constant background of beauty, music and art and the understanding of lovely things, a constant intercourse with people of many different nations and an open doorway into the histories of the past—a sort of rich light illuminating everything with a variety of colours—and I look round, I see how few have been so fortunate: and it seems to me that it is just this richness of civilization which your young men need to make them fit for the delicate business of governing, which is after all nothing more nor less than the dealing with human souls. So, my dear Aidan, I shall settle in Asolo or whatever small ruin is left there, and you can bring your friends and have them mellowed in the atmosphere of an older tradition, which won't do them any harm at all; in fact it should rescue a few from that Moloch of a 'planned economic universe' which is the danger as well as the necessity of our age. We are trying to make everything foolproof—even how to be good—and to do that we have to build on the lowest common denominator in human nature: I can't think that that will lead us to the Communion of Saints, which seems to me still the only possible aim for civilization. Am I talking nonsense? I lie here watching the Canadian clouds blow a hurricane and wonder at the pattern of it all. I wonder if we shall bathe in Tigris ever again? Do you keep up the high standard of our bulletin?

My thoughts were still mostly on the far side of the Atlantic.

11 November 1943

My dear Peter [Coats]
    A school in England could not be got to take an interest in Shakespeare at a time when the air raids were particularly trying—till one day they reached this bit of *Macbeth* in their class:

> The night has been unruly: where we lay
> Our chimneys were blown down; and, as they say,
> Lamentings heard i' the air; strange screams of death,
> And prophesying with accents terrible

> Of dire combustion and confus'd events
> New hatch'd to the woeful time. The obscure bird
> Clamour'd the livelong night: some say the earth
> Was feverous and did shake.

The whole class became interested and the 'obscure bird' was received with broad grins. This is all out of a small book which also quotes a Japanese student's essay on the poems of A. E. Housman. 'I think Housman is quite right. We will do no good to anyone by dying for our country, but we will be admired and we all want to be admired, and anyway we are better dead.' Awfully difficult point of view to fight against!

A week later I was in New York, dazzled by what seemed to me one of the most exciting cities in the world: the blueness of the sky floated about its pencil buildings, and shops, taxis, all human affairs seemed to go on in deep canyon-beds of natural erosion rather than among the excrescences constructed by men. 'It is the only town where one's looks are drawn all the time away from the ground into the sky: the huge buildings are not too close together; they keep their individuality like the towers of San Gimignano or Bologna, and from the shadow of the streets you look to their sunlight and the long vistas of the avenues, and would not be surprised to see clouds trailing about their summits.[1]

Mrs. Otto Kahn[2] sheltered me in her kind and luxurious flat, where the huge outlines by the river looked at night like illuminated sponges, mystery and brilliance combined. The shops in those lean years made one delirious, and I liked the friendly people—the man who said, when I bought a suitcase, 'And I hope you'll come safe from your journey,' and the taxi-drivers whose family affairs one listened to as one went along. 'I live half-days still,' I wrote to Pam, 'but enough to be able to enjoy New York—fantastically beautiful in a Babylonian way and full of the unexpected. A friend of Momo's was stopped in the street by a student "developing his personality", who asked would she mind talking to him as his teacher had told the class to collect eight interviews, each off strangers. The taxi-men talk to you like pure Arabs; the shops are

---

[1] To G. de Gaury 24.11.43.
[2] Momo Marriott's mother.

dazzling and live up to their dim colonial traditions of keeping the community happy; coming here suddenly, the profusion is fantastic—but little holes here and there—only rayon stockings and the end of French lingerie in sight.'[1]

The war seemed very far. I went to hear Toscanini. I had met him over thirty years before, fiery, dark, with a conqueror's profile, and now he came with immense dignity and a most touching, noble head—but a little stoop, and white hair, and tired. 'Perhaps,' I wrote, 'he feels it rather good to be seeing the end of the journey.'

By the middle of November I was drifting gradually into my work. A critical note appears. 'The amount of nonsense talked is phenomenal.' 'I have been hearing about the Negroes in the south, did you know that three whites equal five blacks in voting? And then all this piety over India!' I was 'appalled at the vastness of the job'. 'I don't believe one can combat emotions with mere facts: we always think that anti-British feelings come from ignorance when they actually come from dislike.' I wrote thus to Nigel at the end of November, and there was more disillusion to come.

The collection of letters that follows, written, instead of reports, to inform my Ministry, gives the picture as I saw it, though now, in retrospect, with many obstacles forgotten and the intercourse of fifteen later years remembered, it would probably appear different, and might be a truer picture; yet it would lose the honesty of what was written under the immediate impact of circumstance. Nor was there, as far as I can judge or remember, any preliminary bias. 'We must concentrate on our Atlantic civilization, which must run the world for some time to come,' I had written in November 1941—and it was the belief I took with me. The prejudices that developed were the result of what I found; and as, after a six months' stay, they did not prevent a friendly and grateful recollection, I leave the letters abridged but essentially untouched, with their asperities included: particularly as, from an historic point of view, they coincided with a good deal of English opinion at that time.

[1] 22.11.43.

11

New York to Chicago

NEW YORK *20 November 1943*

My dear Elizabeth,[1]

The basic American prejudice is—I suspect—against us and our so-called imperialism: one sees it in the Lebanon, Indian, Palestine questions, and I never discuss anything without pointing out that the British Empire in the old sense ended when South Africa gained her independence. If we could establish this perfectly truthful view, we should find it easier to get understanding for other individual problems.

My hostess, Mrs. Otto Kahn, and her daughters are all keen to help, and are introducing me to the moderate Jews, not one of whom suspected the existence of the second clause in the Balfour Declaration. So I have distributed copies. It seems important that these moderates should realize that *we have actually fulfilled* the Declaration and I notice that the second clause makes a strong impression.

I met Baroness R. at lunch. Weizmann tells her there is plenty of room for four million people in Palestine. The Arab birth-rate came in useful[2] and left her depressed. She struck me as one who would yield to the evidence of a firm attitude if H.M.G. could only decide to take it: I can't help feeling that a very great number would be in this category. The social treatment of the Jews here is odious.

21 November 1943

This is becoming a diary, but it may be useful, and if not you can throw it away.

I met the bosom friend of Clare Luce (who is now writing regrettably about India) and pointed out that while our Commonwealth revolution is peacefully progressing, and is all so recent, we still have to administer, and must do so with administrators trained in the old school; hence shocks

---

[1] Elizabeth Monroe (Mrs. Neame) of the Middle East Department of the Ministry of Information.

[2] Two to four as against one to six for the Zionists.

to a pure democrat travelling in India who hears Blimpish sentiments that actually misrepresent us. This, Mrs. C. told me, was a new idea to her, and it seems that all new ideas are telephoned to Clare Luce daily.

The French here are simmering and put all their troubles down to British jealousy. That, however, is an easy one to counter: we need never have handed Syria back to them but kept it as military administered territory till the peace. My God, why didn't we?

25 November 1943

It is one of the propagandist's purest pleasures to see his own words come back dressed up as Other People's Ideas, and to do this it does seem important that one should say a few things over and over and all say the same more or less. For instance, I have had two exhausting hours with the most active spirit (I am told) in the moderate Jewish Party which has just seceded from the Zionists. We split upon the White Paper, because he had been convinced by *British* informants that four members of the War Cabinet and Mr. Churchill are in favour of abrogating it. I feel quite certain that this knowledge or supposed knowledge is having a regrettable effect in stiffening the programme of the moderates who are out for just what they think they can get and no more. In fact he admitted to me that if my view were (in his eyes) that of H.M.G. it would make a difference; but they are convinced, so he said, that the Cabinet is with them. Whatever the Cabinet's views may be, it is unfortunate, when bargaining with orientals, that this conviction should have got across to them.

I took the line that the moderate Jews and the British should, in the nature of the circumstances, be co-operative; that the White Paper is so unanimously clung to by all Arab opinion that Great Britain cannot alter it except with Arab consent, or except at the expense of disorders in the Muslim world which are too expensive; and I gave it as a personal opinion that the moderates would serve their cause best by giving Palestinian immigration a rest and building an interim programme for settlement elsewhere which H.M.G. could help in—while Palestine, if the Arabs were given an interval and their unification gradually progressed, might be a much easier problem in a few years' time. I don't think this advice will have the slightest effect.

28 November 1943

At last well enough to spend an afternoon visiting our division here and could not have found them more encouraging, kind and sympathetic. Two long talks with Mrs. McCormick of *The Herald Tribune* and

Mrs. Clare Luce—Mrs. M. twinkling and sparkling with life, fun and sense, I thought one of the nicest women, full of curiosity and soundness: Mrs. Luce 'another pair of sleeves', with lovely eyes fixed on the middle distance when forcibly brought to sit beside me. She opened with the remark that what she believed in was Freedom, resolutely shut down the Middle East, and dragged me to India. She has, they tell me, five secretaries who provide her with facts, so that a war of statistics is to be avoided, but her own were singularly inaccurate. I gave her a little sketch of 'freedom' in Iraq and the years of preparation to prevent its being a massacre of minorities. 'Let there be massacres,' said Clare: 'Why should the white races have a monopoly of murder?' 'Freedom for Fratricide,' I suggested to her for a slogan, which amused the listeners but not her. She interrupted so often that at last I protested and said I must be allowed a 'say'. 'That is our American way.' 'All right,' said I, 'I shall be American and interrupt too'—which strangely enough made her quite friendly. If she carries much weight now, I don't think she will in a few years, she is too much tinkle.

With Miss Case, who is a staunch Republican, discussed Wendell Wilkie's book on the Middle East which, I remarked, omitted to state that all the things he advocated were what we were already trying to do and therefore rather hurt our feelings. She seemed surprised at our having any (feelings); I think they are useful things to mention now and then. After all, why should everyone else have the monopoly?

What a frightful tough job this is! At the moment I feel like an unarmed Christian with no particular method for dealing with lions except a definite wish to side-track India and Hong Kong.

I had a long *tête-à-tête* with one of the chief newspaper owners—very *petite*, all in black velvet, with white curls all over her head, as if she were a young girl suddenly shrunk, and the air of always having been too rich to be happy. She gathered my information in an industrious way, with no *joie de vivre*, and only woke to enthusiasm over new methods of welding in shipyards.

Then went on to a cocktail party of intellectuals and discovered that Liberal and pro-Zionist seem to be considered synonymous. I said I was one but not the other, and Dorothy Thompson (*N.Y. Herald Tribune*) agreed that it is wrong to turn people (Arabs) out of their own country; (she has married a Czech and must know). She was fun: when she starts talking she looks round for an audience as if it were a missing handbag. It was an amusing party—Gipsy Rose Lee the strip-tease artiste side by side with the head of the Chamber of Commerce.

9 December 1943

An epidemic of flu laid me low—but convalescing now. It seems to me a sad failure of medicine that these minor diseases go on for thousands of years causing more accumulated waste of time and spirit than the important ones which doctors attend to; it is like morals—people feel pleased with themselves for not committing murders, thefts, etc., for which the temptation is comparatively rare, whereas if you come to think of it, it would make life much pleasanter if they concentrated on the smaller virtues like kind and pleasant manners even if the strain of doing so made them commit a murder now and then?

We had Dorothy Thompson to tea with a few people. The influential ones don't in the least want to hear about the Middle East as it is they who want to do the talking, but I am learning that delicate methods are no good and I asked her straight out for advice. 'Palestine,' she said, 'is insoluble.' I didn't agree, and, the Balfour Declaration coming up, read the 1922 definition out to them all to show that we have carried it out. I must say it reads very well and obviously made a good impression. I stuck to the line of 'immigration short of coercion', and Dorothy went off with Nuri's brochure under her arm. A little good may have been done. She is a generous creature and I like her and think one would like her more as one knew her better; but she goes by emotion and puts the intellectual touches on afterwards so that one would never be safe unless her emotions were with one.

The night before at dinner I was asked why I had come, and explained that so many things were being said about the Middle East that I had been asked to give facts about it to anyone who wished to hear. 'Thank God,' said my hostess, 'she doesn't say she has just crossed the ocean to see her doctor as most of them do!'

One point of interest I heard indirectly from one of the biggest aircraft factories: it came from a director and he says that the visits paid by our R.A.F. are disliked by the U.S. working man because the officers (when they are being shown over the works) walk 'stiff and proud' and say nothing to anybody. They would surely find it quite easy to chat a bit if the idea were suggested?

I enclose the *Tribune* interview. The horrifying statement that Habbaniya was never fired on is not my fault! I corrected and contradicted it, in writing, and still it went in. What can one do? Another paper—*P.M.*—a pleasing young woman—was deeply interested to hear that we have not been seizing the Irish ports and that South Africa chose to be in the war by free election: I was trying to explain that these facts would give more pleasure and no less instruction than the things they are always publishing about India, and was rather taken aback to find their very existence unknown.

You can tell the dear Establishment that I have had to mortgage two months' salary to get clothes to cover me for the winter.[1]

I have been asked to speak at a private tea party of the Women's Action Committee. Inclining to the heresy that Inaction is a woman's proper sphere, I suppose I must not even think such a thing till the war is over and I have the last committee behind me!

PS. I don't think action matters so long as one realizes that it is unimportant—but so few committee women do!

PPS. I have a rather sad story from an American friend who left Cairo because she couldn't any longer bear the things the 'Bright Young British' said about America. There was a large party in her house the night after Pearl Harbour and one of them arrived rubbing his hands and saying: 'Hurrah, they're in it at last.' This was Randolph Churchill.

10 December 1943

The *P.M.* interviewer went away full of enthusiasm over us in the Middle East and over the White Paper embodying the Atlantic Charter—but her chiefs decided not to publish! It shows, as we guessed, that one goes best through private channels.

My only other business visitor was an intelligent young anti-Zionist. I still believe that these moderate Jews, who are being threatened by the Zionist idea, are the best allies—*the only people in the U.S.A. who have a direct interest in combating the Zionists* and the power to do so.

I forgot to tell you one little point of gossip with Clare Luce. She said that Iraq was not so free as I thought, from things the Iraqi Minister had been telling her. I remarked that he would spend hours telling her frightful things about the British 'if that is what she seemed to enjoy'. It may be just an invention.

The whole of this question is vitiated by a basic misunderstanding of the character of the British political theory; until they get rid of the Empire complex and think of us as a Commonwealth no question which attaches to that concept can find its level. And they don't want to think of us as a Commonwealth, because then America loses her role of liberator. Nothing makes one so unpopular as the showing of Great Britain in a liberal light; they change the subject instantly, like shutting down a lid. It is like preventing a parrot from saying the one thing it says fluently, it

---

[1] Elizabeth had made a gallant but unsuccessful attempt for an allowance to prevent my travelling 'like a Baghdad Sketch'.

naturally hates having it taken away. The only thing to do is to build up, slowly and carefully, another parrot slogan which may say the opposite in time. Until that is done, I believe we shall make no headway for anything dealing with our 'overseas'.

15 December 1943

My dear Stewart,

It was so nice to hear from you, and get a little Baghdad news, of which my friends are very stingy. There is an orphaned feeling which makes letters welcome, and this in spite of kindness here. It is because the world does look different from the opposite side. Or perhaps it is depressing to meet so many people with opinions and no foundations—they gather facts like magpies and never face the idea that two contradictory ones can't be true at the same time. Ladies' luncheons—grey locks and grenadier mouths on solid rectangular bases: they look like a collection of totem poles until they turn into individuals at the end. I can't think why I have been sent here; I have no mass appeal; I hate efficient women; I like truth and am bored by information; and sentimental inaccuracies make me sick. I am tired of being told how bad we are in India by people who can't even keep their own Negroes happy. When they ask me where the poor Jews are to go, I am beginning to ask whether there isn't quite a lot of empty country in the States (there is). My hostess tells me that everyone gets this reaction and I am hoping it may be better as soon as one gets away from the intelligentsia which anyway is awful almost everywhere. How lovely it would be to go for a sail in Mayun!—to sit still now and then and let Allah do the talking...! There will be very little left of your poor little friend after Chicago.

18 December 1943

My dear Elizabeth,

Yesterday I crept out for the first time still feeling very low, and came back shattered, as it was a lunch of fifty ladies of the Foreign Policy Association listening to the foreign editor of *Business Week* on 'Rumblings in the Middle East'. On the invitation the printing said Far East (by mistake) and it is brought home to me that it is better to speak of the Arab World and leave East out of it altogether, as that unlucky word immediately entangles the minds of one's listeners in India. The secretary of the association thinks of involving me in frequent lunches of this kind and, of course, I feel it is just what I am here for and there is nothing for it but to go. With the present fashion in hats one's audience is alarming. When you get near enough to talk you find them full of the milk of human kindness, astonishingly provided with odd bits of information, and with a fund of sentiment all waiting to be poured into the funnels of Foreign Policy that any lecturer provides: except that I have a suspicion that a benevolent view of the British Empire or any of its activities will run counter to so many previous lecturers that it stands little chance of survival. One could do far better if one were an Arab.

Of course what is astonishing is that there should be so many females interested in foreign policy enough to lunch out on it: they think here that everything is everybody's business, unlike our narrow-minded belief in not bothering about jobs which someone else is paid to attend to: but we have some sort of an expert on some remote country in every family almost, and perhaps if we had not we should have to rely on informative luncheons.

Today Miss W. came to tea and told me that she believed in the freedom of Asiatic peoples. I said I believed in the freedom of Arab nations, and the White Paper principle that a nation must consent to its own immigration laws. Palestine, she remarked, is not a nation—but slid away from the subject. She told me how much she regrets the imperialism of Mr. Churchill.

WASHINGTON *23 December 1943*

Delighted with Washington, hills and woods and pleasant houses, to find myself with very dear friends,[1] and also to have advice at hand on this tough job. Apart from our own division, and Mr. Butler, Isaiah Berlin, and Miss McCall,[2] I have been introduced to:

Mrs. Whitehurst, who runs all the women's clubs and thereby wields an instrument of incalculable and terrifying capacities. She, however, is all for guiding its cutting edge into the right direction, and I liked her—warm-hearted, intelligent, not introspective. American female energy is increased enormously by the fact that they don't mind being middle-aged. She was deep in a scheme, now being carried into effect, of providing wedding-dresses sent by the various clubs to the Service girls in England—and far too interested in it to think of Arabs; but gave me a little booklet on how to run women's clubs which I am sending to the Brothers—and hope they will write back to her.

Mr. X I thought a stupid man so anxious to cover it up that nothing from outside has much chance of penetrating: his talk like a conjuror's

[1] Michael and Esther Wright at our Embassy. (Sir Michael Wright, G.C.M.G., Ambassador to Iraq 1954-8).

[2] Then with the Ministry of Information in New York.

patter to hide the (non) workings of his mind. He believed, he told me in a friendly and non-controversial way, in the freedom of India and the emancipation of the Kurds: it seems depressing that anything so simplified should be in a position to deal with the complicated East.

Mr. L, one of the President's special advisers, came and talked in the evening, and asked about Palestine; this was hard going as he is a Jew evidently well supplied with all Zionist ideas, and also had been in Palestine fifteen years ago when the fundamental friendliness of the humble Jews and Arabs struck him and gave him the impression that a change of Arab politicians would solve the whole problem. I countered this by pointing out that in the last fifteen years the Arab world has been *producing a middle class* which looks for outlets in the running of its own countries. I also emphasized the way in which Zionism has lost the great Jewish opportunity for influencing the Middle East. They could have promoted co-operation instead of exclusion, their university could have been Arabic and Hebrew instead of Hebrew only, and their colonies could have benefited Arab and Jew in equal measure. I suggested that this might still happen if the whole question is given a rest, and a new policy taken up later. This line seemed to make some impression (transitory, I fear). His most interesting remark was that the character of our Mandate had been a mistake: it should have provided for 'international control'. I did not wish to make our talk controversial, so omitted to point out that this is exactly what the U.S.A. refused at the time!

Christmas Day 1943

Dearest Nigel,
The thought of semi-public speeches fills me with a feeling only comparable to drowning.

Washington has none of the hard, glittering New York splendour, but a lovely quality, an eighteenth-century colonial air still traceable in and out of its classic avenues and the hills and woods that nestle round it. And how lovely to breathe the cold winter sunlight and see between leafless trees the flat, iced surfaces of streams.

Isaiah Berlin is here, a friend of Bish's and the best talker I have met since his death.

28 December 1943

My dear Elizabeth,
I had a long talk with Colonel Hoskins at the State Department, back from London; he tells me his impression was that no one's mind was

made up and everyone trying to postpone a decision on Palestine. All pressure possible will be brought to bear in America and thence on Britain, but he agrees with me that the interest here is based on votes, so that if we stood firm there would be no eventual damage done to our relations with the U.S.A.; all they want is to say to their electors that they have done what they could for the Jews. Far more depressing is what our Prime Minister has been saying about the White Paper (I have been hearing this from a number of people). I hate to criticize where I so much admire, but if it were the Archangel Gabriel I should feel this as a sabotaging of one's own side. Either the White Paper is our policy or it isn't; it has been publicly confirmed as such by Mr. Eden in the House, and if our representatives now weaken the only effect will be, and already is, to encourage Zionists and even moderates to give a great deal of trouble. I tried to cheer Colonel Hoskins by reminding him that the opinion of everyone whose opinions in the Middle East itself have any weight is unanimous on the necessity of not again upsetting the Arabs, and reminded him that in our history it is usually the Civil Service that wins versus the Cabinet in the long run; I offered to take a bet on it; but it seems rather a pity that this is the light in which the American expert views the London situation!

Colonel H. was tremendously impressed by Ibn Saud; he said the Regent of Iraq was more appreciated in London because 'he can talk about hunting and he wears normal clothes', but he thought we would be wrong not to give first place in the Arab world to the Saudi friendship. At the same time I believe American experts are rather pleased to look upon Ibn Saud as a pet of their own, and with very little encouragement would think they had discovered him.

The Wrights took me to dine at Mrs. V. Bacon's and I there sat between Mr. Eugene Meyer, owner of *The Washington Post,* and Senator Austin. The Senator, great fun and extremely friendly to Britain, said to me: 'You are in a bad mess in Palestine.' It was a very good dinner, excellent champagne, and I said gaily, 'Oh, not really. I could settle it if I were a Dictator.' 'I'll make you a Dictator,' he said: 'Now what do you do?' 'I look round and settle on a principle,' said I, 'and then I don't *wobble.* And the principle is, if you agree, that people should be consulted about the immigrants who go into their countries.' 'Well,' said the Senator, 'I come from Vermont and we're an independent people: I wouldn't quarrel with that.' 'Not with all that tea in Boston harbour,' I said, 'you couldn't, could you?' So we settled the Palestine question.

Mr. Meyer had a French father, banker, and left the firm as a lad because he wanted to make his life without too much help; and having done so, and now retired, took over *The Washington Post* as relaxation. He was a charming man, full of benevolent ideals combined with a certain cynicism as to how human nature carries them out. The story of his life was so long and interesting that I never got to Palestine, but Michael Wright made up the leeway after coffee, and I was asked to go and talk to him in his office. He there told me that Dr. Brandeis years ago had tried to interest him in the Balfour Declaration and that he kept out because he thought 'there were too many Muslims about' (how sensible). But he was perturbed to see how the Jews who arrived in U.S.A. from the ghettos of Europe were without moral guidance, straying into ways of crime, and he had been interested in Palestine as a means of regeneration and an ideal for them to focus on. He looked pained and startled when I remarked that they were rapidly deviating into ways of crime in Palestine also and was very anxious to see the Stern Gang document of which I have some extracts.

My next party was a pleasant affair at the Summerscales where we were all orientalists together except for some journalists who asked me to explain the Middle East 'in two minutes'. Mr. N., very influential in the Press here, with a pretty round little dark wife, listened till he could bear it no longer and then came up and buried me in the 'atrocities' of the Colonial Office. He became so venomous about the Arabs that nothing I could have said could have worked more in their favour and I was sorry the audience were converted already. He came up after to say good-bye in the friendliest manner and said we must meet again as we had only 'scratched the surface'; however I feel that scratching is rather a waste of time.

Mr. Norman Walker was sent out on a survey of lease-lend in the Middle East. He is a business man and anxious for friendly co-operation, but came back with so gloomy a view of the rivalries and difficulties among all except the people at the top that he seemed inclined to advise against lease-lend in those regions altogether. He is the only American I have met so far who fears that the U.S.A. may be left in the cold by a Russo-British friendship if anti-British feeling here continues on its way. He had not entered into Palestine affairs, but was interested in the possible cause of friction there might be for America and Britain, and will do all he can among his business friends to press the points we wish.

Among the orientalists at the Summerscales was Mr. Ireland, very able, of the State Department, also very perturbed about our Prime Minister and his supposed saying to Weizmann that though 'nothing can be done now he would get all he wanted after the war'. I find everyone who is on our side badly in need of reassurance on this score.

Again I had to give the same assurance to Dr. Cleland and the rest of the Middle East division of the O.W.I., with whom I had a long talk—pointing out that our Prime Ministers do not press their views against the advice of all their Government departments. There is such friendly feeling both in the O.W.I. and the State Department. They all seem alert, intelligent, and refreshingly constructive, though kept in by Mr. —— who sits on top of them like a cork.

They all agree that to base our explanations on a democratic theory of consent and no coercion is to find the ears of the Americans, and so I will just go ahead, like Paganini, on the one string, and if my accounts of conversations become incredibly monotonous you must consider that it is nothing to the dreariness of having to *say* the same thing over and over again.

We dined with the Halifaxes[1] and I sat next to Mr. Stimson, a rock-like and benevolent old man who might have stepped out of the *Mayflower*, so shining was he in integrity. I regretted sadly that I could not enjoy myself and talk of this and that but led inexorably to Palestine. My efforts at basing ourselves on the well-worn principles failed, however, for Mr. Stimson said that in the course of a long life he had found that principles caused more trouble than anything else—and pointed out to me how the French and British, divided only by the Channel, flourish the most opposite principles with equal feelings towards each other's inferiority. I couldn't agree more, which shows how unadapted I am for this ghastly job of propaganda. Whatever concessions Mr. Stimson may have made to Zionists, they were certainly not inspired by affection: he told me in a heartfelt way that I little knew them if I thought one could subdue them by being firm. On our standing by our present policy he said, 'it would not seriously ruffle the relations of our Governments, but it would cause a great many pin-pricks to the Secretary of War (himself).' I said it would cause pricks with things much sharper than pins in Arabia if we didn't (stand by our policy), at which he laughed and agreed.

2 January 1944

Mr. Y. of the State Department came to see, and charmed, me. It was he who in 1919 was breakfasting when Weizmann banged his fist on the table and said (of Palestine) that 'unless they give it me I will *break* the

[1] Then British Ambassador in Washington.

British Empire'. I am pleased to have tracked this elusive story at last. He knows a great deal of what went on behind the scenes at the end of the First World War—almost more than actually happened. Even when facts are uncertain, it does not alter their influence if the government departments of a country believe them!

I have been meeting various women journalists who all make one feel as if one's mental processes were very slow. They go about with pencil and pad among blood and tears and revolutions, pinning them down as if they were butterflies with an innocent disarming interest. Miss F. from Nebraska on one side and Mrs. C. on the other took the Middle East down in short snappy sentences and I hear there is something in *The New York Times* and am waiting rather nervously to know what has come out of it all. Mrs. C., I think, wished to talk about brutal imperialism but I got in first and described a lunch at the Emir Abdullah's where I sat next to his Negro prime minister who disapproved of Western women walking in shorts down the public streets: she went away saying that the Arabs were much more democratic than she thought them.

I met the French journalist 'Pertinax' at Walter Lippmann's[1] party and asked him how he liked America. 'A desert,' he said. 'They are lost, not in space but in time.' He blew off his finger-tips into the outer darkness. 'They detest us all, but you British more, because they feel themselves inferior. *Ce n'est pas une civilisation*.' 'But the future,' said I. 'They may be growing into a *civilisation*. How long do you think it will take?' 'I don't know—five hundred years perhaps. It is of no interest.' He shrugged his shoulders, lifted his chin and dismissed the whole continent.

6 January 1944

I am going to write you a prophecy of what will happen if we, to placate the Zionists and by altering the White Paper, arouse the Arabs. When the election here is over and the interest in Saudi Arabia has increased the Americans will gradually begin to pour obloquy upon us as the supporters of a Fascist régime in Palestine and the oppressors of the free and democratic peoples. To gain a very dubious advantage of a few months, we will have forged the ideal weapon for a time when U.S.A. interests may conflict with ours in Arabia.

I saw X. in his office and though not thinking him any more intelligent than before, was touched by his friendliness. He, too, like all his department, was subdued by the remarks of our Prime Minister and asked me how I explained the Zionist fervour among our public men. I said

[1] Of *The New York Herald Tribune*.

'the Bible'. 'Only that?' he asked. He told me his admiration for British colonial methods, a rare and welcome note in this land. He had been thoroughly depressed by Colonel Hoskins's report of London, so I went to the Colonel's office again and did what I could to cheer him as to the eventual firmness of our Government. I also told him about Mr. Stimson's remarks, which pleased him very much as showing him a good deal less Zionist at heart than they had thought, and then went on to dine with the Henry Fields, where we were able to relax into the comparatively peaceful atmosphere of the Stone Age.

On Tuesday I met fourteen ladies at the Iraqi Ambassadress's with a few Americans obviously a little at sea on finding Palestinian, Persian, Iraqi and Turkish females so very like themselves—even the slight loudness in dress struck a familiar note. The Ali Jaudats are doing well and she managed her party splendidly; everyone I have heard speaks well of them.

Mr. Ireland has been telling me he thinks there are no moderate Jews here: I disagree and think that it is only our indecision which makes even moderates think that pressure may pay. A telegram to the Embassy advises us to keep things 'as tranquil as possible': this effort was made by King Canute on the sea-shore in the same sort of circumstances many years ago, with very little effect, and I would much rather have seen a recommendation to 'stand firm till the tide turns'.

I called on Isaiah Berlin who always leads into the most beguiling by-paths of conversation and makes one late for meals (but it is worth it), and in the afternoon I caught the train for Chicago. *If* I have done any good work in Washington it is chiefly through the help of Michael and Esther Wright: this game is like that of a conjuror, and it needs two or more to work together if any rabbits are to come out of the hat. Michael has spent his time bringing useful people and asking useful questions to get them going. I am sure one's success anywhere here will depend on whether one finds people to take this trouble to make the proper setting.

Train to CHICAGO *6 January 1944*

My dearest Jock,

Washington was one of the pleasantest cities—like a huge village losing itself in green avenues (now brown). The Wrights live just above a creek running full of ice in a valley with a zoo arranged at one end— white wolves and grey foxes and bears. My only time off was a walk every fine day in the crisp shining air, with the pale colours of winter all about and the Shoreham Hotel like that Lhassa palace towering above. I am now in the Chicago train, still surrounded by a mass of paper that is slowly rising up and burying me. So that it is very immoral to be writing to you just for pleasure! But I have composed so many minutes on Zionism that I deserve a rest. It is hard to make the Arab popular but even harder to popularize the English. I don't honestly think this is our fault: it is largely puzzled jealousy because this country's business morality can't understand that we combine a different outlook with success. It is a pity. There is no reason in the world why we could not work together for the good of everyone including ourselves; but I don't believe America yet sees that co-operation is better than competition, and we shall probably eventually go hand in hand with Russia while the U.S.A. wonders how her slick methods have failed her. There is a drop in temperature whenever I mention loyalty of Canadians or South Africans. If it weren't for this feeling, so widespread, I should enjoy myself more, and I do love the country as soon as I come on young friendly people keen on the fighting or good tough old boys with Puritan ancestors. I sat next Mr. Stimson and he was lamenting the fact that the war was going to go over his country without coming near enough to teach it.

12

Chicago to Canada

CHICAGO *9 January 1944*

My dear Elizabeth,

Chicago gave me a snowstorm and this morning I walked for an hour on the crisp surface in a world which must be parks and sheets of water in summer: Greek temples scattered about and skyscrapers in the background, and the lake with blocks of ice making a white horizon. Inside the hotel it is like the Balkans grown prosperous—square, squat females with furs and loud cordial voices telling everybody's business in the lounge. It is fun—only appalling to think that these are the people who are to have a hand in the delicate and subtle East.

A Mrs. B. rang up and said she was 'Intellectural' and is coming to call. I think I am going to enjoy the Middle West.

Orientalists are (nearly) always happy together and I had a delightful morning with Dr. Wilson and Dr. Olmstead at the University, looking on what might have been an Oxford quad. Dr. Olmstead is completely scholasticized (if there is such a word) and his eye gleams over potsherds and the inventing of an alphabet but not over minor historical upheavals like the present war: but Dr. Wilson was in the State Department last year and is as worried over his Government and the Zionists as we are over ours.

12 January 1944

The first lecture went off quite smoothly. I recited a Wordsworth sonnet and no one batted an eyelid. A light on what is thought of lecture tours was thrown by a very juvenile flapper reporter who came up and explained that they had sent only her as they 'thought it was just a tour. But this is your first lecture in this country, so you might be *news*, mightn't you, Miss Stark?'

The intellectual Mrs. B. turned out to be an ardently Church of England charming old lady, full of vigour. She and the University are a sort of oasis. The pleasure of conversation is that of exploring—you hope to get a glimpse of the shy and secret creature, the human being you are talking to: you get it in the poorest Arab tent or among the murderers of Luristan but how rarely here! The voice I am hearing in the hotel lounge at the moment is saying: 'I go at eleven o'clock and sit in that picture till three every day.' They talk, they are pleasantly mannered, most friendly, they say 'how interesting', and feel it too, they have collected some new facts for the magpie nest of their mind—but they get up and turn you off as it might be a tap, with no human penetration. Yet many people tell me, and I am noticing it myself, how more adventurous and alive the women here are than the men, and I toy with the theory that on this deathly road of standardization the female element is more refractory and will keep a touch of singularity long after all their husbands are moulded exactly alike. I like their adventurous quality when I find it—as of Goths revelling in the un-understood magnificence of a conquered world: people tossed here by all sorts of poverties and dangers: no wonder that a material universe is all that is needed for their dreams. But what does seem wrong is that there is so little for those that grope after something further. There was a force which in a few generations turned the Goths towards masterpieces like Ravenna: and I don't believe big business will ever provide a motive power of this kind. A girl at dinner last night told me that the religion she belongs to is called *Ethical Culture*.

21 January 1944

I don't know what to do about these newspaper notices: the plainer I tell it the more highly coloured it comes out. And I begin to get letters from Zionists almost inarticulate with fury. It makes me long for private life with a passionate longing.

I like the journalists here: they are anxious to know things and look at them with an eye for the general idea. On the Palestine question they are not only fair, but keen to get it known. If we *did* change our policy on the White Paper, it would be regrettable if the American newspaper men remembered my eloquence and began to write about *coercion* on their own? If there is any chance of this I hope you would send me a wire to recall me as soon as you knew of it, and stop my talking further!

The outstanding events of Wednesday and today were meals with Zionists, shepherded by Dr. Olmstead, who got Rabbi Fox to lunch, one of the most influential Jews here and moderate, and we had a great argument with the usual dead-wall at the end; but it does seem to have roused a certain disturbance in his mind and he afterwards asked Dr. Olmstead to talk on the subject to a gathering of Jews. The Covenant Club manages to combine an atmosphere of modernity, wealth and oriental bazaar. The distressing thing is that I *like* the Jews I meet here and have to argue with, almost better than anyone else I see, and there was a most disarming mixture of sharpness, kindness and humour about the Rabbi. But the little man on my right made me long for a pet pogrom of my own before we were through the soup. He had one of those mouths that you are afraid are going to spit out their teeth, and used it almost exclusively against the Colonial Office. I thought I made no headway, but I may have done, for the Rabbi patted me affectionately on the arm as we parted. As for the little Horror, instead of good-bye I said to him that I regretted he was so shockingly anti-British, and it seemed to cause him the greatest surprise and chagrin. I believe they are delirious and don't know how objectionable they are. The others were nice university people and would not be extreme if one could tell them the facts at leisure. They called in a Judge for dessert, and I left them listening to Dr. Olmstead who has the great art of involving himself in so many learned qualifications that no one knows which side he is on till the end, when he turns out Arab to the core. Rabbi Fox, before we parted, said that he thought Mr. Roosevelt would 'whisper a word or two to Churchill and he'll be afraid to say no'; unfortunately we reached our destination before I could refute this monstrosity.

The consul here gave a dinner at which an enormous rubicund shipping director told me he was founding a Moravian church, and we all sang temperance hymns in broken American. It was a peculiar evening, very matey.

I must bring this rigmarole to a stop. I write at the end of the day and no time to revise, so it may contain all sorts of undesirable things.

Mr. G. has been studying lists of the people here who wish to return to their countries after the war; a few central Europeans, all the French, all the Italians, and almost all the British. The call of civilization is very strong, considering what they go back to. I wonder if it is the 'organizing' of women that makes the blankness here?—the one half of the human race that we still consider as believing in its duties rather than its rights, as being ready for self-sacrifice rather than self-advancement, as having leisure for other people in its life and a mind sufficiently unpruned to be individual—here it is canalized into something hard, bright, competent, quite unendurable, much more intelligent than its average man, and I believe unhappy; or perhaps it just seems to me impossible that it can be happy. I only hope we won't think of 'organizing' women in Europe. The lift girl said to me today: 'Have you seen the *darling* review about you in the paper?' She is such a pretty girl: you would think she ought to know what darling should or shouldn't be used for.

There are exceptions however. I was lunched by a dozen or so women journalists who listened to harim stories and were so cordial that I came away with very warm feelings and the hope that they may yet escape their own efficiency. On the other hand, I had a ghastly evening with Miss P. of *Collier's* magazine. She came all the way from New York to interview me. An interview with *Collier's* seems almost equivalent to an audience with the Pope. Miss P. thought so anyway. She began by being disappointed because I refused to dine anywhere except quietly in my hotel where she drank three old-fashioneds and divided me into paragraphs. After dinner she produced a bouncing young photographer and they spent four hours over me, telling me between whiles what they thought of British rule in India. I got so angry. I detested Miss P; if she wanted to drink I felt she could do so in New York. She had a cold, poor thing, and evidently attributed to that and to the three old-fashioneds the difficulty she had in understanding that I travel for pleasure. Her evening was wasted; and so was mine.

28 January 1944

I have been to Ann Arbor (Michigan University) to lecture. Dr. Ettinghausen had asked me—a gentle, charming man, unhappy both as a German and a Jew. He teaches Islamic art and I had met him in London. He did things so well. I spent the morning talking to his class of Persian students, and lunched with the head of the University and family. They had all been in Egypt and our manners there had made them very anti-British, but the Doctor was invited to England last year and told me he came back with altered views. Next morning I visited their house and the chill seemed to have vanished; with the rest it did not exist—they were all professors and charming friendly people. In the evening we had a symposium and dealt with Palestine; and in the afternoon I met Leland Stowe, the correspondent, whom I thought full of understanding. I talked to him about the vital danger of competition between us in the Middle East and said frankly that as far as I could see we were genuinely anxious to co-operate, and America about seventy per cent out for competition. He was interested and eager to use his influence to counteract. I thought him honest, thoughtful and fair. He has upset his audiences by lecturing on China and saying that the Chinese are behaving quite dreadfully, which is almost as much a heresy as to say that Gandhi and Nehru are not perfect.

Do you think, my dear Elizabeth, that after all this I could be given a little relaxation and allowed to do something I enjoy, for instance among the Italian guerrillas?

I am now sitting in *The Indian Chief*, all shining aluminium or steel with carriages called by Indian and romantic names, filled with white-suited servants offering abundant food to obviously wealthy passengers on their way to California. The middle West is slipping by; as one goes through the little towns their straight streets appear like avenues intersecting a chess board, lined pleasantly with trees; one looks down their whole length and sees them parked solidly from end to end with cars. The country is not a bit flat when you think of flatness in terms of the Indian plains—there is an undulation, a long low ridge of leafless trees here and there, or shoots of maize-sticks long harvested shining in the sun. There is an air of space, big careless patches left to their natural grasses; one cannot help feeling there is room here for far more influx than in poor tiny Palestine! And just now a sudden dip between ridges and here is the Mississippi, wider than anything I have seen except the Indus, and carrying a slush of melting ice on its blue water. I feel extremely happy partly because of the pleasant bigness and variety of the world, but also because for a whole fortnight I shall be able to talk about what I like and not bother about what I say and not lecture to anyone. I can't help feeling that this revolt, which almost every Englishman I see develops out here, is largely due to our *atrocious* task: to go round apologising as we do for being in the war, for being in India, for running the East, for supporting the morale of all the U.S.A., for being courageous, persevering and poor and better than they are—it gets everyone down. Mr. H. came and unburdened himself and my feelings are as nothing compared to his. But if we did not have to follow this bogus humility, we would be able to enjoy the good-humoured nice manners which everyone here has spontaneously, and their friendly curiosity (which I do enjoy), and their obvious pleasure when no one suggests the existence of a world less easy than their own.

PS. The train is now sliding through New Mexico which looks like the uplands of Luristan only less inhabited—and I did think I should have a day of peace. But I was attacked by a Zionist over lunch. He opened nicely, saying he believed in the British virtues and I began to expand and relax until he added 'all except the Colonial Office', and then of course I knew what was coming. He is quite important in the Hebrew University and told me that he cares more for Zionism than for anything in life. I told him he had better save it from its present disastrous path and asked if he really wished to see it pushed in at the point of the bayonet. No, he said, force must not be used: 'all the C.O need do is to be friendly and just!' Reason was of no avail. I begin to have a sort of affection for the Colonial Office, as one has for an ugly baby that nobody loves.

c/o Mrs Beach, LOS ANGELES 31 January 1944

I am now in a haven of quiet on a hillside, with Los Angeles twinkling harmlessly below; a decent house with old things, beautiful and shabby—and my hosts with two boys ready to be 'drafted', who are wearing their old clothes and are glad that there is little butter. Oh my, what a relief!

9 February 1944

My dear Edwin [Ker],

Do you hate typewritten letters? I have been lent this instrument and am playing with it, and I was going in any case to take this leisure—my first in weeks—to tell you how good I thought your Italian poem. I am happy in being able to like people without respecting them and it doesn't worry me to realise that Italy has no public virtues. I am getting a little tired of all things public, virtues included. What I want is to go and fight among guerrillas, and not worry whether or no American soldiers are going to vote.

There is a valley here leading between clefts of green hills to the city, a landscape like that story of Robert Louis Stevenson's *Will o' the Mill*, lovely sunsets, and scrubby hills for walking owned by a Movie Magnate and wired against walkers—a wonderfully big country as everybody says, but so is Asia—and I like Asia better.

11 February 1944

Dearest Pam,

I long for Poverty and Peace, not so much the laying down of weapons, but the peace of people who know through the surface of the world the ties that bind them. I am glad to have come out here, for I shall never more feel the slightest doubt as to the relative worth of our values. The Greeks said that the elements of art are terror and wonder: you can't have any life worth living without that background—and your life's work to turn it into the understanding of love. I seem to be degenerating into a sermon, but so would you if you were here. As for freedom—it is a shallow equality. I remember once going to look for a book on the Hadhramaut in a little slummy shop in Cairo: an old beggar, in tatters, was sitting in a corner and broke into the conversation by saying that what

I wanted was *The Meadows of Gold* by Maqrizi—a medieval author as it might be Marco Polo. We talked this over and parted friends, more free and more equal than the common possession of motor cars could ever make us. Yet in Chicago the skyscrapers are as beautiful as icicles when the sun and the light play about with them. If you look at it, winding beside the ice-bound waters of its lake, and see its blocks and towers in the sunset, it is a very exciting spectacle. All the same I was glad to come away into this human sort of an atmosphere, and have had a quiet happy spell in the room where my mother spent her last year and her little odds and ends are still about. I can't think of her as very far away.

The work has gone pretty well, I believe.

11 February 1944

My dear Elizabeth,

I walked back into the arena last night by lecturing to the California Technological Institute in Pasadena. The president is a world authority on cosmic rays, sufficiently remote to give him a carefree and happy expression. He invited us to a great dinner of fourteen people, all extremely friendly—rich people leading comfortable lives in places like Santa Barbara, with beautifully open minds even on things like India. I had a full audience of two hundred and fifty or so and talked about Aden and the Yemen, and ended with the White Paper—after which a heckler arose, quivering with eloquence and fury. 'If the Arabs were so friendly,' he said, 'why didn't Egypt fight when invaded by the Italians?' I happened to know this answer, and explained our shortage of equipment and how what we required of Egypt were the dull things—guarding, etc.,—which they could do with what they had, and not actual fighting which would have meant supplying them with what we could not spare; the military therefore discouraged any thought of their entering more actively into the war. 'And what about Iraq?' said the heckler. 'That,' I explained, 'was a military revolt against their own Government. It did not include the majority of the country (if it had we could not have quelled it with two battalions) and as soon as Nuri Pasha was back he asked to enter the war on our side. He was again discouraged by our own military—I imagine because of the difficulty of providing sufficient aircraft.' My audience now evidently looked on the heckler as liquidated but he stood up bravely and made a small oration saying that many people call our White Paper a 'black paper', and urged the audience to read what Mr. Churchill himself said about it. I said the answer to this was very short: when Mr. Churchill made that speech, *he was in Opposition.*

Everybody laughed. I said to Dr. Millikin afterwards that the heckler seemed to have been silenced. 'Silenced?' said he. 'He *died*.' I, of course, felt extremely elated as it has never happened to me before to make a Zionist stop talking.

I am asked here to hand in the detailed summaries of all my speeches to be preserved, strangely enough, by the Department of Justice—an awful scale in which to weigh one's casual words.

A wonderfully restful week and I feel stronger again—though with all my mother's things and papers to go through. My hostess is charming, New England descendant from Puritans, her conscience mitigated by goodness and humour—one of the nicest human beings in this world.

19 February 1944

My dear Chief,[1]

Your letter came across all the continents bringing more pleasure than I can say, like a ride in the early Delhi morning (without the possibility of falling off); it made me feel as the Arabs do when you tell them it is a fine day: 'And you are the fineness of the day,' they say.

I was going to write in any case, for *Allenby*[2] reached me just as I was leaving Chicago, and I read him across New Mexico and Arizona and found him as good as I remembered. There is more of yourself in it, and it makes a better book than the first—at least I feel it so.

'Equality is not enough' would be my title for a book on America (a thing I never mean to write. I am passionately longing to get away to any little town of Greece, Italy or England, however poor). Hollywood, however, has a gaiety—you feel it enjoys spending its money as well as making it, and it is new enough to show, here and there, people who still have a trace of the adventure that brought them West in their youth. There is a poem about this West by Bénet that I think you would like:

> The iron in the loadstone of the breast,
> Never to be forgotten nor possessed.

—the mystery of exploration?

Lord Halifax in Washington told me they used to try to get to Simla in time to give one grand banquet with gold plates and bunches of rhododendron all down the table. I hope you will go and see the rhododendrons against the Dalai Lama's snowy land. Some day I should like to ride slowly up the banks of Indus, beginning where the bridge of boats

[1] Field-Marshal Lord Wavell, then Viceroy of India.
[2] A. P. Wavell, *Allenby* (Harrap, 1946).

goes into Baluchistan, and going on till it gets too cold. It would be fun to reach you again while you are all there—who knows? I feel like a discouraged David travelling across this land with one Goliath after another to meet and only a small packet of slingstones which H.M.G. perpetually begs one not to use: and every American seems to think himself born with a capacity to govern India; you would be surprised.

20 February 1944

My dear Elizabeth,

I have a whole week's diary to write and had better begin at the beginning with a speech at a Round Table which has been lunching on Mondays for the last twenty-four years: they are business men, with a judge or two among them. They had planned to form a Rotary Club, but then enjoyed their informal friendly meetings so much more that they decided not to change, and had never had a woman guest except my mother. In this business atmosphere, far from being anti-Semitic, I found I had to stand up for Jews and their doings; there was a virulent feeling against them, the same fear of encroachment which lies at the root of Palestine. The whole trouble of the Jewish question all over the world could be solved if Moses descended with an eleventh commandment for every Jew to share profits with a gentile partner!

On Wednesday I had to address young soldiers being trained for overseas—a pleasant and refreshing audience of about fifty, being taught (at least in part) by a white-haired, energetic female geographer. The hand that rocks the cradle goes on rocking indefinitely in all sorts of unexpected places! However this is a digression—and here is another—for I am writing in the train and the Pacific Ocean has just come into sight for the first time in my life—very exciting, and Japan across the water: the hills are green and round, rolling like the waves of a larger age than ours, and the Sierras are behind, powdered with snow.

But to go back to my day with the students. They were in California University, just beyond the houses and film-star gardens in Beverly Hills, in a college built with very good taste on an Italian Renaissance model—in the most pleasant country of foot-hills all green now in the spring. As they were all soldiers I told them mostly the military story of the Middle East: the fearful odds in numbers and equipment the first two years; the fact that Weygand and his army had been counted on to keep that front, and how General Wavell, when the news was brought that he was left in charge alone said, 'Well, I can't help it,' and finished the last two holes of the game of golf he was playing. I told them of the war in the

Red Sea, and the charge of the Black Watch in Somaliland uphill, pushing back eight times their number; and how the papers in England were so pleased because we lost only two guns, never mentioning that there were only four to lose. I told them how I thought the turning-point in the Middle East was the battle of Crete which lasted eighteen days when the Germans expected to end it in two; and how the loss of their big air transports prevented the sending of troops to assist in the Iraq rebellion, and so enabled us to retake the country with the two battalions which was all that we could spare. I then went on to point out that, with our shortage of manpower, the policing of the Arab world would have been beyond our strength, and that therefore its friendly neutrality was of first importance in preserving the bridge of the Middle East; and gave the example of Palestine, where the Arabs spontaneously stopped their guerrillas—so that in *1939* I had to drive through behind an armoured car and in *1940* could go about in my own little car unescorted. Quite a number of the boys came up after and asked questions, and it was altogether a charming audience. At lunch I met the Dean and the Faculty, and enjoyed the peaceful academic atmosphere of remoteness, and drove back through the sunshine to the endless Hollywood Boulevard, the longest in the world and sordid all its length. Above it is a cemetery where you can pay to have mechanical canaries sing through the funeral services, and luckily no one asked me what I thought of that.

I met two Yorkshiremen— one married to an American and the other the regular sort of retired English colonel whom Americans expect. He told me he came here as a young man because someone sent him advertisements of fruit farming; left everything to join up in the First World War only to find he was over-age and no amount of lying did any good. So he came back, but managed to get taken on a year later and fought in France. This war, his son is in the Navy and he wants to get back to England, but can't get a passage and so decided to fill in time by helping in an aircraft factory as a steel cutter; he got in by saying he was sixty-five instead of seventy-six but—as he explained in a loud voice—you have to be very thorough and forge all the dates from birth certificates to passport. The Los Angeles ladies were hanging about us in groups, listening entranced, while he asked whether I knew So-and-so—'nice fellow, a gentleman— you don't always find them so in that service'—no damned Equality for him. He then went on to reminiscences about the boat-race. I was delighted, with a feeling of fresh air about the conversation; what was more surprising was the warmth with which the Americans spoke of him. I suppose that having created a type, they are pleased when they see us sometimes embodying what they expect. 'He is British,' said my hostess, and he goes down better than many who try harder to please.

I ended my day with a visit to a Hollywood studio in which Merle Oberon was swooning in the arms of a romantic Chopin surrounded by the eyes of the lenses and a tough-looking crowd of advisers.

On Friday I lunched with an engaging young radio commentator who asked what the Arabs would do if Pakistan caused a Hindu-Muslim war. I thought they would give sympathy and no more and might ask advice in London first. 'In that case,' said he, 'one knows what would happen. They would get an evasive reply.'

He was very concerned over the Anglo-American oil rivalry—'entirely America's fault,' I said rather brutally, 'if it comes to competition instead of partnership. Our business world is no doubt equally bad, but our civil service is far less under its thumb and therefore avoids the "slick methods" which too often are put in the place of American statesmanship. To keep a pipe-line going across tribal desert is an affair of experience and careful handling, and they would need and get our help: even when the U.S.A. first got the Bahrein concession, the British political reaction was one of pleasure at finding America at last with an inducement to be interested in Arab affairs.' Mr. L. agreed with all this and said he would do all he could to prevent oil-quarrels, which he looks upon as the gravest threat to our relations.

There were two Mexican guests, father and son, at this luncheon, who came up afterwards with most genuine friendliness, talking about our civilization as if it were a jewel with an ardour pleasant to me but surprising to my hosts.

That was the end of my labours in Los Angeles and I came away feeling as I felt in Chicago only more so: the groundwork of public opinion is open-minded and anxious to be fair; the people who give the news are ready to give it fairly; there is no universal prejudice, as there is against the British: the power one is up against is far more secret and concentrated and I should expect to find it among the politicians (at a guess). Mr. L. said it was far too strong to be prevailed against but admitted that its strength might be not nearly so great after the election.

Apropos of the election, there was quite a ripple over the English Church newspaper that offered its good wishes for Roosevelt. People talked of interference. I was delighted and agreed heartily that interference is damnable; and added how strongly I feel this when every whipper-snapper I meet tells me how to deal with India. They take this very nicely, and seem to see the connection for the first time.

I am now going through the most lovely country, with little houses in orchards sitting by themselves, and hills of green velvet with bits of wood on their slopes. If California had been in the middle, and the Middle West on this far side, I don't believe anyone would have bothered to come so far. The train is called *Daylight*, and has big windows and is painted bright orange; it has an immense streamlined engine like a horse of the Apocalypse and its only drawback, the radio, is just telling me that we are going round the sharpest horsehoe bend in the world.

SAN FRANCISCO *27 February 1944*

This most beautiful of bays has a Golden Gate opening on the sunset, spanned by a spiderweb of bridges that seem a part of the mists of the morning. A pity Turner never painted it.

The Zionists here seem to be more conscious of the danger of my visit than anything I have met before. They shadow me persistently, and when I lectured to the Association of Women Voters there was one solitary man, blond and with the look of a rather obstinate rabbit, who bravely explained his existence by saying that he represented the Society for the Abrogation of the White Paper. He was relying with confidence on Churchill's anti-White Paper speech, which he read out in full when the time came. I am now fairly expert at dealing with it, and remarked that 'political men often speak differently when in opposition: no need to elaborate in an election year' and then asked if Mr. Churchill had made any statement of the kind since he became Prime Minister. 'No', said the young man, rather annoyed, and left the room—whereupon a woman took up the cudgels and said the Zionists were doing wonderful things for the Arabs—giving hospitals, etc. I did not challenge, but told her this seemed to me the right way of dealing with the problem, and if they continued and eschewed the use of force they would probably get good results in time: she looked as if she could have killed me and a third champion now said that Palestine was the only place the refugees could go to. 'Is there nowhere else?' I asked. 'No' (rashly). 'No room in this country?' 'The immigration laws are against it.' 'That is what the Palestinian knows,' I remarked, 'and would also like a voice in his own immigration laws.' This was the end of the controversial matter, and I may say that I never begin any of it of my own accord; but of course Palestine, the White Paper and Oil are inevitable questions and I think the time is coming when H.M.G. will have to make up its mind whether or not it is going to stand behind its own White Paper. We have suffered very much by not being articulate about it. This comes out in almost every talk.

The Council of Churches for instance—I was told by the vice-president—would certainly not have taken its stand if the facts as I explained them had been known.

As for Oil—the Fishers (H.M.'s Consul here) asked an English Shell magnate to dine, who told me that business is business and my hopes for co-operation mere Utopia. I said I was thinking of it not as being more Christian but as being better business—and ended by telling him that he depressed me, for I knew American business men to be worse than ours and he was already so dreadfully bad. He laughed, and I think was just taking the other side for fun. But the oil question has come up again twice and each time the Americans have taken it as an axiom that we would all be 'out-smarting' each other. It is no good denying this on our side; they wouldn't believe one; but I did point out that co-operation in Arabia does more than halve the expenses! I said (at the luncheon-party) that if there was to be cut-throat competition in the oil-fields it would be *entirely the Americans' fault*. To lay down a pipe-line through Arab country meant the setting up of a delicate machine with a huge background of knowledge, personal prestige and goodwill if it was to operate without the equivalent of a military occupation: so that obviously it would be the worst manners, as well as dangerous to themselves, if oil companies were to consider such a thing without talking it over with the British who have so many ties and interests in those lands. The newspaper men present said 'presumably America has her oil-men who give reliable appreciations to the Government'. I said, 'if that is so, the U.S.A. are far more fortunate than we are: I should hate to think that our Government took its political ideas on Arabia from the oil-men who are almost sure to be biased.' I was relieved afterwards to be told by our people that I had done well to speak as strongly as I did: I feel that if there is going to be friction, it is advisable to put our case forcibly before people's minds are hardened.

I feel about my speeches as Louis XIV did about the partridges.

In the evening Miss B. from the Consulate took me across the bay to Berkeley University to lecture on the Yemen—all uncontroversial and encouraging except for two young females who came up without a trace of Victorian modesty and said they wished to challenge my statements about Arab women. Had they been in Arabia? No, but they had read—books about the East in general. By this time there was a chorus of people telling them to stop talking, but they stood firm. 'We have not travelled,' they said; 'but we read authoritative statements, and our point of view is therefore more objective than yours': with which Parthian shot they went off, silenced but not crushed by general disapproval.

I reckon I was actually talking for twelve hours on Friday, beginning with an interview and ending with the most useful meeting of all when I dined with a gathering of moderate non-Zionist Jews, and found them the keenest people I have met here and most aware of the dangers of the whole question, though with the usual absence of any idea on how to do something about it. The Jews are out after ideas more than most people, and I like them so much that it is a pleasure when one can meet on the same side. These had all travelled and knew the Arab world and its menace. They told me that my coming had caused a flutter among the Zionists, who count upon no one's knowing the facts, and who also know that most speakers by the time they reach California are on the verge of a breakdown. I should be over the verge but for the kindness of my pause in Los Angeles and the thought of the few days quiet ahead of me in Canada; but I shall have to take a bit of real leave in England if possible, for I do feel very tired. It gives one a sort of depression to be always struggling with people who try to twist words and facts out of their legitimate paths.

★ ★ ★ ★

I was now across the Canadian border. Already, as one came up from San Francisco, there was a pioneering touch about the land; the miniature townships stood in clearings with their woods still about them and sunburnt farmer-people talked of hiking or fishing as they got in and out of the train. After a night on the boat from Seattle, I reached Victoria on a grey English morning and saw people walking in tweeds; I took a stroll in the park before lunch and two shabby old ladies had trotted out there to look at the pheasants with no useful educational object, but merely for fun. I felt at home. One must come up into Canada from the south to realize how great is the difference made by the border.

VANCOUVER *3 March 1944*

My dear Elizabeth,
I spent the afternoon sleeping like the dead till it was time for the International Affairs at their club—an audience without any of that awful opening of beaks like unreasoning fledglings who expect the punctual worm to follow, but a sprinkling of people who had been in Arab countries and asked about manageable problems like irrigation, leaving

the vaster platitudes alone. It was a refreshment to the weary spirit, and Palestine dealt with in an atmosphere of serenity. I was sorry to leave Victoria that same evening, but, of course, delighted to reach this haven and stay with the Selous[1] who are old friends from Basra. And here again I feel with all the casual people I meet a very pleasant sense of being near home. There is an essential change as one crosses the frontier. Perhaps it was symbolized at the lunch of the Canadian club, which began with grace and ended with a toast to the King and the Canadian anthem? It was the largest meeting they had had and I had to speak into a microphone, and however often I do it, it still makes me feel ill beforehand; but as it was for a British audience—such a relief not to have to bother about being so modest—I really set out to give a picture of our general achievement in the Middle East both before and through the war. An old padre came up afterwards and told me that the churches are being circularized by the Zionists, and asked my opinion. He said that being Scottish he had suspected there might be a snag in their argument and had made no response. As a result, Mr. Selous thought it a good plan to get hold of the Bishop who is a charming man and dealt with Palestine with restful brevity: asked for the number of Jews *v.* Arabs; asked for the Balfour Declaration; remarked on the second clause of it; said: 'Obviously there is a duty to each side': and arranged for me to meet the Bishop of San Francisco, here on a visit today.

A Royal Navy Commander came up, last seen on his tiny gunboat on the Tigris. Everyone practically has a girl or boy overseas. Oh my, what a relief not to have to be tactful about mentioning the fact that we're at war! One more meeting, and I leave for a week of country life tomorrow, just in time to save me from going neurotic.

Train from VANCOUVER *4 March 1944*

It deluged in Vancouver, but I had time and chance to look into Howe's Sound and see the fjords and islands. One last lecture—two Zionist ladies panting to be at me. One of them read out a bit of Van Paassen about the Colonial Office, saying that sooner or later every man has to face the truth. I could not resist interjecting that I hoped this day might come soon to Mr. Van P. and was clapped for this sentiment! I told the heckler that as the C.O. has most of the bother it is obviously not anxious to stir it up, and that all one need do to understand is to pause by one of our Yeomanry lads' graves in Palestine and *think*—whereupon the audience nearly cheered. I added a small rapture over the Zionists' wonderful work, which

[1] Mr. and Mrs. G. H. Selous. He was then Trade Commissioner in Vancouver.

had the usual effect of a soft answer to make the woman look like murder; my hostess, sitting beside her, was appalled at her venom. It is much the best way to smile, and leave it to one's statements to flatten them out.

Now here are no public speeches for a week! A wonderful peace is about me. We are slipping through hour after hour of mountains clothed with pine and cedar, all sleeping in this snow; the clearings, the wooden huts and tidy orchards look minute in such a vastness: there is great gallantry in this western land cut out of the hardness of nature and only just holding its own. The train runs along steep slopes, crossing gullies on trestle bridges made of timber; wind-bitten people come in at the stations, with nice faces.

My father died at Creston in 1931 and I had never been able to reach Canada again to sort out his affairs: Tom Leaman, our groom and gardener in my Devonshire childhood, had looked after them and kept everything for me, and I now wrote from:

BROKEN HILL RANCH, CRESTON, B.C.

I have been here on my ranch three days, splashing about in the thawing orchards and trying to get through an accumulation of business of fifteen years. It is pleasant to get back to the earth and its crops, and to talk about the fruit buds, more fat and prosperous to the eye of the expert than the prospects of Europe. My father came here thirty years ago, and blasted the stumps out of his land with dynamite when there were only a dozen homesteads in the breadth of the valley; now there are over six thousand people in the town and its district, and these older orchards slant down as it might be Herefordshire. But there is still a pioneering feel about the place in spite of its new stores and hotel and cinema; the people are mostly hard up and good to each other; and pretty well every young lad who could possibly be spared is away in the forces. Even here I was badgered into a talk in the grand new school-house to an audience of about five hundred farmers and their wives; even babies were brought. One can see the sort of background out of which the prosperity of the U.S.A. has grown, and it is fascinating to watch these two different stages side by side: also alarming. There is a great storehouse here of tradition, and a far greater unity to start with, and, of course, a reassuring preponderance of Scots! Will this country save something beyond dollars to believe in and keep the qualities it brings with it from home? There is one point which ought to be strongly remembered in Canada, where the greatest interest is taken in the British side of what happens in the Middle East. A number of Canadians have come up to me thrilled by the new conception of Empire based on co-operation and service. Now Lord Halifax's speech and Churchill's (about not liquidating the Empire) assumed this but did not make it plainly understood, and both have come in for a very mixed reception; if the matter is not explained in simple language as I have been doing, the audience is apt to understand something not only different but opposite—an imperialism of the old sort which is unpopular among the young. If we could really make this country realize what we are building into the future, it might be just the inspiration they need. The United States are pulling, I take it, with a very strong economic magnet; their way of life and values have a terrific and, it seems to me, disastrous appeal; our best means of countering is with an idea. These are good people; they are not just 'economic dust'; you need only look at the Home Guard along the railway line, the grey-headed men in their uniforms and old ribbons, all joining again. We must give a vision for rallying. But I don't think just 'Empire' is enough for the young ones: they must and can feel they are building something new and useful to all the world. I think the actual meaning of what we are doing should be so carefully and conscientiously instilled that no *cliché* about imperialism should have a chance of being listened to. We have our opportunity and it may not come again.

I must stop, my dear Elizabeth, and you will now have nearly a week's rest from my diary.

REGINA *15 March 1944*

The fact of my having a farm on the Kootenay made everything go very easily at the Calgary dinner, and a doctor came in who had been an airman in Iraq in the First World War. Only one old diehard stood up and said he still thought 'Britain had made a mistake and Britain ought to pay'. The whole audience, as one man, pointed out that it was Palestine and not Britain who was being asked to pay, but he remained unshaken, full of a rock-like integrity impervious to sense. The rest however were quite convinced and my chairman told me it was a great relief to him to feel that Britain had not gone back on her word. This is what is so pleasant here, the constant meeting with people who are thinking in terms other than profit and loss. Do you think it is the out-of-door life? One knows that a mountaineer will not cut his rope, whatever the pros and cons may be, or that a traveller through the bush will share with his packmen even if it reduces all his chances—it is easy to talk to people like that because there is an unshakeable and simple foundation. Anyway after it was all over I went to the local Rabbi and shook hands, and told him I hoped he would get back to Palestine by peaceful means, and a Russian Jew, his friend, came and held my hands in the warmest manner. It is a horrid job to have to trample on people's dreams, and one is always wishing that cakes could simultaneously be had and eaten.

My chairman walked about with me in the cold starlight till the train was in, and told me of Canadian troubles and of his life here (he was born in Cheshire), and of the joy of building in a new land. And this morning I got to Regina which has prairie all round it, in low waves like the desert.

I wish I knew what an Explorer looks like? Every journalist's first remark is that I don't look like one. 'Oddly,' *The San Francisco Chronicle* says (why oddly?), 'this explorer is no hulking man but a frail, pixie-like woman.' And *The Vancouver Daily Province* says that, as a British agent, I am the 'novelist's dream come true'. Is that flattering, I wonder?

WINNIPEG 16 March 1944

Regina is behind me and we are trundling through the prairie in a snowstorm.

I am always now being asked about the dissension between us and the U.S.A. over the new oil pipe-line. I saw this question coming weeks ahead and asked for guidance and was told not to talk about it if I could avoid it; but naturally one can't avoid it and I do register a wail over this Government habit of giving its children a negative when they ask for bread. I have therefore (as often before) had to make up my own guidance.

In Regina one comes into the Middle West atmosphere, people who—as they themselves say—have come not to live but to make money. But whether it is their comparative poverty, or whether it is the force of more traditional standards still working, it is a temperate atmosphere: the money standard may be the one followed, but one has not got the feeling that no other standard *exists*.

18 March 1944

My chairman here, a most charming lawyer from Toronto, expected me to have a tough time and so I did: there were about forty to fifty men, mostly lawyers, doctors, etc., and at least five Zionists, one a K.C. called Finkelstein who finkled with difficult questions. They were all out to get at Palestine and concentrated on it entirely for over an hour (frightfully exhausting). The fact is, however, that if you base your case solidly on its fundamentals, the details sink into proper perspective. The lawyers came up afterwards and told me I was a good fencer, and there was no doubt which side they were on by the end of the evening. It was exciting, but alarming, to argue with such a trained audience. At the end one of the Zionists dished his case completely by saying that as force was being used to move populations in eastern Europe, why not in Palestine? I said he had described the *only* alternative to a policy of consent, and I left it to the room to judge which was the better of the two. The room was in no doubt. Another point brought up was the relative numbers of Jews and Arabs in the fighting forces—more than three times as many Jews. I said I thought the difference not quite so great, but anyway it seemed to me that a Jew had more than three times as many reasons for fighting the Germans as an Arab had. The last argument was that it would pay Britain to have a strategic point like Palestine in friendly hands. I said the whole area between India and the Mediterranean was strategic and it paid us to have it friendly. I think I enjoyed a rather unfair advantage, being the only woman in that roomful of men all shooting questions at me. Several came up afterwards and said they were ready to come to my assistance, only they saw I didn't need it, and even Mr. Finkelstein came and patted me on the shoulder. One of the Zionists ended by quoting Lloyd George who hoped to see Palestine as Jewish as England is English. I thought this really didn't deserve to be seriously dealt with and remarked that my father had left England and settled in Canada because he disliked Lloyd George, and everyone laughed and cheered.

I went back with my chairman afterwards to end the evening with him and his wife and two friends, drinking sherry in a library filled with old books. There is a pleasant civic pride about the men who run these prairie towns, the sort of feeling you find in Thucydides when he writes of the Greek cities: they have the joy of building, and realize it, stepping easily from their traditions to their future and competent to do it.

Having some time next morning to play with, I spent it in the Hudson Bay Company's little museum, following the romantic history from the first charter given by Charles II. It is fascinating to think that this huge dominion owes its colonization to so small an animal as the beaver, whose fur was fashionable for hats.

WASHINGTON *26 March 1944*

It was an impressive and rather nerve-racking affair to be defending the White Paper under the eye of its author in Ottawa. I stayed with

Malcolm MacDonald and his sister. Everyone likes him across the breadth of Canada; he seems to have all the virtues for a public life and is such a nice person in private.

We had about fifty people at the International Affairs Association and, when my speech was ended, got down to a good hour of questions and answers on Palestine. No other aspect of Arabia even touched on, except the pipe-line. I was so tired I scarce knew what I was saying, but am so imbued with it now that it comes out automatically. The Zionists were ready-prepared with notes, but no question that could not be answered, and the best Canadian orator was there—a Mr. Brockington, listening under a forest of his own eyebrows. He asked all the main Zionist questions with a chortle of satisfaction when they were demolished and made me repeat the Balfour Declaration twice over—had never heard of the second, non-Jewish, proviso before! Malcolm said to me afterwards that I appeared to be one of the very few people who had ever read his White paper, and told me that our argument expresses the intentions of the policy when it was made. He also told me how Weizmann tried to induce him to alter it and, when he saw it was not to be done by fair words, lost all control, using the most violent threats and invective. I have always been convinced that Weizmann's dagger and his silken sheath are two very different substances.

The External Affairs in Ottawa had a Miss MacCallum to keep them posted on the Middle East. She was born in Turkey and happens to be an enthusiast on her own regions, and I dined with her and gave her the latest news I had. It is extraordinary what devotion these scarred and naked lands can still inspire: here she was, a white-haired gentle-faced American with a passion for the rights of people who clamber barefoot behind their camels and mules and donkeys all over the Arabian world and have no idea even that her sort of life exists. The human capacity for being interested is pleasant when you come to think of it.

Just before leaving we discovered a Committee of Canadian-Arab Friendship in existence. It was too late to meet its representatives in Ottawa, but I agreed to dine with them during my three hours' wait in Montreal and when I got there (after dark in a snowstorm) found four grizzled Lebanese preceded by a large bouquet waiting on the platform —wrapped up in tweed coats to which they managed to give an oriental casualness destructive of the most respectable tailoring. They all owned little businesses of various sorts—a candy store, a dress shop, a restaurant. They had brought a car, and had a dinner ready in a private room at the Windsor Hotel; there were two extra places 'in case you had friends' and the bouquet was enthroned in the middle of the table, and we talked Arabic and spoke of villages in the hills they left forty years or more ago. They had banded themselves together and sent a letter with their Arab case to all the Canadian M.P.s: I enclose this document, a feeble slingstone against Goliath. I have long ago come to the conclusion that hardly any Arab should be left to manage his own case! As an afterthought, when dinner was over, they said they must get a few journalists to see me: I had just an hour left, having resisted their optimism, which tried to mesmerize my train into leaving at eleven instead of ten: however one French reporter of *Le Canada* was found and I took him on before they bewildered him into chaos over the Arab cause. They were so decent with it all. The owner of the candy store interrupted his own anti-Zionist oration by reflecting that 'one must do what one can for those poor people: we too have refugees! But,' he added sensibly, 'if you are given three rooms in an hotel, it does not mean you should expect the whole building.' I felt, as I have felt so often, that it is not want of shrewdness or capacity that makes the Arabs so bad at their own case; it is their incurable conviction that pleasant living is worth more than success. I nearly lost my train because a little typewritten speech had to be read out, and we then ploughed through ice and sleet to the station, as the car had been based on the non-existent eleven o'clock train. I left the Canadian-Arab Friendship Committee with a very warm heart.

And that was the end of my circuit. As I am nearly always ill in trains and can't get over the feeling of panic before speeches, I spend practically the whole of a lecture tour in a state of nausea and am glad to have reached the journey's end; but I have enjoyed all my work during the war so much that I feel rather glad to make a sort of offering of something I don't like to do. Events in Washington, Michael Wright tells me, have been busy showing America how sensible we were in what we said: we now sit like Cassandra and watch the Trojan horse and what comes out of it. I cannot believe that the U.S.A. will long remain on the side opposite to Oil.

13
Last of America

The crossing of America over, I spent two months engaged in arrangements for a book published in New York under the title of *The Arabian Isle* and in England as *East is West*. It had been suggested by Dr. Brandt of the Oriental Institute in Chicago and was intended to give an easy but, humanly speaking, accurate picture of the Arabian background to the Palestine question. Even at that eleventh hour one hoped for conciliation. Malcolm MacDonald wrote in May that he felt convinced 'from information received from various quarters that, if only the Jews will accept the policy of seeking agreement, Jewish immigration can continue by consent.'

But the hardening and the urgency of this problem grew sharper as the end of the war began to come in sight. Sir Kinahan wrote from Baghdad (19.4.44): '. . . Those delightful letters describing your doings have interested me very much indeed and your tour has been more than worth while. Our chief danger, as you know, lies in the Palestine settlement—of which the world is so woefully ignorant. So I am very glad to hear that you have been asked to write a book and the sooner you do so the better. Things are much as they were—the cabinet as always tottery and everything pretty expensive . . . Nuri goes faint at intervals and one never knows how much longer he will last.'

A month or two later Christopher Scaife reported a telegram from the Foreign Office supporting our Brotherhood in very strong terms . . . 'They say they realize the British Government is associated in the minds of many people here with old-fashioned and corrupt cliques, with whom they must deal because they are the governing groups; and consider the Brotherhood a valuable means of showing that—though Great Britain cannot intervene to change things—these standards are not ones of which she approves, and she welcomes any movement towards change for the better. The Foreign Office, says the telegram, attaches importance to the continuance of the work after the war ... Honestly, Freya, it really is a triumph. There is no hedging in the language; it's a downright acceptance with no reservation.'

Meanwhile my Washington life resumed its course and while I relaxed with neither a speech nor railway journey at the end of every day, two Rabbis and a Congress member asked for my removal.

WASHINGTON *31 March 1944*

My dear Elizabeth,

I saw them all, like Ulysses *après le long voyage* ... and heard that Mr. Cellor in Congress puts me in the lowest Inferno circle shared only by the Colonial Office. Most of this sound and fury is Election; all we need do is to sit quite quiet and practise that lethargy which comes naturally to government departments. I have always felt the Arab cause safe since it was switched by H.M.G. to the side of inaction.

1 April 1944

Alice Longworth had us all to dinner last night—delightful—full of gaiety and malice—and charmed me as we were talking about physical exercise by lifting her foot with both hands and putting it on her shoulder; she told me she likes to drive in this Yoga position by herself in a car through New York. Her nephew, Archie Roosevelt, sat next me, boiling over Tunis Arab wrongs and I had some difficulty (but succeeded I hope) in persuading him that the best way to help the African Arabs was not a head-on attack on the French but general strengthening and unification in the East.

After dinner I sat in a corner with James Dunn (Mr. Cordell Hull's right-hand man) and was pleased to see what a difference there was in his attitude between this conversation and the one before I started on my journey. He told me he had been watching the predictions then made coming true, and spoke as a full ally, and I inferred he had a little to do with the War Department's intervention against Senators Taft and Wagner. I told him I had just been reading the Book of Judges and noticed how it took the Israelites several centuries and many wars to get settled in the Promised Land even after they had immigrated into it, with their unpopularity rectified by perpetual interventions from Jehovah: it is hard that the Colonial Office should be expected to undertake in a decade or two what it took Jehovah centuries of warfare to accomplish.

The U.S.A. unpopularity among the Arabs is preoccupying them all here, I am glad to see. There is every likelihood, as I wrote before my journey, that an Arab policy will emerge slowly, and it seems to me that our most important job—more even than the Zionists—is to implant co-operation in the minds of all these government departments *now*, while the policy is fluid and the minds that will deal with the Middle East are open to ideas. Competition or co-operation are in the balance, and it may well be a question of individual idiosyncrasies on which side the scales rise or fall; and *now* is the time when diplomacy can act. We have to make converts, not to our ideas on the Middle East but to the fact that they *are* our ideas and not a U.S.A. monopoly: and that it is only together and not separately that we can work them out. I think it pays to point out too what a very good job we have made of the Middle East—a fact which the Zionists tend to make people forget. The Arabian future seems good so long as it can develop in a climate of security; the great achievement of Britain has been to keep a sort of umbrella over these countries to shelter them while their nationalism was young and tender, and the great point of the American entry is that this umbrella can now be made bigger and more protective. But it would be a mistake to let anyone forget that it was a British umbrella in the first place. I have often thought that it would be quite a good plan if we made more of our status as an Arabian government (Aden and Hadhramaut) and had a seat as of right in the meetings of the Arab nations. This might be done now unobtrusively, while later it would probably rouse all sorts of oppositions.

PS. You know the joke that is going about here in the Republican houses—that they would like to lease Churchill and lend Roosevelt?

15 April 1944

I was taken to lunch by two young Arabs from Syria and Iraq, both working for the O.W.I. Amusing to see the different outlook of the two countries, and what a much more congenial spirit we have managed to produce in Iraq. The U.S.A. Government has a lot of these Middle Easterners to draw on, whose influence is worth bearing in mind: it means that their information is that of young men inclined to be antagonistic to the people in office and to spread the feeling, if we are not careful, that Britain is the bulwark of the old fogeys. If the U.S.A. ever came to look upon itself as the champion of the young progressive Arab as against the reactionary governments supported by Britain, it would be largely through the agency of these effendis in offices. This will not happen if we continue to develop the 'young' side of our contacts, as we have been doing lately. I spent most of lunch arguing that it is unreasonable to expect the diplomats to be in intimate touch with *both* sides, as they are not compatible—other bodies, such as the British Council, Public Relations, etc., should foster the young. The Iraqi saw this at once, the Syrian not so easily, being obsessed by French misdeeds to the exclusion of more general ideas, like most Syrians.

No sooner had I lunched with these young men, than Major Snyder arrived to carry me off to the War Department, where twenty-five thousand people are housed in the Pentagon building in a sort of Brave New World apotheosis only mitigated by old-fashioned things like trees on the horizon: one can look out of the office windows and see that the structure of the universe still stands, but for everything to do with ordinary life one can forget it and live in the man-made world.

Major Snyder is the most friendly, sincere man, unbitten by jealousies or inferiorities and therefore all out to help and appreciate: he makes one realize a certain hollowness in other people's ideas of co-operation. His brother-in-law is D.C. in Jaffa and used to be in Iraq and I spent the evening with them pleasantly forgetting who was American and who British. Before this, however, he took me into a room of the War Department with about thirty people from all the services, and I answered questions for two hours. I did this again the next day with the Strategic Services and may as well group the gist of the three meetings together.

The dominant preoccupation seems to be Russia; they asked again and again whether she is being active among the younger people. I said that as far as I knew there was no organized activity, merely the general attaction of young men all over the world. The name of Communism is applied to any leftward movement, often not communistic at all. They evidently thought me optimistic: they expect trouble but seem to think of it as Anglo-Russian, not affecting the U.S.A. The idea that we are treating the menace in a homœopathic way was not received with any enthusiasm (though Mr. Ireland agreed in private that it was the only method which might be successful). At the bottom of it all there seems to be the humiliating conviction that the British can't make themselves liked anywhere, so that if anyone else comes along we are more or less done for; of course no one said this, and in fact may not have consciously thought it, but the whole structure of their theories is built on this assumption. Their information did not seem to take sufficient account of the changes of the last two or three years; these are almost all in British favour, and I stressed them strongly.

The most interesting lunch was with a Captain A. of the State Department who gave me a long and friendly account of all the reasons why Americans distrust the British in the Middle East. The one that seemed to require most attention was a growing feeling that we are encouraging American unpopularity among the Arabs, which I assured him was a mistake and that I had come out to put the Arab case precisely because our people foresaw that the Zionists would make the U.S.A. unpopular and *we* should be blamed.

Americans are discouraged, said the Captain, because they feel we don't really want them in the Middle East; we did not welcome the pipe-line. I again took a strongly non-appeasement view and said: 'Didn't they spring it on us without a word?' He admitted this and agreed that if ever we are to work together it will be essential to make the U.S. public understand that the Middle East is not a field for competition. People are annoyed, he said, because Ibn Saud declared that if he had to choose between us, he would choose British; they look upon his adoption of the American as a switching over rather than as the widening of an old friendship to include a new one. I agreed very heartily in this view and said I had been perturbed for some time to see the sort of 'corner' in Ibn Saud which even people like Colonel H. are inclined to make.

He then pointed out the difficulty for Americans to understand our 'double' policy—the old imperialist and the new (with which he agreed although he 'could not say so here'). I pointed out that it isn't two policies, it is merely that we are like those trees that keep the old leaves while the new are already shooting out and it is up to the observer to see which is which. He agreed and said, acutely I thought, that the British have objectives but no policies, and that our apparent double system still unites in making for the same objective. The Americans would never work with our old-fashioned imperialists but, he agreed, there was far more chance with newer cultural ventures. That would be all right, I said, so long as they did not think of the one as opposite to the other; for the fact is that we do all work for the same and if there is disagreement it is only a minor one of method. 'One would then have to agree on the objectives,' said Captain A. 'Well, what *are* the American objectives in the Middle East?' said I. 'Self-interest and altruism,' said he. I said it was my firm conviction that the two came to the same thing in the long run. He told me that this is where the British and Americans really disagree; the Americans are so generous they can't bear to think of altruism as profitable. 'Well,' said I, 'they must just bring themselves to study the facts and see whether it is or is not so.' 'They can't study facts,' said he.

'They have been dominated by advertisement too long.' It is a gloomy picture.

The bright spot in all this talking was the conversion of Senator G. Virginia Bacon, who is a dear, asked me to a large dinner-party with the Halifaxes and Lippmanns and many whose names I didn't know and sat me next a genial white-haired superabundant old boy, one of those who gaily declare they know nothing about a question and sign documents without a qualm. I thought I would try him with the Bible and began by bringing to his notice the likeness between Ibn Saud and King Solomon—they both kept up their political relationships by marrying numerous wives among the Arab tribes. The Senator had forgotten that Solomon carried conciliation so far as to build temples to Ashtoreth just outside the Jerusalem gate. He did remember that David took refuge with the king of the Philistines below Jaffa: by the time we were through the fish he realized that conciliation had been the only successful policy in Israel. He told me he had to speak on modern Palestine next week and was it true that the Arab feeling was merely artificially fostered? I gave him pictures—of the holy men in Nejf and the peasants in the Yemen sending their pennies to the Palestine guerrillas. He said: 'I'm going to change all my speeches; I'm so glad I heard this in time,' and leaned across our hostess to tell Lord Halifax how glad he was. I got a very quizzical look from H.E. who doubtless expects more protests from rabbis, and I got up filled with admiration over this light-heartedness with the policies of nations. Spent the rest of the evening listening in a peaceful way to Mr. Shapiro who was making all our minds up for us on Russia.

17 April 1944

Oil is being poured on the Zionist waters in a way anything but soothing. If the rival companies here begin to talk about each other, British diplomacy will look pure, by comparison, even to American eyes.

20 April 1944

The latest jewel of American co-operation came to me while lunching with one of the Iraqis. He asked what he was to do, having been requested by someone in the State Department to induce Nuri to foment a protest similar to the recent united Arab anti-American effort[1]—only this one to be directed against the British on the subject of the Yemen-Aden

---

[1] Against the Senators Taft and Wagner.

boundary. I believe this statement because when I was being quizzed by all the Middle East departments, every one of them showed what seemed to me a peculiar interest in the Aden boundary dispute. (I merely answered that I had never known Aden without a boundary dispute and that it was the sort of boundary that always does have disputes, and in fact disappointed them visibly by refusing to consider it of any importance.) It is a sordid tale anyway. When one or two stories of this sort are circulating, it is obviously a waste of breath to talk to the Arab world about Anglo-American solidarity. The feeling it gives me is pure nausea, but there is a certain obtuseness created by the 'businessmen's ethics' which makes it impossible for them even to realize that this is shabby behaviour. I mentioned it to Lord Halifax who looked into the middle distance and said: 'an interesting psychology.'

It is cold and wet, but this town is a lovely sight in its nest of trees; they shimmer like a rainstorm, every drop a bud.

One's heart is in the news as it mounts towards its climax. Someone said that if the invasion suffered a setback this country might be stepping out: I replied rather acidly that in that case she would step out all alone—but he was drowned in a general chorus.

PS. Do you call to mind that our Bible notion of Hell is derived from the Babylonian—i.e. the fire and brimstone of Middle Eastern oil?

1 May 1944

The Irelands say that the reports now coming in are very satisfactory and the interviews of the last few months are showing results. The reports are certainly much more cheerful. *The Daily Telegraph* correspondent tells me that my Jewish friends in San Francisco have been writing to express anti-Zionist feelings and sympathy with our policy. It seems to me that you should now get some *new* person every few months to do a tour, withdraw them when—like me—they become a target, and then start with someone else. Nothing gets so monotonous as invective, and an angry Zionist would soon become an habitual feature of the Congress landscape which no one would notice.

The Rabbis' attack here, Lord Halifax told me, has been dealt with in the 'easy' way and sent to London for burial, and I was amused by Mr. Mander's questions in the House [as to why I had been sent to the U.S.A. and what I was doing there]. I wonder if I can get back in July? There is no chance of going now as everything but the most urgent is clamped down, and all rather doubtful about the summer. It is almost unbearable to be so far away.

I wrote to Brendan Bracken[1] to thank him for his defence of me and to point out that I had never minimized the Jewish achievement and had never yet had an audience that did not agree with my 'very moderate views' by the end of the evening. 'It is possibly this which has upset some extremists? May I add a purely personal opinion which I feel very strongly? I think that if we were to drop our present banner of "keepers of faith" with the Arab world, the U.S.A. would very quickly pick it up and wave it?'

NEW YORK *17 May 1944*

My dear Elizabeth,

I had a party and a dinner given by the dear Wrights, and there said good-bye to the three queens of Washington who have been so kind to me, and on my way here spent a pleasant day with Professor Hitti among his Arabic manuscripts at Princeton. The dogwood was out and the wistaria; there was a Gothic calm—term being over—and they have the finest Arabic manuscript collection in this country, of which even the outer view on rows and rows of shelves was peaceful. They live in an atmosphere of tradition, exclusiveness, and all the things one can indulge when not obsessed by this fetish of equality, and they outrage the democratic principle by selecting small numbers of the most intelligent students only for Princeton.

21 May 1944

A sidelight on my friends in Congress—Mr. Cellor wrote to the American Geographical Society warning against having me as a lecturer—an 'agent of the British'. It appears to have had an excellent effect opposite to what was intended; I can't tell you how nice all the geographers have been. I am also still deeply involved with the Council of Churches and also called on Mr. Sulzberger (publisher of *The New York Times*)—a charming, sad man. He read me a letter he wrote in 1937 speaking of the wish of an American Jew to be nothing but American except in a religious sense. His reluctance to be active against the Zionists comes, I think, from a natural and sorrowful feeling—the wish to tread softly when one is treading on people's dreams: anyone must feel this, and how much more when it is one's own people!

My dear Elizabeth, I can hardly bear the Zionist question any longer! Would you be very angelic and send six of my clothing coupons to

[1] The Minister of Information.

Norman Hartnell, Bruton Street? (If you remember, I left my little lot of coupons to await my return.)

Elsa Maxwell came to lunch with Alyx Rothschild and Chips Channon (just over). It was like sitting under a waterfall—inaccurate but not malicious—a stream of human kindness tossing promiscuously, the first pronoun singular borne up among the waves. I liked her, but my—I hope she never writes about me; her genius for inaccuracy is almost unbelievable. She is giving a big dinner for Clare Luce tonight and I am going.

22 May 1944

An incredible party—a hundred people in the Salle des Perroquets of the Waldorf Astoria. We got lost among naked marble and elevators till the noise guided us and there was everybody—John Gunther, Dorothy Thompson, Anne McCormick, congressmen, journalists, the highbrows of New York, and Mrs. Luce looking beautiful in a sad and bitter way; Elsa Maxwell with her arm round everybody, genuinely rejoicing in having so many friends. I went with the Marriotts (John just out from England seated with a quizzical look beside Elsa). At my table were Colonel Bodley and Henry Luce. Colonel B. has written a book on his seven years among the Sahara Bedouin and we were soon talking nomad shop which I found very interesting; I had not realized that these Sahara Arabs had kept their traditions and their racial character so intact. Soon, however, when I discovered who was on my other side, I tore myself from this pleasant Arab meandering and plunged into Anglo-American tangles with Henry Luce, a tormented soul but likeable. I found him surprisingly sympathetic over the sentimental nonsense about exotic peoples that we suffer from and he evidently does not share his wife's indiscriminate slogans; but about England he expressed disapproval of Winston Churchill in no uncertain terms and refuses to look on him as anything but an old-fashioned imperialist. He made me feel as usual how it is the name and not the thing itself that people out here mind; he was quite passionate about it, with at the same time a great feeling for the English. I said I hoped that we were once again becoming 'Elizabethan' and he leaped upon this as if it were almost too good to be true, only doubting because, he said, it was hard to reconcile with our adoption of government interference of every sort. 'What we Americans dislike is not your buccaneer who goes out into the world and carves it for his own profit, but the man at the desk who makes a slow safe dividend of fifty per cent with no personal adventure.' He had always been able to understand the English, he said—their weakness in 1935–8, their strength in

1939; but in 1942 he went over and could understand them no longer; the 'imperialism' he found there seemed to go with a desire for social security with which it was quite incompatible. I thought he was misled by the word 'imperialism' which was really a desire for the enlargement of the commonwealth idea, and that the desire for social security came from a deep resolve for fundamental unity and an end of the two nations of the English industrial age: a wish for fairness rather than security was at the bottom of it.

By this time speeches were beginning and went on till nearly 2 a.m., and all bad: the crowning horror was that I was dragged in with a question on Arabs in whom nobody was interested and I wished I were in a uniform like John who got out of everything on that score. Mrs. Luce ended the evening with a long and accomplished speech, beginning with her childhood and going right through her friends to the present moment. The smiles, the movements, the pauses, the daisy-schoolgirl innocence were all thought out beforehand and nothing was genuine—but the voice is lovely with a moving quality in it, and she is lovely to look at, and laid the flattery on like butter (unrationed), and everyone was charmed, even I, because it was a work of art. The only thing I thought unforgivable was a reference to her former husband: she said that Elsa Maxwell's friendship had suffered a fifteen-year eclipse while she (Clare) 'was married to a bore'. A ruthless woman! John Marriott's reaction this morning is that he thinks he must leave for England next week. The only real lightness was brought by a comedian (Eddie Cantor) who excused himself from a speech, dived into the hotel and emerged with a shy little blonde in a turquoise toque with whom he sang a song about having a baby which I must say, in that highbrow atmosphere, I found extremely refreshing.

NEWPORT *30 May 1944*

Tomorrow I give my last lecture. After that, apart from one day in New York to try and convert the Federal Council of Churches (which seemed important enough to tear me back into a town) I shall sit in the country until my passage to England materializes; like a happy nation, I hope to have no history, and this diary comes to its end. One day I shall read it and be shocked by the chaos I have hurled at you, but I never had time to write carefully and felt it better to jot down what came at the end of the day than to leave you with no record at all. It is nice of you to tell me that you think the job done satisfactorily; it has been such a nerve-straining affair that I feel rather down and out and unable to judge very clearly myself. My wrists and ankles have developed curious pains and they tell me this is a poison due to strain. Anyway I have now been in the real country for two days and suddenly realized that it is just country—cows, trees, grass, sky that I need and nothing else; I had reached the point when the thought of a platform made me physically sick.

It is fine, however, to end with a week in New England. There is a tradition and a rectitude about it, a difference from the rest of what I have seen as between beads that are threaded and those that lie scattered. One can see it in the Boston faces—nice shabby worn faces that don't mind getting old and look exactly like their great-grandfathers painted by Copley in the Boston museum. I had three days with two good old people in a house crowded with family photographs, samplers, books, Victorian sofas upholstered and held down with red velvet nails, rocking chairs, piety and comfort and a mixture of austerity and benevolence which was charming. I then stayed with the Constables, friends from Asolo—was taken to the Somerset Club, which is the pinnacle of Boston—old ladies with untidy grey hair wearing the fashions of the past in a way that made one feel at home—and Sunday I spent with other old friends at Pride's Crossing, where the woods go back for thirty miles over a sea promontory, and the unassuming rich live in a simple rural and expensive tranquillity. The bungalow was full of pictures and Lowestoft china; cows pastured below the windows by the lake; we bathed with apple blossom and lilac hanging over the water; it was very agreeable. We had the Sedgwicks to lunch (ex-editor of *The Atlantic Monthly*), and talked of Persia, Arabs and France; and went to tea with the Philips who look down an Italian vista to the lake.

Next day I met Miss Williamson of *The Christian Science Monitor* whose heart is in London; she told me that she once arrived to revisit Dr. Johnson's house as the caretaker was just closing it, but he recognized her as a visitor from other years, and left her to browse about alone by lamp-light for an hour or so; she feeds on this memory when the thought of what has been happening in London makes her sad. These are true sorts of friends since they have a passionate wish to preserve the things we also care about, and it seems to me that we can never do too much to make ourselves intelligible and keep these *real* allies with us: no amount of conciliating the other sort of American will make up for the loss of those who genuinely share our views of life, even if they are now in a minority.

I said this to Miss Williamson, and I said it more or less in a short speech of thanks to the 'American Defence' of Harvard where I pointed to what seemed to me the essential likeness between the New and the Old England—the desire to give service rather than to preserve one's rights. It seemed to me that New England is nearer in this to Great Britain than to the rest of the U.S.A.—and I said so and they appeared to like it.

My visit had to end on the more familiar note, with a radio talk for women introduced once a week by the opening bars of 'The Blue Danube'. When I had done I was thanked by a sprightly blonde, "and next week"—she turned to her public through the microphone—"we have another treat in store for you: our Circus of Performing Animals"—a lecture tour's not inappropriate close.

My feelings for England and New England were echoed by Isaiah Berlin:

London is heaven (he wrote) and Oxford seventh heaven. After four days in my own room, and a conversation or two with the Cecils and their friends (Lord Berners, you will be glad to hear, has written a national anthem for Saudi Arabia which he played to me on the piano), I lost all desire to see telegrams, dispatches, important persons, etc., and indeed, although I fear to say it, actually began to lose interest in all the subjects with which they dealt. Before this enchantment could pass, I made a date with my college to return and settle down to a life of contemplation (which genuinely seems to me fuller of tangible and palpable objects than my present existence—certainly no politics are more real than those of academic life, no loves deeper, no hatreds more burning, no principles more sacred).

I shall, if I may, take you at your word about your house in Venetia. Who knows but we may go to the Holy Land together from there one day, but not yet, I hasten to add. As I told Colonel Hoskins the other day, I find I have no stomach for the ingredients of that fearful cauldron and find a position on its edge, scalded from time to time by its fearful exhalations, futile as well as uncomfortable . . . I do envy you your early return. . . .

CONNECTICUT *16 June 1944*

Dear Elizabeth,

Everyone has been kind and helpful; I cannot tell you how easy they made it all. And here I am, miles from the world, at Sharon, Conn., in country lush and green, real farms and lovely houses. A peaceful liking for America creeps into my soul. But it is like a dream to think of London in a fortnight.

14

England in 1944

A woman and I, the only two females on the flying-boat from Baltimore, travelled in the 'honeymoon suite'. From its bedroom, furnished like the Ritz, we saw the Atlantic icebergs in the sun. Daylight met daylight above them, for we destroyed four hours by flying eastwards, drove across Ireland to another airfield, and were in London before dark. And London was fine: empty and shabby among its battered windows and breached thoroughfares, it flourished a sudden unexpected beauty, in the buildings or the quietness of people's faces, or through some odd notice of 'Business as usual' over gashes in walls.

It was good to feel near it, to hear the day's battle spoken direct from the battle-fields every evening (one could hear the excitement in the correspondents' voices and the crackle of the shells behind them). D-Day was over and the invasion of France was on, and the story was going about that the Americans had asked for fifty war correspondents to witness the landing—'the most important event since the Crucifixion,' they said (rather inaccurately). 'And that,' the British had replied when they refused, 'was adequately covered by four reporters.'

The House of Commons, bombed out, was meeting in Dean's Yard among texts such as 'The Fear of the Lord is the beginning of Wisdom', which one hoped they might take to heart for times of peace. I went to listen one day, when Winston Churchill came in to answer questions, and a liveliness followed him, as if fresh water were let into some stagnant pond. He stood with his huge hunched shoulders and head forward, his hands moving with light gestures, almost like a Frenchman's, against the massiveness of everything else about him, as if the delicacy of the artist must show through.

At Chips Channon's one still dined at a marble table with candles and peaches, or with Emerald Cunard among her pictures at the Dorchester (stepping over the splintered glass of its shattered windows), where she received with eyes brilliant with belladonna, infusing into her ancient face a glittering life unrelated to the world around it. A Mme du Deffand out of her century, she was a gallant relic of the *ancien régime* and I liked her—even her complaint about the middle-class war: 'one doesn't know who is getting killed.' Marie Antionette, one felt, could not have done better.

The people who were getting killed were there around one, under the V1, Hitler's 'secret weapon', which in this month of July came chugging with jerks 'like a shopping woman trying to get to a bus', black against the evening sky, with fins triangular as a shark's and a tail of solid and stubby smoke behind it; or rolling under the moon across the housetops, as if a planet had lost its moorings. There was a silence when it descended, and one wondered where its alighting would be, and one could not look upon it as inanimate, it seemed so full of a cheerful inhuman busyness of its own.

It was, I suppose, the first entry of the Sputnik age into our world, the reign of brainless metal, and its significance in retrospect is greater than one felt it at the time; yet I was riveted by it and hated to leave London while that apparition was flaunting through its sky. 'It seems fantastic,' I wrote to Isaiah Berlin (21.1.44), 'that we were lunching in Baltimore so short a time ago and here I am in another world. Which is the real one? Neither, I suppose—but something very curious has happened here with these flying robots. One has gone back into the ages when men saw the inevitable take on a visible shape, and recognized their gods, unpersuadable, unreasonable in human ways, full of fascination and terror. I have a window facing the direction from which they come, and I spent an hour or so watching them last night—about midnight. The sky was still green with faded streaks of twilight. The little droning thing began far off. The houses stood mauve and dark within their outlines: we looked like an uninhabited city, and the drone came nearer—it is quite slow, you hear it from so far. The sky had a few clouds, their tips touched with light. And at last, the drumming loud now like an orchestra working up to the opening of the ballet, the fireball came skimming above the houses whose chimneys seemed to darken under her feet. (Everyone I ask tells me they think of her as feminine.) She did not give one the feeling of being wicked, but rather as if she were a creature of the natural forces which has wilfully left its own appointed circuit and gone wandering, and the destruction comes merely as a result of her unsuitability to the general surroundings. When she comes near, you hear the brazen flapping of her garments, you see that she is shod with flames and "makes the cold air fire". Shelley could have described her, and the Greeks would have known her ancestry. She goes off, hurrying over the human world that cowers as she comes, until she touches it far away across the houses, in a noise of death that seems to fall like a stone into the stillness. It is a strange life, and a strange feeling of fear which, like a touch of black, sets off all other colours. I would not be missing it for anything, nor the sight of London now, very gallant'.

The thing never stopped above me without giving me that peculiar constriction about the middle of one's stomach which is a symptom of fear—yet it was not as dangerous as an ice-slope on the Alps when stones are rolling; it was the silence, and Inevitability made visible, that created the atmosphere of awe—and yet most people I think came to feel that our years on this planet are wasted if something made merely of metal can upset the balance of our minds. The human courage all around was what one saw: a queue in Victoria station (as glassy a place as one can find) and the conversations uninterrupted and not a muscle moving on any face in sight when the explosion came some hundreds of yards away; or the actors playing *Blithe Spirit* to thirty or forty people in an empty theatre with scarcely the shred of a nuance to show when the small red signal of alert went on and off; or the little suburban houses reduced to rubble and the strangely solid figure of a policeman seated amid the matchboard destruction to guard the demolished homes; or the liftman to the flats where I was staying, who had 'only seven chairs, and Hitler's taken five of them, and he can have the other two if he wants them'. The human courage seemed to me something that even God does not compete with, for it is the triumph of Impotence over Power, the prerogative of man.

At the beginning of August I reluctantly tore myself away and travelled to Devonshire in a trainload of children. They wore tabs marked 'Waifs and Strays'—as sad an inscription as that of the L.C.C. carts that carry 'Dust and Ashes'. The country, as we went, subsided into the apparently unbreakable English look of peace, in which, for the next four months, I lived with old friends[1] on the edge of Dartmoor, listening at last to our own bombers as they flew, every night, towards Germany in the darkness. They lulled us, roaring above the silent moors. After the threats and anxieties of the past four years, the deep beat of their engines spoke more of peace than war on our side, for the end was in sight.

In this neighbourhood of my childhood, in the places I knew so well, we seemed wrapped in austerity and time. I wrote to my friends as from an island—to Nigel in Greece among the Andartes; to Lord Wavell in Delhi, whose letters, unlike any others and very like himself, I have kept.

NEW DELHI 10 August 1944

My dear Freya,

I wrote to you the other day and thanked you for Bénet's *Western Star*, but I had not then read the volume. I read it the other day on a long flight back from Assam, and thoroughly enjoyed it. Bénet's poems have the great gift of vitality, which is to my mind the greatest and most attractive quality that man, woman, poet or writer can have. Did you ever know him? I gather he always suffered from ill health but he must have had a great spirit. Thank you so much again.

I went back to the army for a few days this week, and visited troops in the Imphal plain and at Kohima, three pretty strenuous days. Now I'm back again in Delhi, trying to deal with Mr. Gandhi's pronouncements.

Did you ever see the enclosed? And do you know where the lines come from which begin:

'Too late for life, too late for love,
Too late, too late . . .'

30 September 1944

Your letter reached me only a few days ago, you let the poor dear travel steerage on a cattle-boat apparently, and it arrived in strange company with:

[1] Lady Waller and Miss Varwell.

A letter from a religious maniac . . .

Two copies of the Salvation Army journal,

A complaint from a woman who had mislaid her grandfather's Mutiny pension and seemed to think I had it,

A pamphlet on health in the new Turkey.

The annual report of an ophthalmic hospital.

Your charming little letter must have had not only a long but a very boring journey in such company. Send the next ones to the India Office to come by Bag, then they will have a quick passage of a week or so, and will get the low-down on quite a lot of interesting matters from indiscreet self-important official letters.

I liked hearing of your method of dealing with files.[1] When the old War Office was pulled down many years ago, a sort of shaft was found behind the ventilator, down which it had been the custom to shove really inconvenient files.

(Many such intervened: *1.11.44*)

I am sure you were right about the proper occasion for the Valentine hat, it ought to have gone to Paris for the entry *pour jeter au-dessus d'un moulin* . . .

PS. I wish they had a shaft in the Viceroy's house for inconvenient files; and another, a little larger, for really inconvenient Members of Council.

15 April 1944

My dear Chief,

I am sending you a few paragraphs from my book, in which you appear. I hope you will approve, but if not, like the politician's principles, 'they can always be altered.' The book is about two-thirds done now, and is supposed to be a picture of the Young Effendi; it is hard on him to make him stand all by himself in the middle of the canvas, so there is a sort of Cinquecento of the Middle East, with camel caravans walking through history and people fighting in tanks: rather like one of those Persian miniatures with no perspective. I am calling it *East is West*, as it is supposed to make Americans think of Arabs as Effendis instead of Sheikhs. The book has anyway given me pleasant hours remembering far more than I can put down about the days in Cairo and after. . . . Here on these

---

[1] 'One very hot morning in Baghdad I took eight files from my assistant and burnt them: I kept them down, like Richelieu's Academy, to a fixed number, and when they went above it, sacrificed what seemed the least important.' (Letter October 1944.)

high moors everything looks small and remote as if seen through the wrong end of a telescope....

Do you know this poem?

> We feel, at least, that silence here were sin,
> Not ours the fault if we have feeble hosts—
> If easy patrons of their kin
> Have left the last free race with naked coasts!
> They knew the precious things they had to guard:
> For us, we will not spare the tyrant one hard word.
>
> Tho' niggard throats of Manchester may bawl,
> What England was, shall her true sons forget?
> We are not cotton-spinners all,
> But some love England and her honour yet.
> And these in our Thermopylae shall stand,
> And hold against the world this honour of the land.

It sounds like 1940, but it was Tennyson in 1852!

* * * *

The book got written, in spite of that epic autumn's temptations to think of other things. Friends in the Middle East, Reginald Davies, Brigadier Glubb, Bernard Reilly (by then in the Colonial Office), Harold MacMichael and many others, found time to give me help and information, emerging from the war. But the heart was now drawn nearer home. By the end of September the guerrillas were fighting on the mountains in view of my Asolo windows. In November, General Wilson wrote from Caserta:

Dear Miss Freya,

... It is very kind of you to say such nice things about me though I wonder you did not say something about my hide being tough. Certainly include my remark about Missions; I have always had a poor opinion of them. Of course I will send you a photograph and enclose two so that you can choose which you would like for yourself and for the book.

I am sorry to say we have not got sufficiently far north to liberate your house yet. There has been very hard fighting in the Apennines and our progress has been slowed up by torrents of rain. One wonders why people came to Italy to live. Since mid-September the rain has exceeded what one would expect in the west of Ireland and there are bridges washed away which have stood for centuries, not to mention the temporary ones that have been put up to replace demolition. They tell me the Arno is up to its banks in Florence which I believe has rarely been known before.

I have just got back from a three-day visit to Athens. I was almost overwhelmed by the welcome there. They gave Anthony Eden, the Admiral and myself the Freedom of the City on the Acropolis. . . . We were there on the 28th October which was the day the Italians attacked Greece from Albania and which coincided with the March on Rome. There were services in the cathedral and a visit to the tomb of the Unknown Soldier, and the Greeks started by sending a band to play 'Tipperary' under my window at 6.15 a.m. . . .

I hope that when your book is finished you will be able to come east again. Cannot you get the M. of I. to send you out here for a spell?

★   ★   ★   ★

By now the fat hazel nuts were falling out of their sockets and rowan berries like flame licked the old stone walls round the edges of the moors. Cottages tucked away in hollows from the southwest wind grew mosses in their thatch and descended, probably unchanged, from Elizabethan days. Damp and uncomfortable as they were, the mere walking by them inspired peace, 'and the living there must surely do something similar inside one?' I had come home, and felt myself once more, walking and riding, thinking and reading, a part of my own land.

In London, when the book was done, the 1944 winter passed through its squalor; fuel was scarce, service scarcer, and the V2 had added itself to the V1 as an outlet from this world. Complications of rationing made The Antelope pub round the corner the only comfortable way to deal with meals, and one stepped from the snow and the surly blackout into a warm and genial atmosphere of friendliness and beer. What I did in those months I can scarcely remember, except that I was waiting for a chance to reach Italy. Faces are lost in the shadows—friends from the Middle East and others from before—Osbert Lancaster, Harold Nicolson, Victor Cunard with whom one could talk of Venice, Archie John Wavell whose loss in Kenya is one of the saddest landmarks of later years. Here and there a gleam of civilization throws a gentle light as if through the Dark Ages, as when Ronald Storrs asked me to dine in the gloom of his club and I found him beside a bottle of old claret, brought up wrapped in a napkin from the country and warming by an almost invisible fire.

In this interval of suspense, with the allied advance in the Apennines held up, Lady Wavell asked me to work for her in India. A committee of the W.V.S. had been formed there with a programme which, she wrote, 'is beyond me and anyway I have not the time.' A plan was wanted to interest the Indian women, and she asked me out to look at the problem and suggest what I could. The Indian and Pakistan members of her committee welcomed the idea with a friendliness that touched me; and my book was finished. I accepted, with a promise from the Viceroy to be wafted to Venice on the first news of its liberation; and left England in the coldest snap of the winter, in a flying-boat with three generals, held up for five days in Poole Harbour by ice.

15

India

KARACHI *February 1945*

My dear Gerald [de Gaury]

It has taken all this time to get so far, and the *suffering*: sitting on ice for a week and up with false hopes in darkness every morning. I can hardly bear to think of the congealed hands of the poor little Wren coping with frozen ropes on our launch before sunrise every day. A duststorm in Cairo—blurred banks as we touched down; but Owen Tweedy came to meet me and I was carried off to the Embassy which was Arabian Nights—eating off silver, flowers everywhere, a maid to unpack and press one's gown. Jackie was kind as she always is and seven or eight friends were there. Lots of gossip, not for writing. We got into nice weather at Bahrein and for the first time felt comfortable. The Sunderlands are like tame dolphins, their shape a tribute to the designing of nature with all the right fish-lines for swimming. Karachi, the Americans say, 'is half the size of Chicago cemetery and twice as dead': I am spending my one day in bed instead of looking at it, before going on to Delhi where, the Americans also say, 'you needn't be mad but it helps.'

* * * *

An English pattern of W.V.S. was, as Lady Wavell had written, unlikely to appeal to a foreign intelligentsia panting for independence. It was the old story, the need of the Easterners to be dealt with from their own angle—*their* interests supreme and to make it plain to them that they were so. After a two months' experiment we planned a group of four women, Indian and English, whose business it would be not to organize, but to travel about as messengers of goodwill. Mere friendliness had rarely been tried unconnected with any effort to make them do the punctual things they hate; coming from the Vicereine, one could see, even after a short time, that the result could be happy and in the course of three or four years a noticeable change, we felt, might yet be achieved. The plan was blessed by the Indian Treasury with a lakh of rupees, but was born too late to be of service, for the Vicereine herself and her messengers were stepping with British India off the stage. All that remains is a happy unproductive half-year in my memory.

I found Delhi an enchanting landscape of ruins, tombs and fortresses long crumbled, where (I was reading Bernier and the times of Aurungzebe) one could picture Mogul palanquins passing between scarlet pennants of English broadcloth that decorated the gunbarrels of the Indian musketeers. The Wavells were away and had left the Viceregal gardens open to the public. It was extraordinary how alive and agreeable it made them. There is no point in having pomp unless there is a crowd to enjoy it, and the splendour so shut away from everybody had made most of New Delhi seem dead.

A few days after arrival I describe a review where five Victoria Crosses were given to Indian troops.

3 March 1945[1]

It was a gentle, pearl-grey morning, and the regiments of the decorated soldiers were there on the dry grass outside the Mogul fort—its moat and red walls and the mosque of Shah Jehan screened by still leafless trees and a huge crowd round them. The V.C. families sat on two long benches just behind the Viceroy: three were dead, so two widows and a mother were there to take the honour, wrapped in veils. The little Mahratta widow's face was uncovered, one could see how frightened she was, in the arena with the Gurkha band behind her and Baluchis and Punjabis, the most terrific warriors, on either side. The A.D.C.s, looking as if it were agony, walked at a slow step in front of H.E. as he inspected. Then the citations were read in army Hindustani into which a good fourth of English seems to have entered. It must be wonderful to step out to take your decoration with your fellows at attention behind you. In the old days, a year or two ago, this ceremony was performed with only the members of the Government present: can you believe it and then be surprised that we are not popular? Now the troops marched past—the Indian Navy; the British, looking tough in a casual way as if they scarce knew it themselves; the Baluchis, every one like a scimitar out of the

[1] To G. de Gaury.

desert; the Rajputs, magnificent, very slim and straight, with little fierce moustaches; the Gurkhas, throwing out their chests with the quick short step of the hills. The Moguls spent their time watching their armies march and one can see why. We were a very grand party with a charming Rajah in a tobacco-brown redingote, white jodhpurs, gold slippers, and a mauve and yellow muslim turban sweeping like a veil—Rajah of Risalpur I think—with a face like a Persian picture and agreeable company: and Patiala who is six foot four and looks as if he thought nothing at all of any human being and not very much of God! It is very grand to be the 'house party'; the crowd is asked not to move till we do (but it does).

I had a suite in the Viceroy's house and gave little dinners and made no attempt to penetrate Indian politics, but enjoyed Rafiq Anwar dancing in loose silk drawers and a naked torso against a black curtain—the only music (except for two drums played by a man squatting there with fine nervous hands), the sound of Anwar's bare heel on the stage and the small crash of his anklet bells; and in the interlude, an old man in a long black coat with gilt buttons sat cross-legged on a Bokhara rug with a slim ivory-inlaid instrument called a *sitar*. A fretted metal lamp hung above him, as if some Mogul painting were alive.

Another five-hour entertainment was acted for us by the household staff, and we were able to take an hour or two to sup and rest and returned to find the heroine in no worse case than when we left her.

The girls—chosen among the lift-boys—were a tough-looking lot. The sign of a lady was a handkerchief held to the face every few minutes with an enormous hand. There was an Elizabethan character to the play—prose, poetry, songs, comic interludes, length, all in character; and some of the songs were charming. The heroine was carried away by bandits, the prince got into the wrong zenana, nothing could impair their virtue and they said so at improbable length; and Peter Coats and I sat on a sofa in the front, garlanded with blossoms. We went to congratulate, but the cast instantly relapsed into *cawasses* at attention in their incongruous clothes.[1]

A football match was less traditional, between a local team and one descending in parachute from the air—puppets swinging down from the

[1] 9.3.45.

blue sky, shot out of their aeroplane like pellets and turning into men as they came down—one or two landing among a crowd extremely agile in making room. The Air-Marshal was next me, preoccupied till the descent was over because, he said, 'people ask questions if someone gets killed.' The Moguls would have enjoyed the football and probably asked no questions. Their city last-but-one (there have been seven Delhis) made a background of faded walls and turret-pagodas, a gate with blue tiles and a pleasure-dome on a hillock, where once the elephant processions and all the colour must have glowed.[1]

I believe [I wrote at this time],[2] that when the history of the British Empire comes to be written, the reason for its difficulties and perhaps eventual fall will be found in its never having really bothered about education. That control includes everything else—the one thing we should cling to, and the first we let go. I was hearing last night that it was what we first handed over to the provincial Indian Governments and that some of their teachers are paid six rupees a month (what a private gets in the Yemen Army), and the buildings are all falling to ruin. I do think this is a legitimate grievance, and it is the same in other places. In Aden we only recently started the school for young sultans, and it is already affecting the whole country. In Cyprus we never bothered to see that English was taught! Palestine, I remember your telling me, had no technical school available. When you think of the influence of a place like Beirut University, you realize that we could (and should) have kept a guiding hand on all our Empire by education alone. As we don't think it matters much for our own people, I suppose we never think of it as a power among others.

We now have a house crammed with Rajahs and an investiture on Saturday. I wonder whether it is all really passing away? One still has one's nightdress pressed every day, and a *cawass* at the door ready to carry notes (no bells or modern things like showers).

With so much written by more expert pens than mine, and so much knowledge available about these last phases of the English rule in India, it would be an arrogant attempt to give a connected account of my five months there as an amateur. I choose from my letters the vignettes that I best remember—loosely strung as they are and threaded as if by chance, and divided in a sudden and arbitrary way into those written to Lady Wavell about her W.V.S., and those

---

[1] 19.2.45.

[2] To G. de Gaury 19.2.45.

written in a rapture over the novelty of India to other friends. Most of the former are of no interest now and I omit them; my business being to visit the institutions that the Indian women were running for themselves, I was thrown as it were into the arms of philanthropy, for which I have a natural repugnance unless its stern features relax into some human face. Too often it assumes that the benefit is for the recipient, and not for those fortunate enough to be able to *give*. As soon as this occurs, love and kindness die and rancour follows, and the terrible and cruel mask of power. This happened, I thought, more rarely in India than elsewhere, and even in these letters 'cheerfulness', as Dr. Johnson's friend said, 'is always breaking through'; but there was a great deal of the team spirit for someone as solitary as I am to suffer: 'everyone has been helpful and deluged me in the Evidence of Progress. I have visited a model village (swept for the occasion), and milk centres, the women's hospitals, literary classes, recreation centres and deaf and blind and cottage industries. How I dislike it all—not India but philanthropy in general! I am sure, however, that this is the only way; if one doesn't take an interest one may as well be out of India altogether. So I sat about everywhere with garlands round my neck and ended up yesterday by addressing the village industry and enclose my speech because I am most anxious to hear that you approve of it. It has gone down very well and the knowledge that you are anxious to know what they are doing evidently touches them. A middle-aged woman, with a hard philanthropic face, got up and said that it was money and not kindness alone they want from Lady Wavell. I said, "She is not Lakshmi, the goddess of wealth" and this was greeted with joy while the old lady who introduced me, who is the pioneer of the emancipated women here, went for the Congress woman hammer and tongs in Canarese: I don't know what they said, but it seemed all right. I feel sure that, if you can keep half a dozen people of the right sort in touch with all these young and emotional women, you will see quite a strong and friendly feeling in two or three years' time. But what a job! But it would be much more useful than a particular separate venture of your own.'[1]

My tour began in the Central Provinces and went on to Hyderabad,

[1] To Lady Wavell 22.3.45.

where the beautiful Princess of Berar, shut like an imprisoned goddess in her palace, felt like a friend 'and welcomed our plan "if it is kept clearly for our service: if it tries to manage and organize us, it will be only one more burden added". What everyone likes is the idea of having some direct contact with you in Delhi—but the provincial I.C.S. need to have it very gently suggested . . . It is awful to be received as an organizing woman'.[1]

In Madras 'I saw the W.V.S. and a Home for Fallen Women (not that they had anything to do with each other), and pottered round St. Thomas's Mount with Charles Harding who has been very kind and helpful'; then half a day and night in Trichinopoly, and south to Travancore, where the Diwan—a charming person—expounded ideas I had thought of as my own.

I returned by Mysore, and 'what is left of me hopes to be in Delhi on the 10th of April. A delightful morning among the ruins of Seringapatam, fascinated by Scott's bungalow, especially the portraits of Wellington, and tried to be driven to the jungle but they were afraid I might meet an elephant—one longs for elephants after so many good works!'

The second tour took me to Mhow—straight out of Kipling 'with brigadiers' wives not on speaking terms and W.V.S. like Solomon's baby between them. Luckily one was away and the other—very nice—with whom I stayed, invited all the Indian workers with no friction. They kept on saying how wonderful it was of you to think of people working in Mhow. This is very often the reaction and makes me feel it is worth going about, and especially to the smaller places.'[2]

In Udaipur, where I next went, it was hard to tear oneself away to look at schools—'co-education at that, with forty boys and two hundred and thirty girls if you please.' Yet here as in so many of these ventures, in their poverty and enthusiasm, the human spirit was too strong for any committee, and a warm feeling grew for Dr. Mohan Singh Mehta who had started thirteen years before and did all by kindness, with a great deal of dancing, painting, and physical training. 'They have an English woman teacher and an Austrian

[1] To Lady Wavell 28.4.45.
[2] To Lady Wavell 22.4.45.

ex-explorer, and the Indians are genuine and I thought them charming; and though they are out-and-out nationalists, and think everything will be all right when they are independent, the idea of your having sent me just to give a message of goodwill touched them none the less and they said that "it does a great deal of good to create more understanding". You see what nonsense it is when people tell one it is not necessary to go to the States.... As we came away Ranbir Singh, who takes me round, was smoothing down his moustaches and stroking his sword and saying in an angry growl: "I suppose they think Freedom is a thing one can keep by dancing!"'

UDAIPUR *24 April 1945*

I have again seen the headmaster and had the English teacher to tea. She looks almost more like a mouse then a female, with a pointed chin and sharp little teeth and straight black short hair, and here she is all alone in this Indian school, trying to live in a more or less Indian way and bicycling about in the dust; and, with the wonderful imperviousness of our people, might be in Clapham for all the influence India has on her. We went and saw the 'Literacy Centre' where about forty women come to a dilapidated house to learn to read and write. This is run by the *kasturba* fund and is all Gandhi, very ready to be friendly if anyone ever took the trouble to go and visit it. It is run by a middle-aged pair who talk no English. They have a dreary playground with swings for children among heaps of rubble, and a hostel to train women to work in villages. So far there are only three pretty young women and no training as far as I could see, but neat little rooms arranged in the old house and the girls are supposed to spend three years here, and there is a Superintendent. It is touching, and I feel it is a pity not to see these people (without offending them by trying to interfere). Their library is open to men by day and to women in the evening, with lots of Hindi papers, and I thought one might send them a present of books? All this education is going on with such a struggle and against a huge wall of difficulties....

And my last report from Udaipur telling of a tea-party with the Red Cross ladies, sums up the feeling that I have now carried about the East with me for over thirty years—that 'more can be done outside these regular gatherings than in. One has to go among the highways and byways among the people who are out on adventures of their own to do any real good, I think. The P.M.'s wife came, very small in the peculiarly difficult sari of the Mahrattas pulled up between their legs (they say it was so as to ride to war with their husbands, but no one could ever have expected that of Mrs. P.M.); she looked at me with blinking eyes as if your message were part of the sewing bundle she had to take away with her. Because there is no initiative of their own in these meetings, I find the ineffectual things they manage for themselves much more cheerful.'

So far as I am concerned, the note of rapture is absent from committee meetings however tuneful they may be, and what I enjoyed was to write to Gerald de Gaury and describe the asphalt roads of Hyderabad with lamps like round moons, and white villas in gardens, and the Regency Residency with Sir Arthur Lothian rather Regency inside it, and picnic in a garden by the lakeside with the Prime Minister, the Nawab of Chatari, who had been invited from the north (so sensible to bring in ministers when necessary from outside). There he sat, in a coat of apricot satin with a row of gold buttons and a diamond in each down the front, and four smaller of the same pattern on his sleeves, and a narrow face behind a rampart of black moustache, sharply waxed; and enjoyed the sunset hour; and drove me back by ridges where the oldest rocks of the world are tumbled, that have never been under the sea—so he told me—while the ball of the sun went down behind Golconda, its bastions and battlements and inner encircling walls. He told me how Aurungzebe attacked from the direction in which we were driving, and how the King of Golconda was standing by one of his gunners who declared he could kill the Mogul with a shot. The King took him by the arm and said: "Do not shoot; it is not fit for an ordinary man to kill a king." Even so Mr. Pitt, I told the Nawab, sent back a Frenchman who had offered to assassinate Napoleon, though perhaps the King of Golconda would have acted differently if he had known what Aurungzebe was like. I climbed up one enchanted morning to see the sunrise over his Deccan through the open stone windows from the throne which he lost and thought how fortunate I was to see places with names like Golconda!

Because of the size of this book one goes hastily by these places—Trichinopoly for instance—climbing up the inside of its mountain, where the stairs are tunnelled and painted, and columned temple halls are cut out of the rock with hideous gods; and through Travancore to the tip of India where some long, fantastic mountain range dies in a series of improbable outlines. The coconut palms and lagoons disappear, and one stands on a headland where the sun comes

>   up upon our left
>   Out of the sea comes he;
>   And he shines bright and on our right
>   Goes down into the sea.

There, near by, is the old capital—Trivandrum—walled round an empty space with a green mountain behind it, its stones built jutting up into the walls so that the defenders could scramble anywhere inside it; for they were a warlike people, in spite of living in a country where coconut, banana, mango, tapioca, and anything one need desire is within a reach of the hand; they beat the Dutch, and the surrendering major reorganized their army and spent the rest of his life among them. Their old palace is a mass of sloping tiles and sharp carved gables, and the Hindu figures in the frescoed room bring out of their thirteenth century the same smiling gaiety as the archaic Greek marbles—impassive but not comfortable, for no human misery can touch it. The temple towers in this country go up mitre-shaped, as crammed with active little sculptures as anything can be, and feel like the dark wedge-shaped nests of bees that hang from Mogul arches round Delhi. I liked these temples, opened to all castes of Hindu but not to us, so that I could only glance in passing at huge and pillared halls. Round them, in Travancore, there was a cathedral-close atmosphere in the streets and houses, the narrow loggias on wooden columns, and the tiled roofs and sub-roofs over shops. It was beguiling to see paganism believed in.

I sat next the Maharajah last night and asked him if he did not feel very moved by the ceremonies and procession of which he and the gods were the centre during the last few days—and he said, yes, he did—and indeed one could see it by his whole bearing. He is young and very sensitive and gentle and it must be a terrific responsibility to feel that you are the only means by which the gods can do anything for your people—they can't even leave the temple unless he fetches them!

The most fascinating was to see all this mythology come to life in the *Kathakali* dancing—still popular here in any village or temple feast. The court keep it under their wing and it is not being modernized, and boys are trained from eight years old to make their fingers supple for the sixty-four movements they play about with like lightning. We saw it in one of the old royal palaces, where, as we watched with the Maharajah's family, dinner was brought to each on a small table, and the stage was lit by eight or nine wicks floating in oil. Here a chorus stood draped in white from the naked waist downward, chanting the story with a beat now and then of drums. The actors' costumes were red or yellow short crinolines on thin legs ankleted with bells; shoulder-tassels hang for the dancer to play with, and 'halo-hats' and ear-rings big as saucers for the kings. Their masks were rice, creamed and wetted on the face so that it remained supple—a three-hour process—and coloured according to the character—conveying drama by the movements of eyes and eyebrows. The white of the eye is reddened to show in the painted features; and as for the hands, even a country audience would notice the slightest deviation from their traditional gestures: the left wore claw-like nails of metal—the old sign of a gentleman of leisure (I remember as a child in Italy the nails left long on people's little fingers to show they need do no manual work). The saga's climax was the princess's choice of a mortal among four gods wooing her for her beauty (she was a singularly tough-looking boy).

When the scene changed—a curtain held across the middle of the stage for a minute—the four gods were sitting there—a blue-masked god of water, a white-masked god of sky, a red-masked god of fire, and the fearful god of death, their legs tucked away under frills of their skirts and the king in the middle with his feet and their bells on the ground. The princess saw it, and knew that those who do not stand on earth must be immortal and like a sensible heroine chose her king.[1]

In Mysore, among trees with strange and scented flowers and new white domes, I describe a number of institutions 'where people learn to be modern and dependent like those bullocks one sees in carts on dusty roads, leaning against each other because I suppose it makes the yoke seem lighter'. I turned more happily to the ritual of the Indian servants.

[1] To G. de Gaury 8.4.45.

In Delhi, they stand up as you go by (and slow in doing that on a hot afternoon) and only really perform by raising their hands in white gloves above their heads when they each stand behind a chair and H.E. sits down to lunch or dinner. In Travancore everyone holds his fingers in front of his mouth—the Maharajah does this in the presence of the gods and it is a gentle gesture. Here in Mysore as one goes about the palace they stand like statues with arms folded and head bowed. As I drove up the hill to the sunset, an old gate-keeper at the palace at the top knelt and put his forehead to the ground at sight of the Government car. If you are used to burning incense to a bull, you may just as well say your prayers to a governor, and paganism seems to make one very uncertain as to where to draw the line. But even as a very tiny satellite whirling in the divine orbit I can see how boring it must be to be the centre of adoration. Women often find this out without being at all royal, when people fall in love with them and agree with everything they say. Here, the Maharajahs have their domestic goddess 'His Highness's private goddess', the charming gay Brahmin superintendent told me yesterday; she lives in the temple on the hill. A beautiful young Brahmin with very long, fine features and a white coarse wrap thrown about him came out as I went there in the sunset and offered me a scented flower. A line of steps leads up flanked by the square and squat Hindu pillars, and there is a pleasant feeling of worship going on all the time; the peculiar objects don't seem to matter very much—cobras and monkeys and mice come in, and an endless supply of pictures and stories. I think one could get fond of the gentleness and 'earthiness' of it all, though I can't understand shedding our own for something so far back in time.[1]

I flew back from Mysore to Delhi and wrote to Jock (17.4.45) that my work seemed promising, if I could obtain £6,000—'not much if it gets the women of India to like us! I am away again to Rajputana, for a fortnight if I get back at all, as it is a wee Argus I fly in. I believe it has double controls, so I can hold that stick ... What reconciles one with death is that life is so *complicated* with small things —zip-fasteners that get out of order, clothes shrinking in the wash, mourning for Roosevelt, proofs delayed in the post: one will at any rate be clear of all that. The great dancer here says that he sinned with a dancing girl and so has to spend all this incarnation expiating it by dancing (a very pleasant way of doing it too). So

[1] To G. de Gaury 8.4.45.

perhaps all these vexations are just things left over from the Time Before.'

In Rajputana, the whiteness of Udaipur cast its inevitable spell of age and fragility. At any moment, it seemed to me, the cloud-capped palaces might peel, the plaster come away, and the whole thing crumble like a Hollywood creation; yet the eaves of the doll's-house shops were held up by elephants' heads that belonged to times long before the Moguls, and the dim whitewash, streaked by the monsoons, broke everywhere into kiosks or doors of lace-worked arches, where women stood on steps, their bell-like skirts swinging above their anklets and two pitchers at a time upon their heads. All colour was lovely and all movement graceful, even to the pigeons' ballet round the water-palace cupolas in the lake. The white buildings at sunset took on a cloud-like gentleness and two zenanas with their blank white height made the beauty of the view. A princess within them had been so ravishing that both Udaipur and Jaipur wished to marry her, and her father fearing trouble ordered her death; but the jailer himself could not harden his heart; so that she had to take her own poison, and a curse fell for six generations on the reigning house. Every room in the palace must have its story—rooms glass-floored, or lined with Chinese tiles, or roof gardens with marble fountains, or sudden rich pavilions; narrow staircases, and treasuries where clerks squat counting bank-notes as one passes, while elephants painted all over munch their hay in the courts below. In the town, old Rajput noblemen rode through the streets—white eyebrows and a yellow satin turban, and a white beard brushed from a parting to either side; or a wedding, where the bridesmaids wrapped in red and orange walked singing behind the groom. He, in a red coat striped with tinsel and green satin turban, fourteen years old perhaps, rode with a small brother on his crupper and his bride buried among females behind him in a cab. An old Muslim fakir came after, in a rich gown seated in an open gharry, grey hair in waves over his shoulders. Outside the town, where the lake is surrounded like the background of Florentine pictures with low and pleasant but empty hills, the Government feeds the wild pig from a high terrace every afternoon. Out of the scrub they come, grunting and pushing, a Circe crowd, until their heap of maize is eaten and they vanish into the exile of their wildness leaving as it were a Miltonic echo behind them which has insinuated itself ever since into my memory of Udaipur. I think of it too as what India might have been without any Muslim invasion, with its wars and its feasts and its fashions and the good-looking faces of its people; and a talent for painting—walls and houses were decorated with figures of women, elephants, horsemen, tigers; and in the schools a small boy weak on figures had painted a brown mountain with the points of lances showing behind it and a shower of bright green arrows crossing the foreground towards them, an epitome, in a pleasingly natural surrealist manner, of the Rajput history.

The whole of Rajputana carried this enchantment—even Jodhpur, a dull place otherwise, had the hands of its royal widows modelled on a slab within its gate. There they pressed them as they went to be burnt on their husbands' pyres, and the words they said as they did so, whether for blessing or cursing, were bound to come true; in the shadow of the gate, which is huge and its doors studded with spikes against the battering of elephants, there is an eloquence in those tiny hands, so different one from the other and so resigned.

Jaipur, a walled town, was geranium-coloured with geranium gateways, and Sir Mirza Ismail, its Persian Prime Minister, was resuscitating the fancies of bygone Maharajahs, repainting and refurbishing them as new. Brass ornaments again caught the sun on cupolas drawn like eyebrows; the water-maze for swimmers was blue under pink cloisters; the balconies green against cream walls; and the high wall where one walked towards the gates above the traffic was streaked by shadow and sunlight under pagodas painted yellow and pink. The town itself was geranium-coloured by the genial caprice of some ruler long dead; and where the façades had no ornament of whitewashed flags or flowers, the outlines of white windows were painted in for fun. The old palace, now abandoned, was above, in the neck of a valley, and there an elephant would take the ruler's guests.

'Did you know they had pink ears? It was so slow, with a circular motion, while the battlements of Amber drew nearer. They must have seen thousands of elephants in their day. One needn't climb stairs—there is a sloping way built for the palanquins of the zenana.

INDIA

A man with a red sash and a black shield with brass bosses walked behind us. He hadn't shaved for a week or so. I suppose it was the minimum *cortège* an elephant can go out with.'[1]

'It is still a dream. I only came yesterday and it is very hot. I write badly, trying to keep my arm from moistening the paper, with nothing on except a cool little pair of Jaipur slippers embroidered with a gilt ornament over the point. What is so pleasant here is that the beauty is not confined to royal buildings as in most of India, but is just as much in the shops and private houses; one forgets that empty feeling of *nothing* between the Rajah and the Poor.'[2]

My tour so dazzled me that a nostalgia for India has never left me. Many pictures must be lost, but many remain, seen from my Argus —chiefly the endless plains, the spider-webs of village fields thinning to emptiness till the next spider-web begins to appear and life repeated rolls there from the mouth of Time like the Indian river heavy and slow with soil. I remember the crocodile ridges of Rajputana—fortress walls following the contours of their rocks. When we were safe in the air, my pilot allowed me to hold the double control, and I would feel like a leaf in the wind, moving once—when a rainbow met above us and below us—as if in a slanting halo.

By the end of April I was back in Delhi, in the routine that continued while the Viceroy struggled in London with his hard and lonely task. Notes and meetings came dropping in: Peter Fleming over the hump from Chungking; Ronald Storrs, Harold Mac-Michael and many others passing through; Claude Auchinleck our C.-in-C. entertaining his 15th Punjabis; the Caseys, Edith Evans, Joyce Grenfell, friends and acquaintances: one lunched in wet bathing-dresses to keep cool, by the swimming-pool under red umbrellas and a white colonnade, where the noises of the war seemed for a while excluded.

* * * *

On the 6th of May I went up to Simla, where the Colvilles[3] soon came up for a few pleasant weeks during the Viceroy's absence.

[1] To Austen Harrison, April 1945.
[2] To Mrs. Otto Kahn, April 1945.
[3] Then Governor of Bombay (later Lord Clydesmuir).

INDIA

My work is finished [I wrote to Gerald de Gaury], my successor found, nothing further can be done till Their Ex's return and till the Political Secretary rootles round for the necessary funds. It is a good scheme, and the people I think the most intelligent are all keen—so it ought to be all right and able to be left with a blessing a fortnight or so after Lady Wavell is back again. I thought I might as well go into the mountain air, and if I had been fit for it I would have gone off and seen the Himalayas at much closer quarters. But I came back with neuritis in my *feet*, from fatigue they say, so it is better just to go and potter about the rhododendron slopes of Simla.

It is a funny thing, but I am getting more and more frightened as the freeing of Venice comes nearer. So afraid of what misery there may be. They must be in Vicenza, just one hour from my home.

My heart was in Italy now. Scarcely a letter passes without some line of longing.

To Moore Crosthwaite[1] I wrote on May 20, 'I found your letter from Teheran. Glad I was to think of you there, when all the poplar leaves were coming out. Civilizations may be poor human efforts, but *how* one misses them, and welcomes even the poorest, faintest of their footprints. My work here will be handed over on June 15. I call it very clever to persuade any Government to find a lakh of rupees, and the only reward I ask is to be deposited on the Lido aerodrome in a month's time. Dear Moore, if you can find out anything more definite about my poor nephew I will be thankful. They have not heard for *certain*, after all, that he is dead—just vanished into that mist of horror and unknown.'

One has to deal with the agonies of life in literature [I wrote at this time][2] but until they are transmuted into their own serene world, they are not literature. The people who escape them will never write anything permanent, I suppose; but the *whole* process of transmutation has to be gone through, and the artist emerge on the other side. What a subject to begin when the post is just leaving. Soon I hope with a clear conscience to sit in Asolo and forget politics, and write a book of philosophy, quite small and easy and intended for all the world. I shall call it the art of getting old and it is the art I mean to cultivate.

[1] Sir Moore Crosthwaite, K.C.M.G., now our Ambassador to the Lebanon.
[2] To May Sarton 20.5.45.

This book eventually appeared as *Perseus in the Wind*, but meanwhile I chafed on the sophisticated ridge, though I was soon beginning to look and feel normal again. All the things one should do in mountains were beyond the Simla orbit, and one had to be extremely tough to walk, since every path led down immense slopes at great speed and one had to crawl up again. Down below one came into a simple remote mountain world of small tracks and tilted farms all—I found—touchingly decorated for Victory with strings of coloured papers. But I took only one long walk and found it too much for me, and stuck to the Viceroy's terraces designed by the Mintos and curtained by the Himalayas. There was a Scottish feeling about the grandeurs of the Viceregal Lodge in Simla built in tiers of woodwork round a baronial hall.

27 May 1945[1]

It is not the Himalayas or any sort of mountain place at all, but a freak of woods and ridges with houses pouring down their steepness like lava, dilapidated, Victorian, and corrupted by turret and pagoda fancies. There is a funny reminiscence of Venice I could not pin down, till I realized it was the absence of cars and the crowd padding on foot with rickshaws like gondolas calling out as they slip along. When four or five go in a line to a party each with a lantern over the shaft, and the men in red and blue with peaks and turbans all jogging together, it gives a holiday feeling. After all these decades the rickshaw men have not learned to run in step!

June 1945[2]

I am here longing for my own home and still quite ignorant as to what has come to it. The Iveagh's house is all right, though looted. I expect to go and camp and have laid by a blanket, six towels and two rolls of toilet paper to start life with. H.E. is only just back with the future of India hanging round his neck 'like Niobe, all tears'. He is writing to Alexander to ask if I may step on to Italian soil. Alexander seems to be handling Trieste in a very delicate way. My, what a world! I would like to curl up in your pale blue room and talk of the Levant! You will admit that every single forecast has come true? Except that one could never have

[1] To Jeffery Amherst.
[2] To Momo Marriott.

thought that De Gaulle would choose the one moment when everything, the new Arab League in its first gloss, the Security Pact just adolescent, military necessity for the Eastern transport, *everything* combined against a Syrian bonfire.

Here everyone waits with bated breath while the cake is preparing to be cut and everyone will want his slice and to keep the whole cake also.

I made Her Ex. a lovely plan and found a phoenix to work it—but she is going to be divorced and therefore can't appear in court or vice-court circles; this bombshell only just discovered and it seems impossible to find anyone else with charm and efficiency combined. (Why should they be so difficult to find together?)

14 June 1945

My dear Gerald,

There is, in spite of all the trouble seething, a pleasant feeling that a great many people are happy . . . and I hope to be so too. John Wharton brought a soothsayer—the handsomest old Punjabi Muslim you ever saw, with perfect features, very clear and straight. He told me that in about two months' time the best seven years of my life are to begin, with a journey overseas. He also said that I had a tiger-face and, asked what that meant, it appears that no one dares to be impertinent in one's presence. He then said there is a very rare line in my hand which preserves me from telling lies, flatteries, or feeling envy. Nice people, I thought, who feel it comforting to be assured of such virtues; nobody in the West would think anything so non-utilitarian worth mentioning.

There is quiet here at the moment, but the thunder of a tide approaching. Everyone pained at the fact that every secret instantly oozes out of the secret sessions of the Executive Council. I should be much more surprised if it didn't and do wonder how we keep our optimism in the face of years of oriental experience.

H.E. visited Ibn Saud, as I expect you heard, and it sounds as if it had been successful both ways. Ibn Saud was pleased to find another great man with one eye and told him all the story of the conquest of Riyadh. H.E. is broadcasting the future of India tonight. It is an historic occasion, and strange how ordinary one feels in the middle of events. For one thing it is 115° in the shade and difficult to feel at all!

The conference in Simla was the last public event I witnessed during the war.

Into the labyrinth of Indian politics I have no intention and indeed no knowledge to enable me to enter. I had known the Arab world for nearly twenty years, and had seen it in so many of its parts and from such diverse angles that I felt justified in having opinions about it. But the vastness of India was another matter, nor do I think that government palaces can be relied on for presenting general views. Over and over again in history one is surprised to watch the apparent stagnation with which dynasties and sovereignties drift to their destiny amid the tense activity of all the forces round them. In this case it was not so. Very wise and brilliant people were at work, and the Viceroy himself had a soldier's mind for realities; he hoped, he once told me, to be allowed to withdraw in steps, keeping troops in the three chief centres until the transfer was accomplished, to avoid massacres which he foresaw and which eventually happened. But he rarely spoke of these things. Shut away amid the splendid rooms, he came to lunch from the morning's endless negotiations, files and minutes, with his atmosphere about him of unassailable integrity and lonely calm: and every one of us, devoted to him, would try to make the short interval pass lightly, with talk of books or sport or even mild scandal—but never of politics or war. The events which might have filled my diary are absent, and only the husk of the Simla Conference—where the chances of a Muslim-Hindu India rose to their last clash and vanished—remains.

In a letter of the 2nd of July I described it to Gerald de Gaury 'opening with a sort of garden party on the lawn'.

I photographed the leaders of the destinies of India rolling up in rather nondescript rickshaws, the Punjab premier the only elegant one with green runners under white puggarees and dark green pennants, the Congress with that rather dingy 'more important to be good than beautiful' look: but Jinnah was very aristocratic and straight. He has a cruel face at a distance but nice when you come up close and see the delicate features and rather wrought-up glance, like a horse nervous before its race, and blue eyes *speaking* with intelligence. He is against everything both in his party and out of it and it remains to be seen if he plays at all, but has become much gentler to talk to outside business and told Their Ex's that the rather formal little family party they asked him to was the only bit of relaxation he had had. Typically, his venom is for the Muslim in Congress. After discussing neutral and pleasant things like Devonshire cream with him,

I talked to Maulana Azad, the leader of Congress not on speaking terms with Jinnah, who—not talking English—was sitting apart under a tree chatting with white walrus-moustached Pandit Pant. The old Maulana has a charming face and a little pointed beard and goes in and out of prison in a natural way with no fuss—all traits which seemed explained when he told me he was Arab with a father from Mecca. He was pleased (and surprised) to find a woman to chat with in Arabic and would I think have been happy to sit in the shade and forget the troubles of this world. It must be hard to run Congress with Gandhi round the corner limiting himself to 'advice'. Their Ex's now came down and talked to everyone, mollified the Press with a speech, and all went down to business; but came up again for a buffet lunch chosen with care to include the religious, and we all (except Their Ex's) joined those who were not obviously gathered into incubating circles. They could not have been more pleasant and gentle to talk to, and if the future of India is settled it will be greatly due to H.E.'s personality and his goodwill which no one can mistake. One can see it having its effect. The A.D.C.'s too, and Archie John in particular, have been helping to make all happy and at ease. Gandhi, who came to tea in Lady Wavell's private sitting-room before the Conference[1] —and made (the A.D.C. told me) a very quaint picture, one with so many clothes and the other with so few on the same sofa—beamed and melted at the sight of so many handsome and soldierly young men (we have a very nice-looking lot). The only person I felt was not particularly affected was Pandit Nehru, who came—also before the Conference— after a long talk with H.E. He sat with us at a tea-table under the wainscot, with weapons hung ornamentally around and a fire burning, and tables filled with Viceroy and Vicereine photographs, and huge vases of flowers, with Her Ex. on one side of him and me on the other, and secretaries and A.D.C.'s, and H.E. who came down to join us—and everyone made him talk and was as nice as possible, yet I felt he was gnawing some sorrow inside him. He seemed to me a seeking soul, happy to follow a track if he could conscientiously do so; and now by fate, or our unamiability perhaps, is made to oppose so that our pleasantness and all must make it worse. He never relaxed the defensive for a minute, but I would like a talk alone and to get him forgetful and see what is under it all. I may be quite mistaken: it was only female intuition while we sat at tea. He has a good-looking, regular, rather narrow-foreheaded face, very intelligent but without the *apostolic* force of the old Mahatma. The conversation took an unfortunate turn. Somebody mentioned the arrival of a circus

[1] On June 24.

and Her Ex. came to life out of a placid daydream to say that she hated circuses because of the captive animals. 'Captive?' said Mr. Nehru (just out of prison). 'Yes,' said Her Ex. unaware of everybody's frantic but paralysed efforts to think of another topic. 'Behind bars, you know.' 'Yes,' said Nehru, eloquently. An A.D.C. pulled himself together and rescued the conversation just in time.

On the second day of the Conference, Charles Rankin and I went to look at a crowd waiting for the Mahatma to come to his prayers. Politics were blazing from loud-speakers. Everyone was friendly. They seem to regard 'Quit India' as a sort of formula like *Heil Hitler* or *Grüss Gott*. We went on and there, coming out from his house, was the old Gandhi with a man clearing a way for him with a stick, and an Indian woman on one side supporting him and a white-haired English one, elongated, gentle, and the sort who belongs to the S.P.C.A. on the other; and the old man in between, his legs very spindly, his head sunk, his white sheet barrelling in the wind about him, looking neither right nor left, and the noise of the crowd evidently like the sound of grasshoppers that have become a burden. Who would be a Saint? Or at any rate so recognized by contemporaries? When a photographer came and stood right in front of him he could bear it no longer, snatched the man's camera, and tossed it into the air with surprising vigour.

On the third day of the Conference, I went down with blood-poisoning from a silly scratch on my heel (like Achilles). If it weren't for these new drugs I suppose I might be dead; as it is the disease was suppressed in three days, though a horrid gash remains, and I am suffering from the remedy—one of these M & B. things that leave one suicidally minded. When at the lowest, Field-Marshal Alexander's telegram came with 'orders' for me to go to Venice: this would have cheered me in my grave. I leave as soon as the doctor allows and that is, I hope, the 12th, so that I may be in either Rome or Venice in a fortnight's time. I have also good news of my little niece married to a partisan, and comforting news of the poor youngest, who was killed with the partisans, in action and, thank God, not caught.

H.E. has found time to come and sit for a chat by my bedside while I was laid up (I go down to one meal a day now). I shall miss them all. I have never been surrounded by more nice people all at once—everyone is gentle and thoughtful and no one says horrid things about the others—it makes a happy climate.

We are in the monsoon. I went out yesterday in a rickshaw and the rain came pelting down as if a whole series of waterspouts were about us.

INDIA

Roaring brown cataracts fill every creek and gutter, dashing to the plains and filling the slow rivers. The rickshaws are closed with glass windows in front, like Sedan-chairs, and one just sees the eyes of the other rickshaw men as one lurches by them. It rains for hours or drifts in mists, but then all is drawn away like a curtain, mountains appear, the plains shining with Jhelum river, and all the great waves of hillside turn green day by day.

Simla was gloomy when I left on the 11th of July. Jinnah had annoyed H.E., whose patience had seemed unbreakable, by strolling in to him with a lighted cigar in his hand, and had dashed the Conference to the ground.

I asked H.E. when he expected it to finish, and he said "Will it *ever* finish?" I think he is very disappointed. Jinnah does not want a unified India, not with any number of Muslim votes, as it would defeat Pakistan; and the only good of the Conference is that it has made it clear that Britain is not the obstacle; I should say it is also pretty clear that she alone can (if anyone) keep those two parties together at all. If it were not for the anxiety to go to Italy, I should hate to go just at this time. It is sad to leave. And what shall I do without four A.D.C.'s and a secretary or two arranging all our lives? I am, in fact, very tired. Their Ex's have asked me to come back, but I am sure one ought now to do what one can in one's own centre and get ordinary life back to normal if one can.[1]

I flew in a fifteen-hour day from Karachi to Cairo over the Southern Desert and the Nefud[2] where travellers quail, and looked down on its twisted aimless valleys and on Jauf which I had always wondered about and now knew I should never have the slightest wish to visit. In the late afternoon we saw Petra on the wrinkled defencible edge that rings the plateau of Arabia. I had the whole of the Sunderland flying-boat to myself as there were no other passengers, and they let me sit in the control cabin and scan the immense sun-drenched horizon. It seemed strange for so huge a fish to be going so far across dry land (and how dry). I vaguely remembered a Virgilian eclogue that said something about it.

Three days in Cairo with the Bernard Burrows, seeing friends, in

[1] To G. de Gaury 14.6.45.
[2] Sand-dune stretch of the desert of Nejd.

an atmosphere that had lost the precarious zest of the desert war. Then I flew by night, touched at North African and Sicilian airfields piled with wrecks, landed on the 20th of July at Rome, and after a week there with the kind Halfords and several frustrated efforts, was finally landed in Treviso. One third of that little town had been shattered by ten-minute bombing twice repeated, and my heart sank when I saw the skeleton roofs and wondered what home I should find. An army lorry took me next day, and from the southern road my house at the top of the hill appeared intact. The garden gate was open; the front door-bell brought Emma in a white apron, and Caroly, my mother's secretary, behind her:

> Dear God in heaven, it was a joy
> The dead men could not blast.

With many others I was able to think so, in that happy year.

16
Italy 1945

Happiness unattached and unrelated, as if one life had dropped into another from nowhere, followed the months of my return; an atmosphere of safety colours the memory with a comforting familiar and unworldly glow. Every morning, surrounded by desolation, but with the Euganean hills in sight and the Dolomites behind me, and the Venetian plain and its hourly variations stretched at the foot of our hill, I woke enraptured and recognized the security of home, the sweetest and oldest sensation round which the human vine can wrap its tendrils.

This strong impression seemed to grow out of something more basic than facts; for the wings of the world as they moved continued to cast distorted shadows, and the evidence of my letters shows very little security at all.

Most of the old loved presences were missing. Charles Ker and his sisters Car and Penelope had died, and so had Jock's father 'the gentlest man', and my own old people, whose presence continues to linger in their place as if the stream of death were but a brook. But the younger voices reached me. Marina[1] wrote from Switzerland:

LAUSANNE *3 January 1945*

Dearest Freya,

You can't imagine how much joy your postcard gave me. A little of Flora[2] came back to me in her usual consoling and sweet way on this very sad day of Nativity. I have never got over the idea of her death, for the reality of it, I know, will come upon me only when peace will have returned to the world. You probably have had all the news about her—did you read her manuscript on the period of her imprisonment? Everyone loved and admired her in that filthy little place. When at last they allowed

[1] Luling.
[2] My mother.

me to see her, her appearance filled me with admiration: she sailed into the dingy little prison room smiling, serene and dignified. That apparition has remained for ever in my heart as the embodiment of your wonderful country. Against fury and injustice, through darkness and pain, still and ever it will rule, an example, a light, an aim for the whole world to admire and try to reach.

Towards November '43 your home was requisitioned for the neo-Fascist army. Caroly has watched over it as if it had been her own, and so far it has been saved. Now we can only pray God that that dear little corner which your mother so loved, may be spared for you to find again after all the tragedy is over. All she wanted in the world was your happiness, and everything she did was done for you; that is why I am nearly sure that Casa Freia will be saved, she will save it *herself* for you.

Now a little news of myself since you ask for it. We are here in exile, my sister and myself, since last Christmas; the children were here before us, for we were convinced that things could only end in this way and we wished to keep them out of the mess. We were in Italy for the 25th July, and then the ghastly period of awaiting disaster came. After the fall we had to leave Maser very soon for I had added to my old sin of anti-Fascism and my treachery of passionately loving England, the new and active work of the resistance and the formation of guerrillas. They came to fetch me in a very melodramatic way with so many guns and so many Germans, but thank God I was not at Maser but at Pederiva and so I escaped their clutches and came here.

Other news came trickling in: little more than I knew already of my two nephews—the loss of one in Russia, last seen after the terrible Don retreat, and the other's young and brave death in the valleys of Piedmont. The only niece left was married. She had rescued her husband when captured for the third time among the partisans. During the week while the S.S. kept him for information her friends were able to kidnap two German officers to buy him off with, adding two million lire and her gold bracelets for the exchange.

In the south, during the last years of the war, the Allies were moving about and I got letters from Naples now and then.

... Our immediate problems here all centre on food and on transport to distribute what there is. This winter is inevitably going to be cold. A lot of people are inevitably going to be hungry, the only question being how hungry. At present the answer is hungry but not starving. In some cases just not starving. There is also going to be unemployment, particularly if the Germans continue their present policy of destroying the power system; for Italian industry, as you know, is geared to electricity. A combination of cold, hunger and unemployment is liable to be dangerous in any country and we are naturally very preoccupied over this and doing all we can with what we can get to give out. We shall need some luck, so cross your fingers for us.'[1]

In Rome at the end of July 1945 one still heard stray shots every night in the woods of Villa Borghese, and dimly visible the German corpses rotted under Tivoli waterfalls. In the north, where the last wave had not yet passed, 'it seems probable,' Victor Cunard had written, 'that the Germans will hold the Adige for as long as they can'. The Asolo approaches were littered with wreckage.

The Germans had planned, as a matter of fact, to hold, between the rivers of Brenta and Piave, a last defence line running through my garden; their gun, which would have called certain destruction upon us, was half-way up our hill. But the retreat involved it, and its team surrendered, and my maid Emma, running to share in the loot, carried away a suitcase filled with note-paper which was—to Emma —of very little use. Yet already, when I returned, the ancient heart of Italy was beginning to beat again; and 'this country has made an *art* of being vanquished', an exasperated American said to me before the year was out.

In England, too, the thought of peace was creeping like a tardy northern spring. Jock wrote from his R.A.F. station at Old Sarum, 'I have to suppress almost intolerable desires to get back to No. 50. After 11 p.m. I allow myself sometimes to plot and plan for books and publishing, and sometimes I think about Cannon Lodge at Hampstead and wonder whether windows without glass and doors without bolts make an open house. Aeroplanes have made me wish for very simple things—the least simple being a week-end at Asolo.'

Everything is well[2] [I wrote in August], the house shabby but intact, and for the last fortnight things in boxes have been pouring from all their

[1] Letter from Harold Caccia, Caserta, December 1945.
[2] To G. de Gaury.

hiding-places. I found eleven unexploded shells among the roses, and the shrubs cut away for fear of snipers. The partisans, too, used this garden, and their odds and ends were lying about in my room where they hid. The rest of the house has been inhabited by six different lots of Fascists, all destructive and all horrid, and horrid wives took away our kitchen (electric, irreplaceable, but the husband is now in prison for twenty years, and we hope to get the stove back from his villa at Monza). Others cut the window curtains to make frills for a new baby's cradle—a little viper no doubt. They took the inside of my books out to light fires. Caroly and Emma wrestled over every bit of property, and it is practically all there, everything is the same, only older and tireder and a shadow of hunger looms with the winter. If we lived on our rations we would die (rather Irish); we get only half what the Allied Military Government think we get. So it is all black market and Caroly has collected two sacks of corn and 10 lbs of butter and I hope to survive. The silk factory totters on one foot; we are going to open its little shop at Christmas. The garden is desolate, the gardener says it was no satisfaction to work for the *Repubblica*. Everyone is either friend or enemy, it is shocking if one is polite to the wrong people. This tiny place with no rail or air station was chosen as the G.H.Q. of the Fascists after the Italian surrender. A machine-gun post was just outside my gate beside a sixteenth-century fountain, and my tenant, the general, used to walk to and from the cinema with four guards holding guns ready on their hips to shoot any citizen who looked alarming. The Fascists seem to have been as bad as the Germans by that time. Thirty-three trees of the avenue in the next little town are marked with wooden crosses and stiff dry garlands in memory of young men caught in the mountains and hung there on hooks. Most people here were on our side and many gathered in hidden corners to listen to the B.B.C., and their miserable burnt-out houses are about, and a great feeling of bitterness. Our fat, elderly citizens were told they would be hostages, and spent their time in hiding. I can't think there will be any German tourist round Venice for a long time. [How wrong I was!]

Transport and food were our obstacles, and one remembered how great civilizations have ended when their roads were cut.

We have gone back to being a small hill-town trying (successfully) to thwart the regulations from the central government which happens to be A.M.G. but might just as well be the Holy Roman Empire, as the mutual feelings must be much the same. We keep alive by judicious manœuvring

—exchange cloth for butter and so on. I have landed a Yugoslav Governor in jug for blackmail. I have also got the mid-day winter meal for my ten girls; a partisan crossed the Po for us by night as it is forbidden to transport food. I told the A.M.G. I was going to attempt this bit of contraband and all they said was 'don't bring more than you need and don't get caught'.

We are strangely remote. No news to speak of—I haven't had a line from anyone. We live in our own world, intersected by the A.M.G. in jeeps and lorries, who look in, and now and then whisk one to Padua, Treviso, or Venice where I spent a few hours and found a sort of twilight over it, like Shelley's 'Soon shall come a darker day'. It made me sad, but really it is pleasanter than it was, and a very *little* prosperity will make the difference. The female Italians are the most Allied-minded: as I strolled about I saw some young girls watching a gondola with two harmless young lieutenants of the 8th Army lying back inside it enjoying the sun: '*Che aria da padroni; che dominatori!*' they said.

Treviso is a shambles—covered with writings to remind the population that we did it, and as I was standing watching the wreck of a frescoed house, a man passing by said: 'Do you see?' I think it would be a good plan not to allow these slogans, but I suppose we shall not bother. Most people are terrified at the Allies leaving next month, and the local A.M.G. is giving me the present of a pistol. I don't think anything at all will happen. The most depressing thing, far worse than the bombed buildings, is the state of mind of the Italians I see. The middle-aged seem to have thrown up the sponge and the young ones to be in a mental chaos, with no certainty of any values left. It is pathetic how anxious they are for a lead (and how difficult to make them follow when they get it, probably).

25 August 1945

Huge hailstones and a tornado came down on us a week after I got here and we spent the night baling water out of the bedrooms and saw with daylight a landscape like winter, and our last crop and hope after a bad harvest lying flat on the ground. Peasants weeping. There is going to be *very* little food. They (the A.M.G.) seem to think that no civilian British will be allowed in Italy for months. None but the Viceroy's secretariat could have managed such a feat as to land me here now. The shadow of the war still flaps its huge mephistophelian wings and people are far from normal yet. The men far worse than the women (whose morale is kept up by Allied admiration). But the young have had twenty-five years of Fascism and can't stop being Fascist however hard they try and whatever name they call it. Up here they want work and things will improve as coal trickles in and a few factories get going. Naples was one of the most miserable sights I have ever seen: I can't tell you how grateful I am to your brother for making it bearable. He came up to Rome and we stood side by side on the balcony of Palazzo Venezia where the balustrade still has the red velvet for the gesticulating dictatorial hand.[1]

Happiness in spite of all comes breathing through these letters:

How nice the people are! Checchi (the gardener) almost daily brings wheelbarrows of the things that he took away to hide, with the same smile, so many years ago. Emma has just come to say that her salary is too much—she can do with less. These things must surely balance the recording angel's scales? The wilderness of my garden still has the loveliest, gentlest view I know, that winds itself round one's heart. How heavenly it is to look on that landscape: how much more beautiful than anything else anywhere. It is something we have carried inside us for two thousand years, our own sort of civilization, and oh, it is good to get back to.

The army brought civilized life or disrupted it according to its behaviour:

Cart-loads, or rather lorry-loads were carried away from the Iveaghs under a big red cross and they will have to buy all their linen, etc., over again. The S.S. toasted Hitler and smashed the glasses, and slid in boots on the dining-table (beautifully shiny, one can understand the unholy temptation!). The house is now inhabited by a bevy of future parsons who have come to sit and think for a few weeks, and where could one do it better? I introduced their Padre to our Monsignore who immediately said 'Truth is One', and I had to help and remark that the four gospels are all different. The Padre told me he had never thought of this before, which shows how little we know of propaganda even when it is our business. He has been making me do peculiar things, like persuading the female domestics to be passed by an army doctor, one of those regulations that must cause lots of trouble in the more modest parts of the world.

We have a dreadful A.M.G. Yugoslav-American Governor who believes, like the early Arab generals, in possessing the vanquished females

[1] To Charles Rankin.

on every battlefield. But we have a colonel in Treviso whom all adore, and a brigadier in Padua with the heart of Captain Reece (of *The Mantelpiece*). I went to hear them make speeches in Italian to the Treviso authorities and it was a touching, charming affair. Last week the Regent of Iraq, the first swallow, turned up suddenly in Venice and my niece and I went down to help the 13th Corps Liaison entertain him and had four days' luxury in the Grand Hotel, curtseying with that ease which now comes by habit! It seemed very mixed to be talking Arabic in Venice, which has a poor dilapidated air, but is *more* beautiful, with old men sunning themselves on their own piazza. Every week sees more things on the road—and very weird ones! When one goes a distance, as to Milan, one scours the country for a departing lorry, and at vast expense gets a three-day journey on the roof.[1]

It was miraculous to find things in existence, like those Asiatic rivers that reappear suddenly from underground. My house was more or less itself again and the struggle for food well in hand. The silk factory had six girls and we were adding two more, and as there was still a small store of colours left for dyeing we could carry on. I had found enough furniture to last me through the winter, which was lucky as even plain linen sheeting cost £6 a yard; and I amused myself by re-establishing my home, making scrapbooks of the photographs lying around—one of 1896 with Herbert Young, a young man, painting in the garden. It was a pleasure to do this and to think of my niece and her children. 'She has come to stay a few weeks; she is a darling, so pretty, and has had a tough time. Her husband, a gentle, devoted young man came with her, and also Mario who looks too frightful now, like a fraudulent character in a play. I hope I shall not have to see him often'. [My brother-in-law, who died soon after.]

By October the 4th I wrote to Hugh Euston:

I can't tell you my surprise when our A.M.G. drove over with a big bag and deposited two parcels on my table—sugar and coffee and tea, so badly needed. I didn't think it possible for them to get through and am so grateful. It is also the only sign, since Peter's note nearly two months ago, that India still exists. Letters here behave like bullets in a tank and whizz round till they hit their targets by chance.

[1] To the Earl of Euston 14.9.45.

ITALY 1945

I am settling down, not with my own affairs, but with all those that A.M.G. is ceasing to be interested in—people asking for motors, for permits, for houses, for the moon, and sure that any Ally can provide them. Everything is done (or not done) in a welter of six political parties who cook even their macaroni in political party ways. Italy seems to be getting orientalized. The black market must be seen to be believed. I don't in the least mind buying food: it is much less wasted on me than on lots of these ex-Fascists, but I would rather freeze slowly than buy coal which is sent for factories and is bought up by private people. There was forty per cent leakage at first, and now they have halved and hope to get it down to ten per cent. Our own A.M.G. Governor has left, thank God, his latest effort to procure his maid a baby; she came to me to ask what to do about it. Now we have no government. Our third mayor has resigned and we do what we can for ourselves and are relapsing into the chaos which produced the Renaissance: I hope we may produce anything as good.

October 1945

My dear Jeffery [Amherst],

In July I flew back over the dear old deserts and it was rather good to see the wicked but civilized curving shores of Europe and church steeples in the midst of towns. These three months have done wonders: when I came we had no posts, no newspapers except a stray one now and then from Venice, no means except military of getting about, no trains. One lived on what the parish produced and the people who had no geese, corn, fruit or butter of their own got along by selling their household furniture slowly for vast sums. Now every time I go to Venice or Treviso some new thing has burst into life; the steamers have started, the demolished railway stations with their grass-clothed sleepers begin to come to life and the train carries you (without windows and very cold) to Trieste, Turin or even Rome; one sees scaffolding and workmen on the shells of houses and carts carry away the rubble to build with in other places. Rome—looking on me with some disapproval for being in an Italy considered safe and reserved for A.M.G.—told me I should be unable to live as a mere civilian. As forty million Italians were doing it, it seemed that there must be a chance anyway, and I have been existing beautifully, selling a pair of sheets or a sofa when funds got low. I am an Industrialist, though not a Capitalist; it is fascinating to be interested in silkworms and to learn the steps between the worm and the loom and the customer. Out of this lotus-land, this happy haven, the Embassy in Rome have pressed on me a six-months contract to make the Italians democratic; this hopeless task is undertaken in view of the election, but as H.M.G. needs a month to find me a car to *begin* travelling with, I can't think we shall influence the votes. When are you coming out here on your own travel? I think it is the sort of country you will like, not only beautiful but gentle to live in; everyone breaks the law and plays black market, but people are thinking of nicer things than money most of the time. 'Mother's nervy' is a good description (not only of England)—but when you come here you'll forget all that. You won't find anything later than 1920 in my library and very few things belonging to a post-war more recent than the Guelph and Ghibelline affairs in the country round about.

By the middle of October Nigel Clive came for a fortnight's leave from Athens and we walked to Maser over pale gold slopes, and spent two days in Venice, pottering in gondolas through the evenings under the arched bridges, in and out of Middle Ages or Renaissance, watching the sphinx or the marble lion over doorways, spending a morning among the Ducal Palace Tintorettos—the mornings for culture as Adrian Bishop had advised and the afternoons for Recovery and Pleasure. The 13th Corps Liaison with Archie Colquhoun joined us to talk Communism at Florian's, and Venice, gayer and more normal, had her shops filled as if by enchantment with expensive pre-war things. Papers, too, began to spoil one's pleasure. 'Mr. Molotov and all those Belsen faces! Our poor diplomats trying to say it doesn't matter! What a world! and what have we all been doing and saying all these years to make it different? We have debased our words and pay for it by seeing nothing but counterfeit coins. They are forcing me to become a Press Attaché here in the north. It is only for six months and then I hope to get out of it and sit quietly and move softly and love mercy and forget the atom bomb and all—and perhaps write a book or two about non-controversial matters such as the human heart.'

October 1945

Dearest Jock,
    At last your letters come—two of them,
        Breaking the silence of the seas
        Among the farthest Italies.

I was delighted to get them and hope that now our interrupted stream may take its course again.

Everyone says lovely things about the appearance of Mama's diary. It is beautifully done and I am so pleased and grateful.

There are some good young men of the special services now turned observers in Venice. They lunched yesterday, but my pleasure was spoiled by a wasp which dived into my vermouth and stung inside my mouth. I can't think why Sir John Suckling thought it improved a mouth to look as if 'a bee had stung it newly'. I suffered in silence and no one noticed, but it hurt!

October is here, blue days and gold. One wakes to the plain white with frost, the mountains pale turquoise and snow, and there are emerald stretches of spring corn. It is a constant loveliness, and one forgets as one looks how difficult this Beauty is to live with. A.M.G. allows us residents in Italy four thousand lire a month, while an ordinary woollen thing to keep one's top warm costs eight thousand. But the country *is* recovering. Every week some new train starts running and coal is trickling in; the price of silk and oil shows signs of lowering a little; butter is still eight hundred lire a kilo and firewood six hundred and there is no milk to speak of, but *everything* is obtainable to the rich. As for oriental corruption, it is white as snow by comparison. If I become Press attaché I shall get rations and need worry about nothing at all and, dear Jock, couldn't you fly out before or after Christmas for a week?

All through the autumn this life of insecurity and charm persisted. I read Morris's *Earthly Paradise* among food hunts and bandits, who moved in black masks, and two were shot near by and eventually recognized as a local bank manager and a sergeant of police. A band of thirty (or possibly less) surrounded a village café and cleared it of cash, going from table to table like a philanthropic committee collecting. And yet the feeling of stability was there: 'to put things away in the hope of finding them when years and years have rolled by. It is lovely to come upon objects one remembers as soon as one remembers anything, and it makes things like wars and revolutions seem less important when such fragile trifles survive.'[1] 'It is fascinating,' I wrote to Peter Coats in December, 'to watch the old enchantment at work on a new generation that never was brought up on the Continent and the Grand Tour as I was . . . I made a

[1] To Billy Henderson 29.11.45.

speech in Italian. We have started a reading-room in Venice, and this ordeal, with brigadiers and prefects in rows, was hurled at me at the last moment. I felt abject, but suddenly got carried away and forgot the official occasion, and talked about civilization tossed from Greece to Rome, to Mantua and Sirmio and Iona, back and forth with Italy and England in her service, and my audience wept.'

The winter was hard enough and no one had much to keep warm with: most of my friends heated one or two rooms and the poor heated nothing. I had a fire from tea-time and ran about till then. But mails began to come dropping by odd ways—A.M.G. from Padua or Treviso, Embassy from Rome, air mail, or the 6th Armoured Division from Vicenza. A jeep or a lorry would stop, and its inmates come in with letters and a tin or two of army rations, ready for lunch in exchange. 'Did you ever read *The Cloister and the Hearth* and realize that *all those complications* came from an inefficient postal system and the want of facilities for travel? I now have captured a car—like a small Roman triumph rolling along (frequently punctured).'

I was back at my old job of Persuasion, and spent my time touring in discomfort through fifty-one towns where my reading centres were to be started, between the Brenner and Rome. Every new centre was like an exploration. One landed in the unknown with no previous knowledge as to who would wish to benefit by reading the English Press. Sometimes it was easy—the people happily unified in their opinions under Church or Communism, and one meeting-ground, a club or library or school perhaps, could do for all. More often there were three or four different groups and some neutral centre had to be found among them, with quick assessments while the decisions were being taken, and a forecast made in private of the most useful claimants with the future of the little town in sight. Michael Stewart, my chief at the Embassy in Rome, became a friend and is so still—one of that able and kind galaxy under whom it was always my fortune to work during my years of service. He had promised that I need neither keep accounts nor write reports— surely a unique offer in government employment—and gave me the lesser towns, while John Miller—another friend—and others were scattered in more important centres like Venice and Milan. The

ITALY 1945

winter was mercilessly cold and the gloom of the army transit hotels indescribable, but every one of my little cities had some statue, fountain, or picture that one would give a year of one's life to look at.

I would like [I wrote], to be rich enough in my old age to possess one small fifteenth-century madonna with a gold background. The Sienese have black mantles with gold zigzags, obviously woven in Damascus, and I believe there can only have been one of these beautiful weavings and that they borrowed it from each other to paint the models in. It is of course ridiculous to expect Italy to be at home in the modern world: she is deep down medieval right through. If we succeed in building our new Atlantis, she will be a sort of Ireland, an irritation but also a refuge, to the civilization to come: but if the civilization doesn't come off, it may yet be a comfort to find the old and imperfect pattern intact, with its charities and black markets, its political monstrosities and family pities, its art of living in towns so exciting and dramatic and full of their own life that no real interest is taken in the world beyond.

Each small metropolis now calls up in my mind some picture, past or present, of its life. Sometimes it was the beauty of painting or stone, more often at that time some human piety, the disinterested, almost unquenchable, ant-like optimism that builds in the ruined world. The poor were deep in black markets and labour and most of the rich did little; but that heroic educated *bourgeoisie* which Fascism and war had almost obliterated were still eager with their poor resources to do what they could.

Many pictures I remember—too many to describe here. The charm of Pavia's cobbled streets and squares subdued by the University and the atmosphere of Learning, in a setting of pale skies and shallow waters that irrigate the meadows and keep them green. Poplars marked the ditch-sides and smudges of woods the pale meanderings of Ticino, and the old roofed bridge was down; and the Abbé of the Borromeo College sat writing exquisite Italian in a single warmed room beyond his cold high-ceilinged colonnades. He cooked 'imitation' coffee for us, putting a white napkin under each cup by the small electric fire, in a room of stiff high chairs, and books, and a black bed with a red damask cover, a room filled with the decency of study—and found a young-looking man with early-grizzled hair to help us, who had fought all up Italy in the 8th Army and was working for nothing at a 'people's university' in the town. 'I believe Italy will recover more quickly than most other places; I thought this in 1940 and am still convinced of it. There is a passionate wish to get back into civilization and forget this dark interlude.' Before leaving Pavia I discovered the tomb of St. Augustine behind an eleventh-century façade, whither his monks—fleeing before Genseric and the Barbarians, spending enormous sums to convey his bones from place to place—had finally sold them to the Lombard emperor. Here the Augustine friars were chanting evensong under a marble tomb crowded with Renaissance Faiths and Charities in long and modest gowns—and the broken bridge, and Genseric in Carthage, and the whole story seemed to have a single continuity in Pavia.

In the north, discomfort almost outweighed the pleasures of this resurrection. Milan was colder than London in Marina's and her sister's luxury flat on an eighth floor, where neither lift, water, light, telephone nor stove were working and sister, daughter, dogs and friends were all made welcome in the half-demolished town. The Brenner, Trent, Bolzano and Brixen were visited in December. Larches as yellow as pheasants' tails sloped up the hills and snow lay in sun on the tops—but there was still a litter of ruin below. The 5th Army had captured a huge camp of cars, trucks and guns and placed them in rows—all under white frost by the roadside. Now the 5th was no more, but had dissolved without saying anything about its car-park, 'so there it decays inviolable, while the British Embassy is all off the roads for want of cars!' I made a friend here of Father Malden who came from the west of England and ended a rich and varied life as a Dominican missionary in a quiet monastery of the Dolomites among his books, with a view of the mountains.

In the west I pressed up the Valdensian valleys and saw their decent poverty and helpfulness and pride, and the museum of their history where, with his relics round him, is the portrait of an English colonel who devoted his life and resources to this people, after losing a leg on the field of Waterloo.

I followed the coast from Genoa northward, and from the San

Remo casino which had just reopened, with a band where a few dubious women in furs as little genuine as themselves sat listening, I pushed on to see what was left of my cottage at La Mortola.

6 January 1946

You never saw such a mess. The French Navy went for this coast, and poured stuff indiscriminately over Ventimiglia and other towns, and a submarine shot at our walls and blew half the roof off. The R.A.F. blew up the left-hand tunnel and sent rails and sleepers through our gardener's cottage; and the Germans laid mines all over the landscape and garden. Neighbours, peasants, S.S. and Fascists all looted. With this, it still has its charm; the olive trees I planted have grown into a grove, and the cottage is being repaired. I am handing it to my niece as a belated wedding present.

As the spring came, I described the centre of Italy to Lord Wavell,[1]

... from one little town to another, by river and sea-shore and very much mountain-perched with Etruscan citadels: from Cortona a corner of Thrasymenus appears like a plot of forgotten sky and there is a delicate outline of hills through which the baby Tiber winds. In these Etruscan cities every parish tower seems to be flying a red flag, as the peasants have all gone Communist, but I can't help thinking the Russians will be disappointed by them when it comes to the point. Their leader, Togliatti, spoke in Bologna and there were red flags draped over Pope Julius's balcony. He—with his two bronze fingers—blessed it all. Next morning they had a sickle and hammer on their high, thin tower to show they had won the election—it means a change of pocket for strange earnings.

I had fun discovering the ruins of Canossa in the Apennines; the map showed it near my route, and we deviated into enchanting hills with the spring spread over them, geese and pigs and lambs and children, and every clump of trees or group of houses like a 'primitive' background, but no village big enough for an inn. So I lunched in a peasant's co-operative kitchen on all the things the U.S.A. are being told don't exist and the whitest bread you ever saw, and at last found the Canossa ruin on a ridge with a view, and violets and tulips growing wild. It is rather a gloomy thought that a German emperor was doing penance there nearly a thousand years ago and here they are still doing it.

[1] 29.4.46.

The reading centres flourished and Rome was pleased, and the colleagues in the larger centres helped in a valid way. During November I had visited Verona, Vicenza, Padua, Treviso, Mestre and Conegliano; 'from Milan we hear that visits to Pavia and Cremona found our material being used to good advantage'; a cultural club in Brescia, a reading centre in Varese, a *Università Popolare* in Bergamo; Fano and Pesaro and Bologna, Ancona, Piacenza and Ravenna are all mentioned during these months for one thing or another. The uncertainty, as usual, came from London. 'We could get everything working wonderfully here: all we want is to be sure of fifty sets, more or less regularly, of the chief dailies and weeklies, to have north Italy eating out of our hand. This couldn't cost H.M.G. more than £20 to £30 a month, and one person to look after it once it is going would be sufficient for the whole of Italy—you couldn't have any form of effort paying a bigger dividend in results: and yet they seem to be having all sorts of difficulty in getting these few papers. It does seem pathetic that when for once things like *The Daily Mail* could be useful, one can't even get them!'

The starting of my centres was the delicate part of my work and required 'hours and hours of negotiating so that no one party comes off with all the honours'.

I have managed, but only just [I wrote][1] (owing to car accidents) to get to Ferrara and to Ravenna, which seems to be doing beautifully more or less on its own; the young Communists were about and it is a very good thing to have them interested, especially in any town as *red* as Ravenna. Ferrara however is very jittery and politics top-heavy. I had a slight uncertainty before as to the feelings of Signora X.; this time I spent a good while with her looking at the monuments, and as we became more intimate she gradually poured out her difficulties, and asked how it was possible for an Italian to be spontaneously friendly, when they had no means of knowing whom they would have to be friends with in a short while. Rather shocked at this point of view, I suggested that it was better to make up one's mind about one's friends first, and let events happen as they might: sentiments of this sort, I feel, suggest a rather Fascist past?

Everyone complains of the slowness of the dailies in arriving, much

---

[1] To the Embassy in Rome.

more slowly than those on public sale. I suppose it is hopeless to expect the F.O. to send as quickly as the ordinary post?

With spring 1946 the Italian election (which had made everyone nervous) was over, and the agitation for Trieste, with Marshal Tito extremely menacing on the frontier, began to calm down as soon as it looked as if Italy might be allowed to fight it out if she really wished to. I felt that 'if we have to submerge the whole of civilization, I hope it may not be over so *passé* a thing as a frontier'.

The papers are so busy with a political crisis every week that we never get outside them. There are eight principal parties and the only ones that have a chance at the election are those that possess the Ministries of Justice and Interior which manipulate the law courts and police: hence the fearful scramble to get at the vital portfolios in time! I dip into this sordid world when I go to Venice, where the charming Civil Liaison live in an old palazzo with moth'd and dripping arras hung and renovated in a wagon-lit style here and there by the royal house of Genoa. In the midst of all this, they have all, or nearly all, gone Communist and are having an excellent effect counteracting the British passion in Italy for drinking and dining only with duchesses or marchesas.[1]

ASOLO *20 February 1946*

I am glad you are in on the Disunited Nations. For better or worse it is the cauldron in which the future of our world is boiling, and exciting to be inside the orbit of its news. Italy trots along on her butterfly path, no doubt towards some stupendous crash, but with a great many amenities meanwhile. I suppose one's point of view about the Juggernaut depends on whether you are on top of it or in the way of the wheels. Most of the affluent people are clinging rather precariously to the top, with masses of dollars to rat with at the shortest notice; but then you come on someone who has a factory and is doomed in a matter of weeks to close it, or these young people like my nephew-in-law for whom, as far as one can see, there is no likelihood of any sort of job in the future—and as it looks as if no one was doing anything about the future at all, I imagine it is going to be uncomfortable for a long time. We, of course, are all suddenly rich because our salaries are paid in pounds and therefore have gone double overnight, and so I am going to buy a parasol in Venice.

[1] To Charles Rankin.

ITALY 1945

I have been to the Fenice, not yet heated, but what a gem of a theatre —what Venice, and opera and the eighteenth century and all the frills and froth of life should be: arrived by gondola into plum-coloured velvet spangled with stars; turquoise ceiling crowded with shepherdesses in pannier gowns, and everything rounded that can be so; the lights shaded like clusters of candles among the boxes; and *Manon* a travesty of tragedy, on the stage; and gossip, a travesty of comedy, in every one of the semi-dark boxes where events are settled between the acts. It struck me that what makes such a difference between our world and this Mediterranean is the amount of private life we have: here it is almost equally divided and when you go home from opera or café or piazza, it is definitely from one half of life to another; but we in England look upon these things as accidental parts of our private life which goes on all the time.[1]

One was thankful to be through the winter. There were four months yet to the harvest, but there was warmth in the sun, and hens laid eggs and a few green things appeared; and the Italians, who had come through many centuries to mistrust their Government, had learnt that they must do things for themselves. They were being desperately unreasonable over Trieste. 'The whole educated part of the nation insists on being intelligent without knowing, or caring to know, any facts. One sees all the time the fearful effects of a civil war, undermining the machinery by which a country runs. We are now being deluged by troops billeted in all the villas. I imagine because of Tito.'

The thought of writing came back with other normal things:

Foreword to *Baghdad Sketches*[2]—I suppose I could, though I don't feel as if there were anything I wanted to say. I feel like a divorced wife once my book is published and has left me, and hate to be brought back into intimate contact! I thought Connolly's *Unquiet Grave* might be a good book to add to Count C's parcel: you must send six volumes including mine, as rice is really almost worth its weight in literature! John Betjeman is a lovely book too. He has just arrived—thank you so much. I can now deviate from business to thank you and your bronchitis for a nice letter just come—I love receiving gossipy letters here by my fire, with the sun-

[1] To G. de Gaury 20.2.46.

[2] To Jock Murray, 11.2.46, about an enlarged version of the first book which had been published in Iraq by *The Baghdad Times* in 1932.

set outside and no one to disturb; it makes a compound feeling of remoteness and company.

The snowdrops are out—*regiments* down these little steep valleys filled with nut trees and a stream trickling over pudding-stone waterfalls at the bottom. Hepaticas are coming; they call them cows' eyes here, which is silly as their beauty is their quite uncow-like blueness. There is a valley full of Christmas roses, Checchi and I went and dug a sackful of roots to plant in the garden. My two new magnolia trees have furry buds, and narcissus and tulip show their spears—oh blessed spring: it *has* been so cold!

Dear Freya [Lord Wavell wrote from Delhi],[1] I ought to have written long ago, and have meant to, but

> Indeed, indeed a letter oft before
> I swore to write. And then indeed I swore
> As the chuprassi softly entered in
> And brought me more green boxes, and then more.

Work really has been strenuous. I have just finished composing a speech for the jubilee of an Engineering Institution, and now I am told to write one to open a cattle show. I wish you were here to do it...

Now what news can I give you. We are well but a little weary and overworked. The routine seems heavier than ever and the political outlook gloomier, and the carpets redder and the boxes greener, and I have no time to read what I want to read or write what I want to write or meet those I want to meet.

We went up to Assam a week or two ago and did a few days in camp on the northern frontier, beyond the Brahmaputra; and the tribesmen came down from the hills—nice, wild, uncivilized, dirty, happy, mountainy men; and they paraded in front of me and brought little gifts of eggs and hens and sheep and goats, and even a young bison, and bows and arrows and primitive swords and hats and nice little wooden bowls, and two weird dance masks; and they did their national dances and showed us a curious national sport called Bo Bo, which consists of jumping up and down on a bamboo rope between two trees; and gave an exhibition of archery which was a bit dangerous, as they all wanted to shoot at once. You would have enjoyed it all thoroughly. Poor dears, I hope that no one brings them the blessings of civilization for a very long time.

In the hope of brightening this dull letter, I enclose a rather charming

---

[1] 23.12.45.

greeting from the Maharajah of Bhutan which may amuse you. You may also care to hear of a somewhat cryptic telegram I received from the Aga Khan, which read: 'Best thanks gracious permission given for dry fish to my followers'; and of the reply of a charming lady at an official party, when I asked whether she had any family: 'No, your Excellency, I've tried terribly hard, but I've only got dachshunds.'

ASOLO *5 April 1946*

My dear Chief,

I have been wondering what the summer thunder makes a peacock feel. Perhaps it gives him the sort of pleasure that I am finding after all these Eastern years in the thin cool spring rain of Europe; it is snow on the Dolomites behind us, but here it comes down on brown earth and makes the daffodil buds grow. They don't come rushing out in the voluptuous Indian way, but push until they are fat and nearly open, and then wait until they are sure of their weather. They have been doing that for over a fortnight now and I go and look at them every day, trying to tell them that it is quite safe really.

I ought to be touring about but have had the flu and doctor's orders rather conveniently coincided with my feelings, so I have had two weeks of a luxury denied to the poor Viceroy—waking every morning with a day in my lap that I can do with whatever I like. Part of it goes browsing in English history and noticing what a lot of our best kings were foreigners: Cnut, William the Conqueror, Henry II who established our law, which is I suppose the most English thing about us; then the Stuarts, and William III, and our present ones; it is rather remarkable, don't you think? If we annex the U.S.A. and let them rule and think they have annexed us, I feel sure we shall absorb and anglicize them also. The methods never seem to vary either. I have a *Life* of Drake here, in which one finds Queen Elizabeth appeasing Spain for years on end, far worse than Mr. Chamberlain, ruining plan after plan of her poor fuming captains, refusing to let the Armada be nipped in its own waters, waiting till Philip's treachery forced her into a *defensive* war. And the Treasury behaviour was the same also, so that Drake had to organize a private syndicate to procure a proper navy, like Lady Houston with the Spitfire. Do you remember telling me how we evacuated Greece with *twelve* aeroplanes?

Our election was over and there was general relief at being able to rest from pink, white and yellow placards on the walls. 'The monarchists are sad, but I don't know many of them and am not sorry for them. Not one of the house of Savoy fought with the partisans. How to get a tolerably honest president every five years will be the next problem. Do write and tell me about the Victory Day. How lucky to have got it in like a picnic in April before the next storm!'[1]

Asolo had voted for the monarchy, with only a few flags for the republic. They still showed the cross of Savoy, merely because a white centre was so difficult to come by. A woman in Venice who always had to have things explained, asked: "But is the new flag to be *all* white?" "No," said her husband. "We have it so occasionally, but not all the time."

And now the news came from Palestine that Malcolm MacDonald's White Paper was finally defeated—the disappearance as it seemed and still seems to me of our last hope of a settlement there. 'I believe,' I wrote,[2] 'that it seals the fate of the Zionists in the long run. Their only real chance was in conciliation, now they will certainly not disarm, the Arab League will thrive by being kept united with something to fight for, and the Zionists have been given just the necessary rope to make them arrogant enough for their own destruction. But it does make one *ashamed*. The White Paper was the result of twenty years' experience; it is annulled by a commission *chosen because it knew nothing about the question*; what outcome can one expect? It's a poor world where we are impartial through ignorance, prudent through impotence, and equal through mediocrity.' 'How depressed you must be,' I wrote to Jock Jardine.[3] 'The example of Pontius Pilate has been fatally followed by almost every Government ever since!'

Syria was celebrating after the French rule ended: bevies of young beauties driven in cars. 'At a given moment, after speeches, they opened the bosoms of their gowns to let out the soul of liberated Syria disguised as pigeons; the young men shouted "*continuez, continuez,*"' while the dazed allegory settled on the helmets of the gendarmes.'[4]

[1] To Jeffery Amherst, May 1946.
[2] To G. de Gaury 14.5.46.
[3] 11.6.46.
[4] Letter from Stewart Perowne.

ITALY 1945

Old friends now began to drop in. I saw Stewart off and the Simplon Express seemed full of nostalgia for summer holidays long past, when one packed the luggage-racks with haversacks and ice-axe, and woke in the early morning at Vallorbe with a taste of snow in the air and long Alpine days ahead, and no one had anything but a summer holiday to think of. The railway age in Europe had a lot to be said for it! Now it was a sad but gallant little express reduced to one wagon—its coach pinched from central Europe, and a string of day coaches with a coat of paint over bullet-marks and scratchings, and windows still boarded up here and there. An oriental atmosphere of sellers of food and drink had sprung up around it, as every journey meant long hours in sidings; and the wagon-lit attendants were pallid as if emerging from cocoons. The opulent, respectable, invulnerable look had gone from the people who travelled: they were mostly officers' wives, still harassed and shabby, or officers' non-wives not very certain of how the pre-war age and Great European Railway system worked. It was good to see it coming to life again.

New friends as well as old now came to Venice; the Duff Coopers, and most beloved Bernard Berenson with Nicky from Settignano, whose home I now visited twice yearly till his death. His knowledge, so vast in many fields, lapped over with particular happiness into the old Hellenistic fringes of Arabia. Many students of other times and spaces must also have felt his zest, probing and illuminating, and thought of it as peculiar to their own favourite realms. Whatever he said had meaning, and was often unexpected: "I would have been a Saint," he once told me, pulling himself out of a contemplation of the olive-hidden slopes, "a Saint, if I could have loved men as much as I love trees."

23 April 1946

Dearest Freya,

Your note reached me a few busy days before I had to take to my bed. *A quelque chose malheur est bon.* I had the leisure to read your *East is West* and enjoyed it hugely, particularly the earlier part about Imam Iahya, a King David old and full of *mana*. I cannot help sympathizing with your enthusiasm over the Arabophones who take so keenly to the lure of Western knowledge. But the end is clear. It is Levantism. Ever since I can remember I have been fascinated by Arabia, the genuine Arabs and their ways. I have read a great deal about them and about, never a book that pleased me more than your *Southern Gates of Arabia* . . . the vignettes, the pictures, the moods you conjure up so that I forgot I was reading. I was actually living your pages . . . Do not fail to come for a night or more whenever you are near. You will always be welcome. And of course later on at Vallombrosa.

25 April 1946

Thank you for your dear words. You cannot love me more than I love you. And I expect to love you more and more and more.

These letters were dear to me. In Venice Archie Colquhoun and his 13th Corps Liaison left with words that pleased me, because they expressed my own feelings on Asolo, whose influence 'begins to work after a day or so, and one suddenly looks out of window and sees Life waving at one through the branches of the trees, and Happiness glimmering away on the slopes below. Visits to Asolo and your reorganized life, getting its values in order again, a ray of sanity often, when sanity in one's own life has seemed very far away.'

I wished to write. Nothing in particular, but to exercise my mind with words. 'One should not feel, but cannot help feeling, that it might be worth more than all else one does. How many books unwritten lie in dark ages when men were too hard pressed to let their thoughts have play.'

Jock wrote from London,[1] 'The prospect of autobiography is exciting like a morning mist when one knows that a fine summer day is coming. I will set about sorting all pre-eastern journey material of yours here.'

By 1946 much hardness had gone out of summer travelling, though John Miller and I, crawling in my unreliable car up the Spezia headland, still looked for men in masks on the long slope of Bracco. About half a division of deserters of one sort or another had retreated to the Pisan coast, and there in our ignorance we nearly went to lodge and probably come to our end among them; chance took us on, to have the car stolen at San Gimignano by a U.S.A.

[1] 11.10.45.

deserter, who lured it from the public square, during our absence, with its driver inside it: it was the tenth Embassy car to be lost by theft.

'Transport,' I wrote, 'is getting very low: I begin to wonder if it is worth the expense of spirit to go on tour breaking down so often: fourteen punctures on the *Autostrada*! Chauffeurs are becoming like the coachmen of my childhood who would never let one do what one liked with the horses: I had to get up at four a.m. to come from Milan so that the tyres should not get hot.'

Difficulties of this sort were very slow in disappearing and delays in posts, absence of petrol, and the sudden Treasury economics continued. My reading centres, all happily self-supporting, were threatened with the cutting off of the newspapers that fed them. 'Having got over the expense of putting in an irrigation system, H.M.G. now hesitates over supplying the water.' John Miller and I counted up the newspaper expense and made it £1,200 a year; if H.M.G. was too poor, we said, we would collect the money privately ourselves. Michael Stewart stood firm in Rome. I refused to have my salary cut (a nasty trick they like to play on women) but offered to tour while necessary with only travelling expenses paid; and between us all we carried the centres on till the British Council took them over.

31 July 1946

My office sent me away without telling me that one can draw no petrol in Piedmont outside Turin: so we had to slide down the Alps with the engine off, and then make terrific efforts at blandishment with the nearest petrol pump; and today the brakes of the car have collapsed in pools of oil. How I hate mechanics! Half the papers, too, have never reached my centres that now droop and despond; I feel as if I were the mother of orphans, if such a thing were possible. Then just as I had everything ready a cable reached Turin asking me to delay my journey as the sanction for expenses had not arrived. I am not giving any heed to this, as I would far rather pay it myself than let everyone down all the way to Tuscany—but isn't it enough to make anyone tired of doing things for the Government? How right the Italians are in this! On my way, I deviated a little from Torre Pellice in the Valdensian hills, to drop John Miller at the Briançon border where he is doing a walking tour. We asked if one could get across a pass, and the hotel immediately told us how to slip by at night and find one's papers put in order on the other side, all friendly organized sympathy for breakers of the law. We went by the regular route, however, and lunched at Clavières, a disconsolate frontier village —every house pitted like smallpox with bombardment, and a half-demolished hotel from which the proprietor produced butter, ham, macaroni, cutlets cooked in Marsala, and finally an offering of liqueur from himself. This is while the whole of the Italian Press is slanging us over Trieste. The little town at the bottom of the pass was decorated rather pathetically with *Viva Italia* on wide white ribbons across the road.

I am now in an old seigneurial house filled with bric-à-brac, beautiful inlaid furniture and strange Victorian freaks, and two women whose voices go on like simultaneous waterfalls. When I retired at night and listened to a pleasant gurgling stream at the bottom of the garden, I thought how wonderful it is that water doesn't *talk* when it makes a noise!'[1]

That summer, with health again rather low, I took a month among the Dolomites of Val Badia to rest from Information, in a valley 'which old newspapers reach now and then, and in the four days I have been here three cars have passed our door, winding down from the Sella Pass. The people in Rome and Paris are discussing whether this is to be Austrian or Italian, but here the cows are being milked as usual, and one inn is called Gasthof and the other Albergo'.[2]

By that time, Nüremberg was over. 'What can go on in those minds,' I wrote, 'during these last days? Do you remember Montrose, sleeping his peaceful sleep before his execution? Raleigh's letter to his wife? How little people think about how they are to meet that time, which is so sure to come!'

The G.H.Q. from Naples and the troops from Trieste were meeting in one chaos between Venice and Padua and our landscape was again filling with soldiers. 'How many brigadiers' love of Renaissance colonnades will survive the unheated Palladian villas' I wondered. Yet Italy had decided—as she always knows in her heart—that war with Tito, or anyone else, was too expensive. The tumult and the shouting was dying, and in her old untidy way, her surface confusion and underlying order, her medley of vulgarity and beauty, she, too, was stepping into the new and not alluring world.

[1] To G. de Gaury.   [2] To Lord Wavell, 22.6.46.

Epilogue

After the six years' tempest, the destinies of ordinary mortals settled into such uneasy patterns as still confront us, and it has not been possible to find any definite boundary of Peace for the ending of this book. But by Christmas 1946 Western Europe was operating in a rhythm of comparative freedom, trains were threading the continent, and a visit that winter to Paris and London suggests that travel for pleasure was reborn.

A year or more had gone by since the Brothers of Freedom were closed in Iraq. 'We have asked and asked for replacements of staff, without success,' wrote Peggy from Baghdad—and kept the women's side pluckily going for some time longer. In Egypt the end came with more violence.

Ronnie Fay, left by then in sole charge, wrote in May 1947 that 'a bomb exploded outside our Alexandria office... Papers launched the most violent attacks and two of them started publishing "rolls of honour" with the names of a few committee holders who had been "patriotic" enough to leave us. Actually a few were those of people who had been terrorized into doing so but most of them were faked or forged. After six weeks we have only lost about two hundred and fifty committees out of five thousand, and opened one hundred and forty new ones; central meetings have been well attended, and a few people have resigned their jobs rather than leave the organization. The F.O. realize that the Brothers have put up a most incredibly good show while the Anglo-Egyptian Union crumbled to pieces in a moment, as no one had the courage to stand up to a few extremists. Everyone is trying to push the others faster and faster down a road along which none of them want to travel, but in view of the state of feeling, unemployment and Communist intrigues, the result may well be tragedy.'

EPILOGUE

Aware of the dangers and intrigues that surrounded it, the Brotherhood soon recovered the ground it had lost, and indeed grew bigger and stronger than ever, until it finally had more than six thousand committees scattered through every town and in almost every village of the cultivated areas of Egypt. Later, Ronnie Fay described the end:

In the autumn of 1951 the Wafd repudiated the Anglo-Egyptian treaty, and in January 1952 fighting broke out in Ismailia. As a result, on January 14, 1952 the Council of Ministers issued a decree to the police that the Ikhwan el-Hurriya (Brotherhood of Freedom) was to be suppressed, and that they were to take the necessary steps. The Embassy advised me to take refuge in the Canal Zone, but I objected as I thought it might lead to persecution of our members. It was then decided that, to prove that we were complying with the decree, I should leave the country and on the 18th I was escorted by Egyptian police to Alexandria and left Egypt. Eddie Gathorne-Hardy was given diplomatic status and charged with winding up the organization and paying compensation to all the staff. As a result, as far as I know, none of our members were penalized for having belonged to the organization whose closing was solely due to a political situation which could not have been foreseen when the work was started.[1]

By the end of 1952 the totalitarians were back in power and our efforts, nearly everywhere successful in the Middle East in war, had already crumbled with the peace.

I have long pondered over the cause of our failure, and I think that, as far as the Arab world is concerned—and perhaps on a wider orbit also—two reasons were implicit from the start. The first was a lack of clearness and faith in our own values—a fatal flaw, for it meant that the world as we saw it, and offered it to our friends, was an uncertain world in which our integrity felt ill at ease. We were trying to offer a civilization *which we did not believe in*: the Middle East was very quick to feel this weakness.

We did this I think from a genuine desire for unification with the U.S.A. and a rather woolly rejection of bad and good together in our past. I argued this last point at the time with a friend and the

---

[1] Letter from Ronnie Fay.

EPILOGUE

two sides of the question, the honesty of the English doubts and—as I still think—their muddle, are best shown by this correspondence.

ASOLO *10 November 1945*

Dear Lionel (Fielden),[1]

Glad to hear that *East is West* is liked. I wonder if it will do any good? Do you really think it gave too kind a picture of the British Raj? I was thinking about them the other day apropos of General Scobie, who is a thoroughly nice average Englishman, and the Greeks adore him, they think him a sort of god. I puzzled over this till I began to think what the average qualities were that made us take him so for granted: honesty, modesty, truthfulness, courage, integrity, none of which is particularly average in any other Raj we know, and perhaps the Mediterranean, which has lots of other qualities but not so much those in combination, is more correct in assessing them than we are in taking them for granted. Anyway I agree with what you say about the vital necessity of being supernational now: but I think one can do that while caring in a reasonable way for one's own plot of earth. I notice that in the East your intellectual anti-Englander is mistrusted just like your atheist. Why should the love of God make one care less for men, or of our own earth make us care less for that of others? The Jingo people are generally those who care the least about their own country and the people like Henry Lawrence, Nicholson, Gordon, and a dozen I could name living now, passionately English, are the ones who are loved abroad. I suppose that one can only learn to love by loving and to begin by hating in one's own home is a downhill way? Anyhow we are now happily situated as a secondary power, and can watch the great American and Russian empires improving on our ways. I think it will be good for us, and good, too, to be poor.

LONDON *24 November 1945*

Dear Freya,

I was delighted to get your letter which gave me (a) great pleasure, (b) a feeling of guilt and (c) argumentative prickles of the first order. I think that the British Raj as rajahs go is the best, undoubtedly, but I don't like the Raj principle—any more than I like intolerant fathers, headmasters or statesmen. *You* are a kind of arch-fiend of propaganda because you do (or appear to) really act on perfectly equal and equable terms with the desert and its people and if any Raj could be as amusing and intelligent

---

[1] Then Director of Public Relations, Allied Control Commission in Italy.

and friendly as you—well, it should take charge of the world. But I kick violently when you say that Englishmen are 'loved' abroad, and I don't believe it. General Scobie for example is obviously adored by one party in Greece but surely execrated by another. And can you generalize so widely? 'The Greeks adore him'—but how many Greeks, really, has he met? Watching Indians I came to the conclusion that they very very seldom 'adored' Englishmen. They have, of course, a great deal of natural warmth and expansiveness and a real sense of gratitude and—more rarely—loyalty. But take away from an Englishman his money and position and power and how many really 'adore'? I can't help feeling that your qualities (with which you endow him) are not only rare but also a little—what shall I say—tiresome. Tiresome if only because they *are* proclaimed and there *is* an arrogance about the British . . . and it seems to me that on that altar of truth and honesty (so frequently belied by our business men and commercial travellers) is apt to be sacrificed grace of living, gaiety, the arts, humour, tolerance, and even intuition, which I rank high, in spite of Hitler! Of course I do agree that in certain circumstances the Englishman is loved abroad for the qualities you give him, because they are complementary to the qualities of the nation concerned and thus rather endearing (but NOT to be copied!). I think the Anglo-Italian tie is strong because the Englishman thinks 'what picturesque scoundrels these people are' and the Italian says '*questo Phlegm è meraviglioso*' but an Italy *ruled* by England, or the reverse, would be hideous. I am quite certain that all your books do good and I think you've done one of the finest bits of work of our generation—you make everyone, including yourself, lovable! It can't but do good. But I personally feel your spectacles are very rose.

ASOLO *4 March 1946*

Dear Lionel,

I really think that we are only looking at the same landscape from different sides. Admitting that the English virtues only fill half the bill, that our want of gaiety, of a sense of beauty, of *sensitiveness*, is depressing (don't I admit it!) it seems to me that you wrote as one who, having been too much among the British virtues, longs for sunlight—and I as one who, having lived mostly among the other, appreciates solidity. It is the question of the glass half empty or half full. But anyway it seems to me a wrong system to minimize one set of virtues because they don't happen to include another set—and this is what the broad-minded Englishman is always doing. If you flung his own qualities overboard, you would still

EPILOGUE

not furnish the Englishman with Latin graces. The Latin virtues may be superior. I should find that a very difficult point to decide; but in my book I was talking about the other set of qualities and how should I improve a description of burgundy by complaining that it isn't like champagne? You are tired of hearing about the English virtues; any Italian is tired of references to his artistic qualities: but that is merely an argument for mixing and not for throwing our own make-up overboard. I agree that the old-fashioned Jingo who was out to impose his code was a menace; but that is a relic of the past, and I do think that we are ahead of most of the world now in having left the 'possessive' stage, in love, in education, in religion, in administration, behind us. It is only in so far as we wish to serve more than we want to rule that I think we *are* a ruling race—if you see what I mean. Most of the good people I met in the East —not the Blimps—do really want to serve; and if we once realize this as the objective, I think we shall go on ruling by mere force of events. If we don't understand this, then the first nation that does realize it will rule, but so far no one seems to be better at it than we are?

As far as the Arab world was involved, the rejection of our tradition, which was apt to be wholesale when it should have been partial only, was made utterly disastrous by our handling of Israel. It was for this reason and not for any want of admiration for the Jewish achievement that nearly every serious observer in the Middle East looked upon Zionism as our greatest danger. When once the war and its chivalry were over, the trust which individual Englishmen had engendered could not survive, and their personal influence —which should have tided us across our transitions—was unable to stand against what the whole Arab world felt to be an injustice. Here again I shall quote a letter of that time.

ASOLO *9 November 1945*

My dear Harold (Nicolson),

I am not going to quarrel with your feelings for the Effendi: he is raw material, and you are civilized in the rarer and more Latin way, and the Latin seems generally to dislike the Middle Easterner: I think it is partly our British obtuseness, our want of sensibility, which helps us in the modern Arab world. At the same time the fine Arab tradition *is* a fine one, and the genuine product is a complete and satisfactory human being, and the Effendi for all his chaotic stage at present does derive from this background, and will with any luck find a proper balance in some future day. 'Even a caterpillar is beautiful in the eyes of its mother'—not only, for he may become a butterfly: but I am not remonstrating with you for not liking him in his present form.

What I do protest against is the making up of one's mind on the Palestine policy dependent on one's sentiment for or against Arab or Jew. Nor would I make it dependent on policy merely or 'appeasement'. The fundamental problem is a simple one: we took on a mandate which bound us to care for the welfare of an Arab people and we have no right to use it so as to abrogate their chance of sovereignty in their own land. I cannot see any escape from this position and I think the confusion in the mind of many people, and perhaps in yours, comes from the fact that the individuality of Palestine is not realized; it is thought of as a bit of homogeneous Arabian lump, so that people do not look on the taking of it from the Arabs as they would think of New Zealand being taken from the New Zealanders. The two are really quite similar: they both belong to a larger unit, an Arab or a British world, with which they have ties of race, language, etc., but they both have a separate identity and to deny it will offend the very deepest feelings of mankind. For their own Mandatory to do this by *coercion* is not only going to cause trouble, it would be one of those crimes which nearly always have brought a terrible punishment and centuries of revenge.

I don't believe any Arab thinks our decision in their regard will be influenced by fear. They still believe that we are for justice and are convinced of the justice of this position of theirs; and if we admitted their *right* to control the immigration into their country, we could probably *persuade* them to use it in a tolerant way. (I did in fact suggest to Nuri last year that it would be a good plan for the Palestine Arabs spontaneously to offer to take in a number—say one hundred thousand—Jews: this would have put the Zionists in the dilemma of either refusing, or of accepting the principle that the Arabs hold the door—but of course nothing came of my great idea!)

As a nation we are often inclined not to follow a course we think right because we are afraid we might be following it for other reasons—profit and righteousness have so often gone hand in hand that we are shy of the combination. I believe they do eventually go hand in hand but of course it is important to have the proper one leading.

The whole problem seems to be on a wider scale than one of expediency. In a world of Asiatic peoples rapidly becoming self-conscious, I believe Britain has found in her system of 'guidance by advice' the *only* way of retaining influence. If she goes back on this system she is putting herself not only on a losing side but on a side she herself does not believe in.

These two causes, our own want of conviction and our own injustice, were at the root, I think, of our failure. They were not operative during the war, when our beliefs were simpler and firm, and a way out of the Palestine mess still existed; but in the fifteen short following years, from a pinnacle of honour and respect which had never in our history in the Middle East been surpassed, we took one of those downward ways that are said to be paved with good intentions.

In my own story during those years a pattern now seems visible. From the first real sight of the problem and its dangers in the Yemen in 1940, through a gradual search and elaboration in regions far separate—Egypt, Iraq, America, India and Italy—I studied what was involved in the art of Persuasion. The two flaws that have lost us the Middle East were infringements of its basic rules—one's own integrity in the first place—in this case a scale of values from which we swerved—and in the second place the neglect of *disinterested* service towards those with whom we speak—which, in the eyes of the Arabs, our policy with Israel destroyed. We therefore had no chance as soon as the war was over.

What are we to do, we may ask, when those two, or even one of these basic foundations are missing, and for the good of our country we are asked to spread a gospel either unhelpful to the people for whom it is destined or unconvincing to ourselves? We should in this case, I think, refuse; such a baseless building is anyway, in the long run, sure to fall.

Yet I am not a pessimist to think of this defeat as final. Re-established as a trading nation we have, I hope, reverted to strength. No longer clogged with too much power, we might perhaps develop the best of civilizations yet known and, reverting to a perennial policy which is, in effect, a neutrality that favours the weaker, we could still lead the smaller and peace-loving nations of the world. Since 1943 I have thought that this should be our role, and I watch it slowly emerging.

The evils of over-centralization too must soon be realized and most probably be cured, and men of ability lured back into services now more and more deserted. (The speed of communication always offered as an argument *for* can equally be used *against* centralization, since it allows the periphery to act with knowledge.)

These are external matters though they are vital enough; whereas the use of words, with which I am chiefly concerned and with which this book chiefly deals, is at the heart of thought and therefore of action. Attention to it is not to be deferred for times of crisis, since its neglect hatches the crisis in itself. In an age prosperous as this promises to be if violence can be avoided, the importance of words, their management and their reality, becomes supreme. If they are mishandled or abused, even for the simplest purposes, they produce corruption and decay, for it must never be forgotten that they are the vesture of something greater than themselves—doorkeepers to a sanctuary as the evangelist saw them, and as indeed they are.

We have failed in part. And yet we have no wish to recapture the material trappings of a past that has moved on: but during that past, in our need, the spirit of our words did not fail; we held its sharpness by the handle; and nothing but the integrity of what we say and the belief in our saying can give us that handle again in whatever its future form may be.

Table of Main Chronological Events 1938-1945

1938

March. Hitler occupies Austria
Sept. Chamberlain goes to Munich for conversations with Hitler on Czechoslovakia. Agreement signed 29th
Oct. 1 German troops occupy Sudetenland

1939

March 15 German troops cross Czech frontier
April 1 Spanish War ends
April 4 King Ghazi of Iraq killed in motor accident; succeeded by three-year-old Feisal
April 7 Italy occupies Albania
August 23 Soviet-German Non-aggression Pact signed at Moscow
Sept. 1 Poland invaded
Sept. 3 Britain and France declare war on Germany
Sept. 11 Iraq breaks off relations with Germany
Sept. 27 Warsaw surrenders
Nov. 30 Finland invaded

1940

March 12 Russo-Finnish peace Pact signed in Moscow
April 9 German invasion of Denmark and Norway
May 10 Germany invades Holland, Belgium and Luxembourg
May 10 Resignation of Mr Chamberlain. Coalition formed with Mr Churchill as Prime Minister
May 15 Dutch Army capitulates
May 27/28 Belgian Army capitulates
May 28 Dunkirk evacuation
June 10 Italy declares war on Britain and France
June 17 Petain announces that France has asked for armistice
July 3 British attack French ships at Oran
July 10 Battle of Britain begins
Sept. 7 Start of London blitz
Sept. 13 Italians occupy Sollum
Oct. 28 Italians cross Greek frontier
Dec. 9 First Western Desert offensive opens

1941

Jan. 22 Australians enter Tobruk
Feb. 6 British enter Benghazi
March 11 Lease-Lend Bill approved by House of Representatives
March 30 Enemy counter-offensive in North Africa

TABLE OF MAIN CHRONOLOGICAL EVENTS 1938-1945

April 22 Evacuation from Greece begins
May 2 Iraqi forces attack Habbaniya
May 30 Iraqi revolt collapses
June 1 British forces withdraw from Crete
June 8 Imperial and Free French forces enter Syria
June 22 Germany invades U.S.S.R.
July 12 Anglo-Soviet Agreement signed in Moscow
July 12 Syrian armistice terms initialled at Acre
August 14 The Atlantic Charter
August 25 British and Russian troops enter Iran
Sept. 16 Shah of Iran abdicates
Oct. 9 New Iraqi Cabinet under General Nuri as-Said
Dec. 7 Japan attacks Pearl Harbour
Dec. 7 Japanese High Command declares war on Britain and the U.S.A.
Dec. 11 Italy and Germany declare war on U.S.A.
Dec. 22 First Washington Conference

1942

Jan. 21 Second German counter-offensive in North Africa
Feb. 15 Singapore falls
May 4 Battle of the Coral Sea
May 26 Third German counter-offensive in Western Desert
June 4 Battle of Midway Island
June 21 Tobruk falls
July 1 Germans reach El Alamein
Aug. 12 First Moscow Conference

Oct. 23/24 Battle of Alamein opens
Nov. 7/8 Allied landing in North Africa
Nov. 22 Stalingrad counter-offensive

1943

Jan. 18 Siege of Leningrad raised
Jan. 23 Eighth Army enters Tripoli
Feb. 2 Germans capitulate at Stalingrad
May 12 Organized resistance in Tunisia ends
July 9/10 Allied landing in Sicily
July 25 Mussolini resigns
August 17 First Quebec Conference
Sept. 3 Allied landing in Italy
Sept. 8 Italy surrenders
Sept. 9 Landing at Salerno
Sept. 10 German troops occupy Rome
Oct. 18 Second Moscow Conference
Nov. 22 First Conference at Cairo
Nov. 28 Teheran Conference
Dec. 4 Second Cairo Conference

1944

Jan. 22 Anzio Landings
June 5/6 D Day
June 13 First flying-bomb lands in England
August 15 Allied Forces land on south coast of France
August 23 Paris liberated
August 23 Rumania accepts Russian armistice terms
Sept. 10 Second Quebec Conference

TABLE OF MAIN CHRONOLOGICAL EVENTS 1938-1945

Oct. 9 Third Moscow Conference
Dec. 16 German Ardennes offensive

1945

Jan. 11 Warsaw entered by Russians
Feb. 4 Yalta Conference
March 7 U.S. first Army cross the Rhine
April 1 Okinawa invaded
April 12 Death of President Roosevelt
April 13 Vienna liberated
April 28 Death of Mussolini
April 30 Death of Hitler
May 2 Berlin surrenders to Russian armies
May 2 German armies in Italy surrender
May 7 Unconditional surrender of Germany
May 8 VE Day
July 17 Potsdam Conference
August 6 Atomic bomb on Hiroshima
August 8 Russia declares war on Japan
August 9 Atomic bomb dropped on Nagasaki
August 15 VJ Day

Index

Abd el Qadir Gailani, 78, 98
Abdullah, Emir of Transjordan, later King, 57
Abdullah, Emir, Regent of Iraq, 76-8, 107-10, 113-14, 120
Abu'l Huda, Lulie, 63, 69, 158
Abu Simbel, 55
Abyssinia, 7, 20-21
Aden, 2, 10-21, 23-5, 27, 29, 31, 34, 36-7, 39, 41-50, 52, 54, 63, 65-6, 68, 73, 97, 118, 195, 212, 216
    Crater, 14, 46
    Little Aden, 11
Aleppo, 7-8, 123
Alexander, Field-Marshal Earl, 249
Alexandretta, 8
Alexandria, 60-61, 69-70, 134, 276-7
Algiers, 161
Altounian, Dr. and Mrs. Ernest, 8
Alwiyah, 155, 121
Aly Khan (d. 1960), 60, 117, 136
    Joan Aly Khan, 136
America, 3, 61, 138, 141, 149, 151, 165-221, 192, 196, 199, 201, 209-21, 278, 282
Amherst, Earl (see also under author's letters), 59
Anatolia, 119

Ankara, 100
Anti-Semitism, 165
Antonius, George (d. 1941), author of *The Arab Awakening*, 77, 79-80, 129
Aosta, Duke of, 52
Aqqa Kuf, 110
Arabia and Arabs, 3, 11-14, 16, 18, 21, 23, 39, 41, 43, 49, 57-8, 62, 68-9, 113, 128, 130, 141, 146, 159-60, 165-6, 176-7, 181-6, 195-6, 198-9, 201-3, 207-20, 226, 246-7, 251, 271-3, 277, 280-2
    Saudi Arabia, 12-14, 157, 183, 186, 221
Arabian Isle, The (in England, *East is West*), 210
Asolo, 45-46, 172, 220, 227, 244, 254, 267, 270-1, 273, 278-80
Astor, Viscount (William), 117
Athens, 117, 156, 228, 260
Atlantic Charter, 179
Auchinleck, Field-Marshal Sir Claude, 58-9, 243
Austen, General Godwin, 50
Austin, Senator, 183
Azerbaijan, 119

B.B.C. (broadcasts), 25, 42-3, 92, 95, 98-9, 101, 105, 108, 110, 117, 255

INDEX

Bacon, Virginia, 183, 215
Baghdad, 61, 73–135, 138, 141–2, 148–9, 153, 156, 160–1, 210, 226, 276
Baghdad Sketches, 268
Bailey, William, 91, 112, 115
Basra, 76–8, 89, 96, 101, 105, 108, 110, 115–16, 124, 144, 146, 152, 203
Beach, John and Lucy, 72, 133, 152
Beirut, 135, 145
Bentinck, Count Arthur, 13, 16
Berenson, Bernard, 3, 272
Berlin, Sir Isaiah, 181–2, 221, 223
Berry, Mary, 158
Besse, Sir Anton and Lady, 14, 54
Birdwood, Lord (2nd Baron), 141–2
    Author of *Nuri as-Said*, 141–2
Bishop, Adrian (d. 1942), 3, 93, 95, 98–9, 101–2, 105, 118, 130, 138, 160, 172, 260
Bodley, Colonel, 218
Borland, Miss, 81
Boston, 220
Bracken, Viscount (Brendan) (d. 1958), 217
Brandeis, Dr., 184
Brandt, Dr., 210
British Council, 118, 137–8, 213, 274
British Institute, 118, 130, 149–50, 159
Brockington, Leonard, 208
Brotherhood of Freedom, 67–71, 75, 84, 117–21, 125, 128–35, 139–41, 145–6, 149–51, 158–60, 210–11, 276–7
Bullard, Sir Reader, 85, 149
Burma, 129

Burrows, Sir Bernard and Lady, 250

Caccia, Sir Harold, 161, 253–4
    letter to author, 253–4
Cairo, 20, 22, 50, 52–4, 56–73, 79, 84, 89, 109, 116–18, 127, 129, 133–4, 139–40, 145, 151, 158–9, 161, 179, 194, 226, 230, 250
Calgary, 205
California, 194–202
Canada, 3, 165, 202–9
Cantor, Eddie, 219
Carmel, 121–2
Casey, Lord and Lady, 130, 243
Catroux, General Georges, 117
Cattaro Harbour, 86
Cawthorn, Major-General Sir Walter, 116
Cecil Lord David, viii
Champion, the Rev. Sir Reginald, 34, 37–9
Channon, Sir Henry (d. 1959), 171, 218, 222–3
Chapman, John, 157
Chicago, 180, 187–92, 195-6, 199, 210, 230
    Oriental Institute in, 189, 210
Cholmondeley, Marchioness of, viii
Churchill, Randolph, 179
Churchill, Sir Winston, 86, 119, 123, 176, 181, 184, 186, 191, 195, 200, 205, 212, 218, 222
Clayton, Brigadier, Sir Iltyd (d. 1955), 3, 68, 158–60, 171
Cleland, Dr., 185
Clive, Nigel, 125–6, 131, 133–4, 160, 174, 182, 225, 260

[288]

INDEX

Coats, Peter, 172–3, 232, 258, 261
Cockerell, Sir Sydney, 138
Colonial Office, 19, 21, 34, 184, 191, 193–4, 203, 211, 227
Colquhoun, Archie, 273
Connecticut, 221
Cornwallis, Sir Kinahan and Lady, 3, 19, 62, 75–78, 80–81, 83, 90, 93, 99, 102–3, 105, 107–8, 110–15, 118, 124, 141, 160, 210
Council of Churches, 201, 217, 219
Creston, B.C. (ranch), 204–5
Crete, 88, 106, 108, 110, 112, 117, 136, 198
Crosthwaite, Sir Moore, 244
Cunard, Lady (Emerald) (d. 1948), 223
Cunard, Victor (d. 1960), 228, 254
Cyprus, 52, 134, 136–8, 233

Davies, Reginald, 53, 63, 69, 137, 227
De Gaulle, General, later President of French Republic, 58, 246
Delhi, 105, 149, 196, 225, 230–1, 233, 235, 238, 240, 243, 269
Dhala, 15
Djibouti, 14, 49
Domvile, Group-Captain Patrick, 89, 92, 98, 105, 109, 113, 142
Drower, Lady (Stefana), 80, 125
Drower, Peggie (Mrs. Hackforth-Jones), 125, 138, 276
Duff Cooper, Alfred (d. 1954), and Lady Diana, later Viscount and Viscountess Norwich, 272
Dunn, James, 211

East is West (in America, *The Arabian Isle*), 2, 64, 76, 166, 210, 226, 272, 278
Eden, Anthony, later the Earl of Avon, 58, 107, 183, 228
Edmonds, C. J., 93, 97
Egypt, 3, 12, 21, 28, 41, 52, 56, 63, 70, 72–3, 103, 119, 127–8, 132, 139–40, 143, 150–1, 192, 195, 276–7, 282
  Anglo-Egyptian Treaty, 145, 277
Eisenhower, General, later President of the U.S.A., 161
Elmhurst, Air Marshal Sir Thomas, 125
England, 2, 7, 10–11, 13, 16, 29, 42, 54, 77, 80, 132, 144, 161, 166, 172, 196, 198, 202, 207, 210, 218–19, 221–9, 253, 260, 262, 264, 268
Eritrea, 21
Ettinghausen, Dr., 192
Euphrates, 123, 150–2
Euston, Earl of, 257–9
Evans, Edith, 243

Fakhri, Nashashibi, 124
Fallujah, 89–90, 98, 106–7, 109, 116
Famagusta, 136–8
Farouk crisis, 129
Fascists, 2, 7, 19–40, 45, 52–4, 63, 254, 256–7, 263, 265
Fay, Ronald, 69–71, 117, 151, 158, 276–7
Feisal, King of Iraq, 57, 111, 115
Feversham, Earl of, 137–8
Fielden, Lionel, 278–80
Fleming, Peter, 243

[289]

INDEX

Foreign Office, 7, 19, 210–11, 267, 276
Fox, Rabbi, 190–1

Gandhi, Mahatma (d. 1948), 192, 225, 236, 248–9
Gathorne-Hardy, Hon. Ralph Edward, 158, 277
de Gaury, Lieut.-Col. Gerald (see also under author's letters), 86, 107, 112–15, 237
Germany and Germans, 2, 7, 10, 16, 18–20, 22, 28–30, 32, 44, 60–2, 76, 79, 87–8, 97, 99, 102, 104, 106–7, 119, 133, 192, 198, 225, 253–4, 265
Glubb, Lieut.-General Sir John, 114, 227
Golconda, 237
Grafftey-Smith, Sir Laurence, 63
Graham, Barbara, 125
Graziani, Marshal, 52
Greece, 7, 10, 58, 160, 225, 262
Grenfell, Joyce, 243
Grobba, Dr. (German Ambassador), 76, 101–2, 104, 113
Gunther, John, 218

Habbaniya, 76–7, 88–91, 93, 95–6, 101, 107–8, 112, 116, 128, 178
Hadhramaut, 19, 21, 24, 49, 157, 194, 212
Halabja, 154–5
Halford, Aubrey, and Mrs., 251
Halifax, 166, 168
Halifax, 1st Earl of (d. 1959), and Countess of, 185, 196, 205, 215–16

Hama, 7
Hamadan, 85
Hamilton, John A. de Courcy, 53
Harding, Charles, 235
Harrison, Austen, 243
Hawtrey, Air Vice-Marshal J. G. (d. 1954), 120, 128, 146–9
Hitler, Adolf, 43, 74, 76, 83, 129, 223–4, 257, 279
Hitti, Professor, 217
Hodeidah, 20–1, 33, 39–40
Holman, Sir Adrian, 105, 114, 150
Holt, Sir Vyvyan (d. 1960), 83, 89–90, 93–4, 96–101, 103–4, 106–7, 109, 112, 115–16, 124, 126
Hong Kong, 177
Horder, Lord, viii
Hore-Ruthven, The Hon. Mrs. (Pamela) (see also under author's letters), 57, 63, 69–70, 117, 121, 124, 126, 139, 161–2, 173–4
death of husband, 139, 161–2
Hoskins, Colonel, 182–3, 187, 221
Hull, Cordell, 211
Hyderabad, 234, 237

Ibn Saud, King (d. 1953), 183, 214, 246
Riyadh, 246
India, 56, 58, 124, 146, 175–7, 192, 195, 197, 199, 229–51, 258, 283
Information, Ministry of 10, 15, 138, 169, 175, 181, 228
Ingrams, Harold, 13, 46, 52, 54
Ingrams, Doreen, 13

[290]

INDEX

Iraq, vii, 3, 12, 70, 73, 75–9, 81–82, 88–9, 91, 93, 97, 100–4, 108, 111, 118–19, 125, 129, 131–2, 139–41, 143, 145, 150–1, 153, 158–9, 177, 195, 198, 205, 212–13, 258, 282
Ireland, Mr. (orientalist), 184, 187, 213, 216
Isfahan, 86, 147–9
Ismail, Sir Mirza, 242
Israel, 140, 280, 282
Istanbul, 10, 156
Italy and Italians, 2–3, 7, 10, 19, 21–5, 34, 37, 41, 43, 45, 52–3, 59, 72, 111, 160, 191, 195–6, 228, 239, 244, 252–75, 279, 282

Jaipur, 241–3
Jamil Madfa'i, 116
Japan, 119, 197
Jardine, John, 138, 271
Jerusalem, 73, 116–17, 129, 135, 215
Jews (see also *Zionism*), 16, 31, 62, 108, 114, 133, 159, 165, 176, 179–80, 182–4, 192, 197, 202–3, 206–8, 210, 217, 280–1
Jinnah, 247–8, 250
Jodhpur, 242

Kadhimain, 110, 114, 116, 126
Kahn, Mrs. Otto, 173, 175
Karachi, 147, 250
Kassem, 141, 143
Ker, Edwin, 144
Kermanshah, 84, 86–7, 157
Kahn Nuqta, 107, 110
Khanikin, 87–8, 91, 112
Khunum, Adela, 154–5

Kirkuk, 108, 145, 153, 156–7
Kurdistan, 144, 152–7

Lake, Col. Henry (d. 1940), 13, 15–16, 21, 23, 25, 33, 38, 43
Lampson, Sir Miles and Lady, later Lord and Lady Killearn, 57, 70, 72, 230
Lancaster, Osbert, 228
Latakia, 123
Lebanon, 9, 15, 135, 161, 171, 175, 244
Libya, 21, 52, 61, 80, 123, 133
Lippmann, Walter, 186, 215
Lloyd, Seton, 92–4, 109, 113, 118
London, 7, 10, 41, 43, 52, 58, 69, 144, 182, 187, 199, 221–4, 228, 243, 266, 273, 276
Longmore, Air Chief Marshal Sir Arthur, 58, 63
Longworth, Alice, 211
Los Angeles, 194–9, 202
Lothian, Sir Arthur, 237
Luce, Clare, 175–7, 179, 218–19
Luce, Henry, 218–19
Luling-Volpi, Contessa Marina, 72–3, 252–3, 264
Luxor, 55, 70
Lyttelton, Sir Oliver, later Viscount Chandos, 58

MacCallum, Miss, 208
McCall, Miss, 181
McCormick, Anne, 218
MacDonald, Rt. Hon. Malcolm, 165, 207–8, 210, 271
White Paper, 165–6, 176, 181, 183, 186, 191, 195, 200, 207–8, 271
MacMichael, Sir Harold and Lady, 74, 227, 243

[291]

INDEX

Macmillan, M.P., Rt. Hon. Harold, 161
Macrae, John, 105
Madras, 235
Main, Ernest, 92, 113–15
Makins, later Sir Roger, 161
Malaya, 129
Malta, 132
Marriott, Major-General Sir John, and Lady, 55, 57, 173, 218–19, 245–6
Maugham, Viscount (Robin), 171
Maxwell, Elsa, 218–19
Meshed, 147–9
Meyer, Eugene, 183–4
Mhow, 235
Miller, John, 273–4
Mississippi, 193
Monckton, Sir Walter, later Viscount Monckton, 71
Monroe, Elizabeth (Mrs. Neame) (see also under author's letters), 175
Mosul, 101–2, 112–13, 115, 120, 145, 151
Mufti, the, 77, 81, 83, 97–9, 111
Muhammed Ali, Prince, 57
Muhammed Baban, 153
Murray, John Grey (Jock) (see also under author's letters), viii, 10, 15, 44, 161, 240, 252, 254, 273
Mussolini, 20, 22, 26, 53
Mysore, 235, 239–40

Napier, A. N. Williamson, 63
Nehru, Pandit, 192, 249
New England, 220–1
New Mexico, 193, 196
New York, 173–82, 192, 210–11, 217–19

Nicolson, Hon. Sir Harold, 228, 280–1
Nicosia, 137
Nuri as-Said Pasha, 3, 109, 113, 141, 143, 158, 160, 178, 195, 210, 215
    murder of, 109, 141–2

Olmstead, Dr., 189
Ottawa, 207–9

Pakistan, 199, 229
Palestine, 12, 25, 29, 52, 62, 74, 89, 94, 103, 124, 130, 134–6, 158–9, 161, 165–6, 175–6, 178, 181–7, 190, 192–3, 197–8, 200, 203, 205–8, 210, 215, 233, 271, 281–2
Pasadena, 195
Pavia, 263–4, 266
    tomb of St. Augustine, 264
Pearl Harbour, 61, 179
Pennefeather, Harold, 109
Perim, 11, 51, 53, 55
Perowne, Stewart (see also under author's letters), 10, 14, 16–17, 20, 45, 47–8, 52, 54, 118, 123, 126, 131, 161, 166, 271–2
Perseus in the Wind, 245
Persia, 84, 86–87, 119, 124, 129, 146–7, 149, 157, 220
Philip, Aidan, 118, 172
Political Officers (work of), 118, 143
Port Sudan, 54–5
Pott, Leslie, 89
    Mrs. Pott, 101
Pritchard, Sir Fred (Judge), 115, 125
Pumphrey, Phyllida, 69, 117

[292]

Qadhi al Amri, 38–9
Qadhi Muhammad Raghib, 22, 24–5, 29–31, 36
  Madame Qadhi, 22–4
Quetta, 112, 146–7
Qurna, 109, 152

Rajputana, 240–3
Ramadi, 98, 106, 109
Ramzi Bey, 63
Ranfurly, Countess of, 125
Rankin, Charles, 249, 267
Rashid Airfield, 91, 103–4
Rashid Ali al Gailani, 76–80, 94–5, 104, 106, 111, 114, 142
Ravenna, 190, 266
Red Sea, 11, 14, 41, 49, 51, 55, 198
Regina, 205–6
Reid, Air Vice-Marshal Sir R. Macfarlane, 14
Reilly, Sir Bernard, 13, 20, 25, 227
Resafa, 123
Rome, 34, 228, 249, 251, 254, 259, 262, 266, 274–5
Roosevelt, President (d. 1945), 191, 199, 212, 240
Rothschild, Alyx, 218
Russell Pasha, Sir Thomas (d. 1954), 53
Russell, Vaughan, Mr. and Mrs., 87
Russia, 60, 123, 125, 134, 140, 147, 149, 188, 213, 215, 253, 278

Salamis, 137
Samaha, Mr., 69
San'a, 20, 22, 25, 28–30
  letters written from, 22–40
San Francisco, 200–3, 216
Sarton, May, 244

Scaife, Christopher, 71, 134–5, 145, 151, 158, 210–11
Scobie, General, 279
Sebastopol, 119
Selous, G. H., and Mrs., 203
Shearer, Brigadier Eric, 64
Sheba, 28
Simla, 244–50
  Simla Conference, 246–50
Sinderson, Dr., later Sir Harry, 88, 96
Singapore, 119, 128–9, 132
Skrine, Sir Claremont and Lady, 147
Smart, Sir Walter, 53
Snyder, Major, 213
Somaliland, British, 43, 50, 52, 198
Southern Gates of Arabia, 273
Spears, Major-General Sir Edward, and Lady, 135
Stark, Freya
  difficulty of writing autobiography, 1–2
  her task of propaganda or 'persuasion', 3
  her friendships, 3–4, 160
  Italy and Fascists, 2
  her mother (see also under *Letters*) 3, 43, 72, 138, 251–3
  in Syria, 7–10
  Templars' castles and fortresses of Assassins, 7, 9
  in Greece, 10
  tragic news received in Aleppo, 7
  her reading, 7
  lecture at Chatham House, 12–13
  in Aden under Ministry of Information, 10–18

INDEX

Stark, Freya—*(continued)*
  goes to the Yemen, 20–40
  'persuasion' in the Yemen, 22–40
  cinema films, 23-4, 26–34, 36–9
  visits harims, 26, 28, 30, 32–3, 36, 38
  returns to Aden from the Yemen, 40
  begins to keep diary, 42
  bad news from France, 43
  working under difficulties, 45
  hears of war with Italy and surrender of France, 46–7
  air raids in Aden, 48
  translates papers captured by Royal Navy, 48–9
  goes Cairo for liaison and consultations, 50–4
  flies to Aden, 54
  returns to Cairo, 55
  stays Cairo, September 1940 to April 1941 and subsequently at intervals, 56–73
  kindness from British Embassy in Cairo, 57
  her life in Cairo, 56–73
  the Desert War, 52, 56, 58, 61, 75
  visits General Wavell at G.H.Q., 59
  methods of 'persuasion', 64–8
  founds Brotherhood of Freedom (q.v.), 63–71
  spends two Christmases in Luxor, 70
  her mother's imprisonment and release, 72
  constant headaches, 72
  moves to Baghdad, 73
  friendship with British Ambassador and family, 75–6
  Iraqi crises, 77–116
  discussion with George Antonius, 79–80
  describes problems of propaganda in Iraq, 81–2
  spends five days in Teheran, 84–7
  description of landscapes on journey, 84–6
  returns hurriedly to Baghdad, 86
  siege of Embassy in Baghdad, 88–116
  shortage of food during siege, 94, 111
  R.A.F. activities in Iraq, 91, 96, 98–100, 102–4, 106, 111–12
  armistice arranged, 111–13
  flies to Jerusalem, 116
  in Cairo for a month, then returns to Iraq, 118
  life and work in Baghdad, 1941/2, 119–34
  holiday on Carmel, 121–3
  description of landscape, 122
  returns to Baghdad along Euphrates, 123
  her 'private life had become singularly pleasant', 125
  writes to Minister of State in Cairo, 130
  two months' leave in Cyprus, 134–8
  declines to go to America, 138
  death of her mother, 138
  writes of visit to Iraq in 1957, 142
  lecture tours during 1941/2, 143–4
  leaves Middle East, 1943, 146

INDEX

visits India and Persia, 146–9
writes report to Owen Tweedy, 149–51
tour through Kurdistan, 153–7
'my earliest friend in Iraq—Muhammad Baban', 153
leaves Baghdad, 153
description of journey, 153–4
is awarded R.G.S. gold medal, 157
flies to England, 161
attitude to Zionism, 165–6
passage to America, 165–73
develops acute appendicitis, 167–8
after recovery, stays in New York with Mrs. Otto Kahn, 173–4
describes work in letters, 175–209
goes to Washington, 181
work and life in Washington, 181–7
meets journalists, 186
goes to Chicago, 188
meets Zionists, 190–1
lectures, 192, 195, 200–1, 206–7
in California, 194–201
goes to Vancouver, 202–3
visits ranch at Creston, B.C., 204–5
in Winnipeg, 206–7
stays with Malcolm Macdonald and sister in Ottawa, 207–8
meets Canadian-Arab Friendship Committee, 208–9
lecture-tour ends, 209
arranges publication in New York of *The Arabian Isle*, 210
meetings and talks in Washington, 211–17

questions about her asked in House of Commons, 216
sees Arabic manuscripts at Princeton, 217
discussions, lectures and parties in New York, 217–21
clothing coupons, 217–18
'incredible' party given by Elsa Maxwell, 218–19
week in New England, 220
letter from Isaiah Berlin, 221
in England in 1944, 222–9
'human courage all around', 224
spends four months in Devonshire, 225
accepts invitation from Lady Wavell to work in India, 229
five months in India, 'a happy, unproductive half-year', 230–50
sees presentation of Victoria Crosses, 231
education in India, 233
tours in India, 234–50
'a nostalgia for India has never left me', 243
flies to Treviso, 250–1
Italy in 1945, 252–75
a hard winter, 262–3
describes places visited, 256, 259–60, 263
reading centres, 262–6, 274
a 'pattern' in her life, 282
the 'art of Persuasion', 282–3

LETTERS to:
Lord Amherst, 245, 259–60, 270–1
Lucy Beach, 152
Isaiah Berlin, 223–4
Henry Channon, 170–1
Brigadier Clayton, 170–1

INDEX

Stark, Freya—(*continued*)
　Nigel Clive, 174, 182
　Peter Coats, 172–3, 261–2
　Sir Kinahan Cornwallis, 19–20
　Sir Moore Crosthwaite, 244
　Lord Euston, 257–9
　Lional Fielden, 278–80
　Gerald de Gaury, 148, 173, 230–3,
　　238–40, 244, 246–50, 254–6,
　　267–8, 271, 274–5
　Austen Harrison, 242–3
　Pamela Hore-Ruthven, 169–70,
　　173–4, 194–5
　Mrs. Otto Kahn, 243
　Edwin Ker, 194
　Lady Marriott ('Momo'), 245–6
　Robin Maugham, 171
　Elizabeth Monroe, 175–87, 189–
　　209, 211–21
　Jock Murray, 41, 169 187–8,
　　260–1, 268–8
　Sir Harold Nicolson, 280–2
　Stewart Perowne, 22–40, 180
　Aiden Philip, 172
　Charles Rankin, 256–7, 267
　May Sarton, 244
　Flora Stark (author's mother),
　　8–10, 15–16, 27, 29, 31, 35,
　　41–2, 44–6, 60–1, 70–3, 121–4,
　　127–9, 131–4
　Owen Tweedy, 149–51
　Lord Wavell, 196–7, 226–7, 265,
　　270, 275
　Lady Wavell, 234–5
　Rushbrook Williams, 16, 83–4

EXTRACTS FROM DIARY
(chronological)
　in Aden, 42–5, 47
　in Cairo, 61
　in Baghdad, 77–82, 86, 89–116
　in Halabja, 154–7
　in Udaipur, 236
　in Asolo, 263
Stark, Mrs. Flora (d. 1942) (see
　also under author's letters), 3,
　43, 72, 123, 138, 251–3
　An Italian Diary, 72, 252–3, 261
Stern gang, 184
Stewart, Michael, 262, 274
Stimson, Mr., 185, 188
Storrs, Sir Ronald, 137, 229, 243
Stowe, Leland, 192
Suez Canal, 2, 58, 145
Suleimaniya, 153–6
Sulzberger, Mr., 217
Sykes, Capt. Christopher, 53
Syria, 7–10, 58, 76, 103, 107, 117,
　119, 130, 135, 161, 176, 212,
　271

Tartous, 9
Taurus mountains, 8
Tedder, Lord, Marshal of the Royal
　Air Force, 58
Teheran, 84–6, 89, 147–9, 244
Thompson, Dorothy, 177–8, 218
Thornhill, Colonel C.M. (d. 1952),
　53, 71–2
Tigris, 115, 126, 152, 172, 203
Tobruk, 75, 119, 129, 132
Transjordan, 57, 74, 89, 120, 123,
　161
Tranvancore, 235, 238
Treviso, 72, 251, 256, 258–9, 262
Trichinopoly, 235, 237
Trieste, 245, 259, 267–8, 275
Trivandrum, 238
Turkey and Turks, 8, 22, 25, 58,
　68, 109, 136, 208, 226

[296]

INDEX

Tweedy, Owen (see also under author's letters), 71, 74, 135, 230
letters to author, 151, 158

Udaipur, 235-6, 241-2

Vancouver, 202-3
Varwell, Miss, 225
Venice, 10, 73, 255-6, 259-61, 267-8, 272-3, 275
Vichy, 76, 103, 123-4

Walker, Norman, 184
Waller, Lady, 225
Washington, 181-7, 196, 209, 211-17
Waterhouse, Major-General G. G. 90
Wavell, later Field-Marshal Earl (d. 1950) (see also under author's letters) 3, 41, 52-3, 58-9, 72, 77, 119, 128, 146, 160, 225, 244, 246-50, 269
letters to author, 225-6, 269
Lady Wavell, 229-35, 244, 246-50
Wavell, 2nd Earl (d. 1953), 228-9
Weizmann, Dr. Chaim (d. 1952), 175, 134-6, 208
Weygand, General, 124, 197
Wharton, Lord, 246

Williams, Laurence Rushbrook, 16, 52, 69, 82-4
letter to author, 82-3
Wilson, Dr., 189
Wilson, Field-Marshal Lord Wilson, 117, 139, 160, 227-8
Winnipeg, 206-7
Women's Voluntary Service, 229-30, 233, 235
Woollcombe, R., author of *The Campaigns of Wavell*, 41, 52
Woolley, Sir Charles and Lady, 137
World War I, 13, 186, 198, 205
World War II, 1, *et seq*
Wright, Sir Michael and Lady, 181, 183-4, 187, 209, 217

Yafa'i, 15-16
Yemen, 11-12, 15, 17, 19-41, 63-4, 195, 201, 215, 233
H.H. the Imam, 21, 24-8, 30-1, 36-9
Prince Qasim, 23-4
Young, Herbert (d. 1941), 43, 72, 258

Zionism and Zionists, 138, 165-6, 175-7, 179, 182-90, 193-4, 196, 200, 202-3, 206-9, 212, 214-17, 271, 280-1
Balfour Declaration, 175, 178, 184, 203, 208